"TORPEDO IN THE WATER, CAPTAIN!"

Plummeting downward from the ocean surface, the Mark 48 torpedo's run to target took just under five seconds. There was no time for fear, no time to react, but time enough to understand. A sense of loss, of sadness, would follow later, given time to reflect.

Entering the water nose down, directly above the *Georgia* at a range of one hundred fifty feet, the torpedo's sonar locked on target with the first ping. Guided now by its sonar seeker, the pump jet propulsor engaged, plunging the torpedo downward on a near vertical intercept track.

Although brief, the sound reverberating inside the *Georgia* was one no submariner ever forgets.

Ping . . . ping . . . ping-ping-pi-pi-pi-pi-pi-p-p-ping—THUNK! followed by a cold stillness closing in around them, a stillness experienced only in death . . .

Berkley Books by Bill Buchanan

VIRUS
CLEARWATER

CLEARWATER

BY

BILL BUCHANAN

BERKLEY BOOKS, NEW YORK

This is a work of fiction. Names, characters, places, and incidents are either the product of the author's imagination or are used fictitiously, and any resemblance to actual persons, living or dead, business establishments, events or locales is entirely coincidental.

CLEARWATER

A Berkley Book / published by arrangement with the author

PRINTING HISTORY
Berkley edition / March 2000

The Penguin Putnam Inc. World Wide Web site address is http://www.penguinputnam.com

ISBN: 0-425-17364-X

BERKLEY®
Berkley Books are published by The Berkley Publishing Group, a division of Penguin Putnam Inc., 375 Hudson Street, New York, New York 10014. BERKLEY and the "B" logo are trademarks belonging to Penguin Putnam Inc.

PRINTED IN THE UNITED STATES OF AMERICA

10 9 8 7 6 5 4 3 2 1

"The idea," Victor Hugo said, speaking of liberty, "it is everything."

Today, the French author is remembered for his novels *The Hunchback of Notre Dame* and *Les Miserables.*

For Mom and Dad

This book was written as a reminder that people are the most important asset we have protecting our freedom.

ACKNOWLEDGMENTS

My heartfelt appreciation to LCDR Bob Klimetz, U.S. Navy (Ret.), for his ideas, exhilarating stories, and the reality that comes from having been there. And to Mark Gatlin, acquisitions editor for the Naval Institute Press. Your "I think you're on to something" encouragement gave me the confidence to forge ahead and never look back.

With sincere thanks to Jake Elwell, Tom Colgan, George Wieser, Olga Wieser, and Leslie Gelbman. Jake for his insightful feedback; Tom Colgan, "the world's best editor"[1], for substantially improving the story; George for his unstoppable spirit and enthusiasm; Olga for being the wonderful, inspirational person she is; and Leslie Gelbman, for without her this novel would not exist.

Very special thanks to my lifelong friend Marlo Horne, for reviewing the manuscript in its early stages. Your comments regarding character solidified the story's foundation.

For their kindness and help: My daughter, Laura, for articulating the essence of the story in a few well chosen words: In clear water, there's no place to hide; my daughter, Amy, for crafting some of the story's most memorable lines; my brother, Alan, for his handgun expertise and great sense of humor; my sister-in-law, Suzie, for underscoring the importance of story context; David Rhodes for my first introduction to Slim Mason; Dr. Gary Alley for

---

[1] C. A. Mobley said it first in her novel *Rules of Command*, and she's right.

patient explanation of low-phase noise in doppler radar and love of technology; Jim Blodgett for proficiency with P-3C aircraft engine controls; Don Richardson for explanation of air handling on a submarine; Ralph Noel for first-hand experience with sonar, churned-up surface water due to weather, and dummy torpedoes; Wally Debus for revealing the gut-wrenching terror of his first submarine shakedown cruise; CDR Cyndy Mobley, USNR, for a sanity check on naval operations; Harry Stephens for correcting misinformation about submarine communication; Mike Goodwin for his enthusiastic story conversations and suggestions; Denny Carroll for acoustic research; Tim Walker for information regarding bird behavior in winter; Mrs. Marion Olesch for introducing me to *Traci with an i;* and Mr. Charles Stevens for the most memorable story conversation I ever had.

My thanks to Ensign Wendy Snyder at the Navy Office of Information and LCDR Mark McCaffrey, SUBLANT public affairs officer, for their willingness to help where possible.

And to my wife, Janet, for her helpful story conversations.

My objective was to produce a good story—a technically and operationally viable work of submarine fiction—within the bounds of possibility. To the extent someone outside our closed submarine community can achieve this, I have tried. Please understand, stories like this can't be written without the help of many generous people, so let me say up front, the credit belongs to those mentioned here—family, friends, and subject matter experts who guided me along the way.

GLOSSARY

Technical Terms

ADCAP—ADvanced CAPability torpedo is the latest and greatest version of the Mark 48, the world's smartest homing torpedo.

ASCII—Pronounced "ask-key," American Standard Code for Information Interchange. Industry standard for information exchange between computing equipment, typically binary patterns that define alphanumeric characters.

ASW—All Seems Well

ASW—AntiSubmarine Warfare

AUDIX—"Your phone is being answered by AUDIX," trademark of Lucent Bell Labs

boomer—Naval jargon for a nuclear powered ballistic missile submarine

CD-ROM—Compact Disk Read-Only Memory

CIC—Combat Information Center

COMSUBPAC—COMmander SUBmarine PACific Fleet

DoD—Department of Defense

DSRV—Deep Submergence Rescue Vehicle

EAB—Emergency Air Breather. Much like a gas mask, submarine crews wear them to get good air if their onboard air's fouled. An umbilical breathing tube is connected from the mask to an air duct that supplies safe, fresh air.

EAM—Emergency Action Message

EBA—Emergency Breathing Apparatus. Another name for the Emergency Air Breather mask.

ECM—Electronic CounterMeasures

ELF—Extremely Low Frequency

ELF station—Extremely Low Frequency radio station used for slow, reliable, one-way submarine communication. Site locations include Clam Lake, Wisconsin, and Michigan's upper peninsula, near Republic and Sawyer Air Force Base.

fast attack—Naval jargon for a nuclear powered attack submarine

GPS—Global Positioning System that uses Navstar satellites

IUSS—Integrated Undersea Surveillance System (formerly SOSUS)

LaserLink—Registered trademark of Lucent Bell Labs

MAD—Magnetic Anomaly Detector

MCC—Missile Control Center

NAVSTAR GPS—Global Positioning System that uses Navstar satellites. Navigational aid that uses satellite and hyperbolic fixing technology to accurately determine position, latitude, longitude, and height above sea level.

OOD—Officer Of the Deck

Pri-Fly—Primary Flight tower with unobstructed view of aircraft carrier flight deck

RF—Radio Frequency

SAT—SATellite

SAT break—SATellite communications break

SEASAT—Nicknamed the flying boxcar, the Trade Winds–class I satellite was described as an environmental monitoring satellite whose actual purpose was submerged submarine detection.

SEC—Submarine Element Coordinator

SLCSAT—The Submarine Laser Communications SATellite, called a SLCSAT (pronounced slick-sat), is used for communicating with submerged submarines from space. Typically, target positions are downloaded in real time to guided missile submarines.

This Trade Winds–class II satellite is one of two different, but complementary, types of satellites used for orchestrating submarine surgical strikes.

SLOT—Submarine Launched One-way Transmitter

SPARCstation—UNIX-based workstation and trademark of Sun Microsystems

SPO—Special Project Officer

SSBN—Nuclear powered ballistic missile submarine

SSGN—Nuclear powered guided missile submarine

SSN—Nuclear powered attack submarine

SUBOPS—Submarine Operations

SUBROC—SUBmarine-launched antisubmarine ROCket

SUBTRACK—SUBmarine TRACK data, including position, speed, and direction

SUBTRACKER—The name of the supercomputer that tracks submarine positions, above and below the surface, around the world.

TBD—To Be Determined

TCP/IP—Internet Protocols

Trade Winds–class satellite—Trade Winds–class I satellite, called SEASAT, detects submerged submarines. Trade Winds–class II satellite, called SLCSAT, downloads target coordinates to submerged submarines.

UHF—Ultra High Frequency

URL—Uniform Resource Locator

USSPACECOM—United States SPACE COMmand

VLF—Very Low Frequency

XO—Executive Officer

PREFACE

In February 1993, *Scientific American*[1] reported the effectiveness of our ballistic missile submarines as a nuclear deterrent may be in doubt because they could no longer hide beneath the black veil of the sea. Using the latest advances in remote-sensing technology, submerged submarine wakes may be detected by measuring microwave reflections off the ocean's surface. Later that same year, once the Naval Institute Press published its politically controversial *Submarine Detection from Space*[2], the highly classified world of undersea operations changed forever. It didn't happen overnight, but it was inevitable.

Wake detection principles had been understood for years, but not until the mid-nineties did newly emerging technology begin delivering the horsepower required to make this submarine tracking satellite network feasible. Ultimately, advances in ionospheric physics, remote-sensing, communication, and computer technology converged to the point where global deployment of this space-based ocean surveillance system was considered viable. As a result, the United States military cleverly developed its remote-sensing satel-

---

[1] Beardsley, Tim. 1993. "Making Waves," *Scientific American*, February, page 32.

[2] Nguyen, Hung P. 1993. "Submarine Detection from Space: A Study of Russian Capabilities," The Naval Institute Press.

lites under the guise of a civilian ocean surveillance program; nevertheless, the world took notice.

Officially, the purpose of the U.S. government's Trade
Winds project was tracking ocean surface currents, and
fortunately for everyone concerned, this information had
enormous commercial value. Cost savings in shipboard
fuel alone more than paid for the satellite program. CORE-
SAT's microwave division in Lexington, Massachusetts,
was awarded a contract for tooling the radars carried
onboard each prototype satellite. On paper, radar resolution requirements were coarse, but adequate for tracking
ocean surface currents. But more intriguing than this—the
contract contained an off-the-record, word-of-mouth set of
radar requirements that deserve closer examination.

Unofficially, resolution requirements were sufficiently
rigorous for tracking 2.3-centimeter waves—"Bragg scat-
terers"—on the ocean surface, waves created as part of a
submerged submarine surface wake. Following Trade
Winds' preliminary success, the ocean surveillance program expanded, emerging as the ClearWater project, and
a new Trade Winds–class of low-orbit satellites entered
the U.S. military's operational inventory. Once folded into
the budget catch-all category of missile defense, the ocean
surveillance program achieved top priority and Trade
Winds-class satellites rapidly proliferated. Long before
the program concluded, submerged submarine detection
from space was an unspoken reality. Like most first-generation surveillance systems, however, its operational
capabilities were notably limited. Typically, surface
storms overwhelmed radar wake sensors, temporarily
reducing the coverage footprint. Even in average seas,
Trade Winds–class surveillance satellites rendered the
ocean transparent—but only to a depth of one hundred
meters. Below one hundred meters, the ocean remained

opaque to all. Not surprisingly, advances in technology would illuminate the black ocean depths in stages, one layer at a time.

Since satellites rendered the surface layer transparent, the problem for submarines now shifted and became one of reliable communications at deeper depths. This was particularly important to SSBNs (strategic ballistic missile submarines, nuclear powered) because their mission demands uninterrupted reception of communications, quick reaction to command messages, and remaining undetected throughout their patrol.

Both the U.S. and Russian navies reacted well in advance to this impending detection capability, thereby averting any communications crisis with their submarine fleets. During the last two decades of the twentieth century, both navies set up new ELF (extremely low frequency) broadcasting stations to back up their primary VLF (very low frequency) systems. Although the data rate transmitted is only a few bits per minute, this rate is adequate to send a signal for triggering some previously agreed on plan of action. In addition, ELF can be used as a "bell ringer" for calling a submarine shallow to receive longer, more informative VLF messages. Unlike VLF, this new communications system proved impervious to noise and, as a result, far more dependable. Specifically, ELF can be received much farther below the surface and, in addition, reliably penetrates polar ice.

By the year 2004, the only place a ballistic missile submarine could hide from the U.S. and her allies was beneath the polar ice or at depths greater than one hundred meters. Understand too that this detection capability impacted a great many nations. As early as 1999, forty-three countries maintained submarine fleets around the world, and of these, ten maintained missile boats.

Invariably, the logic of politics and strategic military thought dictated that once you had the capability to detect submerged ballistic missile submarines in real time, you would most certainly develop the capability to destroy them—on demand—before any had the opportunity to launch their lethal payload. Otherwise, why bother detecting them at all?

So our course was set. Predictably, one capability led inescapably to the other. Given our state-of-the-art detection capability, the logic of politics and national security demanded an "SSBN surgical-strike" counterpart; our scientists said it was possible; most of our military leaders endorsed the idea from the get-go—and so it came to pass.

Sea trials began mid-year—2008. Strategically, the world was divided into two operational theaters—poles and oceans. Allied air forces patrolled both ice-covered poles. Combined submarine, surface, and naval air forces—guided by real-time target downloads from space—embodied the firepower made ready against opposing missile boats moving beneath the black veil of the open sea.

As it turned out, though the technical solution was often described as elegant, there were worldwide political problems with our unilaterally advancing state-of-the-art submarine communication and detection technology.

Not every nation shared America's heartfelt enthusiasm for furthering her own security, and equally important, not every American believed it the right thing to do. Some forty-one countries held their own best interests above that of the United States, and as such, they felt disadvantaged—even threatened—by this new "detect, track, and destroy" capability. Lesser developed countries viewed America's newfound military prowess with grave misgivings. Others engaged in blustery bouts of saber rattling, but in the final analysis, spineless diplomacy proved ineffective.

So one small country, a mere David, hurled a stone toward the American Goliath, executing a premeditated, well-rehearsed course of action. Although many nations soberly interpreted America's "SSBN surgical strike" capability as the next step up the nuclear escalation ladder, David began preparing for this eventuality as early as 1993—following *Scientific American*'s article entitled "Making Waves."

And one day in December, the world held its breath.

PART ONE

Hijacked

The Week Following Christmas—December 2008

CHAPTER ONE

Isn't Technology Wonderful? 12/26/2008, Fri., 04:38 A.M.
Off Russia's Kamchatka Peninsula
Onboard Sierra Eleven

Officially, so his U.S. Navy records had said, he was a loner. Unofficially and unspoken, the real reason he was put out to pasture had to do with his book and classified testimony before the Senate Armed Services Committee. Unofficially, Lieutenant Commander Mike Mandrone had cost the Navy any prospects for new missile submarines now, or in the foreseeable future.

An Annapolis graduate, former missile boat XO (executive officer), and CIA naval analyst, Mike Mandrone felt betrayed, stabbed in the back by his own country, after the IRS brought him to court on trumped-up charges of tax evasion laced with unfounded hints of womanizing. During his trial, government officials presented persuasive paper evidence—suspicious motel bills, restaurant bills for two, and the like—most of it planted, of course, but seemingly solid, convincing evidence that closely correlated with the actual time he'd spent away from his family on business—and official government business at that.

Mandrone was a beaten man. Before his trial was through, the Mike Mandrone his friends and family had known died, drowned in a backwash of rumor, accusation, and innuendo. *What about the constitution I swore to defend? . . . How about the Bill of Rights? . . . Free speech, pursuit of life, liberty, and justice for all? If they want to get you,* Mandrone concluded bitterly, *they'll get you.* Mike wasn't perfect. In his younger married days, he'd experienced an indiscretion or two in Singapore, but he wasn't the cheating, slithering snake in the grass they'd made him out to be. Besides, the soft sights and smells of Singapore were massive overload for almost any young, red-blooded, American male fresh off the boat.

Personally, he'd never recovered, and vowed revenge. He'd been right. He knew it, they knew it, and he'd show 'em once and for all. In testimony before the Senate Armed Forces Committee, he'd claimed that the effectiveness of the missile boat as a deterrent was in doubt. With the advent of submerged submarine detection from space, missile boats weren't only vulnerable targets, but subject to hijacking as well. His book on the subject, testimony, and subsequent trial cost Mike everything he valued in life— his wife, family, house, and livelihood. He'd heard about the long arm of the law, always believed it independent of politics, but in the end, he'd become a victim of the system he'd sworn to defend. He did what he believed was right, then had hell to pay, finding himself in over his head, isolated, out of step with the admiralty, American industry, and East Coast politicians. On the one hand, he'd helped save taxpayers several billion dollars, but on the downside, he'd cost East Coast shipyards hundreds of desperately needed jobs. New England's submarine manufacturing community had been especially hard hit.

He'd learned through bitter experience that some agencies within the federal government are living, breathing, political organisms. They don't get mad, they get even—

destroying lives and careers in the process. If East Coast politicians and the Navy's big guns decide to settle a score, by the power vested in money, fear, and intimidation, they've got the connections, they're utterly relentless, and woe be to anyone who stands in their way.

"Who'd believe it?" former Lieutenant Commander Mike Mandrone wondered out loud from the bridge of Sierra Eleven, an old Russian Andreyev-class civilian research ship. *Life's what you make it, but it doesn't always turn out the way you plan.* Sierra Eleven, renamed the *Kansong* by the North Korean Navy, had been reoutfitted with a new sonar and mini-submarine, a Chinese DSRV (Deep Submergence Rescue Vehicle), sitting on its rack inside an internal compartment with access doors on the port side.

Inside the bridge of Sierra Eleven, Mandrone heard the muffled sound of a phone ringing. *Right on the money,* the former XO thought, checking his watch. A distinctive click signaled telephone pickup, followed by the high-pitched chirping of modem-to-modem communication. Sounded like FAX machine chatter to Mandrone, but he knew otherwise. That call was one in a series of calls relayed halfway around the world over Motorola's Iridium satellite network.

Turning toward the sound, he eyed his laptop computer display fastened to the ship's plotting table. From outward appearances, the navigator's station looked makeshift, an antiquated stack of NAVSTAR global positioning system receivers bolted willy-nilly into place on a shoestring budget, but for Mandrone's purposes, appearances mattered not at all. This hodgepodge of tried-and-true technology worked flawlessly.

Mandrone studied the laptop's display screen. Pictured, he saw a full-color map showing the Bering Sea coastline off Russia's Kamchatka Peninsula plus the course and position plotted for two naval vessels, one labeled *Kansong,* the other USS *Maine.*

Isn't technology wonderful? Mandrone mused.

At first inspection, nothing about this situation seemed extraordinary, the mood on the bridge felt pretty laid back; however, if any admiral in the United States Navy had seen the USS *Maine*'s course and current position plotted on screen, he'd have gone ballistic. The *Maine* was a newly modified, Ohio-class guided missile submarine—one of the finest submarines in the fleet—and as far as the Navy was concerned, only they knew its whereabouts, and sometimes they weren't sure. Like a fast-attack submarine, the *Maine*'s mission was to destroy intercontinental ballistic missile submarines before they launched their lethal payloads, and like a ballistic missile submarine, the *Maine*'s patrol location off the Kamchatka Peninsula was one of America's most diligently guarded secrets.

On the bottom of the display, an indicator flashed phone busy. Mandrone knew in advance the call would be brief, less than one minute in duration, and it was. Thirty seconds later, the chirping fell silent, signaling Mandrone to focus once again on the screen. The navigator's GPS radios updated the *Kansong*'s position, while the phone call updated the *Maine*'s.

The Maine*'s submerged thirty miles due east, steering a random zigzag course,* he concluded. *Nothing out of the ordinary about that; no clue she's onto us, just another day at the office.*

Fish Out of Water, 12/26/2008, Fri., 03:41 A.M.
Destroyer USS *Yorktown*

Steaming several hundred miles southeast of the *Maine,* Air Force liaison officer Captain Linda Scott stood braced inside the CIC (Combat Information Center) of the USS *Yorktown,* an Arleigh Burke–class guided missile destroyer. The mood in CIC could best be described as somber, one of serious-minded respect for the sea, punctuated by bouts of nausea.

Outside, during the darkest part of the night, a violent Pacific storm was raging, battering the *Yorktown* fore and aft. The captain cut across the swells diagonally, walking them like a tightrope to minimize stresses in the hull.

Heaving upward, Scott sensed the ship cresting, teetering on a peak, rolling to starboard. For a brief moment she held fast, then suddenly the bottom dropped out. Plummeting down with a crash, their bow plowed under forty-foot swells. Feeling mixed emotions of reverence, respect, dread, and wonder, Scott stood in silent awe of the sea. Pitted against the might of this storm, their ship seemed pathetically small.

Judging from the age and rank of those inside CIC, most were veterans who would've experienced storms at sea before. Studying their faces, especially the older ones, didn't make her feel any better. In the dim red light, they looked grim, wrinkled, and hollow-eyed. Anyone could see they were deeply concerned. Occasionally, there was the muffled sound of someone suppressing a gag, or retching, but no talking. The place reeked of vomit.

Tonight, Scott surmised from the crew's expressions, *there are no atheists onboard the* Yorktown.

As the deck pitched beneath her feet, Scott felt fear, and she wasn't alone. Admitting it, she felt better. After all, feeling apprehension at a time like this was perfectly normal. But worse than apprehension, fear had a debilitating grip on her spirit she couldn't shake. She'd never experienced anything like this in her life, and hoped she'd never go through it again.

Scott purposefully distracted herself, allowing her thoughts to stray to her childhood.

Throughout her adult life, Scott had carried a photograph which reminded her at a glance who she was and where she'd come from. Taken on a salt lake runway at Edwards when she was six years old, the photo had come to symbolize her love of flying and family. In essence, that photograph had cast an outline for her life. At first glance, you saw only blue sky, lake bed, and black airplane. On closer inspection, the picture revealed an engaging father-daughter team, dressed in flight suits bearing identical logo patches. Scott thought *they were so cool!*

And if you looked closely, you could see that the little girl was standing on the forward tires of her father's SR-71, hugging the front tricycle gear. Across the photo, her father had written, *Awesome! Life doesn't get any better than this!* As an adult, Scott had come to understand what he meant. He loved flying and his family.

Like her father, she loved flying and wanted children, but continuous weeks of separation had strained her marriage. Today, she was an Air Force pilot stuck on a year-long ground assignment flying a desk. Given the reality of fiscally austere defense budgets, every pilot took their turn out of the cockpit. Funny thing was, temporary sea duty didn't look that bad on paper. Sounded more like a vacation, a see-the-world travel adventure.

From Scott's perspective as a thirty-year-old pilot, temporary duty onboard a U.S. Navy destroyer sounded more interesting than any desk job pushing paper. Further, as her commanding officer—Colonel Mason—had explained, this job was important. Three months earlier, sea duty had looked pretty good from the dry, lonely land surrounding USSPACECOM, Colorado. Her husband, Captain Jay Fayhee, was already stationed in Alabama for three months anyway, and besides, Colonel Mason believed this assignment could goose up her chances for a space plane slot at Edwards. This job demanded all the right ingredients—high visibility, leadership, teamwork, leading edge technology, pressure, press and politics.

And intuitively, Mason sensed she had the right stuff.

Scott was a pilot, one of the best, and for as long as she could remember, she'd dreamed of flying the XR-30, the fastest air and space plane ever flown across the face of the earth. Her father knew she could do it, never questioned her ability. She was a natural, best he'd ever seen, bar none. If he'd told her this story once, he'd told her a hundred times: The single dream remaining in his life was to stand on the salt flats at Edwards and feel the ground shake when his daughter punched the burners of the fastest plane ever flown. It was Scott's dream first, but over the years, especially since her father had retired, it had become their dream.

Feeling a little queasy, Scott's thoughts wandered back to the cockpit. In a way, flying happened in a serene, almost sterile environment. If a pilot is inexperienced or doesn't treat a storm with the respect it deserves, weather like this will kill you quick enough, but more often than not, you simply flew around it. Now, between moments of fear and nausea, she longed for dry land, long runways, and Christmas leave.

Scott's reverie ended with a jolt as the bow came crashing down, seemingly devoured by the sea.

What kind of desk job is this? she thought. Shaking her head from side to side, Scott forced a tight-lipped grin and studied her colleague's face. Normally, his expression was only a heartbeat away from a smile, but he wasn't smiling now.

Dr. Tristan Roberts, their ClearWater expert from Lawrence Livermore Laboratory, hunched over a chart table, struggling to concentrate, trying to make sense out of the mountains of test data they'd collected during the past few weeks. He looked up, perturbed. It was absolutely impossible to think under these conditions. The data would have to wait.

Two weeks ago, Tristan would have traded everything he owned to be here. Now, he too was ready to go home. For the most part, he felt they'd accomplished what they'd set out to do.

A tall, impressive man in his late thirties, Dr. Roberts served as the visiting senior civilian scientist onboard. Born in Orlando, Florida, Tristan had grown up in the shadow of "the Mouse," working his way through school thanks largely to summer jobs inside the Disney organization. He'd started off in the Magic Kingdom, loved it, and by the time he finished school, he'd become one of Disney's imagineers. For Tristan, life never got better than this—doing cool stuff to make people happy, pushing the technology envelope to show what could be done, and getting paid for it. For Roberts—two-thirds scientist blended with one-third child—the Disney magic never faded. Someday, he hoped to go back again, but for now, he was conducting ClearWater sea trials for the United States government. It was important work and, in a way, helped make the Walt Disney Worlds possible.

Scott couldn't tell for sure under the low lights in CIC, but she thought Tristan looked ashen. "What're we doing here?" she wondered out loud.

"We must be crazy," Tristan quipped, allowing his

expression to soften. "This storm's not in my job description."

"I could never get used to it," she added, letting out a sigh.

"With any luck, we won't be out here much longer," he reassured her.

"You're satisfied, then?"

"Well, yes and no. For a first-generation system, it's working better than anyone has a right to expect. On the other hand, any first-generation system's gonna have limits, and this one's got its share. It's the hype, the promise of more bang for the buck, that'll kill a system like this one. The Navy tried to warn 'em early on, but Congress was sold a bill of goods."

"Sometimes people hear what they want to hear," Scott lamented. "But you've got to admit, ClearWater's hype is irresistible—high-tech jobs plus military cost reduction. What politician could say no?" About that time, she noticed motion in the seat ahead of her and cringed. Strapped securely in his combat director chair was the submarine element coordinator, a senior naval officer, white-haired, distinguished, and slight of stature. After hearing Tristan's comments, the admiral swiveled his chair around, then began probing shortcomings of the ClearWater ocean surveillance system. Most people observe social courtesies in conversation and avoid an abrupt approach to anything unpleasant. The admiral, however, had trained himself to do just the opposite, coming directly to the point without wasting words.

"What exactly are these limits, Roberts?" the admiral asked without preliminaries.

"You already know most of them, sir," Tristan responded, taken aback. He'd been grilled by the admiral before, but because of the storm, he hadn't seen this one coming. "We can't detect subs deeper than a hundred meters and we lose 'em if they run too slow."

"How slow?" snapped the admiral.

"Typically, three to five knots, depending on sea conditions, especially ocean currents."

"Why not slower? Five knots's a good clip."

"It's got to do with wavelength, Doppler shift, and phase noise, sir. ClearWater's got lower phase noise than any system in production today, and three to five knots is the absolute best we can do."

The admiral narrowly scrutinized Tristan. "What's the theoretical limit?"

"We're approaching theoretical performance with this system as is."

"I see." The admiral's tone—skeptical. "Any other limitations?"

"Ice," Tristan responded nervously. "We can't see very well under ice, sir, and with all due respect, I doubt we ever will."

The admiral's eyes narrowed to a close. He sat silently, without comment for a moment, then spoke to both Tristan and Scott. "It's not perfect, but no system ever is."

"It's working better than I expected," Tristan said with a bit of pride.

"That's fine, just fine," the admiral snapped with biting sarcasm. "It damn sure better work!" They watched with dismay as the admiral's voice rose and his face turned purple. "My antisubmarine forces have been decimated, and I'm stuck waiting on technology to take up the slack." The admiral's voice had an emotional tremor to it. He was clearly displeased with the decision cutting his ASW forces, and didn't believe technology would ever make good his losses. "Back-fill the hole with technology—like hell." His words sounded loathsome and seemed to stick in his throat. "Personally, I think this program's one big mistake."

Initially, Tristan was left shaken, not knowing what to say.

After a few moments' silence, Scott quietly voiced her opinion. "Technology's pretty remarkable . . . I mean, it's amazing what we can do and all, but people are the most important asset we have."

Hearing her words, Dr. Roberts nodded agreement, then spoke in a somber, almost apologetic tone."I've given this dilemma a great deal of thought, Admiral, and I agree, your people should never have been cut. Technology's an enabler, but people must remain the most significant term in our defense equation."

Remember the Maine, 12/26/2008, Fri., 12:11 P.M.
Submerged Off the Kamchatka Peninsula
USS *Maine* (SSGN 741)

Petty Officer Ash Wilson lived on the edge. Wholly dedicated to his cause, Ash's greatest God-given talent was his uncanny chameleon-like ability to become whomever he wanted, whenever he needed. Working as an electronic technician specialist, Ash maintained the guided missile boat's atmosphere control system and fan room, including all equipment used to measure and maintain the quality of air circulating throughout the USS *Maine*. On paper, Ash was part of a nine-man team responsible for the crew's breathing air. In reality, he was a spy.

And onboard a guided missile submarine, espionage is an especially dangerous line of work.

Crossing a long corridor lined with missile tubes, Ash stepped through a hatchway, passing by the boat's mess. Judging from the smell of freshly cooked fried seafood,

Petty Officer Wilson confirmed for the fourth time that it was Friday—traditionally seafood day onboard the *Maine*. Ash smiled amiably at the seamen enjoying their meal, knowing his shipmates did not appreciate the fact that their patrol beneath the Northern Pacific would be like no other.

Ash passed into the crew's berthing area, headed for his bunk. Living quarters for enlisted men on Ohio-class boats were nestled between the twenty-four missile tubes. The *Maine* provided crewmen living space divided into nine-man rooms. Each sleeping station had a bunk with a storage locker equipped under it, and blackout curtains forming an outside wall for privacy. Silently surveying his dorm room, Ash concluded his shipmates were either on duty, sleeping, or eating. All was quiet for now. *A rare sight indeed,* Ash thought. Raising his bunk exposed the contents of his locker, and one glance revealed a sizable teddy bear. Retrieving the stuffed bear, Ash gingerly placed it on his bunk. Stripping to his skivvies, one by one he slipped off his shoes, unbuttoned his shirt, hung his uniform in the clothing locker, then climbed onto his bunk. Situated belly up, he closed the curtains and turned on the overhead reading lamp.

Seldom did Petty Officer Wilson respond visibly to stress, but now Ash heard the pounding of his own heart. Closing his eyes, he tried to relax. Listening to air whistling through his nostrils, he noticed his breathing faster than normal and made a conscious effort to control it. Thumping the brown bear with his middle finger reassured Ash, but only slightly. The bear's large distended stomach was hard and had a distinctly metallic ring to it.

Once his breathing slowed, he grabbed the bear by both arms, removing them with a snap. Inside one hollowed arm he found a syringe and two sleeping pills, from the other he removed a small cylindrical vial. After collecting saliva on his tongue—his mouth felt bone-dry—he swallowed the pills without water. Assembling the syringe, Ash noticed his hands trembling. Try as he might, he could not steady them while extracting the drug from the vial. Once the syringe was filled, with all air bubbles removed, Ash inserted the vial and reattached one of the bear's arms. Using a white sock damp with spit, Ash cleaned off a spot on his upper thigh then inserted the needle with a wince. The pain of the needle was insignificant relative to the searing heat subsequently flowing into his leg. Once the injection was complete and the burning subsided, Ash felt a calmness overtaking him. As he checked his watch, his arms seemed to take on weight. He found himself fumbling to take the syringe apart, then struggling to reassemble the bear. After several feeble attempts, the bear's arm snapped back in place. Only after switching off the overhead bunk light did he feel relief. Knowing full well that this could be the last sleep he would get for several days only made matters worse. Closing his eyes, Ash allowed the sounds onboard the *Maine* to clear his mind—at least for the moment—of coming events. Relaxed by the monotonous whirring tones from the missile boat's power plant, Ash drifted off to an uneasy, drug-induced sleep.

Precious, 12/25/2008, Thu., 11:36 P.M.
Falcon AFB, CO
U.S. Space Command (USSPACECOM) Computer Center

What was so insidious about the scene was that it looked so ordinary. Just another DoD (Department of Defense) data center megaplex, like tens of others scattered across the country, only larger. Several second-generation optical supercomputers stood clustered in the center of the room providing the nerve center's brain. Tens of networked Sun SPARCstations, arranged in rows, lined the outside walls.

On the surface, everything looked and behaved perfectly normal.

But one of these workstations had a little something extra connected to its external expansion bus. Disguised to look and sound exactly like an external hard disk, the appearance of this particular desktop box gave no clue to its covert function. In fact, the desktop box had started life as an external disk drive, but had been modified to support an adjunct one-way communications function. Without technical information describing the change, the illicit communications function would remain forever hidden. To the typical workstation user or system administrator, the modifications were transparent. Neither could detect the difference without additional hardware addressing and control information. Yet any trained technical person who knew exactly where to look could detect the difference immediately and enable the low-power, frequency-agile transmitter.

A second and even more remarkable characteristic of this covert RF (Radio Frequency) transmitter was that its output was impossible to detect buried in the noisy RF environment of the computer center. Its radio frequency output signal looked like the background noise present in every computer center. In short, it looked like random noise appearing first on one frequency, then on another. This method of spreading the transmitted data over time and frequency made the signal difficult to detect because only the transmitter and receiver knew where to tune and when to listen.

Spread-spectrum technology is expensive to be sure, but for strategically sensitive operations, North Korea's dictator, Kim Jong Il, and his Pyongyang regime had spared no expense. Their intelligence gathering arsenal was stocked full of the finest high-tech tools Russian rubles could buy, and for this clandestine operation in particular, the value of the information transmitted proved well worth the expense.

This information consisted of minimum data with maximum value to any ready and worthy adversary. Judiciously chosen, strategically sensitive, real-time submarine position information transmitted as low-bit-rate data, disguised as noise.

All this activity was dedicated to accessing sensitive information; specifically, accessing the "Submarine Wake Track Object" for the USS *Maine*, SSGN 741, then transmitting the position information to a receiver located nearby inside some treasonous officer's home on Falcon AFB.

Submarine Wake Track Object

```
1.  Submarine Wake Track (SUBWAKE)
*   wake track ID
2   sub ID
2   country ID
.   posX
.   posY
.   velX
.   velY
.   accX
.   accY
```

```
/ / take wake track snapshots all day
/ / Thursday, Friday, Saturday, and Sunday
do for all (12/25/2008 && 12/26/2008 &&
12/27/2008 && 12/28/2008) {
      / / take sub position snapshot at
      / / random intervals every 300 to
      / / 600 seconds
      sleep ( iuniform [ 300 - 600 ] ) ;
      / / find the sub wake track for
      / / USS Maine
```

```
Find 'Submarine Wake Track' with
('sub ID' == "SSGN 741" &&
'country ID' == "USA") {
    / / copy SSGN 741 position
    Create 'Submarine Posit' =
    this.'wake track ID' ;
}
/ / copy 'Submarine Posit' object
/ / to file named precious,
/ / then encrypt
. . .
. . .
/ / enable transmitter
iocntl( tx_on ) ;
/ / send file via direct connect
/ / RF transmitter
cat precious > /dev/scsi/sd10h ;
/ / disable transmitter
iocntl( tx_off ) ;
}
done
```

Every five to ten minutes, the offending workstation
would take a snapshot of the USS *Maine*'s position, then
transmit the forty-byte descriptive packet to a nearby
receiver located inside the perpetrator's home. Upon
receipt of every new position packet, the receiver sent a
message to the traitor's home computer announcing its
arrival. Once retrieved, the home computer placed a toll
call via Motorola's Iridium satellite to a surface ship—
designated sonar contact Sierra Eleven by the USS
Maine—halfway around the world, off the Kamchatka
Peninsula. After the remote modem answered, forty bytes
were transferred in a burst less than one second in dura-

tion. Following a brief error checking protocol exchange, the call terminated.

And all the while, no one was home. The perpetrator, a female Air Force officer and computer networking specialist, was a thousand miles away enjoying Christmas leave.

Stalked, 12/26/2008, Fri., 06:44 P.M.
USS *Maine*

In the *Maine*'s command center, Skipper Clay McCullough went about the business of covertly maneuvering under the veil of the North Pacific. A quick glance at the plotting table was all he needed to check their position.

Hovering over the charts, McCullough held his lower jaw firmly in one hand, then slid it gently to one side. He could feel it coming; that painful catch brought back memories of his buddy Hawk and high school football, but he'd learned to live with his injury long ago. He closed his mouth slowly, clenched his teeth, and the pain eased.

Football, Clay thought and chuckled, remembering Slay Hawkins, his longtime friend and skipper of the USS *Topeka.* During a high school scrimmage twenty-odd years ago, Hawk accidently blindsided McCullough, slamming his helmet into Clay's lower jaw, dropping him flat on his back. Even today, Clay cringed thinking about it.

He knew he should've been protecting himself instead of watching the play develop across the field, but he'd learned his lesson the hard way. If you want to stay in the play, always keep ahead of the situation. He'd learned this principle then, and had used it to survive ever since. Even now, with a surface warship possibly trailing them, McCullough struggled to stay ahead of their situation.

The deep water of the Kuril Trench gave Clay ample room to maneuver. Surrounded by more than a dozen seamen inside the spacious compartment that was the command center, the skipper prepared the crew for yet another thorough sonar search. Below periscope depth, McCullough's primary sensory input was sonar. Without an exchange of words, his chief sonarman knew exactly what he wanted to know. Was the *Maine* still being stalked by Sierra Eleven or had they shaken her?

Forward in the sonar room, the chief sonarman was on the move, helping classify contacts. Poised behind a row of four technicians, he studied their consoles, shifting from one to another. As the submarine moved slowly forward, his sonar team listened using hydrophones—underwater microphones fitted on the bow, both sides of the hull, and towed inside a long thick cable. Off to the left, an equipment rack filled with Mercury computers collated every sound detected by the ship's hydrophones, then translated them to the sonarman's display as vertical lines.

Chewing his black grease pencil, the chief sonarman saw no sign of Sierra Eleven topside . . . so far. Instinctively, he requested a course change from due east to northwest. This maneuver allowed his team to listen for contacts in their blind stern arc, the relatively small cone of silence directly behind them.

Searching for anyone in their area, the sonar team listened and watched as sounds separated into discrete bands, vertically lining their waterfall displays. It took several minutes for the towed cable array to straighten out following the course change, but once it ran true, the chief sonarman grimaced. No need to check the pattern library. Without a doubt, the maneuver had revealed Sierra Eleven concealed by their baffle. After analyzing Sierra Eleven's motion nearly thirty minutes, it became clear that she was tailing them from a range of roughly twenty miles. No ambiguity, her active sonar signature was clear and, by now, easily recognized.

"Sierra Eleven was covering our six, Captain. Best bearing is due west at two seven zero."

"Very well. Have you got a definite sound I.D. on their sonar yet?"

"Negative, Captain. Sierra Eleven is believed to be a warship based on her active sonar signature, but she's not one of ours. Origin unknown. Not American, NATO, or Russian. Type unknown, but she's a warbler . . . sounds like a rippled chirp. One-second pulse similar to a British 2020 but tinny . . . some sort of cheap imitation. We're searching for a match, but no hits so far. I think she's one for the books." Sierra Eleven was using an active sonar of unknown origin to scan the area and, as such, must be assumed hostile. The *Maine*'s orders: avoid all contacts.

"Record her signature, everything you can get. Sounds like one for the boys back home."

Meanwhile, Commander McCullough pondered the stalking warship. Haunting questions concerning ocean surveillance technology dominated his thoughts. Was Sierra Eleven being drawn to the *Maine* by information other than her sonar? It wasn't likely, but it was possible. America had done it. So had the Russians. Building on Russian ocean surveillance research conducted throughout the eighties, America and Russia had succeeded in illuminating the ocean depths in such a way that only they could peer beneath the surface. Other countries would certainly follow in time. The admiralty projected a five-year lead. Scientists, on the other hand, felt a five-year lead was optimistic because much of the original research had long since been publicly available over the internet.

The surveillance technology which rendered the oceans

transparent revolutionized the world of submarine operations. McCullough's best intelligence confirmed only America, her allies, and Russia possessed it. *But what about Russia?* the skipper wondered. *They had the technology. Would they share it? Hell no . . . but they'd sell it if the price was right!*

If Sierra Eleven's ocean surveillance wasn't limited to sonar only, McCullough's evasion tactic would ultimately prove ineffective. Nevertheless, he had no intelligence that would lead him to believe otherwise and he did hold a considerable speed advantage over any surface warship afloat. Clay's mind was made up. He would outrun Sierra Eleven, but quietly, using a recent modernization to the *Maine,* her new screw—a pump jet propulsor system adopted from the British Swiftsure-class submarine—designed to reduce cavitation by compressing, or squeezing, the gas bubbles back into the water. Once he'd decided on his evasion tactic, his heart rate quickened. Anytime an eighteen-ton, four-story-tall, 560-foot-long guided missile submarine accelerates from a near standstill to speeds in excess of thirty knots, the awesome power—the feel of the boat—invigorates the crew and the rush is contagious. When altering course at speeds greater than twelve knots, a submerged submarine handles like an aircraft in flight. As such, once a large wheel order is given, the helmsman and planesman work closely together. While the helmsman wheels her nose about, the planesman pulls her nose up, avoiding a downward, spiraling dive.

"Gentlemen," McCullough spoke to the men in the control room. "It is my intent to shake Sierra Eleven, so whatever you're doing, do it quietly." Catching the glance of the OOD, the skipper began issuing orders with a reassuring tone of calm precision. "Officer of the Deck, we're breaking contact."

"Quartermaster, plot our best course for egress from this area avoiding all contacts. We're getting the hell out of Houston."

"Aye, aye, Captain. Best course is zero nine zero."

"Engineering, we need a slow, controlled acceleration ramp. Stand by for full power. We'll engage the pump jet, sprint awhile, then listen."

"Reactor room's standing by for full power, Captain. Pump jet impellers on line."

"Very well, Engineering," the skipper said. "Helm, make your course zero nine zero."

"Aye, aye, Captain, coming about to course zero nine zero."

The skipper scanned the status board, then nodded approval. "Engage impellers."

Sounds of rushing water were punctuated with "Aye, aye, Captain."

"Engineering, all ahead full."

More than sixty thousand horsepower accelerated the *Maine* forward with incredible force. Biting into the water as the pump jet impellers spun up, force from the rudder rolled the boat twenty degrees about its long axis. Anything not secured shifted quietly without mishap. Within half an hour, they were moving over thirty-five knots and still picking up steam.

Spooked Her, 12/26/2008, Fri., 07:31 P.M.
Onboard Sierra Eleven

From a TV monitor inside the bridge of Sierra Eleven, Mandrone watched sailors in the sonar room pinging away, trailing the *Maine* twenty miles due east. *A respectable distance,* he thought with a confidence that suddenly eroded in the blink of an eye.

For a few moments that seemed to drag on forever, he felt perplexed, surprised by what he saw displayed on screen. Had he overlooked something? What was happening down there? Then it became clear.

They'd spooked her. The *Maine*'s skipper had gotten anxious and was making a run for it—oldest evasion tactic in the book for breaking contact. *Well, not to worry,* Mandrone thought. *This run's not altogether unexpected.* Six minutes later, when the next SUBTRACK data came in via phone, he confirmed his suspicion—the *Maine*'s speed and direction had indeed changed. The plot advancing across his computer monitor told the whole story. In his mind's eye, Mandrone was submerged with the *Maine*'s crew, pondering the skipper's situation, his every thought. He could visualize it clearly now. The sub had checked her baffled area, detected the *Kansong,* and run. *She can run,* Mandrone thought sardonically, *but she can't hide.*

After studying the *Maine*'s new speed and heading, he alerted the captain. Fifteen minutes later, after receiving two additional sub posit updates, the *Kansong* altered direction, running an intercept course on the *Maine.* They couldn't match her speed knot for knot, but Mandrone knew they'd eventually catch up with that dark, mysterious lady of the evening.

Never Happened, 12/25/2008, Thu., 09:58 P.M.
Ford Island, Pearl Harbor
Integrated Undersea Surveillance System (IUSS) Command

Inside IUSS Command Headquarters (formerly SOSUS), the situation was reasonably clear. One of their onshore listening posts, a station in Northern Hokkaido, Japan, had detected the classified frequency signature of an American submarine off Russia's Kamchatka Peninsula. Judging from their latest USSPACECOM information, the submarine was probably SSGN 741, the USS *Maine*.

Based on the active sonar transmissions from a surface ship scouring the seafloor behind her, she may have been detected. It wasn't likely, but it was possible. It was hard to know for sure. What else was known about the surface ship? Very little at this stage; an unidentified or little known class, very likely of Russian origin based on the harmonic frequencies detected, probably Russian or North Korean Navy. At this juncture, it didn't seem important really.

Only two things mattered. The guided missile boat had broken contact, and officially, the American submarine was never there.

CHAPTER TWO

Red Tag, 12/26/2008, Fri., 08:02 P.M.
USS *Maine*

Ash Wilson's blackout curtains were quietly drawn open by a seaman making his wake-up calls. Shining his flashlight inside Ash's bunk, Wilson's call was delivered by a patient, soft male voice. "Ash. Wake up, man. Time to get ready for your watch." Wilson woke with a start, scrunched his face, silently acknowledging the call, then slowly began to stir.

Wilson removed his flashlight from a small wall-mounted utility pouch hanging by his head, then pulled himself out of his coffin-sized bunk. Next, he propped up his hinged bed—revealing the contents of his locker—and carefully tucked the bear away in his resting place. Ash noticed the fiber-optic cleaning kit he'd borrowed and decided to come back for it. After a shave, shower, and breakfast, he was ready to face the workday.

Before taking over his watch, Ash took the short walk from the crew's mess through Sherwood Forest—the missile deck—back to his bunk to pick up the cleaning kit he'd signed out. He had borrowed the kit from the air-conditioning room toolbox, allegedly for cleaning his laptop computer keyboard, and was on the hook to return it ASAP.

Entering his dorm room cubical, he was relieved to notice everyone either asleep, eating, on watch, or occupied elsewhere. Once again, Ash propped open his locker, but this time he removed the cleaning kit he'd used last evening. The kit consisted of a can of pressurized air, alcohol, Q-tips, plastic carrying case, and a small packet of lint-free tissues. Laying the kit at the head of his bunk, Ash's heart raced so fast his ears were pounding. No doubt about it—espionage was a stressful business. After a deep, slow, calming breath, he lifted his bear from his resting place and, without hesitation, began taking him apart. First, he removed the bear's head with a twist. Through the opening created by the bear's thick neck, he removed a metal can seemingly identical to the can of pressurized air contained in the cleaning kit. Having efficiently swapped the two cans, with no wasted motion, he quickly replaced the bear's head. Next, he removed the syringe and drug vial from the bear's arms, squirreling them away in his pants pocket. Once reassembled, he carefully tucked the bear away inside his locker, where he would rest undisturbed.

Walking from his cubical in Sherwood Forest, Petty Officer Ash Wilson entered the air-conditioning room down the corridor, across from the crew's mess.

After taking over his watch, Ash's job for the next six hours—along with his three-man team—was a combination of equipment calibration, maintenance, and atmosphere control. On a submarine, atmosphere control means to monitor and mix the breathing air constantly circulating throughout the boat. On paper, the Navy's job description for atmosphere control somehow sounded profoundly dynamic—almost like an adventure. In reality, the duty involved monitoring gauges which never changed and periodically recording readings which were always the same. Although one of the most important jobs on the boat, atmosphere control is perhaps the most boring. Air quality on a nuclear submarine is rigorously measured around the clock for radioactivity, temperature, moisture content, and gaseous concentrations of oxygen, carbon dioxide, water, hydrogen, freon, methane, and carbon monoxide. Since the breathing air is the crew's lifeblood and since it must be manufactured from seawater, nothing can be taken for granted about the process—so the book says.

Ash Wilson well understood that the key to atmosphere control onboard the *Maine* was good monitoring equipment, but like all sensitive measurement gear, it required routine calibration. The *Maine*'s atmosphere monitoring system was the best money could buy—a mass spectrometer centrally located in a fixed cabinet. This system continuously measured all gas levels in the boat and prominently displayed the results in the command center.

But this watch, Ash intended to red tag the mass spectrometer as out of calibration and take it off line—a situation not unusual for sensitive gas analysis equipment. As standard operating procedure, when the mass spectrometer goes down for calibration, a manual backup method is used, where operators with portable analyzers move about the boat, log the results, and then report them to the skipper.

Weekly fan room filter maintenance and round-the-clock air quality testing is a routine, but absolutely necessary way of life on a nuclear submarine. Every submariner knows that his life depends on others performing their jobs without error. On a submarine, there is little room for error and no room whatsoever for malice.

Ash scanned an array of gauges and digital readouts that filled the room. The breathing air on the *Maine* was carefully created, blended, and monitored by equipment in this room. In addition, the humidity and temperature were constantly adjusted to keep the missiles healthy. Fortunately for the crew, the missiles were happy in a reasonably dry and cool environment. Except for cigarettes, anything that would contaminate the breathing air—aerosol cans, glow-in-the-dark watches, shoe polish—were excluded from the boat. To the extent possible, every cubic foot of breathing air inside the *Maine* was kept constantly moving, circulated throughout the boat by a series of large overhead ducts fed from the fan room.

After completing an uneventful six-hour watch, Ash began his equipment calibration and maintenance duties. Every Saturday, he and two other air handlers performed mass spectrometer calibration plus preventive maintenance on the fan room. Ash intended, however, that this week's procedure would prove anything but routine.

Gary Ellie, 12/26/2008, Fri., 02:07 A.M.
USSPACECOM

During the normally quiet week following Christmas, Second Lieutenant Gary Ellie was performing routine maintenance inside the Space Warfare main computer center. The mission of the Space Warfare computer center involved collecting and collating real-time data from every Trade Winds–class ocean surveillance satellite operating in low earth orbit. As the official story goes, Trade Winds–class satellites map ocean surface currents, which results in enormous fuel savings for the U.S Navy and friendly navies around the world. Savings in fuel costs alone more than paid for the satellite program. All this was true; however, the heart of the matter was omitted.

Unofficially, Trade Winds–class satellites track submerged submarines, and therein lies the crown jewel. Within operational limits imposed by depth, speed, and salinity, the wake from a submerged submarine could be detected from space in real time and relayed to the Space Warfare computer center.

The young second lieutenant was eager to impress his new bosses, having been assigned to the comp center for only two weeks. Gary Ellie was a computer system administrator, a techie, and considering his age and experience, there was none better. He believed, like many young engineers, that he could get ahead of the game by working long, hard hours, but in his heart, he did the work because he loved it. Like flying to a pilot, he had high-performance computers in his blood. Along with millions of others, Gary Ellie was addicted to the allure of high tech. He needed it near; to touch, to feel and caress.

At this time in his life, he was young, optimistic, and had almost limitless energy. Like most engineers, Gary Ellie possessed one great gift: his curiosity. It wasn't enough for him to know something worked, he was compelled to understand how and why it worked. When discussing computers, some said they'd seen Gary Ellie's appearance transform, his eyes glazed over with thoughts of high tech.

Standing on the raised floor of the computer center, he gazed mesmerized, awed by the most powerful collection of computers under one roof in the world. Never resting, linked to hundreds of lesser computer centers worldwide, the nerve center operated around the clock. Working inside the Space Command comp center was a profound experience for Gary Ellie. He found the environment thrilling, almost sexual. He'd thought his infatuation with technology was strange at first, worrying he might be a little bit crazy. Throughout his college years, he'd learned that he might be crazy, but the good news was he wasn't alone. All the young people he'd met since arriving—the entire comp center support staff—loved it. They were nuts . . . as crazy as he was. Most important of all, he'd found a group of kindred spirits. *My kind of people,* Gary Ellie thought, believing he'd found where he was meant to be.

Gary Ellie couldn't wait for the Christmas holidays. The week between Christmas and New Year's was the best time for a techie to have fun in the comp center—practically deserted, no people—only computers wall-to-wall. While nearly everyone else went home on leave, he enjoyed having the most powerful computer system in the world at his disposal.

Working through the night into the early morning hours, Gary Ellie was cleaning up old programs—programs that no one had run for two years or more—making room for new ones. A routine administrative task for any super-user, but one which had been neglected for years. From Gary's point of view, this cleaning exercise gave him a chance to learn his way around the supercomputer named SUBTRACKER, an awesome machine if ever there was one.

This is so cool! Gary Ellie thought sitting behind his console terminal perusing all the software available. He'd been there for hours, enamored by the almost endless collection of programs. *Is this heaven, or what?*

Slowly, his eyes began glazing over. It was late. Focusing on the flashing time stamp he read:

```
26 December 2008
2:11 A.M. Friday
```

After working twenty hours straight, he'd lost track of time. He yawned, drowsiness getting the best of him. *Well, it's about time I let the computer do the walking,* he thought. Out of habit, he typed a cryptic command into SUBTRACKER's keyboard requesting a process activity report.

What Gary Ellie saw was exhausting. Hundreds of active processes scrolled by on screen. The renegade sub posit database query program was asleep when he scanned the active program list, but in all honesty, even if it had been running, it wouldn't have made any difference. With a seemingly endless number· of programs on SUB-TRACKER's process queue, all waiting in line to run, the renegade program wouldn't have been detected on casual observation no matter what he had done. Even if he'd been a project software expert, there were simply too many programs running concurrently for one person to assimilate the big picture, comprehend all the intricate details, correlate the relevant clues, and piece together what was happening.

Follow the Yellow Brick Road, 12/26/2008, Fri., 08:20 P.M.
Pyongyang, North Korea
Mission Planning Facility

From a distance, the Mission Planning Facility could have been any of the high-tech industrial buildings scattered outside Boston, off the 128 loop. From a distance, they could have manufactured computers, software, radio components, power supplies, or who knows what else there. Only on closer inspection did it become clear that this facility provided one of the most important support functions necessary for the North Korean Army, Navy, and Air Force to run a war—cruise missile mission software development. This manned, computerized facility was a uniquely specialized software development house—one which painstakingly planned cruise missile flight paths in almost unimaginable detail, wrote all the customized guidance system software used to fly every mission, and simulated each mission before it was flown. Their final product, when all was said and done, was a CD-ROM containing the software required to fly each cruise missile mission sponsored by Kim's regime.

Inside Kim's revitalized military machine, cruise missiles were one of the linchpin, top priority technologies for anyone seeking career advancement. Everybody in the North Korean military who was anybody had, at one time or another, been associated with the cruise missile program. As a result, the entire vertical organization well understood the priceless value of terrain intelligence in planning any land attack. The need for this type of information drove the expansion of Kim's intelligence network around the world, with specific emphasis on Russia and the United States. For in these countries, terrain information was collected via satellite, updated, and stored on a daily basis; not only the terrain of Russia and the United States, but every square foot of terrain of interest to anyone anywhere around the world.

At least for now, the plant manager felt this latest crisis was nearly behind them. He'd seen this frenzy coming to a head over the past six months, but in the final analysis, it's not over till it's over. Their mission software was in the can, shipped out the door, and there was nothing, well almost nothing, left to chance. From a cruise missile software and systems perspective, the chances of success were excellent—exceeding ninety percent. You don't normally get six months to plan, program, and simulate a cruise missile attack, but according to the plant manager's orders, the importance of this mission could not be overstated. Everything they needed, all the necessary terrain information, had been made available over the last six months—he'd never asked how. If any mission ever deserved to succeed, this was the one. The plant manager felt a great deal of pride in that they'd had the chance to do it right the first time, and they'd taken advantage of it. In his gut, he believed the mission would succeed beyond all expectations. Their Dear Leader would be pleased.

The hours demanded by this place were impossible; still he enjoyed this type of work compared to the agricultural life of his parents. If he ever left the business, he'd miss the action—no doubt about it.

It was late, after eight Friday evening, when leaders from Kim's Pyongyang regime entered the building. Before greeting the group face to face, the plant manager placed his hand over his chest, felt a familiar round button about the size of a quarter, and breathed a sigh of relief. His Dear Leader pin was in place, prominently displayed over his heart. Quickly skirting his visiting government authorities around three security checkpoints, he guided them inside the mission simulation room. Huang Kŏn, the supreme commander of North Korea's military forces, headed the small entourage, followed by the foreign intelligence chief.

Upon entering the room, they saw a large satellite view of Wisconsin, Michigan's Upper Peninsula, and the south Canadian border projected on the conference room screen. After adjusting the focus of the overhead projector, the plant manager took his position behind the podium and began his presentation.

The viewgraph projector was attached to a laptop PC on the speaker podium and projected the computer's display onto the large wall-mounted screen. Initially, the plant manager ran a goosed-up CD-ROM version of the *Rand McNally Road Atlas* for navigating around his maps. Following a sequence of mouse clicks, he zoomed in on the Upper Peninsula of Michigan, drawing attention to their target area with a red circle. Inside the red circle, a clear aerial view of ELF Station Michigan emerged in ever enlarging detail.

Remarkably, the ELF transmit station stood out like a sore thumb in the photograph, looking exactly like a plus sign from the air, with the transmitter building located at the intersection of the two crossroads. Located in the rural woodlands near Munising, on Michigan's Upper Peninsula, the station's visible transmitter antenna consisted of two orthogonal wire runs, several miles long, supported above ground by two rows of suspension towers. From the air, this plus shape resembled two wide belts carved into the dense woods— much like a power line right-of-way scarring the landscape.

"Visually," the plant manager began quietly, "targets don't get much easier to spot from the air than this." Once he had the undivided attention of his audience, he continued. "In addition, the target designated ELF Station Wisconsin is nearly identical in appearance and readily accessible from numerous rural locations within our seven-hundred-mile operating radius. Once airborne, en route to target, our chances for success exceed ninety percent."

"Your simulations confirm these claims?" Kŏn asked cautiously.

"Our simulations project a probability of success greater than ninety-eight percent, General."

"Once the ELF transmitters are neutralized," the supreme commander said clearly, not to the plant manager, but to the foreign intell chief, "have you confirmed how the American missile boats respond to this situation? What's their standard operating procedure if they lose their ELF comm link?"

"As you're aware, General, we have several sources of information regarding how they'll respond. Lieutenant Commander Mike Mandrone, for one, assures us they'll come shallow, they'll carry on as they did before deploying deep-water ELF communications. Depending on their operational situation, they'll attempt to establish communications by any means possible, first trying VLF, and if that fails, their UHF satellite link. They must minimize their probability of detection, so before exposing their UHF comm mast above the surface, their submarines will come shallow, deploy their VLF buoyant wire antenna, and listen, awaiting further instructions."

"And what will their VLF instructions be, given this scenario?"

"Operationally, the Americans have worked through this ELF comm lost scenario many times over. Mandrone knows these procedures backwards and forwards. The SSBNs will be ordered to stay deep while the details of our ELF attack are sorted out. As a matter of policy, they're always told to stay deep during politically volatile periods, probably for a matter of hours."

"But initially, they'll come shallow, at least for a time."

"They will. We are sure of this."

"It looks almost too easy," a young aide observed, speaking softly into the intell chief's ear.

The supreme commander overheard his whisper and quickly took exception. "These types of operations require long-term planning," Kŏn corrected. "Dear Leader's magnificent vision coupled with years of preparation put us in this favorable position today. It's not easy and it's no accident."

The intell chief was not so abrupt, but agreed. "The supreme commander is right. Without Dear Leader's guiding vision, planning, and long-term commitment, we would not be in this position today. When we need the ELF transmitters neutralized, we can deliver with a high probability of success, but collectively, it took many years to establish this capability."

Nodding approval, the supreme commander allowed the plant manager to continue his presentation.

Over the course of the next thirty minutes, the manager

reviewed the boost, cruise, and terminal phases of the cruise missile mission. After running through a visual simulation showing each missile's flight path, the plant manager concluded. "Once the cruise missiles enter the terminal phase of their mission, they'll follow the long wire antenna like a road map to target."

Coming About, 12/27/2008, Sat., 12:02 A.M.
Sierra Eleven

Once the *Maine* completed her high-speed run, she gradually slowed to a crawl, reducing her flow noise and allowing her sonar to operate once again. If the area was found clear of contacts, the *Maine* would come to periscope depth, raise her UHF communications mast, and take her satellite communications break. At this time, Sierra Eleven was due west of the *Maine,* approximately 120 miles back.

On his computer monitor inside the bridge of Sierra Eleven, former Lieutenant Commander Mike Mandrone watched the *Maine*'s speed drop over the course of thirty minutes. Mentally, Mandrone was submerged with the crew. *They're rigging for ultra quiet,* he thought. *Setting up for a sonar search.*

Mandrone checked his watch . . . again. Barely five minutes had passed since his last read. He didn't know when exactly, but he knew something was going to happen soon.

He could feel it.

Deathwatch, 12/27/2008, Sat., 02:51 A.M.
USS *Maine*

Toward the end of Ash's watch, he collected the tools, filters, and cleanup gear he'd need to perform fan room maintenance. Although there were no fiber-optic cable connectors in the fan room, he made sure his toolbox contained the cleaning kit. Once relieved from watch, Petty Officer Wilson and two sailors departed, descending one deck into the fan room directly below. After they'd oiled every blower motor and cleaned each scrubber filter, Ash meticulously inspected the resulting work, one station at a time. Dragging out his inspection, Ash sensed both seamen becoming anxious to leave. He expected this, of course. Then, Ash added an extra step to the maintenance procedure.

Once Petty Officer Wilson completed his inspection, the two seamen began buttoning up the blower room, nicknamed the wind tunnel. About the time they began sealing the wind tunnel's access hatch, Ash feigned losing his filter wrench to remain behind. Simultaneously, both sailors checked their watches, having not eaten for eight hours. Looking into the eyes of both young seamen, Ash concluded they were anxious, tired, and hungry, so he dismissed them by pointing across the aisle to the crew's mess. Immediately their faces brightened as they scurried off. *Kids,* Ash thought with a straight face. *Predictable as hell.*

Not wasting any time, Ash opened the access hatch and again entered the wind tunnel. A very strong wind dominated the corridor. Opening the connector cleaning kit, Ash's hands trembled as he removed the generic white can marked *Pressurized Air.* On first inspection, the extraordinary thing about the canister was weight—it felt like a lead brick. Ash guessed it must weigh eight pounds or so—about the same as a gallon of milk. Shaking it near his ear, he heard the muted sound of sloshing liquid above the wind. In reality, the canister contained one of Russia's most lethal tools of chemical war—a two-part nerve agent, stored under enormous pressure, ten times more toxic than anything in the U.S. inventory. Gaseous at atmospheric pressure, undetectable by the onboard air monitoring equipment, this agent entered the body through the skin and inhalation. It was considered a designer agent by professionals, and Ash's accomplices had done their homework before acquiring this toxin. Programmed at the time of manufacture, it would remain lethal for twenty-four hours after activation; the average lethal dose—comparable to ricin—a minuscule $^1/_{5,000}$ of a gram. Regarded by some as quick and merciful (by others as cheap and effective), without the antidote the toxin killed five minutes after initial contact. Characteristically, unconsciousness preceded death by one or two minutes.

Ghost Ship, 12/27/2008, Sat., 04:57 A.M.
USS *Maine*

Time to gas the sewer pipe, Ash thought, feeling a paralyzing sense of trepidation. In the early days of submarines, submariners were referred to as sewer pipe sailors.

Ash examined the generic white can for the final time, then double-checked to make sure he had the syringe and antidote vial. Feeling the hard lump in his pants pocket, Ash twisted the base of the can one half turn, opening an internal passageway allowing the two separate parts of the agent to mix freely, thereby activating the toxin. Once he'd given it a good shake, he threaded an air nozzle onto the canister with a spin. Clutching the valve with his right hand, he twisted several turns, eventually piercing the top of the pressure vessel. When he felt the top of the canister yield, he wedged it alongside a whirring blower assembly, backing the threaded valve out one quarter turn. As Ash expected, the background noise of the droning fans and howling gale drowned out the *hissssssing* sound of escaping toxin. Immediately, he exited the wind tunnel, sealed the access hatch, and carried his toolbox back to the AC room.

Checking his watch, Ash hurriedly performed some mental arithmetic. Thirty seconds to saturate the control room—closest to the fan room, the people there would go down first—three to four minutes for the toxic air to travel the boat's length into the engine room, four minutes for the crew to pass out, plus two minutes tops till death. In less than ten minutes, he'd be completely alone inside the *Maine,* submerged underneath the Northern Pacific, somewhere off the Kamchatka Peninsula. Briefly contemplating the irreversible consequences of what he'd done, Ash Wilson felt the satisfaction that comes with fulfilling one's destiny. Nothing could stop him now. Concerned for the safety of the ship, Ash imagined the next few minutes inside the control room. Once the skipper dropped, he'd steer and work the planes.

Approaching the control room, he felt a heightened sense of awareness unlike anything he'd ever experienced. He became acutely aware of everything around him—the stench of hydraulic fluid, the smell of bacon from the galley, the muted laughter of sleepy sailors at breakfast, the glare from overhead lights, the throbbing of the power plant—all signs of life on the boat. For a moment, he felt sadness that much of this would be stilled. But what choice did he have? These men chose their vocation as he'd chosen his. They'd volunteered for duty aboard this weapon of Armageddon, they weren't drafted. *Isn't it fitting, almost ironic in a way,* Ash thought. *This ship of death will itself become a ghost ship, forever lost at sea.*

Before stepping into the shadow of death, Ash paused

for a moment outside the control room hatch, sensing the ever slowing pulse of the situation. At first he heard sniffing sounds, followed by the sounds of deep breathing all around him. Gazing through the hatch, the first thing he saw was the weapons systems officer rubbing his nose. The sniffing sounds increased from the control room, then the officer of the deck took in several deep gulps of air trying to catch his breath. For Ash Wilson, time seemed to stand still.

Within fifteen seconds, the OOD's arm jerked in a spasm. Bewildered, Skipper Clay McCullough looked on, but didn't speak. *What should I do?* he thought, overwhelmed by indecision. *What's wrong with everyone? The air . . . something's wrong with the air.* Scanning the air quality indicator panel, all seemed normal—*No, it was red tagged, wasn't it? Maybe . . . I'm not sure, but something's wrong somewhere. It has to be the air, it must be. Nothing else makes sense, but nothing's making sense anyway. What the hell's wrong with me? Damn runny nose.* Squinting, he gazed around the control room. *What's wrong with this picture?*

Grabbing the handrail in a death grip, McCullough suddenly felt his knees giving way. Looking at his XO through narrow slits, he tried to speak coherently. "Something's wrong with the air."

"Maybe you're right." The XO sniffed, scanning the same indicator panel. He couldn't make up his mind. "Are you sure, Skipper? All lights green."

"Uh . . . Spectrometer's red tagged."

As his XO froze with indecision, Clay knew what to do—*save the crew.*

After stabbing at the intercom several times, McCullough finally made contact, mustering his remaining strength to issue one final order. "This is the captain.

Everyone's having trouble breathing, grab your EBA and suck rubber."

But it was already too late.

Within a matter of seconds, McCullough's nervous system failed completely, electrically disconnecting his brain from his body. Every nerve was open, severed by the toxin, and as a consequence, he lost all muscle control.

Clay McCullough's face went slack, losing all expression. The muscles in his hands stopped working, his legs let go, and he collapsed into a jelly-like heap, eyes wide open, face down on the floor. His bladder emptied, his bowels moved, and his difficulty breathing reached desperation levels. Gulping air didn't help. He felt panic, trapped inside a body that didn't work, but never took another breath. Before his field of vision completely tunneled in, he saw Ash entering the control room and for a time watched his every move. Over the next minute, Clay suffered a relentless series of convulsive spasms, his life ending in death by suffocation. Although his last thoughts were scattered, in his heart he wondered *why . . . why was this happening?*

During the next three minutes, one hundred fifty-nine men, many of them newly married, many of them fathers, all of them good men looking forward to the rest of their lives, were mercilessly torn from their families.

Ash needed to take the wheel, but the helmsman, planesman, and diving officer were in the way, strapped snugly to their seats. Ash disconnected the helmsman's seat belt and dragged his massive frame to the periscope pedestal. Winded, he found himself now gasping for air, and gagging in the process. *What a stench! The place smells like a sewer pipe.* This was something he hadn't planned on, but his nose would adjust. It would have to.

Returning to the boat's control station, Ash repeated

the process, moving the smaller, lighter weight planesman out of his way. Nauseated by the inescapable stench engulfing the boat, Ash unbuckled the diving officer's seat belt and shoved the large man sprawling onto the floor. Exhausted from the exertion, he wanted to move him, but simply didn't have the strength to drag the limp, two-hundred-plus-pound man away. Although clear of the control console, the diving officer lay spread-eagle, faceup alongside Ash's feet in the confined space of the three-man control station.

Ash cleaned off the wet bucket seats with an oily rag, took center position at the helmsman's control wheel, then trimmed it. "Driving the *Maine*," he thought out loud. "Can't rest yet . . . no time for that." Facing a wall of indicators, he had much to think about and a great deal to do. He'd worked through it all many times before, and with a little luck, he'd keep the number of surprises down to a precious few.

Suddenly, the diving officer's leg twitched in a death seizure, kicking Ash hard on the shin. Panicked, he looked down, saw the diving officer staring wide-eyed at him, and almost jumped out of his skin. Instantly, nausea overwhelmed him. Ash retched uncontrollably, covering everything in a six-foot range with a foul coating of slimy, brownish-yellow grunge. After a time, he found himself on his hands and knees, throwing up alongside the diving officer's body, his vomiting punctuated with dry heaves. Exhausted by the ordeal, he rolled over on his back and gazed around the control room, trying to regain his equilibrium.

Thirteen open-eyed men, many slumped forward in their seats, stared lifelessly into space, keeping watch over their precious weapon of Armageddon. From his vantage point on the floor, Ash thought the scene looked horrific, even larger than life. But once the shock wore off, he began studying the control room scene analytically, meticulously dissecting each element. Following some additional consideration, he corrected himself out loud. "No . . . there's no life here. None at all. The scene looks frightening, larger than reality . . . maybe, but certainly not larger than life." He stood slowly, feeling light-headed, but good enough to take account of the boat.

Once his dry heaves stopped, Ash didn't notice the sewer pipe stench as much anymore. As the shock of the control room scene wore off, the face of death didn't bother him as much either. *They aren't people really, not anymore, just bodies, and most of them in the way.*

Humans are remarkably adaptable creatures when they need to be. In a matter of minutes, Ash's nose, eyes, and mind completely adjusted to the rancid stench of death. He was alone, without fear, and he liked it. Ash knew that soon, probably very soon, he'd be the most hunted man on the face of the earth. Lesser men would have withered at his prospects, but he felt exhilaration, for Ash was a hunter, and one of the finest. The thrill of the chase was afoot and for the next several days, time was on his side. Unless the United States Navy knew where to look and began searching immediately, they'd never find him. The *Maine* was that quiet. Only way they'd ever find her was if he did something noisy, or frankly—stupid. Once his final deed was done, Ash expected they'd find him. Revealing his location was unavoidable, but it would be on his own terms, in his own time and a place of his own choosing.

Resuming his center seat position behind the control wheel, Ash went about the business of driving the boat. Looking left, checking the *Maine*'s depth to keel and dive angle, Ash read 300 feet, level bubble. *That's a break,* he thought, feeling some relief. Scanning right, he saw the automatic depth and speed controls. *Speed, 18 knots and falling . . . slowly. Good depth and speed. Simplifies my life a little. Setting up for a sonar search I expect. If things go as planned, and the weather's good topside, Mandrone should see me on screen, heading due east.*

Now, where am I exactly? Ash couldn't see the map laid out on the plotting table, but that was no surprise. For the second time, he checked the control wheel's trim, tweaked it just a bit, then slowly eased his hands away. "Steady as she goes," he whispered as the boat held true to course. "And keep your nose up."

She did.

"So far, so good."

Hunched over the plotting table, Ash carefully studied their position. The good news—he was in the box, within a few hundred miles of where he'd hoped, well off the Kamchatka Peninsula. The water was deep here, no IUSS hydrophone arrays for three hundred miles. *Excellent!* All he need do now was secure the boat, then signal Mandrone. Securing the boat wasn't easy, but one man could handle it as long as there was no emergency.

Pulling a checklist from his pants pocket, Ash Wilson read over his remaining to-dos. On top of his list:

FIRE: *kitchen*
reactor
gas
shot
sonar
  . . .
   . . .
    . . .

First thing, he'd shut off every kitchen stove. Any fire, even a small one, could put him out of business. Next, he'd clear a path to the maneuvering room, close the toxic gas canister, then take another antidote injection. *The antidote,* he thought, feeling a flash of panic. Patting his pants leg pocket, he found that the hard lump remained intact. "Good," he grunted. Once secured from fire and flood, he'd steer his "come and get me" course, a prearranged gear-tooth-like pattern, to signal Mandrone. After signaling six hours, he'd slow the screw, and wait.

Ash dreaded the waiting. Only time would tell, but he expected the wait for his rendezvous would prove the most stressful time of his journey. If all had gone as planned, Ash would have been right. But in real life, things seldom work out exactly as planned—there are simply too many significant factors unaccounted for, too many first-order variables left to chance. Ash knew adapting quickly to the unexpected improved his chances for survival. It had nothing to do with right or wrong, really; nothing to do with morals or ethics; it's simply a law of survival: either adapt quickly or perish.

As it turned out, Ash's wait was of little consequence compared to the events that followed his rendezvous. Not surprisingly, many people take notice once a guided missile boat turns up missing.

CHAPTER THREE

Approximately six hours after he began steering his square-wave-shaped course, Ash Wilson took account of his situation. Glancing at the gauges to his left and right, he surmised: level bubble, two-hundred-ninety foot depth to keel, at twelve knots. *Good.*

Should he change depth and dive below the layer? Maneuvering was simpler if he maintained his current buoyancy, besides the DSRV could easily operate at this depth. Mandrone expected him deeper but why risk it? Everything had gone reasonably smooth until now. *Don't push your luck, Ash ole boy. You've got nothing to prove.* Generally, the *Maine*'s greatest vulnerability was during times of depth transition. His last sonar check revealed no one actively pinging topside. As best he could determine, there was no surface traffic in the immediate area, but he couldn't be sure. So Ash's answer was a no-brainer. He'd maintain his current depth; that was challenge enough.

Next topic, Ash thought. As he mentally shifted gears, his jaw muscles tensed. Unfortunately, he had to get into the maneuvering room—no option there. He didn't like working in the maneuvering room, but once inside, reducing the output power and slowing the *Maine* was easy enough. In preparation for his departure, Ash trimmed the control wheel again, making her ready for hands-off operation, tweaking her ever so slightly for good measure, then switching in the autopilot. After more than six hours behind the wheel, the excitement of steering the *Maine* was gone. Ash eased his hands away from the wheel, then visualized what he must do. He'd cut the reactor back, reducing her speed to a crawl, thus reducing her wake below ClearWater minimums.

Just do it. Unbuckling his seat belt, Ash stood and stretched. More than anything else, he wanted to take a ten-minute breather, but there was no time for that. Turning, he headed aft, out of the control room, toward the stern, to the reactor compartment and maneuvering room.

Thirty minutes later, Ash was back behind the wheel. The USS *Maine* crept along, drifting slowly with just enough speed to maintain steering, lying in state, perfectly silent, waiting.

Lost Track, 12/26/2008, Fri., 04:23 P.M.
USSPACECOM

In these days of fiscal austerity, the Navy spent the lion's share of its funding on ships and personnel, comparatively little on shore base facilities. As a result, Falcon AFB provided land-based headquarters for the Naval Space Reconnaissance *Wing,* as the Air Force liked to call them. In the name of joint cooperation and lean budgets, the Air Force provided office space and equipment, while the Navy provided the staff that made up the Pacific screening room— the place where all the surface ships and submarines in the

Pacific were tracked continuously round the clock, twenty-four hours a day.

Ensign Eion Macke stood at his watch station overlooking a room filled with sailors, each gazing blank faced at a series of large computer monitor screens. To a newly commissioned Navy man such as the young ensign, Falcon Air Force Base, Colorado, felt like a foreign land—no ocean, no ships, mainly dry air and dust. Fresh out of Naval ROTC and stuck in the Midwest on his first tour of duty. In his letters home, he described this period of his life facetiously as his great desert adventure. Where was the justice in this world?

Focusing his gaze, the ensign noticed some activity on the floor. One of the sailors monitoring the water off the Kamchatka Peninsula had been tracking the *Maine* several hours, when suddenly, the slowly moving track crawled to a standstill. A few seconds later, the icon labeled USS *Maine* began flashing on screen, indicating track had been lost. In the overall scheme of things, however, this lost track condition wasn't all that unusual. The space-based detection system was still in its infancy insofar as naval operations were concerned. Being relatively new, the sailors operating the detection system called it buggy because typically they couldn't believe what they saw displayed on screen. On the other hand, government contractors, engineers in particular, argued the system hadn't been properly tuned. From their perspective, critical ocean environmental parameters such as surface currents, salinity, and temperature weren't known as accurately as their system required for reliable submarine detection. In addition, performance parameters hadn't been optimized; thresholds for detection were still being refined based on live data collected on a daily basis. All this was true, but the sailors operating the system still called it flaky. Operationally speaking, submarine detection had come a long way, but still remained more of an art than a science.

Once they lost the *Maine*'s track, standard operating procedure required the sailor to first check the weather conditions in the area. Normally, a submarine track might be lost for any number of reasons, bad weather among the most common. In addition, the submarine might slow down below minimum detectable speed or dive below illumination depth, so there was no cause for alarm—not yet anyway. If the seas were average or better, the submarine's immediate vicinity would be closely monitored to see if track could be acquired once again. If the submarine hadn't been detected after ten minutes, the boat would be assumed to have dived below their one-hundred-meter depth limit, and the lost track was reported—as a matter of routine.

And so, once ten minutes had passed, the sailor left his station and reported to the ensign in charge of the watch. "We've lost track on the *Maine,* sir."

"What's the weather in the area?" Eion's tone was matter-of-fact.

"Average seas, sir."

"I see," the ensign replied, pausing for a moment, thinking through the myriad of conditions that might have caused loss of track. "Anything else unusual or out of the ordinary?"

"Her course seemed a little odd, sir. Not what I'd expected, somewhat erratic."

"How do you mean—erratic?"

"Sort of blocky, like the shape of zipper teeth."

"You mean a saw-toothed sort of pattern?"

"I'm not much of an artist," the sailor said, hurriedly sketching the *Maine*'s course. "Not exactly a pointed shark tooth pattern; more of a blunt-nose, broken tooth pattern, something like this."

"Don't worry about it," Eion replied after scanning the line drawing. "Looks more like a sloppy zigzag pattern."

"I don't trust this system, sir, not yet anyway."

"We're even on that score," the ensign smiled, "but I think we'll get there eventually. Besides, it's the best we've got, and from what I read, it's the best in the world. There's one hell of a lot of water out there, and we monitor it with fewer people than anyone would have believed possible ten or fifteen years ago. Anything else in the immediate area?"

"All clear, sir."

"She's probably trailing her cable array, running an extended sonar search. Normally, we might lose track for any number of reasons. Offhand, I'd guess she probably dove deep, below our illumination depth. Just to be on the safe side, I'll give Pac Comm a heads up, get the *Maine*'s satellite break schedule, and get back to you. That way, Pac Comm can put a tracer on her and we'll know when she's scheduled to come shallow. They'll detect her downlink going active during her SAT break, then get back to us." The ensign checked his watch, then subtracted five hours from mountain standard time to account for the *Maine*'s difference in time zones. One thing about this job that took getting accustomed to—you had to keep your days and nights straight. "If they don't detect her SAT break overnight, and we don't detect her within fifteen hours, then we'll start to worry."

"Aye, aye, sir."

A Rock and a Hard Place, 12/27/2008, Sat., 07:12 P.M.
Sierra Eleven

Inside the bridge of Sierra Eleven, Mike Mandrone gazed at the display on his laptop computer. The idea behind his animated computer simulation was simple enough—identify which reconnaissance satellites could see them while off-loading their DSRV, which country owned them, then synchronize their launch operation to minimize their exposure. To no one's surprise, the timing and execution of the DSRV off-load were critical. The skies overhead were literally swarming with satellite eyes.

After scrutinizing both the American and Russian reconnaissance satellite schedule tables for the fourth time, Mandrone furrowed his brow. Their situation wasn't a pretty one. The decision as to when they should deploy the DSRV was his. The decision as to where to deploy the DSRV was in the captain's hands, working in conjunction with his sonar team.

Mandrone felt wedged between a rock and a hard place. Using his best estimates of the *Maine*'s position, along with their most likely intercept time, he'd taken his best shot at a DSRV launch scenario and didn't like the looks of it. Everyone had expected to work in blackout conditions during the darkest part of the night. That came as no surprise. But until now, no one fully appreciated the fact that even their ship's position, its north-to-south orientation on the ocean surface, was critical.

Because of the high density of satellites orbiting overhead, Sierra Eleven must deploy her DSRV oriented with her bow heading approximately twenty-five degrees east of north, parallel the SEASAT's orbital path. In addition, the timing of the DSRV launch must be precise, and it must occur quickly, to minimize their exposure to satellite eyes. As the simulation numbers clearly showed, there was no time, none whatsoever, they could operate in this region of the Pacific unseen by satellite eyes. Given this undesirable, but inescapable, reality, the best they could do was expose their port side to Russian satellite eyes while deploying the DSRV. In summary, as Russian eyes watched Sierra

Eleven's port side, American cameras would no doubt photograph her starboard.

Not great, Mandrone thought, *but good enough.* Her starboard view gave no clue as to the off-load in progress, because the DSRV compartment and launching crane were both located behind a pair of large access doors on her port side. Mandrone knew firsthand the deeply rooted distrust that existed between these two countries and fully expected their mutual suspicion would play out to his advantage. In fact, his plan's success now depended on it.

All things considered, Mandrone's observation was accurate, but unremarkable. Neither the United States nor the Russians could directly share photographic reconnaissance without revealing classified secrets regarding strengths and weaknesses of their orbiting satellites.

As a result, before any photographic information exchange ever took place between the two countries, reconnaissance photos would be rasterized and filtered, a form of image transformation which serves to reduce information content, blur, and somewhat distort the original high-quality prints. In addition, this process can be, and had been, used to modify the photograph's original content, much like adding special digital effects to a Hollywood movie. Not surprisingly, any photographic intelligence shared between the two countries was immediately suspect, subject to days, sometimes even months, of technical scrutiny and expert opinion regarding its validity.

Final Preparations, 12/27/2008, Sat., 08:07 P.M.
Sierra Eleven

From outward appearances, the *Kansong* was an old, Andreyev-class, Russian civilian research ship, originally christened the *Konstantinov* in 1989, now flying North Korean colors. In truth, Sierra Eleven was North Korea's only submarine rescue ship, modified to find a sunken submarine, then, if possible, rescue her crew. The *Kansong* was outfitted with two key pieces of equipment, each optimized for the sub rescue task at hand: a new, more powerful, Chinese sonar—modeled after the British 2020 system—for precisely locating the downed sub, and the *Cha-ho,* a Chinese DSRV—first tested in 1986—for reaching the crew.

Inside the *Kansong*'s concealed DSRV compartment, Mike Mandrone watched as his crew loaded the fifteen-meter-long *Cha-ho* with tools; power converters; antenna adapter cables; marine, ELF, and VLF receivers; and a young, healthy spider monkey. Storage space inside the DSRV was tight, but Mandrone knew everything and everyone would fit. Both he and his nine-man North Korean crew had worked through this final prep checklist many times before. Originally designed for a complement of four crew and six survivors, the *Cha-ho* had been gutted of most sophisticated electronic equipment in preparation for its final, one-way rendezvous with the *Maine.*

Once loading was complete and all their DSRV diagnostic tests had passed, Mandrone checked his watch, satisfied they were ready. In a matter of hours, the *Cha-ho* would make its last dive, moving Mandrone plus nine seasoned, extensively trained SSBN crewmen into the *Maine.*

CHAPTER FOUR

Before boarding the *Cha-ho* for his final crawl-through inspection, Mandrone reviewed his checklist one final time. Highlighted with fluorescent yellow so it couldn't be missed, he frowned at the words "antidote injection." Mandrone hated shots, but more than that, he hated the possibility—however remote—of needlessly dying from poison gas. Of all the things about this mission that worried Mandrone and his crew, entering a submarine saturated with an active, horrifically lethal, toxic gas topped the list. To make matters worse, as if breathing the stuff wasn't bad enough, touching anything exposed to the gas would kill you if you were not protected in advance by the antidote. *Man, that's nasty stuff*, Mandrone thought. *Why worry about nuclear bombs or terrorists when you've got vats of this stuff aging in leaky storage vaults somewhere inside mother Russia?*

"Bridge, Sonar. Contact bearing dead ahead."

Scanning with radar for surface ships, the captain saw only endless miles of ocean ahead. "Sonar, this is the captain. Bearing is clear. Report what you've got."

"Contact is shallow, Captain, above the layer; drifting,

dead in the water; no detectable ambient noise. Range: approximately ten miles."

"Do you advise any change in intercept course or speed?"

"Negative, Captain. Estimated time to intercept—forty minutes."

"Very well, Sonar. Will maintain course and speed. Inform me immediately if the situation changes."

"Aye, aye, Captain."

Inside the bridge, the captain's gaze shifted to Mandrone. The captain's weathered face looked almost expressionless, but from the glimmer in his eyes, Mandrone knew the old man was quietly pleased. Precious few surface ship captains on the face of the earth had ever detected, tracked, and closed on an American nuclear-powered guided missile submarine. Overall, the sense inside the bridge was one of quiet anticipation, almost subdued surprise. In his heart, the captain had never really believed they'd get this far, but now it looked as if they just might pull it off. At least one thousand things could still go wrong, but they had a chance, a good one so long as the *Maine* was unaccompanied, drifting out here all alone. And with each passing minute, the odds were shifting in their favor—the Pacific's an enormous ocean. *Amazing,* the captain thought. Dear Leader's visionary prophecy was unfolding before his very eyes, and he was an instrument, a major actor in their unification play.

"Your time is short, Commander," the captain said in an even tone. "As you requested, we'll close, come about, then deploy the *Cha-ho* with the *Maine* one hundred yards off our port bow."

"Very well, Captain. Once in position, our launch window's short—can't miss it." Walking toward the hatch, a sense of déjà vu engulfed Mandrone like an inescapable backwash. Somehow, maybe in a dream, he'd been here before. DSRV scenes from Tom Clancy's *The Hunt for Red October* flooded his mind, flashing back with all the freshness, all the vividly real sensation of a fleeting dream—just past. Then, in the blink of an eye, his fantasy faded. He approached the captain, very possibly for the last time.

"Remember, Captain, Ash is expecting our signal. He's got to be exhausted, could be sleeping. Put a practice torpedo in her side to wake him up, then once we're in position, give him a one second chirp—full power."

"Very well, Commander."

Their eyes connected briefly. The captain recognized a distant emptiness in Mandrone's expression unlike any he'd ever seen. Though raised generations, even worlds, apart, they shared one thing in common: an awe of the sea. Beyond that, the captain found Mandrone a man without family or country. His judgment was accurate as far as it went, but nevertheless incomplete.

Former Lieutenant Commander Mike Mandrone was driven by revenge, money, and an unyielding need to vindicate himself. He considered himself a rogue warrior, a mercenary in a high-stakes game of vengeance and diversion. His plan was to hit fast, divert the Seventh Fleet, and run for the money. North Korea had bankrolled their expedition, set up him and his crew for life, and he had no intention of risking it all or dying in the process. He knew he was singularly qualified for this job, but six years earlier, he couldn't have anticipated any set of circumstances that would have led him here. *If you beat a man with a stick long enough,* he mused sardonically, *he starts to like it.*

Looking back, Mandrone believed his troubles all started with a book.

Admiral Conrad Quintana, U.S. Navy mover and shaker, hired Mandrone to write a book describing the strategic implications of submarine detection from space, a book the Navy subsequently went to great lengths to discredit and block from publication. Following a series of suits and countersuits filed by Mandrone, a New York publishing house, and the Navy, the United States Government intervened by engaging Dr. Tristan Roberts and other Lawrence Livermore experts as a technical arbitration team. To the Navy's dismay, Livermore found Mandrone's work rigorously precise, citing his work as technically legitimate, repeatable, and well substantiated by supporting data.

Mandrone could clearly see in retrospect that at that moment he won the battle and lost the war.

As a result of the Livermore hearings, the Senate Armed Services Committee put pressure on the Pentagon to explain—in plain English—the practical consequences of Mandrone's work. The U.S. Navy and Central Intelligence Agency, anxious to not appear complacent, decided to play along for a while and retaliate later.

Eventually, the book led to Mandrone's testimony before the Senate Armed Services Committee, which ultimately shut down the Navy's submarine building program, after much gnashing of teeth. Less than one year later, an IRS judge convicted him of tax evasion with implications of womanizing—a trumped-up charge of which he was completely and totally innocent. Before East Coast politicians and Admiral Conrad Quintana had finished with Mike Mandrone, he found himself bankrupt, a marked man with a blacklisted social security number, a man without country, family, or prospects in the United States.

For a former U.S. Naval Academy graduate (class of 1984) with a once promising future, Mandrone's options looked pretty dismal. Officially, the United States government didn't want him, government contractors and universities couldn't hire him, so what could he do?

He didn't have to wait long.

CIA professionals following Mandrone's case contacted him once they'd determined his prospects had shifted from bad to worse. For nearly two years, he worked without incident in Hokkaido, Japan, for the CIA as a naval technology analyst, and then one day, field officers would later speculate, Mike Mandrone met the competition.

North Korean agents initially contacted him off campus, then after several "getting to know you" meetings, they described an upcoming sea duty assignment they had in mind. Their plan sounded too fantastic to take seriously at first, but eventually, it struck a cord with Mandrone.

In fact, for diversionary reasons of their own, they planned to do exactly what Mandrone had predicted would be done. It was only a matter of time; their resources had been in position for years. He could either join 'em or watch from the sidelines. Months later, he resigned from the CIA, apparently taking another job, with the government communications division of Sony. As police investigators would later confirm, this was in fact true, but after three weeks at Sony, Mike Mandrone simply vanished, disappeared off the CIA's radar screen.

But that was then, Mandrone thought, stiffening his spine, *and this is now. Time to face the music.*

As he walked from the cool, air-conditioned bridge, through the hatch into the humid night air, Mandrone's stomach suddenly knotted into an icy ball.

He knew why, didn't have to think about it—that bloody Russian gas made his skin crawl.

Mandrone was the last man down and closed the *Cha-ho*'s hatch behind him. He felt the *Kansong* changing direction, coming about to a northerly heading. *We're close. Won't be long now.* Moments later, through the DSRV's forward viewing port, he saw the outside compartment lights fade to black. Stooping, he worked his way forward through the cramped confines of crew and equipment. After folding down his bulkhead-mounted seat, he studied the now familiar faces of his crew. Each man had been handpicked, not by Mandrone, but by the North Korean admiralty. This worried Mandrone initially, and as a result, each man's service record was translated, then made available for his review.

At first read, he'd been impressed, but after spending the last four months together with the men, working as a team, he'd become a believer. If this mission could be pulled off at all, his crew could do it. Occasionally, often when you least expect it, life deals you a winning hand, one that can't miss. Mandrone had that hand now; he was sure of it. In some technical respects, his crew was smarter, or at least knew much more, than he did. Each spoke fluent English and possessed at least four technical specialities. They were specialists, true enough, their jobs demanded it, but the scope, the breadth of their skill set was extraordinary. Each crewman had the equivalent of a master's degree in engineering, two had nuclear degrees, three electrical, one mechanical, with the remainder holding advanced degrees in computer science. To top it off, they had all trained for missile boats in the Chinese Navy and had extensive operational experience onboard their SSBNs.

On the personal front, these men weren't spring chickens. Ranging in age from thirty-nine to forty-seven, they were first and foremost professional adventurers of fortune. Although having their own reasons for coming aboard, they shared several things in common. All were well-educated mercenaries, freelance fighters old enough to have lived and loved, yet most had chosen to keep their personal lives uncluttered and free of serious commitments. None had any relationships he wasn't willing to sever. Perhaps most important of all, these men were survivors. When the chips were down, you'd want them around you. In addition, every man among them believed in Korean unification as if it were preordained. And finally, as computer scientists and engineers, they fully understood the unthinkable effects of nuclear weapons, as if they'd experienced them firsthand. Rather than bury their heads in the sand, they hated nuclear weapons with such fervor they were risking their lives doing something about it.

At this early juncture, each believed they'd be successful, not because of youthful optimism—their days of invulnerability, of living forever, had long since passed—but because they had what it took to get the job done; they felt it in their souls. Above all else, they had faith in themselves. Collectively, they had the training, skills, equipment, and courage required to pull this thing off, and in this, they bound together as one.

Whether or not they'd succeed, only God knew, but time would tell.

Sealed inside the *Cha-ho,* Mike Mandrone heard an outside gearbox grinding as the crane gingerly lifted their DSRV off her cradle. *Launch sequence under way.* Outside, he saw only inky blackness. In a matter of seconds, he sensed lateral motion, movement toward the access doors. As the crane's twin horizontal displacement motors slowly traversed the pair of I-beams overhead, the mood inside the DSRV was much the same as any training mission—quiet, no nonsense, but not overly tense. Submariners fight like they train.

Overhead, once both displacement motors rolled over access door proximity switches, the pace of the programmed launch sequence picked up and massive things started moving—quickly. The loud hissing, whining sound of hydraulics told Mandrone the enormous outside access doors were opening. He knew, but couldn't see, what was happening. Outside, in the darkness, the two thick, tensile steel access doors were pivoting about their hinges—the bottom door swinging out and down, the upper swinging out, then locking horizontally, exposing the DSRV to the open sea air, thirty feet above the ocean surface.

Mandrone checked his watch. *Excellent! An omen of good things to come!* The *Kansong*'s DSRV launch operation was now exposed to prying satellite eyes, but both her orientation and launch time were perfect. *This is the best we can do and it's good enough!*

As predicted by Mandrone's simulation, satellites hurled by overhead on course and on schedule to within a fraction of a second, scanning all the earth they could see with clockwork precision. Then, even as additional image frames were collected, these same satellites simultaneously transmitted digitized representations of their pictures to ground stations waiting below. Ground stations in Russia, the United States, and around the world recorded these data streams as fast as their eyes in the sky could spew them out.

In the intelligence business, recording unthinkably vast amounts of information is straightforward compared to analyzing it.

And Mike Mandrone's plan took full advantage of this fact.

Immediately after the access doors began creaking open, the *Cha-ho* began her final horizontal traverse toward the sea, seemingly throwing the doors open, erupting from the bowels of the ship like some alien form of mechanical birth. The free fall, carnival ride part of their minimum-time launch sequence was near. Mandrone and his crew knew what to expect and would have preferred to skip it—tough on the stomach. Once their lateral motion abruptly stopped with a metallic clang, Mandrone spoke to the crew.

"Take a deep breath and hold on to your seats."

The crane brake released and they plummeted thirty feet, suddenly slowing during the last five feet of the drop. As programmed, they entered the water with a controlled crash, in near record time.

Seconds later, after the *Kansong* pulled away, an auxiliary crane lowered a tethered practice torpedo nose down into the sea. Manning a joystick control inside the sonar room, a plainclothes weapons officer guided the torpedo on its fifty-knot terminal run toward the *Maine*.

Once the launch crane retracted and the *Kansong*'s oversized hydraulic cylinders slammed the access doors shut, the following message was relayed to the bridge:

"Torpedo away, Captain. DSRV is clear."

The captain checked his stopwatch. *Near record time. Mandrone will be pleased.*

Buckled into the helmsman's padded seat inside the *Maine,* Ash Wilson slumped forward, fast asleep.

Ping . . . ping . . . ping . . . pi-pi-pi-pi-p i i i i n n n n n g g g g g !!!
"Torpedo is closing, Captain."
B A A M M M ! ! !

Ash jumped out of his skin.

This *CLANG* from the high-speed collision reverberated about the *Maine*'s steel hull for several seconds with such tremendous mechanical force that the submarine shuddered.

Now fully conscious, Ash raced forward to the sonar room, piping the passive hydrophones over the intercom.

Minutes later, the *Kansong*'s sonar room contacted the bridge.

"Captain, the *Cha-ho* is approaching the *Maine* . . . hovering above her bow."

"Sonar, this is the captain. Focus a one-second, max-power chirp on her side."

"Aye, aye, Captain. One wake-up call, coming up."

An earthshakingly powerful, explosive ping followed, consisting of not one audio tone, but a continuously increasing sweep of tones, each seemingly louder than its predecessor. The ear-piercing sound heard inside the *Maine* was similar to the sound heard when tuning the earliest oscillator based, shortwave radios—a whistle with ever increasing pitch.

Inside the sonar room, Ash Wilson heard the sound he'd been waiting for all these hours. Before leaving port, he'd heard a recording of that chirped ping, but the recorded version paled in comparison to the real thing. *Amazing,* Ash thought. That ping had frequency components so low and powerful it'd rip a sea lion in two, so powerful the *Maine*'s floor shook and her lights rattled. Technically, her floor wasn't supposed to shake. It was acoustically and mechanically isolated from her outer hull, but apparently, even the quietest submarine in the world had its design limits.

After rallying from his ear-ringing wake-up call, Ash Wilson stared at his pistol. *What good's it going to do?* He had to trust them. He had no alternative.

• • •

The *Cha-ho* was hovering above the sonar's main beam, out of earshot, in a low-power side-lobe region. Be that as it may, the crew heard the wake-up call anyway—bouncing off the *Maine*.

Following the *Kansong*'s ping, Mandrone spoke out loud, to no one in particular.

"Hello, Ash!"

A few seconds pause as the echo decayed, then a crewman spoke.

"Think he heard that, sir?"

Mandrone lifted his right eyebrow. "Count on it. If he's alive, he heard it . . . and we've got every reason to think he's alive."

Mandrone shifted his gaze to the caged spider monkey sitting aft. *Better you than me, little buddy,* he thought, then addressed his crew. "Everyone's injection set?"

A groan punctuated without enthusiasm.

Looking toward the DSRV pilot, he continued. "Very well, set her down."

Hovering above and to one side of the *Maine*'s forward escape trunk, the *Cha-ho* began her descent through the inky black seawater. From a distance, the DSRV looked like a tiny shuttle spacecraft docking with its gargantuan mother ship.

Using a combination of low-power sonar and high-intensity headlights, the DSRV pilot navigated within sight of the *Maine*. The first thing Mandrone made out was the *Maine*'s massive sail. Visibility at this depth was dismal, but the DSRV pilot was good with the maneuvering screws. As a result, his maneuvers were slow, deliberate, but sure. Using the sail's leading edge as a guide, he soon positioned their docking collar over the forward escape hatch. After gingerly touching down, the diving officer

secured the collar, then blew out the water with pressurized air.

Below, in the control room, Ash Wilson heard the commotion topside—someone banging on the hatch of the
escape trunk.

Climbing up the ladder into the escape trunk, Ash sealed
the lower entry hatch behind him. Once inside, he slowly
turned an overhead flood valve, a pressure-equalization
valve which opened through the escape hatch to the outside. With the DSRV seated, resting securely on the escape
trunk hatch, the overhead valve served to equalize the pressure between the DSRV and the escape trunk. As Ash
opened the valve, he heard air hissing, occasionally gurgling from the DSRV back into the escape trunk. Mandrone
had made absolutely sure they'd docked with positive pressure, guaranteeing no toxic air from the escape trunk would
initially enter the DSRV. But not to worry. Most important
of all, the seal was good. Remarkably little seawater—only
a gallon or so—poured in as the gurgling stopped. Gradually spinning the hatch open, Ash again listened for the
sound of rushing water—potentially lethal at this depth.
There was none. The seal held fast and the hatch opened
without complication.

When Mandrone saw the scared dog look on Ash's face,
he recognized at once the reason behind it—*fear.* Mike
would've been worried for his life were he in Wilson's
place. *He must've been through hell,* Mandrone thought,
although he couldn't really imagine what Ash'd been
through; no one could. He spoke calmly, trying to put him
at ease, all the while feeling a combination of fear and anxiety himself. "Ash, we're here to help you."

Maybe Ash was simply too strung out to react ration-
ally, but Mike's comment caught him off guard—mentally
reset him—throwing him into an emotional tailspin. For a

few moments, Ash found himself at a complete loss, not knowing what to say. His gaze went blank, his expression slack. At first, he didn't know what he felt, then suddenly, a kaleidoscope of feeling washed over him. For a fleeting moment, he felt like crying. Every death he'd caused came crashing down on his consciousness. His self-protection circuits tripped into massive overload extinguishing any spark of humanity left in his eyes; then, it was over. He felt nothing at all. Ash's darting black eyes revealed a quick, curious mind, but once again mirrored the pitiless soul of an animal.

Ash smiled, but said nothing, apparently finding some humor in this extraordinary situation. He'd been alone now over eighteen hours, with no one to talk to but himself. Now, encountering real live people, he couldn't think of anything of consequence to say.

Watching Ash Wilson's gaze clear, Mike Mandrone directed his crew to pass the monkey cage forward. As the cage passed hand to hand, Mike felt concern. The wide-eyed little spider monkey panicked, screeching in terror, instinctively sensing danger and the crew's fear. Mike placed the caged animal on the floor alongside the hatch-way opening into the *Maine*. He spoke calmly to the monkey, as if he could understand. "Settle down there, little fella. You'll be fine—Ash here's living proof—that anti-dote works." It was the sound of his voice, not the meaning of his words, that soothed the harried creature. Although quiet now, Mandrone knew the little animal was scared, his small lungs working overtime.

After a brief discussion, Ash climbed down the hatch, back into the escape trunk. Reaching up, he retrieved the cage from overhead, closed and sealed the hatch to the DSRV, then took the monkey below to the control room.

Sensing the death that permeated the *Maine,* the tiny

monkey drew into himself, hugging himself tightly in a fetal position, trembling slightly, but otherwise absolutely still. Ash read the monkey's reaction as absolute terror. Five minutes later, the monkey was still balled up, but breathing, and Ash reported this fact to the commander.

Mandrone entered the *Maine*'s control room alone and surveyed the scene. Gazing at the dead crewmen, he regretted their deaths, but they wouldn't be the last. Figuring one million dead per sea-launched ballistic missile, and twenty missiles or more per boat, a crew of 160 men was expendable. Biting his lip, he chided himself. *Get a grip on it, Mike!* Looking away, the spider monkey caught his eye. Watching the little monkey tremble, he felt compassion, but then suddenly, above all else, he felt nauseous from the stench. Still, the antidote worked and they had a job to do.

Returning to the forward escape trunk, he spoke to his sonarman onboard the DSRV. "Signal the *Kansong*—vacate posthaste."

The calvary had arrived.

Mandrone's crew knew in advance what to expect onboard the *Maine,* but knowing didn't make it any easier. They adjusted to the death onboard the *Maine,* eventually they adjusted to its stench, but none of them, not one, adjusted to the face of death staring at them with open eyes. Somehow, the unseeing gaze of these dead men, these former guardians of Armageddon, seemed to penetrate the very souls of Mandrone's crew. After all, they were sailors too. Even Mandrone found working under a dead man's watchful eye a bit unnerving. Nevertheless, they couldn't take time to rearrange the body furniture now—maybe later, once they'd moved well clear of the area.

Once the crew and equipment were off-loaded, Mandrone ordered the DSRV scuttled. Timed incinerator charges were set to weaken the hull, she was flooded, and the docking collar seal was broken. As the *Maine* rolled slightly about her long axis, the *Cha-ho* slid off the bow, starting her final descent to the blackest depths of the Pacific floor.

Free of the *Cha-ho,* Mandrone ordered the *Maine* to take on additional ballast. His objective was to shift her buoyancy slightly negative, then have her sink—not dive—below the layer to an undetectable, five-hundred-foot depth. He knew sinking in a controlled, near vertical drop produced no detectable wake. In a matter of minutes, she'd slipped below the temperature inversion layer and below the hundred-meter visibility limit of Trade Winds–class surveillance satellites. Leveling off around five hundred feet, Mandrone engaged the impellers and began a passive sonar search of the area.

She was now—and would remain—invisible, until they chose to reveal her position in their own time and place. Other than a few remarkably maneuverable whales and the fading sound of the *Kansong*'s screws, they were alone— nothing detected within a fifty-mile radius.

Less than two hours after the *Cha-ho* was ditched, the *Maine* was running like a bat out of hell—thirty-five knots plus and blind, her sensors swamped by flow noise.

No Show, 12/27/2008, Sat., 07:15 A.M.
San Diego, CA
Pacific Fleet Communications Headquarters (Pac Comm)

A lieutenant junior grade nervously checked his watch for the fifth time in fifteen minutes—and it wasn't due to boredom. The *Maine* was overdue—missed her SAT break. She should have come shallow sometime during the last two hours and activated her downlink, but she had not. Typing at his computer keyboard, he entered an efficient, but cryptic command which allowed him to query the downlink message status of all submarines on patrol, then search the list for only those overdue.

```
$ dnlk -stat -sort 'OVERDUE'
```

Staring at his computer monitor, he grimaced as the expected result scrolled on screen again for the hundredth time. Anyone looking over his shoulder during the last fifteen minutes would have immediately noticed his monitor screen filled with seemingly countless occurrences of this same message. Try as he might, the lieutenant couldn't will the *Maine* to raise her UHF communications mast and activate her satellite downlink.

```
SAT Break Status:    MAINE OVERDUE
                     Maine Downlink Message
                     Status: IN QUEUE
                     Maine SAT Break Window:
                     1300 - 1500 Zulu
Current Time:        1515 Zulu
```

Finally, after staring at the screen over fifteen minutes, the lieutenant decided it was time to spread the word. An overdue SAT break was a rare thing in the world of submarine operations—not unheard of, hostile surface traffic had been known to keep a sub deep—but very unusual nevertheless. Had the lieutenant covered all his bases? As far as he knew, but at this early morning hour, there was no one he could pass his alert message by for a sanity check. His best bet was to play it safe, not overstate the situation, treat it as a matter-of-fact. In the pit of his stomach, he had a bad feeling about this one—couldn't put his finger on why—but in his heart, he hoped they wouldn't shoot the messenger.

Then out of habit, almost without thinking, the lieutenant did a screen capture, taking a snapshot of the text on screen, converting it into a bitmap file with an .xwd file name extension—an X Windows Dump file format understood readily by UNIX workstations, but not by other types of computers without special file transformation software. Next, he appended the file behind his FYI comment in an e-mail dispatch to USSPACECOM, COMSUBPAC Operations, and the Pentagon—everyone who needed to know. When he hit the final SEND key, it was with a feeling of reluctance. Somehow, almost instinctively, he knew this e-mail would come back to haunt him. Once his e-mail was en route, he printed out a hard copy of the message, just to be on the safe side.

Maybe what bothered him was the e-mail. He'd never trusted it. E-mail worked for some people, if they were computer literate and bound to their terminals on a daily basis. For others, e-mail didn't work at all. If you wanted to get your message through, you had to see them face-to-face, or talk to them over the phone. Standing, the lieutenant left his desk and walked across the room, to where a yeoman was seated alongside a secure telephone. For his own peace of mind, he asked the yeoman to call USSPACECOM over the secure phone and relay his message, person-to-person.

So the yeoman called the newly commissioned ensign inside USSPACECOM, then spoke directly, person-to-person, to Eion's answering machine. Disgusted, the yeoman looked into the telephone handset and shook his head in disbelief.

Technology—isn't it wonderful? Eliminate the people and reduce costs. You don't need people really—like hell you don't! You don't need people unless you need something done!

Never had so many depended on so much from so few.

Unsupported File Format, 12/27/2008, Sat., 05:21 A.M.
Pearl Harbor, HI
COMSUBPAC Operations

Inside COMSUBPAC Operations, the yeoman screening their incoming e-mail was running their mail program on his PC. He monitored their e-mail's priority; if it was hot, he made sure it got to the right people without delay. When the e-mail from Pacific Communications Headquarters scrolled on screen, first thing he noticed was the e-mail's FYI priority. *Nothing hot here.*

```
TO: pacscreen@usspacecom.mil
CC: comsubpac@subpac.mil,
    comsub@pentagon.mil
FM: paccomm@paccommhqt.mil
SUBJECT: FYI: Break Status
```

```
                Unsupported File Format.
    Picture will be displayed as a gray box.
```

After seeing the file incompatibility problem, he noted its time of arrival in his incoming message log, stored it away on disk, and put it on his list of things to do. Once their UNIX guru arrived on site, later, much later that morning, he'd take a number and wait in line for Mr. Wizard's attention.

And so ended Round One of their information exchange.

PART TWO

Surgical Strike

Two Weeks Earlier

CHAPTER FIVE

What was unfolding on the plot board inside the USS *Yorktown*'s CIC had been thirty years in the making.

All eyes, including those of Captain Linda Scott focused on a slowly moving V-shaped pair of lines—submerged submarine tracks—displayed on the naval operations tactical screen. ASW (Anti-Submarine Warfare) was the name of the game, but unlike most games, this one cost billions to win.

Cruising the Pacific northwest of the Hawaiian Islands, Captain Linda Scott stood in front of a large screen inside the CIC. Everyone felt apprehensive. For one person in particular, Dr. Tristan Roberts, this new submarine detect, track, and destroy capability represented the fruition of his life's work. He, for one, believed they were making history.

Seated center stage, occupying the two combat director consoles in front of Scott, were the submarine element coordinator, a no-nonsense admiral from Missouri, and Dr. Tristan Roberts, the visiting civilian chiefly responsible for demonstrating America's new submerged submarine surgical strike capability. Both men studied the submarine tracks labeled USS *Maine* displayed on screen, then checked the weather maps for the hundredth time. The weather was holding—average seas with clear skies over both the *Maine* and her target area. This was important because submarine detection from space and satellite-to-submarine downlinks require good weather for reliable operation. Submarine detection works best in calm or average seas; laser downlinks to submerged submarines need clear skies.

Crossing his fingers on one hand, Tristan shot the admiral a thumbs-up with the other. "Conditions are perfect. The *Maine*'s ready for download. Let's do it."

The admiral returned a skeptical *I'll believe it when I see it* glance, then spoke into his headset to their shore-based Operational Control authority. "OPCON One, OPCON One, this is Yorktown Seven Three. *Georgia* patrol area is clear, I repeat clear of contacts. Bring her to launch depth and commence missile drill."

"Roger Yorktown Seven Three," echoed the reply via secure satellite link. "Placing emergency action message in transmission queue—now." A brief pause followed, as a muffled, background conversation took place back at OPCON One. "FYI: we've got a last-minute change of plan. Colonel Mason wants one final manual walk-through before initiating the posit download and spotlight sequences. He requests you report in once the *Georgia*'s detected on screen."

"Roger that OPCON One," the admiral chuckled to himself. "Tell Slim not to worry. If and when we see her coming shallow, you'll be the first to know."

Glancing away from the admiral, Tristan Roberts turned and spoke quietly to Scott. "Tonight, I think we've got her."

Even in low light, Scott could see the glimmer of excitement in his eyes. Scott acknowledged Tristan's comment with a forced tight-lipped grin, then in the darkness of the CIC, she felt underneath her flight suit and rubbed something about the size of a dog tag. Around her neck, she wore a tiny four-leaf clover sealed in a case of clear acrylic; a gift her husband, Jay Fayhee, had given her back in high school—for luck.

The admiral acknowledged Tristan's comment, but remained skeptical.

Undaunted, Tristan announced, "We're headed topside to see the show."

"Make tracks," the admiral responded, pointing toward the bulkhead. "I'll inform the captain."

After clearing his screen, the admiral held down his press-to-talk button. "Bridge, CIC."

"Bridge," the captain's baritone voice boomed over the intercom speaker.

"Roberts and Scott are on their way."

"Very well, will maintain course and speed. Please keep advised."

Tristan and Scott raced out the bulkhead, up a series of ladders to the bridge. Quickly winded by their dash upstream, Tristan spoke to Scott between gasps. "There's going to be a light show here tonight you won't believe!"

Waiting in Line, 12/12/2008, Fri., 05:24 A.M.
USSPACECOM Headquarters

Colonel Daniel "Slim" Mason, ClearWater's special project officer, stared patiently at a large, almost empty projection screen, calmly waiting for the USS *Georgia* to show herself. He didn't know exactly where she was inside grid square B, but he knew she was patrolling deep, well below their hundred-meter visibility limit. He couldn't know exactly how long he might expect to wait because in the world of one-way submarine communication, it's difficult to rearrange submarines quickly, or for that matter, do anything fast. While running deep, one-way ELF radio communications to the USS *Georgia* were slow, but sure, with a data transmission rate of only a few bits of information per minute. To further complicate the timing of their sea trial, these extremely low-frequency bands were shared across the entire submarine fleet. As a result, their orders to the *Georgia* were in queue, waiting in line for transmission, and would be scheduled for repeated broadcasts many times. Normally, the folks at OPCON assume the submarine reads the message on the last rerun, because acting on any other assumption might put two boats in the same water. Trouble was . . . the last message rerun was hours away.

But tonight's sea trial was extraordinary in that grid square B had recently been sanitized by three Orions operating in conjunction with a pair of Los Angeles–class fast attacks, the *Topeka* (commanded by McCullough's buddy Hawk) and the *Cheyenne*. Other than the *Georgia,* there were no other submarines in grid square B, only the surface ship USS *Yorktown*.

After twenty minutes or so, OPCON One's radio operator tapped his headset then spoke to Colonel Mason. "ELF station Wisconsin reports our first emergency action message transmission is complete, sir."

"Very well," Mason responded, starting the mission clock mounted on the wall. Projected on screen, the USS *Maine* and USS *Yorktown* icons were labeled, their speeds and headings displayed, but because of the screen's vast scale, they appeared motionless.

Slim Mason was optimistic about their prospects. He believed, and had hard data to back it up, that the *Georgia* would respond within ten minutes of receiving their first

EAM transmission, and furthermore, he fully expected they'd see her appear on screen as she came shallow.

Turned out, he was right.

The Target, 12/12/2008, Fri., 02:46 A.M.
An Ohio-class Trident Ballistic Missile Submarine
USS *Georgia* (SSBN 729)

On patrol somewhere in grid square B northwest of the Hawaiian Islands, the USS *Georgia*'s crew was interrupted by OPCON's call to action. Inside her communications shack, the Extremely Low Frequency (ELF) receiver began flashing three red letters—EAM. Grabbing the telephone-like handset, the radio operator suddenly sat erect as if his back were made of spring steel. "Conn, radio, we are receiving an exercise emergency action message."

"Radio, conn, aye," replied the OOD. Activating the boat intercom, he spoke to the crew. "Alert one, alert one. Sound general alarm. Man battle stations missile drill." Suddenly, the inescapable earsplitting bong of the general alarm reverberated throughout the boat.

Only moments after the bonging silenced, the OOD, skipper, and XO met back by the communications shack in a cramped compartment containing two locked steel safes.

From this point forward, for the duration of the exercise, everything the three-man team did and said was dictated by the launch manual, a master checklist specifying the sequence of events and dialogue that defined their missile drill. After reading the emergency action message and consulting the book, the XO spoke to the skipper. "We received a properly formatted emergency action message, sir."

"I agree," added the OOD. "Request permission to decode."

"Very well." The captain nodded.

After unlocking their safes, the two officers first pulled out the sub's individualized code book and began matching it against their six-character emergency action message. The first three characters, CBE, represented the sub's ID or address; the last three characters, ATA, made up the sub-specific encoded message.

"Charlie, Bravo, Echo, Alpha, Tango, Alpha," said the XO.

The OOD repeated this sequence exactly, spurring the XO to remove the skipper's SPECIAL ORDERS from the safe and hand them over to him. "We have an authentic message invoking our Special Orders, sir."

The skipper read their orders carefully, then addressed the team. "This is the sub strike sea trial we've been expecting. Looks like the boys topside finally got their act together. Strictly speaking, we're what you'd call—the target." The team nodded understanding, then the XO handed the skipper his fake missile key.

After hanging the key around his neck, the skipper spoke to his team. "Let's get on with it."

The skipper and XO returned to their missile drill positions alongside the launch panel adjoining the control room; the OOD resumed watch on the periscope pedestal.

The menacing threat wired to the launch panel was something the skipper never took casually. Like a law of physics that can't be broken, when the *Georgia*'s launch panel lit up, the skipper's mood was serious and this feeling permeated the entire crew. Even the mathematical, ordered array-like look of the launch panel was intimidating. Displayed were four labeled columns of lighted, one-inch-square push-button switches, duplicated in step-and-repeat pattern forming twenty-four horizontal rows. Labeled left to right, marked by column, the switches read MSL 1SQ,

DENOTE, PREPARE, and AWAY. Although abbreviated so their ominous meaning wasn't clear, these four words conveyed the operational state for each of the twenty-four Trident missiles onboard.

Positioned alongside the launch panel, the skipper addressed the crew over the intercom. His tone—no nonsense. "This is the special exercise you've been briefed on. I say again. This is the special exercise we've been expecting. Set condition 1SQ for weapons system readiness test."

After killing the intercom, the skipper spoke directly to the diving officer. "Proceed to launch depth, then make ready to hover."

"Aye, sir."

Feeling the angle of the deck shift beneath his feet, the skipper addressed his weapons systems officer as the boat came shallow. "Pressurize all missile tubes to normal launch depth."

Immediately, the missile indicator panel sparked to life with red and green lights. "How long until the weapons are warm and ready to fire?"

"Sixteen minutes, sir."

Looking into the eyes of his XO, the skipper spoke quietly, uncharacteristically allowing his anxiety to surface. "It's going to be the longest sixteen minutes of my life." After giving their situation a good think, he whittled down what he wanted to say into the fewest possible words. "This could mark the beginning of the end for the boomer."

"It could, sir, but I doubt it." Inwardly, the XO grimaced, a gut reaction consistent with his opinion set years ago, an opinion established independent of the facts or hard data. Outwardly, he delayed his skeptical kneejerk a few moments in order to appear reflective. After all, he had his career to think about . . . wouldn't want to come across as half-cocked. "The idea of illuminating black water sounds intriguing, like the Holy Grail, but it's a hell of a tough nut to crack. They've been working space-based ASW since Vietnam and nothing's worked yet. The way I see it, sir, nature's on our side with this one and she's in it for the long haul."

"You could be right," the skipper acknowledged willingly, his tone—almost optimistic. "And in a selfish sort of way, I hope you are."

Orbiting Boxcar, 12/12/2008, Fri., 02:54 A.M.
Orbital Inclination: 65 Degrees
Passing Over the North Pacific

Orbiting the earth at a height of one hundred seventy miles, the American-made Trade Winds 8 satellite, called a SEASAT, passed over grid square B in the North Pacific at 2:54 A.M. local time. As it rose above the horizon, the USS *Yorktown*'s tracking system locked on its position, pointing its high-powered electronic jammers purposely skyward in an effort to obscure the satellite's view.

But this powerful electronic interference was all for naught. In less than one second, the boxcar-sized Trade Winds 8 electronically steered an antenna null—a blind spot—over the USS *Yorktown,* effectively removing the jammer by punching a tiny hole in its vast picture of the sea.

As quickly as the jammer had been squelched, Trade Winds 8 radar detected the submerged wake of the USS *Georgia* coming to launch depth.

After monitoring the wake track for a few seconds, making sure it wasn't a false alarm, Trade Winds 8 transmitted the location, direction, and apparent speed of the submerged submarine via geostationary relay satellite to

OPCON One, the headquarters for United States Space Command, located on Falcon AFB, Colorado.

Environmental monitoring was the politically acceptable description for this Trade Winds–class of satellite because the words sounded almost wholesome. In reality, environmental monitoring was bureaucratic techno-speak for surface ship and submerged submarine detection. Powered by a compact nuclear reactor, SEASATs carry every type of sensor necessary to fulfill their ocean reconnaissance mission—a three-frequency synthetic aperture radar, microwave and IR radiometers, a two-frequency scatterometer, plus an electro-optic scanner to boot. In average seas, using this extensive combination of sensors, SEASATs track submerged submarines to a depth of one hundred meters by detecting surface wake and thermal scars.

Fully fueled, weighing in at twenty tons, comparable in size to a boxcar, the Trade Winds–class of ocean environmental monitoring satellite was an awesome thing to behold. Those people who'd seen it on the ground couldn't believe it would fly at all. Most believed, and rightfully so, that trains don't fly.

But this one did.

Detection, 12/12/2008, Fri., 05:54 A.M.
USSPACECOM

Roughly eight minutes after the emergency action message ELF transmission completed, a second submarine icon appeared on screen in USSPACECOM headquarters. Almost immediately, the projection screen operator clicked the icon, labeling her

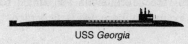

USS *Georgia*

Moments later, their ship-to-shore satellite radio link crackled over the conference room speaker.

"OPCON One, OPCON One, this is Yorktown Seven Three. *Georgia* is coming shallow. We make her posit five miles off our starboard." Once on deterrent patrol, missile boats—like the *Maine* and *Georgia*—never transmit, to avoid revealing their location. Their standing orders: avoid all contacts and remain undetected. Fully half the ASW battle is detecting the submerged submarine; the remaining problem becomes guiding ordnance into the moving target. In the limit, this problem becomes one of response time, and as such, a problem of automation pitting machine against machine.

"Roger Yorktown Seven Three. We confirm *Georgia*'s posit. Does your sonar room still show grid square B all clear?"

After a few moments' pause, the reply came back loud and clear. "Affirmative OPCON One. Area remains sanitized, clear of all contacts."

"And the weather?"

Another pause. "Clear skies and average seas holding over both the *Georgia* and *Maine*. Dr. Roberts recommends we run hands-off, closed-loop in real time, and I agree. If it's ever going to work, tonight's the night. We're go for download, go for spotlight."

Mason took the admiral to mean computers would run the sea trial without human intervention. Walking up behind OPCON One's radio operator, Mason passed him a note. After a quick read, he spoke into his headset. "Yorktown Seven Three. Yorktown Seven Three. You are go for hands-off, go for real time. We wish you God's speed and good luck!"

An Elegant Sister, 12/12/2008, Fri., 02:55 A.M.
Orbital Inclination: 65 Degrees
Onboard a Submarine Laser Communication SATellite

The United States uses two different, but complementary types of satellite—a brother-and-sister pair—to carry out its mission of submarine detection, tracking, and strike. The brother, a flying boxcar called a SEASAT, detects and tracks submerged ballistic missile submarines. The sister, a Submarine Laser Communication SATellite, called a SLC-SAT (pronounced slick-sat), relays target position information directly to friendly naval forces . . . including submerged submarines running shallow. Of the two satellites, Big Brother's a massive brute, while the baby sister's considered a machine of exquisite beauty, precision, and grace.

The genesis of the SLCSAT lay in two physical principals. First, blue-green laser wavelengths penetrate seawater to a limited extent. Second, the laser's enormous information transport capacity makes it an attractive carrier for high-speed data downloads to submerged submarines and surface ships. On the downside, the laser's beam is visible and susceptible to cloud cover. In normal operations, the SLCSAT's big brother guides her laser to the download site—often onto the back of a submerged submarine—but unfortunately, dwelling too long on site with a column of blue-green light, risks focusing enemy attention there.

• • •

Immediately below the southwestern horizon of the USS *Yorktown,* an American-made SLCSAT fired its station-keeping microthruster, fine-tuning its altitude, keeping its orbital period exactly 93.3 minutes. Seconds later, from an altitude of two hundred seventy miles, the SLCSAT passed over the same piece of ocean—grid square B—as her brother passed over only a few minutes before. As she rose above the horizon, the USS *Yorktown*'s ECM (Electronic CounterMeasures) officer felt duty bound to jam her reception of ground control signals. But again, his best efforts were to no avail. The ECM officer knew in advance he couldn't successfully interfere with the SLCSAT's mission—only extensive cloud cover could do that—but he had to try because any enemy worth their salt would do the same. The ECM officer understood the SLCSAT received ground control signals relayed from geostationary satellites operating over its head, so in effect, the SLCSAT looked skyward for instruction, not toward earth or his jamming source.

Seconds before the download began, the SLCSAT received a `laser_comm_enable` message from ground control. After she transmitted an acknowledge in return, a wondrously delicate sequence of events occurred with blinding, almost imperceptible speed.

In less than one second lapsed time, the SLCSAT received download site information—the USS *Maine*'s position—from her brother, sparking her onboard computer to life and causing her parabolic mirror to pivot smoothly into position. Within a matter of seconds, the SLCSAT had the *Maine* locked in her sights. Once on track, brother and sister electronically joined at the hip such that the SLCSAT's laser communication and mirror pointing systems ran slaved to the SEASAT. With control loops closed, the SEASAT barraged his sister with a rapid-fire sequence of instructions describing the position, heading, and speed of the target submarine—the USS *Georgia*.

And so began their graceful, electronically intimate, space-based ballet.

CHAPTER SIX

The Hummingbird's Ballet, 12/12/2008, Fri., 02:55 A.M.
USS *Yorktown*

It was the darkest part of the night when Scott and Tristan entered the bridge. The first thing Scott noticed was how hard it was to see. Her sense was of an unknown place filled with dark, hollow-eyed faces she couldn't quite make out. Rigged for night operations, the bridge was illuminated by dim red light. Having lost her night vision moving about the ship, she had to feel her way to the starboard side. Her second impression . . . *music*—Tchaikovsky's *Nutcracker* playing softly in the background. The combination of soft red light with the *Nutcracker*'s intrada had an oddly dreamlike quality about it. Not threatening really, simply surreal.

Once positioned starboard, Scott and Tristan found themselves gazing out the window into an endless black void.

Nine minutes after OPCON One's ELF transmission to the *Georgia,* the admiral's voice squawked over the intercom. "Bridge, CIC."

"Bridge," the captain responded immediately, his baritone voice booming about the room.

"*Georgia*'s posit is five miles off our starboard side."

"Very well; we're set here. Let's see what you got."

Traces of the captain's deep baritone voice still lingered in the air when suddenly, a ballet of blue-green spotlights began dancing across the night sky, reflecting off blackened swells of rolling ocean, leaping to one spot, dwelling only for a moment, then flitting off to another. Visually, the agility of the exquisite beams skipping across the shimmering ocean surface, the glistening blue-green columns slashing through the black veil of night, was breathtakingly stunning . . . a delightful, even wondrous sight to behold.

Completely at a loss for words, Tristan's reaction was one of heartfelt emotion whispered under his breath. "Awesome."

"All this orchestration. All this intricate, delicate motion," Scott observed with a quiet sense of reverence. "It reminds me of a hummingbird's flight from flower to flower, sort of a hummingbird's ballet."

"Brilliant iridescent columns of light, capable of hover and very rapid, almost instantaneous motion," Tristan replied, still enamored by the spectacle unfolding before him. "An eloquent observation . . . the flight of the hummingbird."

"No . . . you said it better," Scott remarked, her eyes twinkling. "It's awesome . . . totally awesome."

"I like your analogy . . . hummingbird ballet. It might stick. Mind if I steal it?"

"Go right ahead." Scott chuckled to herself, tickled by Tristan's sudden shift from tongue-tied kid to wordy Ph.D. "The flight of the hummingbird may sound artistic, but pilots call this maneuver touch and go." She watched the ballet a few moments longer, fondly remembering her childhood days, then continued. Her tone only modestly more serious, she said, "Looks a little like the light show at Disney World, only the stage is bigger . . . horizon to horizon, as far as the eye can see."

"I suppose you're right," Tristan said with just a hint of sadness. "The real world finally caught up with Walt Disney Imagineering."

Target Posit Download, 12/12/2008, Fri., 02:55 A.M.
USS Maine

The USS *Maine,* four stories high, nearly two football fields in length, listened attentively, waiting for her call to arms from OPCON One. Born a Trident missile submarine, now converted for guided missile attack, the modified Ohio-class boat crept along at launch depth, biding her time, awaiting her download via satellite laser link. She'd been in position about two hours, fifty miles due west of the USS *Georgia,* with her dorsal doors open, exposing her laser-sensitive comm panel to black seawater.

Clay McCullough, the skipper of the USS *Maine*'s Gold crew, lifted his phone and patched into the communications shack. "Downlink status?"

"No change, Cap'n. LaserLink receiver's fully operational, sir."

"And the radios?"

"Both VHF and ELF fully operational. If any message is transmitted our way sir, we're ready."

"Very well. We'll stand by until download commences . . . or they call the whole thing off." In a small way, the skipper felt relieved to be on the attacking end of this sea trial. From firsthand experience, he understood that driving a submarine, like flying a plane, loses its appeal when people start shooting at you.

Suddenly, an array of lights flashed green back in the radio room. "Incoming message off LaserLink, Captain. Satellite download in progress."

"Radio, conn, aye," replied the captain. Activating the

boat intercom, the skipper spoke to the crew. "Alert one. Man battle stations missile." The earsplitting bong of the general alarm called everyone to station while McCullough, the OOD, and the XO met back by the communications shack.

Once the download had been authenticated by the three-man team, the XO typed his decryption key into the computer. Immediately afterward, a human-readable form of the download header scrolled on screen.

```
/*
Z1255 12 Dec 2008
TOP SECRET
FR: OPCON ONE
TO: USS MAINE
1. Target USS Georgia posit 50 miles due
east.
2. Operate hands-off. Use discretion as
necessary.
3. God's speed and good hunting. Col Mason
Sends.
*/
```

"The computers are running the show, sir," observed the XO. "We're out of the loop unless there's a problem."

"Fully automatic," the skipper directed returning to station. "Stay one step ahead of it." To his relief, the transition to software control was a smooth one.

"Weapon download in progress, Captain," the OOD reported. "Missile three assimilating both flight profile and torpedo parameter data." The OOD reviewed a laundry list of torpedo presets flashing on screen: seeker activation set, search depth set, target track set, search zone set, circular run enabled. Nodding approval, he continued. "Practice torpedo loaded with all data required for a near vertical, sixty-knot run."

The skipper stood silent, ready by the phone, staring intently at the missile launch panel. Both he and his XO checked the payload of missile three's onboard torpedo . . . for the third time. Its status display read simply

meaning *not* a warshot.

"Guidance system update complete, Captain. Missile three status now 1SQ—warm and ready to fire." Immediately, one set of missile indicators flashed a bright lethal green, then the hull of the *Maine* echoed with the rush of water and air.

"Missile three is ready in all respects," the OOD continued. "Outer door opened."

Picking up this handset, the skipper addressed his crew over the intercom. "This is the captain. Missile three carries no warhead. It is not a warshot. Status is 1SQ."

The XO repeated McCullough's words over the intercom.

"Captain, launch cycle in progress," interrupted the OOD.

The explosive sound of expanding gases ramming the weapon into the sea echoed around the hull.

Outside, a Trident-sized cruise missile packaged inside a blunt-nosed launch cylinder sped toward the surface. Once clear of the water, the missile hovered momentarily, then fired its booster rocket, erupting skyward from its watertight cocoon. Now airborne, with its oversized spring-loaded wings extended, the missile tilted over, ignited its air breathing engine, and headed for the USS *Georgia* making about five hundred knots.

Meanwhile, the rolling thunder overhead convinced McCullough their launch was successful. Instinctively, without conscious thought, he started his stopwatch . . . six minutes until impact and counting.

What's Happening, 12/12/2008, Fri., 02:58 A.M.
USS Yorktown

Scott, Tristan, and the captain of the USS *Yorktown* gazed to starboard, spellbound by the blue-green beams dancing across the waves. Then, as suddenly as they started, they finished.

Inside the bridge, the trio's focus shifted immediately to a tactical map—labeled "SLCSAT Laser Footprint"—prominently displayed on the screen of a large NEC monitor. Superimposed over a background showing the *Maine, Georgia,* and *Yorktown,* the screen displayed laser tracks, marking footprints of the agile beam as a series of dots and dashes. The telling feature about the image was the seemingly random location of each track, and Scott picked up on the significance immediately.

"Excellent," she remarked, delighted by the widely scattered tracks. "Colonel Mason will be relieved to see this. There's no way anyone could infer the *Maine*'s whereabouts from this chaotic set of prints."

"As best I can see, there's no indication of backtracking," the captain observed after studying the image.

"My read exactly, Captain," Scott replied. "We never touched the same place twice."

"Look's like your Livermore buddies took care of that problem," he continued, looking at Roberts.

"Touch it once," Tristan quipped, shooting Scott a grin. "That's our motto. We thought randomizing the dance should mask our boat's position, but it's always a relief to see theory confirmed in practice."

"I still think laser downlinks to subs should remain a backup capability," the captain maintained. "It simply is not reliable."

With some reluctance, Tristan acknowledged the captain's point. "It's a first-generation system, sir. What else can I say. It's got its limitations. If the cloud cover doesn't absorb the laser beam, losses due to reflection at the air-water interface kill you."

"Satellite radio links to our surface fleet's the way to go. Use the fleet for sub downloads. The *Yorktown*'s already equipped with a sub comm laser mounted below her waterline."

"This direct downlink approach is driven by one prime mover, Captain—minimum time to target. Speed is everything. The undisputed, fastest way to get ordnance on target is direct downloads running fully automatic launch cycles . . . That means no hops through the surface fleet. We're not there yet, but in my opinion, we're well along the way. The fewer people in the loop, the faster the response. We've got to catch them flat-footed . . . hovering . . . before their missile doors open."

"So with people out of the control loop, it's a battle between machines," the captain observed, looking for confirmation.

"That's the way I see it, sir. Blow them out of the water with their missiles still in the tubes," Tristan said and nodded. "Once their missiles fly, nothing we've got can stop them."

The captain listened, understood where Tristan was coming from, but did not agree. "So now, with the *Maine*'s download complete, how long till she cuts loose?"

"Once they confirm the download's error free and authentic, only a matter of seconds."

"Time to target?"

"Approximately six minutes," Tristan said, his thoughts now focused on the *Georgia*. "But a minute or so before the missile closes, the SLCSAT will spotlight the *Georgia*'s exact position to compensate for any position errors. We'll see the beam from here."

"X marks the spot," the captain responded succinctly. "As I understand it, the satellite download programs the missile for a fixed target position, while the spotlight compensates for the fact that the *Georgia*'s actually moving."

"Right," Scott added, speaking toward the dimly lit, hollowed-eyed form. "That's not the only way to compensate for a moving target, sir, but that's the mode we're testing tonight." After a brief pause, she continued. "In the final moments of approach, the missile reduces its air speed, jettisons the bomb bay door, then drops its payload."

"What's the payload? What's dropped once the shroud's blown off?"

"The missile's a one-way torpedo bomber, sir . . . carrying the smartest homing torpedo in the world."

"A Mark 48 ADCAP?"

"Yes, sir. A parachute slows its water entry, but once wet, it's warm and ready to run."

"Sounds like a SUBROC or Sea Lance." Scott took this to mean the first- and second-generation rocket-propelled torpedoes used by the United States.

"Pretty much, sir. Nothing's really new under the missile's hood, but it's optimized for the sub hunt. It's all been done before, only this third-generation missile system's quieter on launch, longer range, perfect for a sea-skimming run against a moving missile boat."

"Sounds damn effective," the captain conceded. "A long-range homing torpedo with real time enemy position updates."

"We're expecting to catch the *Georgia* flat-footed sir . . . dead in the water," Tristan added. "If all goes as planned, we can't miss."

"Oh, you can miss all right," the captain observed in a dry, acerbic tone. "A Mark 48's hit rate runs about eighty percent. There's plenty that can go wrong, believe me."

"The torpedo will enter the water in a near vertical, nose-down attitude, directly above the *Georgia* . . . within two hundred feet of the target." After a brief pause, Tristan continued. "Figuratively speaking, sir, it'll come down her stacks."

X Marks the Spot, 12/12/2008, Fri., 03:02 A.M.
Onboard a SLCSAT

Once the missile closed within thirty miles of the *Georgia,* the SLCSAT racing overhead received a `spotlight_lock` message from ground control. After transmitting its acknowledge, the SLCSAT received updated spotlight site information—the USS *Georgia*'s position—from her brother. Again, her parabolic mirror pivoted . . . this time locking the *Georgia* in her sights. Sixty seconds before impact, the SLCSAT received a `spotlight_enable` message, instantly turning her beam on like a light switch. Big Brother detected the beam's position immediately, calculated a steering signal in real time, then electronically guided the beam to target as the SLCSAT hurled by overhead.

Beam Off Starboard, 12/12/2008, Fri., 03:02 A.M.
USS *Yorktown*

"Spotlight off the starboard, Captain," Scott announced, catching the flash out of the corner of her eye.

As seconds ticked away, the blue-green beam swept out a pattern shaped like an enormous piece of pie. The source of the beam—the SLCSAT—was traveling through an arc, orbiting overhead at over sixteen thousand miles an hour, while the beam's base remained rigidly fixed, seemingly hinged to the ocean's surface, firmly anchored on the *Georgia*'s back.

"Missile should arrive in fifty seconds or so," Tristan added, "approaching from our right."

About that time, a computer-enhanced moving picture appeared on the large NEC monitor. The image displayed was a light-amplified video picture showing a washed-out image of the beam's base pinned to the ocean surface. Every light source was amplified in intensity so even the stars appeared as burned-out greenish spots on screen. As the SLCSAT raced overhead, the persistent screen stored the beam's motion, smearing a sweeping triangular-shaped pattern across its display.

Almost on queue, with the *Nutcracker* grand finale playing quietly in the background, a ghostly green image streaked across the screen toward the beam. Within seconds, a flash registered the explosive bolts firing, releasing the bomb bay doors. Following the flash, the moving image transitioned into a blurry form of slow motion as the nose of the missile pitched up in a bunt release maneuver, lobbing the torpedo forward in an arc toward the blinding light. As the parachute deployed, the torpedo's descent slowed dramatically, hovering midair near the surface, selecting exactly the right spot. Releasing its chute, the homing torpedo nose-dived, plummeting into the ocean like an Olympic diver, seemingly without a ripple, disappearing beneath the surface without a trace.

No Place to Hide, 12/12/2008, Fri., 03:03 A.M.
Submarine USS *Georgia*

"Torpedo in the water, Captain!"

Plummeting downward from the ocean surface, the Mark 48 torpedo's run to target took just under five seconds. There was no time for fear, no time to react, but time enough to understand. A sense of loss, of sadness, would follow later, given time to reflect.

Entering the water nose down, directly above the *Georgia* at a range of one hundred fifty feet, the torpedo's sonar locked on target with the first ping. Guided now by its sonar seeker, the pump jet propulsor engaged, plunging the torpedo downward on a near vertical intercept track.

Although brief, the sound reverberating inside the *Georgia* was one no submariner ever forgets.

Ping . . . ping . . . ping-ping-pi-pi-pi-pi-pi-p-p-ping—THUNK!!! followed by a cold stillness closing in around them, a stillness experienced only in death.

Streaking inside its fifty-foot safety limit, the practice torpedo's brain called off the endgame, deflecting its rudders hard at the last moment, though not in time to avert collision. As for the crew, the damage was done.

"No place to hide," the XO sighed in resignation. "No time to react . . ."

"Inescapable," the skipper spoke quietly, cutting to the crux. Instinctively, he checked his stopwatch. What he read seemed to knock the breath out of the old man. "We weren't even close," he lamented. His gaze saddened, turning distant . . . unfocused. "Game's over."

For years, from the project's very inception, ClearWater critics claimed the world's oceans would forever remain opaque to all.

But the critics were wrong.

CHAPTER SEVEN

The Plan, 12/13/2008, Sat., 10:07 A.M.
Pyongyang, North Korea

Following the death of North Korean dictator Kim Il Sung in 1994, the son of the Great Leader, Kim Jong Il, emerged as his father incarnate—patient, ruthless, dangerous, and wholly dedicated to a single goal: Korean unification. The Dear Leader, as he was known to his people and North Korean press, outlived his father's old political and military rivals, survived a nationwide famine, then united his empire with promises of hope—a brighter tomorrow built on expansion and self-reliance—while secretly he began modernizing his military forces as Hitler had done before the start of the Second World War. Initially, their economy suffered for lack of Russian subsidies, but shortly after the revitalization program began, North Korean military, industrial, and economic factions rallied behind Dear Leader with their eyes focused firmly on the South. Their loyalty had nothing to do with love of country, but everything to do with the wealth that was now South Korea. Eventually, even North Korean workers began seeing evidence of Kim's promise for a better life. School systems improved markedly. Every able-bodied worker who wanted work, found work—and good high-tech work at that—inside Kim's revitalized military order.

Like his father's, Dear Leader's destiny lay in the richness of South Korea. Kim bet his Pyongyang regime on his military modernization program, which included developing both a nuclear deterrent and an extensive intelligence network. Secretly maneuvering behind the scenes, carrying on in the unpredictable fashion of his father, Dear Leader also negotiated a Secret Naval Protocol Agreement with China. As far as his people, the North Korean Press, and Western intelligence analysts were concerned, Dear Leader was the embodiment of his father spiritually, mentally, even physically in appearance.

In a very personal sense, Dear Leader had been preparing for this morning's meeting all his political life—since February 1993, the date *Scientific American* published Tim Beardsley's article entitled "Making Waves." His single agenda item—unification. For Kim and the North Korean military, unification meant a Stalinist dictatorship—an authoritarian communist government—for the whole peninsula, complete with the nationalization of South Korea's capitalist wealth.

As Kim meandered slowly through the Piwon (Secret Garden) on his palace grounds, memories of his father came flooding back. It was here, in this place, Kim felt closest to his father. In the garden, beautifully landscaped with ponds, pavilions, and very old wooded areas, Kim drew strength from the thousand-year-old trees, as had his father. During his father's reign, these gardens were used by his family as a place for rejuvenation. Strolling this garden prior to any important decision-making meeting had become a common, but very necessary, practice for Kim. In this garden, Kim found a peaceful place, a place he could feel the presence of his family, a special place only he could go to remember exactly who he was.

Feeling an almost righteous sense of his father's blessing, Kim walked with renewed vigor into the People's Royal Shrine, a very old stone pagoda built around 1400, during the Chosŏn Dynasty. Entering the meeting room, Kim studied the small group gathered before him. Everyone who needed to be there was there. Only the highest-level officers from Kim's military, intelligence, and foreign services were present—and no one else.

Once their traditional greetings were exchanged, the wiry-built admiral of the fleet spoke first. "Our sources on the American mainland have confirmed your visionary prophecy, Dear Leader. Their satellite system for guiding sea-launched cruise missiles to mobile targets now appears operational. This space-based detection and guidance system will certainly be used for the destruction of submerged submarines . . . primarily submerged missile submarines at first, but all types are now vulnerable."

Having been briefed in advance, Kim nodded understanding without emotion. "This capability comes as no surprise to anyone in this room. It took longer to achieve than anticipated, but we've been expecting this for many years." Considering the political and strategic consequences of this technical breakthrough, he spoke first to his foreign ambassador to China. "What do they think in Beijing?"

"The Chinese claim this capability is the next logical step up the ladder of nuclear escalation."

"That is good," Kim smiled. "They're repeating the Russian party line. It is well known . . . Russians have held that position for many years. Their posturing will be useful for us when the time comes."

"Even today, they're demanding a special meeting of the United Nations Security Council in protest."

"We will support their position, of course."

Kim's ambassador to China respectfully nodded agreement.

After a few moments' reflection, Kim elected to shift their focus to his agenda. Addressing his comments to the head of his intelligence organization, he continued. "Now that their detection capability is operational, I must assume our people on the American continent remain steadfast, committed to unification, and ready to act."

"Many of our agents were raised on American soil by your finest loyal families, Dear Leader. Many have been in your service since childhood."

Kim raised a skeptical eye. "Historically, our network of foreign assets represent our biggest risk."

"Our agents are small in number, wholly dedicated in spirit, and strategically placed," the intell chief argued quietly, without pretense. "Many would die to unite the land of their ancestors. I would stake my life on this."

And you will, Kim thought, but did not say. "It is important that you believe in your people." Concerned, he looked across the table to his supreme commander for support.

Huang Kŏn, North Korea's supreme commander, had been quiet until now, but on hearing Kim's words, he felt obligated to speak, and speak clearly. To Kim, Kŏn was family from his father's old guerrilla days in Manchuria, as were all his general staff. Kŏn, the grandson of a guerrilla comrade of Kim Il Sung, was tall by eastern standards and commanded respect. When he spoke, Kim took his advice and his general staff listened. "Our unification plans are based on three principals: surprise, deception, and speed. All three depend extensively on accurate intelligence. It's both our key to success and Achilles' heel. Unification, the very success of our campaign, pivots about timely, precise information. We absolutely must have it. There is no alternative."

Respectfully acknowledging the supreme commander's point with a deliberate slow nod, the intell chief paused for a moment, then framed his response succinctly. "I understand."

Reading his intell chief's expression, Kim elected to back off . . . his point now clear, articulately reinforced by his supreme commander. "Even now, the Americans withdraw their forces from South Korea."

Silently, the intell chief breathed a sigh of relief, sensing that, for now at least, he was off the hot seat. All the others present politely smiled, then engaged in a brief roundtable discussion. Once their conversation quieted, the diminutive commanding general of the North Korean People's Army relayed the group's consensus. Kim knew well, the elder general's delicate stature camouflaged his formidable spirit. "The American President wants another term in office."

"Your observations are well known," Kim said, his expression shifting to no-nonsense. "Our Great Leader's strategy on foreign policy has served us well. We create a problem, then demand concessions from the spineless Americans." Grinning like a Cheshire cat, Kim reflected proudly on his father's leadership for a few moments, then continued his query. "Report the latest information you have concerning withdrawal plans for United States forces."

Once again, the feisty general of the Army spoke. "The U.S. Air Force pulled out first, leaving nothing but empty hangar space behind. The United States withdrew its armored and infantry divisions before their Thanksgiving holiday, reducing the total number of army forces from twelve divisions to one, just under forty-two thousand troops."

"In many respects, the United States is fading as a superpower," Kim observed perceptively. "All technology, but no teeth . . . no commitment to die for what they believe."

Kŏn expanded Kim's point because he felt it important. Having studied the United States many years, his words cut to the heart of the matter. "Americans don't know what they believe anymore."

Kim felt pious satisfaction hearing about America's problems, then again queried his intell chief. "How does the United States government feel about this withdrawal?"

"Publicly, they boast confidence, claiming the South Koreans are capable, well armed, and well trained. Bear in mind, however, they maintain the U.S. Seventh Fleet in the Sea of Japan and have forces on Japan and Okinawa for backup."

"What about the Seventh Fleet?" the wiry admiral interrupted.

"They'll be diverted, I assure you, occupied elsewhere in the Pacific," the supreme commander responded evenly. "Once they understand what we're about, it'll be too late."

"War boils down to resupply by sea—moving men and material to the front," the admiral offered in summary. "Any sustained offensive requires resupply from the sea and therefore control of the sea lanes. If you divert the Seventh Fleet, there is no way to resupply South Korea. The vast majority of resupply always goes by sea. Always. Air lifts will be ineffective and there is no way Americans can resupply South Korea by sea. Effective ASW is both a man and material intensive activity. Their ASW forces are inadequate. Their submarine detection system has serious operational limitations and we'll use these to our advantage. Our naval forces are defensive, well trained, and optimized for cutting resupply lanes to the South."

"Once the Seventh Fleet is diverted, we must move quickly," the supreme commander added in a matter-of-fact tone. "Gas the DMZ, gain air superiority, cut the sea lanes, occupy Seoul, surround retreating ground forces, and sue for peace. Our forces will overwhelm the South in less than eight days. This war must end before it begins."

The group sat quietly as Kim pondered his generals' war plan. Focusing on the political aspect of the question, he addressed his intell chief. "How does South Korea view this American withdrawal?"

The intell chief had anticipated this query, so he spoke confidently, without hesitation. "Publicly, they are proud to have the destiny of their country under command of a South Korean general. Privately, they are going through an understandable phase of threat denial. Economically and industrially they are very powerful and take comfort in this. They downplay our threat in view of their capitalist wealth. They too hope for reunification, but feel extensive money for defense is unnecessary. They aren't prepared and don't expect another war. Off the record, South Korean officials view this withdrawal with grave misgivings, but still, they believe help only a phone call away."

"I would not want the fate of our nation depending on Washington."

The council nodded agreement.

"Understand too, under no circumstances are nuclear weapons a viable alternative in this civil war. We will occupy the South, unify our country, not devastate it."

"Surprise, deception, and speed are paramount, Dear Leader," the supreme commander reaffirmed. "Our yearly winter maneuvers will mask our troop movements from surveillance satellites. We must complete our preparations, then keep to schedule."

As they judiciously weighed the gains against the risks, a long period of silence followed, while Kim pondered the countless unknowns of war. Once he sorted the problem into mathematical terms, his mind cleared of irrelevant clutter. He spoke decisively, with the calm reassurance that comes with knowing who you are and what you believe. "Once the Seventh Fleet is diverted, we unleash our forces on Seoul."

North Korea had been expected to collapse for twenty years, ever since the Russian bear lumbered back into his cave.

Trouble was . . . North Koreans seemingly draw strength from doing the unexpected.

PART THREE

Investigation

Present Day

CHAPTER EIGHT

Advil, 12/27/2008, Sat., 08:35 A.M.
USSPACECOM

Fifteen minutes after Pac Comm left their "*Maine*'s Over-due" message, Ensign Eion Macke reported in for watch duty on the Pacific screening room floor. First thing, he filled his large Dunkin Donut coffee mug, then gulped down four more Advil. Looking back, he would think this had been a good thing. As it turned out, he'd need the painkiller and caffeine.

Glare, any kind of bright light, hurt his eyes; sound, even background noise, hurt his ears; and his head pounded like he'd been battered by a wooden mallet. Glancing at his reflection off a nearby computer monitor, he thought, *How can anybody so young and pretty as me feel this bad?* Everything hurt. He couldn't remember many details from last night, but maybe that was just as well. *Ugh! Ain't worth it. That officer's club's going to kill me if I don't back off.*

Entering the Pacific screening room, he surveyed the large, wall-mounted projection map displaying the location of every surface ship and submarine known operating in the Pacific. For stability, he held on to a desk. Everywhere he looked, he gazed through squinting, bloodshot eyes. Every sound pounded his sensitive ears, causing his head to throb—relentlessly. At first glance, things seemed normal enough considering it was three days following Christmas, on a sleepy, hungover, Sunday morning. Everyone of importance in Eion's known world, his immediate family and best friends, had the good sense to return home for Christmas. But not the young ensign. He'd joined the Navy to see the world—*it's an adventure,* he reminded himself. To date, his adventure had carried him barely two states northwest of his Amarillo, Texas, hometown.

Eion already knew about dirt farming, already knew about flatlands, sunflowers, springtime dust storms, and desert. In his mind's eye, he could still taste the dry Texas dust, still feel the grit in his teeth like it was only yesterday. He'd joined the Navy to see water and women, but seeing images of the Pacific continuously displayed on the walls around him was like adding insult to injury. He wanted to go to sea so bad he could almost taste, smell, and touch it. More to the point, he wasn't intrigued by the seamanship aspects so much as by the promise of lusty women—the forbidden fruit of foreign ports. He'd heard about Singapore, about the luscious women there, and more than anything else in the world, he'd wanted to experience these wonderful, wild women firsthand. At this time in his life, sex, the prospect of sex, even the thought of that word was seldom more than four seconds away from his consciousness. What else mattered in life? What else made life worth living? Work begets money, money begets girls, and girls—girls make life worth the work.

Walking across the room toward his desk, coffee cup in hand, Eion saw the message light flashing on his phone. *What's this all about?* he wondered. *Nothing's going on now*—then suddenly, reality hit home in real time—he remembered the *Maine.* Cutting his eyes back toward the big board, he absorbed the name of every icon, every vessel in the Pacific, searching. *Nothing—she's not up there!* Disgusted with himself because he'd known he'd forgotten something, he picked up the phone to get his messages. Over the phone, the AUDIX answering system spoke without inflection.

"Message from," followed by a long, heart stopping pause, "Pacific Fleet Communications Headquarters." A sick feeling formed in the pit of his stomach.

In a fraction of a second, the O Club, lusty women, and Singapore were shoved on the back burner.

Now it's time to worry!

Focusing his gaze from his watch station overlooking the Pacific screening room, the young Navy ensign scanned the floor looking for the sailor monitoring the water off the Kamchatka Peninsula. Bingo . . . same sailor, same station. After moving down the stairs—gripping the stair rail like a vise—the ensign walked across the floor and approached the sailor. The sailor didn't notice, busily pecking away at his workstation, preoccupied reading his computer display. Judging from his still open briefcase, full coffee cup, and uneaten doughnut, the sailor hadn't been on station very long.

One glance and Eion knew what the sailor was doing—searching USSPACECOM computer logs, looking for reports on the USS *Maine*'s whereabouts. Looking over the sailor's shoulder, Eion read the result of his search on screen:

```
Maine Not Found.
```

Without skipping a beat, the sailor opened a new window and remotely logged into Pac Comm's database server in

San Diego. Once logged on, he queried for the downlink
message status of all submarines on patrol, then dumped
them into a file for his perusal. His method wasn't elegant,
but it worked. Displaying the file on screen, he used his text
editor to search for the string "Maine."

And there she was, squirreled away, buried in the seemingly countless lines of data:

```
   . . . :MAINE OVERDUE:IN QUEUE:1300 - 1500
Zulu: . . .
```

The ensign checked his watch. *Let's see . . . it's 8:45
here; she's forty-five minutes overdue . . . Hmm. . . . it's
early there . . . 3:45 in the morning,* Maine *time. Still dark
there. Good. That could be useful.*

Eion tapped the sailor on his shoulder to get his attention. "Whaddaya think?"

The sailor wasn't one to beat around the bush. "I think
we got trouble staring us in the face."

"Any suggestions?"

"CYA. Somebody needs to know about this, someone
important, someone local with a vested interest."

"You're right," Eion replied, scanning the floor. "Seems
like the place is deserted. Nearly everyone's on leave. How
about pulling up the duty roster. Let's see who's left in
town, on duty, and in charge."

The sailor displayed the org chart on screen, and at first
glance, their prospects looked pretty thin. Their two-man
naval chain of command was out on leave, and the Air
Force chain didn't look much better.

"Well, judging from the duty roster, it's not clear who to
call," Ensign Macke observed, a little bewildered.

"What about Colonel Mason? He's in charge of this
ClearWater project isn't he? He'd have a great deal to lose

if this problem was due to some idiosyncrasy in his pet project."

"Yeah . . . that's true, isn't it? In an indirect way, we report to him, don't we? . . . Dotted line, I think. I can't keep these crazy org charts straight. Seems like they're changing every other day."

"There's no seems-like to it," the sailor snarled. "They do change every other day. That's a fact, not fiction. The way I see it, nobody's really responsible for anything anymore. There's no sense of ownership."

"Funny," the ensign offered, rubbing his aching head. "You said what I've often thought, but didn't want to say."

"If someone slips up and takes responsibility, rest assured, we'll reorganize and they won't be responsible for the same thing tomorrow. That way, nobody's to blame. Nobody's responsible for anything long enough to get saddled with the blame when it gets screwed up. It's like a big shell game."

"I hear what you're saying," Eion added cautiously, "but from what I've seen and heard, Mason's different. He's been responsible for ClearWater from the get-go. Even pitched this project before the Senate Armed Forces Committee . . . got it funded from what I heard. Judging from what I've seen firsthand, he believes in what we're about here."

The sailor pulled up a list of all the people, officers and enlisted, reporting to Colonel Mason. "All his direct reports are blue-suiters—Air Force types. We're not in his direct line of responsibility."

"Screw the org chart," the ensign argued. "The longer we talk, the more convinced I am that Mason's our man. He's been behind ClearWater from its inception, he wants it to succeed and he's bet his career on us." The ensign heard himself speaking and gained confidence from his own words. "I don't know what he'll do, but he'll help us."

There was a pause as the sailor queried the computer for Mason's duty status. He looked up, obviously disappointed. "He's signed out to his home on base—with his family on Christmas leave."

That knocked the wind out of Eion's sail for a moment. The young man sat down and held his throbbing head in his hands. *What to do? Mason would need to know about this no matter what, right? But I hate screwing up anyone's vacation, especially a full-bird colonel's. Oh man, I wish I'd gone home for Christmas. It figures we'd have some kind of Christmas crisis.* The ensign raised his head, having come to his decision. "The ClearWater buck stops with the colonel."

The sailor grinned, then spoke with a little dance— more of a soft-shoe—in his voice. "Right, sir, and you've got the duty!"

The ensign paused, reviewing the essence of what he needed to say, then concluded, "He's a good man, a fair man. He'll help us. You'll see."

Across the base, about a mile's walk away, a sleepy-eyed family man sat quietly in a rocking chair, holding his first grandchild absolutely still. The tiny baby Slim Mason held in his arms was not much bigger than a pot roast; only four months old, his grandson was named Alexander—affectionately referred to as Alexander *the Great*. Slim had been up much of the night with the Great one. For whatever reason, probably colic, Alex had had a tough night with his stomach. It had taken several hours, but the colic medicine seemed to be helping—finally.

In Slim's eyes, Alex was the best there ever was. He'd promised himself that he was going to love his grandchildren unconditionally, without reservation, and they'd feel this in their hearts and know this by his actions. Slim

Mason'd had grandparents like this. They were gone now, but during Mason's life, he'd never known any happier feeling than those instilled by his grandparents. Looking back, Mason could see things more clearly now; he'd been one of the most fortunate people he'd ever known. It had nothing whatsoever to do with money, but everything to do with people—a sense of place, of family, of friends, neighbors, and home. Since the day he first left home, he'd yearned to return to his grandparents' farm, to live where he'd enjoyed his happiest times as a child. He'd get there someday, but for Slim, someday couldn't come soon enough. The farm wasn't much to look at, his grandparents never had much money, but everything they had they'd always shared with him. Their kindness nearly defied description, but Slim knew he'd go to his grave with memories of their love entrenched in his heart. He remembered that the happiest days of his life, summer vacations on the farm, Christmas times on the farm, the best things that ever happened to him in his life—the only things that ever really mattered in the long run—happened to him on the farm.

Slim Mason wanted to give his grandchildren the same sense of *wonderful life* that his grandparents had given him. And when he was dead, he hoped Alexander would remember him as he remembered his grandfather—the grandfather who was always there, always willing to stop whatever he was doing, the kindest, most unselfish man he had ever known. When Alex grew up, if he could look back on his childhood days and have a sense of acceptance, of unconditional love, of being a very lucky fella, then Slim Mason's mission as a grandfather would have been fulfilled.

But for now, like many grandparents, Slim Mason pulled the night shift while his son and daughter-in-law caught up on countless hours of lost sleep. Colicky babies can be rough on new parents. Pulling the night shift also upped their chances, however slightly, that there might be other tiny grandchildren on the way. He couldn't influence this directly, of course, but he had no reservations about voicing his opinion on grandchildren when asked.

Looking back over his life, Mason also felt fortunate to have been blessed with wonderful, life-long friends. In his heart, he believed they were gifts from God, and should be treated with all the care and respect that he gave his family—and then some. As it had turned out, Mason's oldest son married one of Sam Napper's daughters, and Sam Napper was Mason's dearest friend. Life's funny sometimes, if you live long enough to see it through. Mason and Napper had grown up in the same small hometown, gone to the same university, and to date, gone through much of their Air Force career together. They'd been separated off and on over the years, but in the main, they'd always made the effort to stay close. Together, they'd learned that life's ups and downs were much easier to live through with friends. Besides, Mason and Napper had been good for each other. Over their twenty years in the Air Force, as a rule, wherever Mason would go, Napper would follow some months later. Sort of a buddy system—Slim would check out a new place, and if it looked good, Sam would follow. Mason had learned the hard way that he was happiest if he never strayed very far away from who he was as a boy. And Sam Napper reminded him of this; fact was, Sam wouldn't let him forget who he'd been even if he'd wanted to.

Together, they'd learned everything they'd needed to know about people by the time they got out of high school; the most important stuff they'd picked up by the end of the ninth grade. And between the ninth and twelfth grades, they'd learned about girls. Not everything—they'd never figure it all out because some things were simply incomprehensible; but nevertheless, they'd gotten a handle on the most important girl stuff by the end of high school.

Looking down at Alex, Mason smiled. The little baby held Slim's first finger in his tiny hand. Slim couldn't remember ever seeing fingers so small as these. Four tiny fingers rolled around his first finger, holding him in a snug, baby grip-lock. He'd forgotten what it meant to be so small. *The world must look a great deal different from your point of view, little man. Everything must seem mighty big.*

When you're awake much of the night, rocking a tiny infant in your arms, you have time to reminisce about these things. And they're important to remember—otherwise you become what you're told you're supposed to be. And Slim knew better than that now. He'd learned that sometimes losing yourself is like dying—something you don't want to go through, something you want to put off as long as possible.

About that time, Slim heard the sound of a distant, muted phone ringing. Didn't need to check his watch; he knew it was early, before breakfast on Saturday morning. Instinctively, he sensed the call was for him and his whole body tensed. Saturday A.M. calls never brought good news.

Alex picked up on the tension in his grandfather's finger, opened his eyes, but continued to rest—for now—quietly.

Mason heard the sound of his wife's footsteps coming down the hall. The door opened. Rays of light flooded into the darkened room, causing Slim to squint. Looking up, Mason saw the backlit form of his wife holding the portable phone. He couldn't make out her expression, but it didn't matter. He'd heard her sigh.

Mason stood slowly, never making a sound, and walked across the room to the baby's crib. Leaning forward over the crib, he gently laid the young man down, nestled between a collection of blankets and soft foam pads. Alex didn't make a sound through it all, but his eyes were open wide, taking in his change of situation.

Alex lay in the crib now, face up, but never let go of Slim's finger. To the uninitiated, this situation might have posed a *what-to-do-to-keep-the-baby-from-crying* kind of dilemma. But Slim had been in similar grip-lock situations before with Alex, and knew what to do.

Using his free hand, Mason quietly lowered the crib's side rail. Once the rail was out of the way, he leaned over young Alex and gently kissed him on his cheek. When Alex felt the warm breath of his grandfather near, he released Slim's finger and used both hands to rub the rough, unshaven stubble on his grandfather's face. As early as four months, Mason sensed Alex had a kind heart.

You and I will be the best of friends, little man, Mason thought, his eyes tearing slightly. He kissed the tiny fingers, then, reluctantly, he stood upright and raised the crib rail. In a way, he felt a deep resentment for this intrusion into his home life, and in his heart, he wished he could hurl that portable phone out the window.

Quietly, he and his wife left the room—portable phone in hand. Outside in the light of the hallway, Mason read the look in his wife's eyes and knew his instincts were right.

"It's the Pacific Screening Room, Slim. They said it's important."

Slim took a deep breath, allowing his mind to shift to business. He hadn't thought about work for two glorious weeks and dreaded the prospects of being drawn into some quagmire now. He'd hoped to get back into work a bit more easily. Show up for work physically one day, then arrive mentally several days later. At least that had been his plan until now.

Slim put the portable to his ear. "This is Colonel Mason." In less than thirty seconds, Mason knew his vacation was over. "OK. Let me make sure I've got this straight. How long's it been since you lost the *Maine*'s track?"

Ensign Macke replied succinctly. "She dropped off the big board eighteen hours ago, sir. We lost track about two hours after her last SAT break. As I said, she missed her last scheduled SAT break and's now an hour overdue."

"Who else knows about this?"

"You're the only person we've called, sir, but Pac Comm knows. They called us with a heads-up."

"If they called us, then COMSUBPAC must be in the loop by now."

"Maybe so, sir, but we haven't heard one word from COMSUBPAC, nothing from Hawaii at all."

"That's strange. Admiral Eastwood should be all over this one. He watches ClearWater like a hawk." Mason recalled Admiral Ozzie Eastwood breathing down his neck the last two years. As a rule, nothing of consequence ever slipped by that man or his organization. Mason would have to call him, no way around it. He'd keep his boss, Brigadier General Robert Craven, in the loop, but he'd need to call Ozzie ASAP. This was one of Ozzie's first-line boats, and a nuclear-powered, guided missile boat at that. *Yeah, Ozzie must be going ballistic about now. Christmastime with Ozzie.* Mason cringed, imagining the tension mounting inside COMSUBPAC. *His lights at Pearl must've been burning all night.* "What's your recommendation?" Mason asked.

"It's still dark over the *Maine,* sir, and if we move fast, we can take full advantage of it. Call the admiral. Tell him to order her shallow for her SAT break or else."

"Or else, what?"

The ensign paused. "Or else we send the whole Pacific fleet out to find her, Colonel."

Mason was taken aback by the prospects of sending the entire fleet, and responded with a knee jerk. "Hold on here. What if she can't communicate because of some equipment failure? What if the *Maine*'s UHF equipment's out of order? What if her communications mast was somehow damaged?"

There was a silence over the line, followed by a subdued, "Uh . . . I see what you mean, Colonel."

"I didn't mean to throttle your feedback, son, don't get me wrong. I'm with you, it's just you're navy, I'm not . . . help me out here. What do I tell the admiral when he asks these questions?"

"Just a minute, sir. I put a call into Norfolk SUBOPS— they're coming on line now. Let me run something by them." Mason heard the sound of muted conversation over the phone. He couldn't make out everything the ensign said, and only heard one side of the conversation, but what he heard went something like "You've got to be kidding me! This is unbelievable! It's our own sub. You know—an American . . . You can confirm that much, can't you? Give us a sanity check . . . For crying out loud . . . We don't have time to clear this through channels . . . It's dark over the *Maine* now! We only have a couple hours of darkness left." A few moments later, the ensign returned in a huff. "It's like this, Colonel. Order the *Maine* to establish communications immediately, any way she possibly can. If she can't radio Pac Comm directly, have her release an emergency locator buoy."

"Can she hear our signal?"

"Yes, sir."

"You're absolutely certain of that?"

"Rest assured, Colonel, the *Maine* can hear us. We've got full UHF, ELF, and VLF coverage in her patrol area. If she's listening, and her equipments operational, she'll hear us. Even if her receiving or crypto gear fails, her standing orders are to establish communications any way she possibly can."

Mason listened, then asked, "Your SUBOPS buddy backs you up on this recommendation, right?"

"Well, sir, he said my proposal was reasonable, but that's all he'd say. Bubbleheads are a funny lot. Maybe they've got their reasons and all, but frankly—well, let me put it like this. SUBOPS is a closed community. They won't talk about the specifics of submarine operations at all, even when one of their own is missing. Strikes me as Neanderthal, an anachronism like something left over from another era. The way I see it, we watch them go about their business twenty-four hours a day, and still, they won't talk to us about it."

"I know what you mean. I'm constantly running into that brick wall myself. Our business is an open book, subject to SUBOPS scrutiny anytime, anyplace, but it's a one-way street. We should be fair about it though. We're talking about good, well-intentioned people here—our own people, not machines, Sometimes technology changes so fast, our people and operations can't keep up."

"I think I know what you mean, sir." the ensign confirmed. "If we weren't in this business day-in and day-out, I don't know how we'd ever keep up. Things change so quickly here in Oz." His tone confirmed what Mason already suspected. The young man had a good sense of humor.

"Tell me again though . . . It's important: On the whole, Norfolk bought into your recommendation as reasonable?"

"Yes, sir. So long as the situation topside remains status quo, our recommendation makes operational sense. And if the admiral doesn't like our proposal for whatever reason, he can change it." He sounded convincing.

"Good. I'll take it to him as is."

"Excellent!"

"And I need to ask you to do one more thing for me."

"Name it, sir."

"Please bring my staff onboard for me. Major Sam Napper's at home on leave. Captain Linda Scott and Tristan Roberts are on the *Yorktown* concluding sea trials. Contact them, bring them up to speed; I've got a hunch we're going to need 'em."

"Yes, sir. I'm on it."

Mason paused, playing the coming events over in his mind, and one final point occurred to him. "By the way, please keep at least one line open for the next couple of hours—until I get in there. I might need to call you in for backup."

"Will do, sir. You have my number. Don't hesitate to call. I'll be here." There was the distinctive ring of optimism in his voice.

"I'll get back in touch within the hour and let you know where the admiral's going with this. We need to stay in the loop with this one . . . period. We'll do whatever it takes."

"Thank you, sir. We knew we could depend on you."

"By the way, I'm glad you called about this. I owe you one."

"Let's call it even, sir."

"Thanks, son. Talk to you soon."

Hanging up the phone, Eion looked across the desk at the sailor and nodded his head in the affirmative. "He's going to help us." The young ensign felt as if the weight of the world had been lifted off his shoulders.

Unbelievable, 12/27/2008, Sat., 06:15 A.M.
COMSUBPAC Operations

It was dark, 6:15 in the morning Hawaiian time. Inside COMSUBPAC Headquarters, Admiral Ozzie Eastwood's secure phone rang in the front corner office overlooking Pearl Harbor. As was normally the case, a yeoman—not an answering machine—picked up for the admiral.

"Admiral Eastwood's office; may I help you?"

The voice at the other end sounded matter-of-fact. "Hello. This is Colonel Daniel Mason calling from USSPACECOM in Colorado. I need to speak with the admiral on a matter of immediate importance."

There was a pause, as if the yeoman didn't know what to say, then the words came to him. "But, Colonel . . . it's early Saturday morning here, sir. The admiral won't be in until Monday. Should I take a message or will you call back?"

"Oh, I see," Mason said, surprised Eastwood wasn't in. After collecting his thoughts, he continued. "I understand it's early Saturday morning in Hawaii, but I'd expected the admiral and his staff would have been there much of last night. There's a significant problem under the Pacific. This situation demands his attention—immediately. Apparently, there was a communications failure somewhere along the line, but your office should have been informed about this situation long before my call."

"Sir, with all due respect, it's just after Christmas. This place is as quiet as a cemetery."

"I don't think you understand, so let me be clear. I need

to speak with the admiral, and I need to speak with him now."

"Yes sir . . . I'll . . . uh . . . I'll connect you with the duty officer."

After obtaining buy-in from the local officer in charge, Mason was patched through to the admiral's home.

Following Mason's introduction, the admiral asked, "What is it?"

"Is this line secure?"

"It is."

"The *Maine*'s overdue. She's an hour and a half late for her SAT break now. We lost track of her about eighteen hours ago and haven't seen her since."

"What about surface traffic? Hostile surface ships would keep her deep."

"Her situation is status quo. On average, her patrol area's clear of contacts."

"We could get a fast attack on her trail," Ozzie thought out loud. "Say again, how long since you lost her?"

"Eighteen hours."

Ozzie sighed. "Her fresh water trail may have already grown cold. Depends on the current." Nuclear submarines, especially nuclear missile submarines, produce freshwater from the sea, more than they can possibly use or store. Consequently, as long as their distillation plant's running, they continually discharge freshwater into the sea. One aspect of hunting missile submarines that is seldom discussed concerns sniffing out and following this freshwater trail. Given a reasonably calm mixing current, this trail can often be detected by a fast attack hours after the missile sub has passed.

A few moments later, Mason sensed Ozzie's blood pressure rising an ocean away. "Unbelievable. Why wasn't I notified earlier?" A pause. "Never mind that now; that's a separate, internal problem. What about the *Maine*? What'd our people propose?"

Mason summarized the Norfolk SUBOPS situation over the phone and offered the ensign's proposal.

"Sounds all right. We'll signal the *Maine* and get working here immediately on contingency plans. If the *Maine* talks to us, we're out of the woods. If she doesn't, we're going to need all the help we can get."

Fifty-five minutes after Mason hung up, a top priority emergency action message preempted the ELF message queue and began transmission. Once decoded, the six character message read:

```
Z271733ZDEC
EMERGENCY ACTION MESSAGE
FM: COMSUBPAC
TO: USS MAINE (SSGN 741)
1. ESTABLISH COMMUNICATIONS NOW.
      A. EXECUTE SAT BREAK IF POSSIBLE.
      B. OTHERWISE, LAUNCH LOCATOR BUOY
      IMMEDIATELY.
2. VADM EASTWOOD SENDS.
3. AUTHENTICATION: ALPHA ECHO ECHO BRAVO
ALPHA ALPHA
```

Rigor Mortis, 12/28/2008, Sun., 04:33 A.M.
USS *Maine*

Making twenty knots straight and level, passing over the southernmost range of the Emperor Seamounts, Mandrone constantly checked his depth to optimize passive sonar performance, all the while operating at depths below ClearWater minimums. For now, his goal, like that of every missile boat skipper, was to maneuver where he wanted to go, yet remain undetected. He had slightly less than three days to close on his final launch position, and unless he did something stupid, or ran across some bad luck, they'd make it.

About that time, the *Maine*'s radio room was interrupted by Admiral Eastwood's emergency action message. Inside her communications shack, the ELF receiver began flashing EAM. Normally, the crew's pattern of life would be preempted by any message from National Command Authority, but Mandrone's North Korean radio engineer paid little heed. He was occupied with problems of his own, rigging the *Maine* with Chinese radio equipment.

After wiring power, the radioman ran a series of tests on every receiver, making sure each was operating to spec. Satisfied with his progress, he mentally worked through his remaining tasks. Once the antennas were connected to the radios, matching impedances was theoretically, and in practice, the most difficult thing to get right, but he wasn't worried. He'd worked through this installation procedure many times over, and knew he had all the cables, connectors, and tools he needed to get the job done. He'd practiced this critical phase so often, he could do it in his sleep. Gazing at the two-foot-wide radio bay stacked top to bottom with rack-mounted equipment, the radioman sighed. There was much to do; nevertheless, once he was tuned and connected to the *Maine*'s antennas, his installation job was done. *Maybe eight to ten hours per radio,* he thought. *Two days' work remaining, max. Excellent, plenty of margin.*

On reaching this conclusion, the radioman took a break, printing out Eastwood's six-character message. After matching it with an entry in the *Maine*'s code book, he signaled Mandrone.

Forward, in the control room, the intercom squawked.

"Conn, radio. We received an emergency message. They've missed us, Captain."

Mandrone punched PUSH TO TALK. "Radio, conn, aye." As he checked his watch, the corners of Mandrone's mouth turned up slightly. He'd expected this *missing you* message several hours before now. "They're running a little late, topside. Read it for me."

The radioman did so.

Mandrone was quietly pleased, knowing time was on their side. This delay was a break he'd hoped for, but hadn't planned on. The longer the Navy waited before starting their search, the more difficult they'd be to find. The Pacific was a big ocean and the *Maine* was quite literally quieter than the ocean background noise. With this extra few hours' lead time, their chances for success soared.

Mandrone squinted, looking about the control room, gazing silently as bright overhead lights glared down on the ashen faces of the dead. He saw every wild-eyed expression, imagined their screams, then took a deep calming breath, struggling to clear his mind. *Now's the time to take account of the boat,* he thought with a grimace. *What do you do with one hundred fifty-eight dead men? Nearly two-thirds of the crew died in their bunks—not a problem—but the rest are in the way. We can't bury them, can't dump 'em, can't freeze 'em. Moving fifty-plus men would take time we don't have and energy we can't spare. No way around it. Even with four men pulling morgue duty around the clock, it'd take twenty-five hours to get 'em in the freezer. Face reality, Mandrone. It's a big boat, three and four decks. Besides, if we bury them at sea, we risk detection . . . could jeopardize the mission. And we've got one hell of a lot left to do! I don't like it, but we'll stick with the*

*original plan. Bag the bodies, trip points first, and drag
'em out of the way.*

The air reeked with the rancid stench of raw sewage and
urine. His nose had adjusted, but there was something in
the air, probably methane gas, burning his eyes.

The gas irritated his eyes, harsh glare made it worse, yet
every overhead light was on. Everyone wanted it that way.
No one talked about it, but Mandrone understood fear of
the dark. Being surrounded by death's worse if you can't
see it.

Closing his eyes, Mandrone struggled to concentrate.
Open-eyed visions of death haunted him, relentlessly tormented him, distracting him from the task at hand. *Focus,
Mandrone, shake it off.* As he punched the intercom, his
voice sounded stilted. "Sonar, conn. Any contacts?"

"One unidentified contact, sir. Bearing zero-three-zero.
Probably a surface ship, twin screws. Range unknown . . .
probably greater than eleven thousand meters."

"Very well, sonar. Will plot egress course to avoid contact." Shorthanded, running without a navigator, Mandrone filled the ticket. Safe practice and common sense
told him to triple-check their current position before rec-
ommending a course change. Hovering over the navigation plotting table, Mike checked their latest recorded
position, then read his watch. After running through a
short series of calculations, he plotted his best estimate of
the *Maine*'s current location. Next, he compared it against
latitude and longitude readouts from two independent
Navaids: the Ships Inertial Navigation System and NAV-
STAR, their Global Positioning System. *Close enough,*
Mandrone thought, feeling satisfied. *Dead reckoning's
only off by a couple of clicks. All things considered, a reasonable margin of error.*

Mandrone, Ash, and thirteen dead men manned the control room. Ash drove the boat, Mandrone took the conn. Projecting his voice across the room, Mandrone spoke to Ash. "Come to bearing two seven zero. Bring her about quietly, slow to one third."

"Aye, aye, Captain." Ash's voice—flat, lacking vigor.

Stepping across two bodies lying face up, Mandrone nearly tripped maneuvering toward Ash. In the process, he determined he couldn't stand it any longer and rolled the men over, face down on the floor. Touching one dead man's outstretched arm, Mike recoiled at the disquieting, cold fleshy feel. Rigor mortis. The sailor's limbs felt stiff, making him awkward to roll; his temperature, maybe seventy degrees, felt chilled to that of the cool, tile floor. Wrestling the dead man's arm down, strapping it to his side, was a struggle, catching Mandrone by surprise. He unbuckled the man's belt from his urine-soaked pants, then forced his arm inside the loop, using the belt as a tie strap. Mike grimaced, feeling the man's shoulder separate with a snap, yielding with a final *curr-rack*.

Minutes later, with both men secured face down, Mandrone stood breathing heavily. Punching PUSH TO TALK, he repeated his change-of-course order for the sonarman, giving him a heads-up regarding their new direction.

Mandrone moved toward Ash, all the while scanning instruments normally monitored by the diving officer. *Slight bank to starboard, feels about right; speed decreasing, falling under nineteen knots; heading west, good. Slight dive angle.*

"Umm." Mandrone frowned. *Depth's nearly six hundred feet—that's a problem. Ash is exhausted.*

Mike decided to take the planesmen's wheel on Ash's left. *Take a little angle off the dive planes, pull her nose up, pump water out of her trim tanks and let the autopilot maintain depth.*

Eyes caged ahead, riveted on the depth gauge, Mandrone hurriedly approached the planesman's bucket seat from the rear. Closing quickly, concentrating on what to do next, his toe suddenly caught fast. Trying to catch himself, both feet wedged beneath something massive; carried forward by his own momentum, he hurled face first over the diving officer's body. Fortunately for Mike, the seat was padded. He bounced off the seat back, slowing his fall, then came down hard, shoulder first, on the cold tile floor. His only sound a low, primeval grunt.

But he'd been lucky, missing the plate glass on the control console.

From his vantage point on the floor, Mandrone opened his eyes to find himself lying head-to-head alongside the diving officer. Stunned, he lay still a moment, staring at that ashen face. The dead man's gaze, an insane grin, cut right through him.

"Been there, done that," Ash quipped without expression.

Mike heard, but did not speak.

Bruised, but otherwise unharmed, Mandrone concluded enough was enough. His shoulder throbbed, but he wasn't hurt so much as he was mad. He'd behaved stupidly . . . become engrossed, tripped over a body, nearly jeopardized the mission.

"I tripped over him too." Ash explained. His tone—pitiless. "He was too heavy for me to move . . . couldn't lift him alone."

"We're gonna take care of this once and for all." Mandrone growled. He stood slowly, buckling himself into the planesman's chair with a groan. Once oriented behind the wheel, he gingerly brought the boat to five hundred feet, pumped the trim tanks, then placed depth control on autopilot. Throughout the process, he thought ahead, considering what he should do next. *Survey the boat, take account of the crew, and bag the bodies.*

Some minutes later, after their depth stabilized, he spoke again to Ash. "Maintain current heading. I'll return shortly."

Mandrone stepped across the diving officer to his periscope station and punched the intercom, broadcasting his voice to all parts of the ship. "This is the captain. It's time to take care of the dead. We'll stick with the original plan . . . Bag the bodies, working in pairs."

He paused, listening. Within seconds, the clatter of ratchet wrenches, drills, pots, and pans fell silent. The boat sounded eerily quiet, like the final stillness of a tomb. Pulling a pencil and small notepad from his pocket, he continued.

"Radio, conn. Deal with the trip-points first. How many?"

"Conn, radio."

A pause. Mike heard only air whistling through his nostrils.

"Four."

"Weapons, how many?"

"Six."

"Sonar?"

"Eight."

"Torpedo room?"

"Three."

"Engine room?"

"Four."

Mandrone took a deep breath, then released it slowly. "Galley?" His tone—apprehensive.

"Eighteen, sir. I'm practically buried here." A tense pause. "And they're stiff."

"You'll need help in the mess. I'll make my rounds, drop off the bags, then circle back . . . give you a hand."

"Aye, Captain."

Mandrone detected a distinct sense of relief in the cook's voice.

Heading aft, Mandrone's first stop was the MCC (Missile Control Center), one deck below.

"Gangway, men," Mandrone barked down the hole. "Clear down ladder." Tossing two boxes of body bags down ahead of him, Mike slid down the ladder rails. Entering the MCC, he saw one missileman pulling safecracker duty, methodically twirling the tumblers on a double combination safe. A second missileman lifted his hand, signaling Mike to stand fast.

The safecracker had attached a collarlike microphone array around one of the safe's combination dials. By his left hand, Mandrone noticed the microphones connected to an audio amplifier and laptop computer. He paused a few seconds, and heard the amplified metallic sound of the tumblers clicking into place. Nodding an affirmative, the safecracker pulled his hand slowly away from the dial. Taking a deep breath, he looked over his shoulder at Mandrone, made eye contact, then opened the safe door.

The weapons system officer's safe held the pistol-shaped missile firing trigger which plugged into the main missile console—one of the three essential ingredients necessary to complete the launch circuits.

Outwardly pleased, the safecracker spoke. "You arrived just in time, Captain."

"So I see. Nice work. You're both well ahead of schedule."

"We'll tackle the captain's safe next."

"Excellent. Nothing'll stop us now."

CHAPTER NINE

Lunchtime at Space Town, Mason thought, feeling a little down about calling his friend, Sam Napper, back from Christmas leave. Knowing Gary Ellie, Eion, Scott, and Roberts were already on duty the week after Christmas helped his feelings, but only slightly. With lunch tray in hand, Mason walked across the building to their video conference room and took his seat. To his left, Ensign Eion Macke and Lieutenant Gary Ellie concluded their subdued discussion concerning the *Maine*. To his right, Lieutenant Colonel Napper sat silent, staring at his food. All in all, the group's mood seemed pretty somber.

Looking across the table at their video screen, Mason greeted Scott and Roberts onboard the *Yorktown*. Scott worked for Mason directly, Roberts attended as an observer and ClearWater technical expert.

Once introductions were exchanged, Sam Napper announced he was never going to eat again. After this Christmas holiday, he was sick of eating—tired of it. Sam didn't get any sympathy from the *Yorktown*. Scott reported the storm at sea had passed, then offered to change places

with him. Slim acknowledged Sam's condition as understandable aware of the eating binge he'd been on all week,
but considered this a transient condition, one that would
pass in time.

After Mason offered an apology for screwing up Sam's
vacation, Napper attempted to put him at ease. "We knew it
was serious, or you wouldn't have called. Eion briefed us
on the *Maine*'s situation and we're wondering . . . where do
we go from here?"

Mason's expression shifted to *getting down to business*.
"I've been giving that question a great deal of thought this
morning and wanted to run an approach by you folks."
Watching their eyes, Mason saw the mood of his key players changing. These people were as good as they get . . .
self-starters, ready to help, wanting to contribute and get
their hands around this situation. Just point them in a reasonable direction, and stand back. "I don't like being pessimistic," Mason paused. "I could be wrong, and I hope I
am—but in our situation, I think we should assume the
worst and prioritize our efforts accordingly. If we're
wrong, no one gets hurt and our problem solves itself. But
if we're right, we must prepare for what we're up against."

"I don't care for pessimists either," Scott confirmed,
"but I think you're right with your approach on this one.
Concentrate on the worst case."

Gary Ellie, the new kid on the block, nodded agreement.

Dr. Roberts thought a moment, then added, "I take
worst case to mean one of two alternatives. Either the
Maine's down or she's been hijacked." Frowning, he
rubbed his forehead. Clearly, he didn't like the sound of his
own words.

Sam Napper sat for a time apparently studying the ceiling, both hands on his head, thinking through the consequences of his friend's proposal. After deciding what he

thought, he offered an opinion. "Let me make sure we're all on the same wavelength here, Slim. You're saying we should assume the *Maine*'s been hijacked, assume she's in hostile hands for reasons unknown."

"I'm saying exactly that. The Navy hasn't faced this possibility yet, but I think we should. Given this worst case starting assumption, we answer two questions, and two questions only. First, why it happened . . . the motive behind it, and second, how it happened." Mason paused, reading a puzzled looked in Sam's expression. "I don't mean to say we resolve this problem down to a single motive—I'd expect we might find a dozen or more possible motives before we're through. And I don't mean to say we identify the way it happened; we identify as many ways as we can imagine, then rank order them."

"With all due respect, Colonel," Sam offered almost apologetically, "what's this got to do with ClearWater?"

"I don't like biasing your investigation in advance, but as I see it, I don't have any choice. If our efforts are to be useful at all, we don't have much time. How much time? . . . I haven't a clue, but if this worst case scenario plays out as legitimate, we're running on borrowed time already." Mason shifted his gaze toward Gary Ellie. "This renegade sub situation may have nothing whatsoever to do with ClearWater, or it may have everything to do with it. If the *Maine* doesn't show in the next couple of hours, she's either a renegade or lost at sea. Neither alternative's attractive, but if she's a renegade, ClearWater's very likely involved. The connection's too obvious to imagine otherwise. Somehow, someway, ClearWater's been compromised."

Gary Ellie's face looked despondent. He hadn't been on the project very long, but already thought of ClearWater as his own. "I can't believe it, sir. I understand what you're saying and all . . . Just doesn't seem possible . . . too fan-

tastic. ClearWater's only been deployed a little over a year
. . . been operational less than that . . . six months or so.
And the system's still in major flux. We install bug fixes
every day . . . new software releases, every month. We
change operational software so often it'd make your head
spin . . . have trouble enough keeping it straight among
ourselves. It's hard to imagine how anyone could compromise such a moving target."

Mason nodded understanding, then stated something
both obvious and undeniable. "Try considering the problem from another point of view. You're wrapped up in the
most important business of all—making the system
work—and you're really good at it, but try considering our
renegade sub problem from Admiral Eastwood's perspective." Mason smiled, hoping to shift Gary Ellie's position
off the defensive. "Look at the problem from one hundred
thousand feet. The sky's clear; you can see a great many
things, but none of them in fine detail. The oxygen's thin
there, not much air, so if you cruise this altitude very long,
you'll lose your ability to think at all. Happens to upper
management all the time." Mason chuckled, all the while
studying Gary Ellie's face. At first and second read, he
appeared receptive. The tension around his mouth now
relaxed.

"What I'm trying to say is this. From Admiral Eastwood's perspective, the U.S. Navy's driven submarines all
his life. They've lost precious few in that time, and never
had one hijacked—until now . . . until ClearWater came on
line."

Gary Ellie reiterated Slim's point. "ClearWater comes
on line and we lose a submarine."

"And a nuclear-powered, guided missile submarine at
that . . . one of the finest in the fleet. She was converted for

guided missile attack two years ago as a direct result of the ClearWater program."

"What you're saying makes sense, sir," Gary Ellie reluctantly agreed. "I can see where you're coming from. My problem's technical, I guess. I don't see . . . I can't begin to imagine how anyone'd compromise a moving target."

Dr. Roberts had been quiet until now, imagining how he'd compromise the ClearWater system. He spoke quietly as the room hushed. "In my opinion, it wouldn't be easy, but it's certainly possible to compromise our surveillance data." A long, silent pause. He had their attention now. "Someone on the inside could do it."

Mason agreed. "Perhaps together, you can come up with something. Scotty's a jet jockey, but don't let that fool you. She's a tech-head too, a computer type at heart . . . two degrees in computer science . . . one from the Air Force academy, and a master's from Cal Tech."

"Really—cool!" the young lieutenant responded enthusiastically. "For a minute, I was feeling all alone here, surrounded by flight wings and blue suiters. What'd you do at Cal Tech, Captain Scott? What was it like?"

Scotty shook her head, dredging up bad memories she didn't want to recall. "I don't mean to sound trite, but I studied—that's all I did was study—and it was hard. In retrospect, I learned a great deal, but I had to put my life on hold to do it. That's not unusual for Cal Tech though . . . at least in computer science, it's not unusual. As far as I could tell, no one in the Computer Science Department had a life."

"Sounds awful."

"Awful is a good single-word synopsis," the captain agreed, "but most of the people going there think it's worth the price. Maybe they love knowledge, maybe they love prestige, maybe they love school and want to go all their lives. I can't say that I understand why people love it, but undeniably, some people can't get enough of that place. As for my call on Cal Tech, I'm glad it's behind me."

"What was your interest?"

"Computer networking . . . the internet . . . hooking systems together all over the world through high-performance links and making them sing in unison."

"Do you know much about computer network administration?"

"More than I ever wanted to know, but it's pretty neat stuff, really. TCP/IP network administration was one of the few bright spots for me at school . . . worked part-time in their comp center as a network administrator. It was good practical exposure to the real world. And we got our hands dirty . . . fighting hacker fires I mean. Around Cal Tech, everyone thinks they know more than the comp center staff and that's an excellent incentive . . . helped keep us on our toes. On a technical level, it was like a war. Our lives were never threatened, nothing like that, but on a technical plane, it was the comp center staff versus the world."

"Any ideas about ClearWater?"

"A few . . . maybe we can talk about them off line."

"Excellent, Captain Scott," Gary Ellie said, taking his *back off until later* cue from the captain.

"And please, call me Scotty."

"With pleasure, Scotty," he grinned. "Works for me."

Mason sat silent, inwardly pleased with his group's interaction. Scott, Eion, Tristan, and Gary Ellie were his core technical team on this problem and it was important they should work well together. To Mason's delight, though separated by thousands of miles, his core team had willingly coalesced before his eyes within the span of a few minutes. No one could have hoped for more. He knew firsthand that sometimes when technical people come together to focus on a problem, ego and face time often get in the way. More often than not, egos must be stroked while every one involved gets face time in front of the big guns. *Not a problem with Gary Ellie, Eion, or Scott though. Good.* Mason didn't know Roberts that well, but Scott thought highly of him. *If he's good enough for her, he's good enough for me,* Mason thought, giving Tristan the benefit of the doubt.

Shifting his gaze to the young lieutenant, Mason spoke quietly. "I propose that you show Dr. Roberts and Captain Scott anything they want to see."

Gary Ellie nodded. Looking at Scott and Tristan on screen, he asked, "Any ideas?"

They talked the question over among themselves, then Tristan replied, "We'd suggest starting with ClearWater surveillance recordings and accounting records."

"Turns out," Ensign Macke grinned sheepishly, "I was playing back surveillance tapes when you called this meeting, sir." Eion had intentionally stayed in the background until now, learning the ropes, measuring personalities.

"We'll be wrapping up here pretty shortly, son." Mason's blue eyes smiled. "Could you pick up where you left off and let us know if anything turns up?"

"Yes, sir," Eion replied with a smile. He stood, shot Mason a thumbs-up, then left the room.

Mason shifted his focus to Gary Ellie, Scott, and Roberts. "Once you've covered accounting, focus on our computer network; pick it apart. Run through Tristan's scenario. Assume ClearWater's been compromised by someone on the inside. Think through how you'd do it and let me know."

Scott and Gary Ellie looked at each other in disbelief.

"This is the most pessimistic scenario, people," Mason continued, "but we've got to face it or we'll never move forward. Assume someone on the comp center staff, for reasons unknown, has compromised our system. If this is the case . . . how'd they do it? We've got to find out."

Gary Ellie, Roberts, and Scott nodded agreement, knowing what to do next.

Mason shifted his gaze toward Sam Napper. "Let's you and I focus on motive first thing. I'm not sure about this, but my hunch is that we can treat motive independent of method. Intuitively, it would seem the reason behind Clear-Water's compromise should be independent of how they did it."

"Seems like a reasonable place to start, Slim. Dissect the problem into independent, separable parts."

"Right, but remember, somehow, some way, people are behind this problem." Mason paused, then summarized his proposal. "Once we've brainstormed a list of motives together, I want you and your group to work with the Navy personnel department . . . review the records of everyone on the *Maine*. Somehow, somewhere, we must find some clue as to who's behind this."

"She's got a crew of a hundred sixty men, Slim. Gaining access to those records, let alone reviewing them's, going to take some time . . . I'm talking hours, maybe days." Sam gazed directly into his friend's eyes. "You know, I don't mean to sound like a broken record, but if any of the officers or crew had even a hint of some problem identified in their records, they wouldn't have been onboard the *Maine* in the first place. I don't think it's very likely that we'll find anything buried in the records that the *Maine*'s skipper would've missed."

"Unless the skipper's involved."

"We'll check him out first thing, sir . . . and the XO second, but you know as well as I do, this is no *Hunt for Red October*. We already live in the finest country on the face of the earth. Besides, our skippers are impeccable. If the *Maine*'s actually been hijacked, this situation's deadly serious, almost too frightening to contemplate."

"So what are you saying?"

"We'll check the records, but be realistic about our prospects. Expect in advance, we're going to need some legwork—there's no way around it—some background investigations to find out the truth behind this situation."

"What do you recommend?"

"Grease the skids with the FBI up front, and don't pull any punches. Tell 'em what we know and get them onboard ASAP. The only way these background investigations could possibly be of any value to us in our short-fuse situation is if they were completed immediately, right?"

Mason nodded agreement.

"Since our time is short, have the FBI jump-start a hundred sixty background investigations in parallel."

Mason grimaced. "I see where you're coming from, and what you say makes sense, but in reality, we're the federal government. We don't do anything fast." Slim thought for a few seconds, then his expression turned brighter. "I'll take this one up my chain of command. Craven's a real mover and shaker. If anyone can make this happen, he can."

"Don't forget the record reviews . . ."

"I'll set it up through Admiral Eastwood's office. He'll arrange on-line access to these records for us. You won't need to travel—we'll work them from here. Break up the records into smaller groups and divide them among your staff. If you need more people, let me know." Mason thought for a moment, then asked, "Sam, you got any more ideas as to how we should proceed? Any other suggestions? Things we might be missing?"

"This task is almost overwhelming. Where on earth do we start looking for this needle in a haystack?" Sam Napper rubbed his eyes, blocking out the visual distractions around him. There was a protracted pause as Sam thought through the problem of *what to do,* then he began making notes. Sam Napper had learned over the years that he didn't really know what he thought unless he could write it down, read it back, and see if he agreed with it. Mason didn't pressure Sam and understood how he operated. After reading over his notes several minutes later, Sam offered his suggestion. "What I think is this. We've got to approach this problem like peeling back the layers of an onion. We may or may not find someone on the *Maine* with a suspicious background. In advance, my guess is we won't. The Navy's mighty particular about their submarine crews. Screening and regular psychological testing weeds out the unstable types early on. Honestly, I find it hard to believe there'd be one traitor on the *Maine,* and besides, what could one man do alone?" He paused . . . looked determined. "Matter of fact, I find it impossible to believe there'd ever be more than one traitor onboard unless the skipper or XO were involved. The probability of more than one traitor onboard the *Maine* must be absurdly low— practically speaking, it must be zero." Sam shrugged; his expression was not optimistic.

"I can't believe there'd ever be a team of conspirators," Scott affirmed. "Not onboard a nuclear-powered American submarine. It just doesn't make any sense. What possible motivation could unite a band of independent-thinking Americans to do such a thing?"

"Money?" Gary Ellie offered.

Scott disagreed.

"A truckload of money?" the young lieutenant countered.

"I don't think there's enough money in this world," she responded.

"I hope you're right, Scotty," Sam acknowledged. "And

I believe you are. As I understand it, even a submariner's finances are routinely scrutinized. No one in desperate financial shape sails these boats."

"Mutiny?" Gary Ellie was full of ideas.

"Like I said," Sam responded, "we'll check out the skipper and XO first thing, but in my opinion, the likelihood of mutiny in peacetime conditions is absolute zero . . . period."

"One fact is undeniable," Mason observed. "If the *Maine*'s been hijacked, people are behind it."

The group shrugged agreement, but did not speak.

"So where does that leave us?" Mason asked.

Gary Ellie looked at Scott and quipped, "I think we've got the easy job."

"The technical problem's a cinch compared to the people problem," Scott confirmed.

"My point exactly," Napper said. "And because of the problem's complexity, I recommend we make some simplifying assumptions from the start. First, let's assume there might be—at most—one bad apple on the *Maine*."

"Very well." Mason supported the idea. "Where does that lead us?"

"Our bad apple's gotta have outside help." Scott paused, concentrating on the fallout from the lite colonel's assumption. "More important than that, he'd need well-organized, well-supported . . . well-connected . . . well-coordinated outside help. And a pretty sizable organization at that . . . probably naval support . . . maybe submarines, surface ships, aircraft, special forces, who knows? And some intelligence organization to support their connection here."

"Seems altogether reasonable," Mason responded evenly, concealing his personal delight. "I'd assumed organized topside help as well, but you're revealing insight as to what type organization we could be up against—and more. First off, this doesn't come across like any half-cocked terrorist activity. Sounds more like something we might do . . . no, that didn't come out right, did it? I mean it's more like some premeditated CIA plot." Mason surveyed the group, looking for traction.

"So we're pitted against some country, somewhere, with a navy?" the second lieutenant asked. His expression conveyed disbelief.

"After considering Sam's *one bad apple* assumption, I'd say that's about the size of it," Scott confirmed. Her tone remained sure. "Probably a country with some Pacific coastline . . . maybe one on the Pacific Rim."

"But there's more good news here in my opinion," Mason added. "In this type situation, there's always a question about the mental stability of the opposition. Are they rational or not? Thank God we're not dealing with terrorists. We're probably dealing with some hostile foreign government, one with a navy, special forces, and spies. That's what we do—we're geared for it. We may not like it, but unless they're desperate, hostile countries operate like we do—motivated by self-interest."

"But I can't see the light at the end of the tunnel, Slim." Sam sighed, sounding lost. "That's what's bothering me. The problem's mind boggling. The Pacific's an enormous ocean. Too many countries with oceanfront property. Too many unknowns."

"So let's eliminate as many unknowns as we possibly can. How about this? We work through our list of possible motives, review the crew's records, then meet again tonight as a group and see what we've got."

"I like it in that it gets us moving, heading in some direction anyway. If our direction's off course, we'll correct it along the way."

"Good. Let's get on with it and meet up again . . . say six-thirty tonight. By the way," Mason looked to Scott,

Roberts, and Gary Ellie, "don't discuss this exercise with anyone, and I mean anyone. No one on the comp center staff must know what we're about here."

"I understand, sir," Gary Ellie affirmed. "In the computer networking world of cyberspace, it doesn't take long to cover your tracks."

Within two hours, Gary Ellie discovered something subtly out of order with comp center accounting. Somehow, for some reason, the books didn't quite balance. There was an eighty-seven-cent accounting discrepancy that defied explanation. Apparently, someone had used a few seconds of USSPACECOM computing time without paying for it. This could be something significant, it could be nothing at all. Thousand-dollar errors aren't hard to find, but smaller, seemingly insignificant, errors are insidiously difficult to nail down. More often than not, these problems are either mired in the computer's operating internals or malice.

Body Bags, 12/28/2008, Sun., 06:47 A.M.
USS Maine

Mandrone entered the crew's mess, body bags in hand, to find the dining area littered with corpses. Six dropped dead in their tracks by the soft ice cream and soda dispensers. Two cooks collapsed preparing food, one by the griddle, the other died running the kitchen mixer. Judging from the batter left standing in the mixer bowl, Mandrone concluded the cook had chocolate chip cookies in mind when he'd been struck down. Mandrone couldn't put his finger on it exactly, but he found these suspended signs of life most disturbing of all.

To make matters worse, one of the chiefs had apparently been teaching a class in the dining area when the gas let go. As a result, the dining area looked like a high school classroom from the Twilight Zone, filled with young men, frozen in time. The chief had collapsed in a heap by his white board, while students looked on, slack-jawed. Some sat open-eyed, heads rolled back, staring at the ceiling; others appeared to be resting, face down on the dining tables.

On further inspection, Mandrone noticed a rash of white paper straw wrappers strewn about the floor, concentrated around two students in particular. From all visual indications, these dutiful student warriors had enjoyed annoying each other, and were engaging in a protracted spitball war before their prank callously drew to a close.

Mandrone looked away, feeling he'd seen the death of a hundred lifetimes. Ahead, he saw three of his men pulling morgue duty, dragging corpses into the open walkway space between the galley and dining area. Mike counted seven bodies, neatly arranged face down on the floor, arms tied using brown cooking twine. *Sides of beef, bound up, awaiting the meat hook.* Mandrone grimaced.

Seeing one of his men struggling with a particularly large sailor, Mandrone decided to lend a hand. Setting his body bags on the dining table, Mike grabbed the dead crewman's arms, lifting him into an open space where he could be bound without interference. Once free of obstructions, Mike grabbed the sailor's stiff open hand, working it halfway down his side. Having coerced the dead sailor's arm partway, Mike spoke to his crewman, a middle-aged reactor expert, kneeling at the dead man's feet.

"Pull it down. I'll tie it off." Breathing heavily, he sounded winded.

The nuclear engineer evaluated the situation, grabbing the corpse's arm with one hand, holding the dead man's torso with the other. Feeling the man's shoulder separating, the crewman recoiled, allowing it to spring back like a green sapling.

During its sweeping arc, the dead man's hand snapped back in Mandrone's face, the thumbnail catching his right eye. Stunned, unable to duck quickly enough, he felt the sting. Batting the dead man's arm away, his eye flushed with tears seconds later. Instinctively, Mandrone blinked, then squinted. Mike knew he'd been hurt, his eye felt uncomfortable when he blinked, but he believed that within a few minutes, a few hours worst case, he'd be good as new.

What he didn't know was that the dead man's thumbnail had severed forty percent of his cornea, leaving only a thin flap of loose skin dangling in its place.

CHAPTER TEN

From his watch station overlooking the Pacific screening room, Ensign Eion Macke escorted Gary Ellie through a maze of cubicles, back to his office. At first glance, the ensign's office struck Gary Ellie as in transition. Half-unpacked book boxes sat alongside the ensign's partially filled bookcase; government-issue pictures of naval aircraft and submarines lined his cubical walls, creating a checker-board-like effect surrounding the cramped space. Following an apology for the disarray, the ensign took his seat behind a large-screen workstation located in the back corner of his office. Standing behind him—there was no other place to sit—the lieutenant watched over Eion's shoulder as he set up their conference call with the *Yorktown*.

Eion clicked on a camera icon, loading his video conference software. Using his Conference Configuration menu, Eion set up three windows. The first he titled "Eion," the second "Gary," and the third "Play Back Monitor." Next, he reset their speakerphone, a desktop black box located alongside his monitor. The speakerphone responded by sounding an audio sweep, a series of increasingly high-pitched tones, then went quiet. Finally, Eion positioned one camera on himself, another on Gary, then selected Yorktown from the Connect menu. Following some unseen computer networking magic, Scotty appeared in a fourth window.

"I'm glad you could come on such short notice," Eion opened, "but where's Dr. Roberts?"

"He's working our accounting problem," Scott replied. "That missing eighty-seven cents intrigues him."

"Divide and conquer," Gary Ellie added. "I sent him the files."

"Sounds good to me," Eion concluded. "I'd wanted you to see what I found. It may not amount to anything, but after the *Maine* didn't show this morning, I took a second look at our log files. Her course struck a couple of us here as a little odd." Eion clattered away at the keyboard a moment, searching for a copy of a file he'd squirreled away. Once he'd found the right directory, he double clicked the log file icon he'd created earlier.

In a matter of seconds, his computer screen turned deep ocean blue. Displayed prominently to the left of the screen, a slowly moving submarine-shaped icon flashed. It was labeled USS *Maine*. Distributed across the bottom of the screen were a series of buttons, or soft keys, looking something like VCR controls. Everything Eion saw on screen, Scott saw mirrored on her monitor in CIC.

"Take a look at this," Eion said, clicking a FAST FOR-WARD button on screen. "This display plots the *Maine*'s course during the last twelve hours we tracked her. If the *Maine* hadn't disappeared, I wouldn't have given her course a second thought. In fact, to be honest about it, I didn't give it a second thought until she missed her SAT break this morning. Then I went back and took another look."

There was a pause while the computer displayed the

Maine's course over a twelve-hour period. At times during the first six hours of playback, the *Maine*'s heading seemed determined by a random roll of the dice, marked by straight, deliberate legs of arbitrary length. Then for some reason, during the last six hours of her recorded journey, her course didn't seem random at all. In fact, her course took on more the appearance of a square wave—straight, equal-length legs marked by near-right-angle, ninety-degree turns.

Circling the square wave pattern with his finger, Eion continued. "When I first saw her course, it struck me as a sloppy zigzag pattern. Random zigzag courses are common among our submarine fleet, see 'em all the time, but they're usually shark-toothed affairs, more triangular shaped."

"The course is interesting," Gary Ellie said, "but I don't see that it tells us anything."

"We need a little ramp up here, Eion," Scott added. "We're not familiar with patrol courses, typical or otherwise. What do you see in her course that strikes you as unusual? Is it the blunt, flat-topped tooth shape? . . . The similar length of each leg, her right-angle turns, her speed, duration, or what?"

"In a nutshell, the *Maine*'s course was too . . . too regular and squared off to be a sloppy zigzag course, and the duration's too long. She should've mixed it up a little . . . don't know why she didn't. Generally, a guided missile boat's course should be unpredictable . . . same's true for a boomer. That's the whole idea behind remaining undetected on patrol. They roam randomly about their patrol areas—we're talking sectors of ocean the size of states here—always steering clear from other contacts. Fact is, they avoid contacts like the plague."

"Got it," Scott closed. "The *Maine*'s course struck you

as out of the ordinary because for six hours, it was predictable. Thanks for the snapshot . . . could be meaningful."

"I've got a sinking feeling about this one," Eion sighed.

"Yeah, me too. I'm afraid we're missing something." Scott thought for a moment, gazing at the VCR-like control buttons across the bottom of Eion's large monitor screen. She ran the controls round and round in her mind . . . REVERSE, STOP, PLAY, FAST FORWARD. *Something's missing from this picture,* Scott thought. *What's ClearWater all about? Submarine detection. Right, but there's more. ClearWater detects surface ships as well, all classes. Yeah, and then what? That's it! That's what's missing . . . The RECORD button's missing. ClearWater not only detects oceangoing traffic, it operates like the world's largest VCR recorder. It records everything it detects like a digital tape recorder! Why didn't I think of this before?*

Scott read Eion's face. He was staring at the screen, lost in his thoughts.

"Let me ask you a question." Scott spoke softly to get Eion's attention. "Judging from what you've shown us, ClearWater records everything it detects, right? . . . Above and below the ocean's surface."

"That's about the size of it. ClearWater logs span the last six months."

Gary Ellie immediately caught on and looked Scott in the eyes. "So if any naval support forces were involved, we should have a record of it."

Scott nodded, rolling her lips between her teeth. *Unless it's been erased,* she didn't say.

Eion sat silently for a moment, thinking through the consequences of the lieutenant's comment. He appeared puzzled at first, then became concerned. "I think I see where you're heading." Eion's inflection was tentative. Naval support forces likely meant one thing. "If you're thinking the *Maine*'s been hijacked, we'll have a record of it."

Scott raised both eyebrows. "We don't know what's happened to the *Maine,* but we've got to consider this possibility, however remote."

Eion's eyes narrowed. After giving the hijacking possibility a good think, his face relaxed. "The idea's impossible to take very seriously, but we can check it out easy enough, no sweat."

"The logs are tangible, recorded evidence. I like the idea. Should keep us on the right track," Gary Ellie added while Eion clattered away on his keyboard.

"Here's a recording that spans the last thirty-two hours." Eion studied a series of event markers laid out across a time line displayed on screen. "Let's see . . . roughly twenty-two hours since we first lost her track plus a six-hour segment with her sailing that squared-off course."

"Excellent," Scott replied. "Now we need to set up some boundary conditions. First, can you program this thing to display a circle that grows with the passing of time?"

"Absolutely. We do it all the time. Even got a drawing tool for it."

"How 'bout a teardrop?"

"No problem."

"All right. We'll need a teardrop and circle overlaid on your recording, both centered over the point where the *Maine* was last detected." Scott studied the display, then asked, "Can you tell the speed and direction of undersea currents where the *Maine* was lost?"

"Sure, we've got to know that or the detection system won't work." Using his mouse and cursor, Eion swept out the shape of a small box centered about the *Maine*'s last known position, then double clicked. Immediately, a new window popped up showing ocean currents and temperatures in the area.

"As I understand it, ClearWater detects the velocity of the water shoved aside by the advancing submarine's hull . . . sort of a submerged wake." Scott looked to Eion for agreement.

"Yep, that's about the size of it."

"What if a sub's drifting? . . . I mean, what happens to her wake if she trails her screw and drifts with the current? Could ClearWater detect it?"

"First off—and this is important—we'd detect her slowing down. Her residual momentum's enormous! Say, for example, if she's making twenty knots and kills her throttles, she'd still be logging five knots twenty minutes later. Eventually though, her wake'd disappear, drop below our detectable minimum, and we lose track. It's as simple as that."

Scott pointed to the screen. "Let's assume the *Maine*'s drifting. Use the speed and direction of the current along with that . . ."

"I'm with you, Scotty," Eion interrupted. "I'll create a region showing where she may have drifted over the last twenty-two hours." A few keystrokes later, an oblong, teardropped-shaped pattern appeared on screen. As Eion fast-forwarded through the recording, their teardrop grew about five miles in length every hour. Satisfied, he looked up. "OK We're set."

"No, not quite yet," Scott countered. "Next, assume she's running flat out and deep—below one hundred meters."

"That's right. We'd never detect her running deep." Eion nodded, clicking and dragging all the while. "Any heading in particular?"

Scott thought a few seconds, then shook her head. "No.

Assume she could be heading any direction on the map, any direction at all."

Using his cursor and drawing tool, Eion created a circle centered where the *Maine* was last detected, then ran his animation. As he fast-forwarded through ClearWater's recording, the circular shape grew eighty miles in diameter every hour.

"That hummer's moving," Gary Ellie observed.

"If she's a renegade running deep . . . no way anyone could find her." Scott bit her lip. At the end of the twenty-six-hour video clip, the circle expanded to encompass over two million square miles of ocean.

Eion sighed. "Not unless she wanted to be found or did something stupid."

"Whoever they are, if they've got the *Maine,* they're professionals." Scott's tone was final. "They won't make mistakes." She shook her head slowly as if to clear it, then pressed ahead. "Let's put all the elements together now. Overlay the animation on the ClearWater clip. We'll examine it frame by frame where we need to."

Eion displayed each element on screen, then clicked the FAST FORWARD button. The *Maine* sailed through the last legs of her square-wave course again. Seconds later, shortly before ClearWater lost track of the USS *Maine,* Eion pressed STOP and read her speed. "Hmmm . . . ," he thought out loud. "She's creeping through here . . . barely logging eight knots." He rewound the recording, backed up fifteen minutes of play time, and checked her speed. "Eight knots . . . hmmm." Backed it up a full hour and checked her speed again. *Ten knots,* he thought. "You know, the *Maine* sailed that square wave running only eight to ten knots . . . never noticed it before, never thought of it really. She's barely detectable through here. We have maybe four knots margin, tops."

"Margin? What do you mean exactly?" Gary Ellie asked.

"Like I said earlier, if she runs too slow, below three knots or so, we generally can't see her. Her wake drops below our minimums."

"I don't know what to make of her speed, Eion, not yet anyway." Scott sighed. "Let's run the clip forward looking for submerged and surface traffic cutting across our animation." She paused, sorting through what they might expect to find. "The way I see it's like this. If we detect anything cutting across the max speed circle, then we've got a suspect."

"It's a big ocean," Eion observed with a grimace. "After twenty-six hours, that circle encompasses millions of square miles."

"I understand that," Scott responded evenly. "The longer we run your animation, the more ocean we must include when looking for suspects—but I don't want to think about that now. As far as this analysis is concerned, that max speed circle represents our most pessimistic view. If we dwell on the worst case first thing, it's overwhelming . . . we'd never make any progress." Speaking with both hands—she was emphatic on this point.

Eion yielded, acknowledging she was right.

Gary Ellie looked on, impressed. The woman was focused and would not be distracted by irrelevant concern or fear of the unknown.

Scott continued in a measured tone. "But if anyone cuts across the teardrop at any time, we've got a prime suspect."

"I understand where you're heading," Eion affirmed. "Look for the obvious intercept before sweating the long shots."

"Exactly." Scott closed her eyes, blocking out all distrac- tions, struggling to phrase her point in as few words as possible. "And finally, if anyone seems to intercept the *Maine*— I mean where the *Maine* would be if she were drifting—then in all probability, we've got a big, big problem."

"This whole idea's too fantastic to lose any sleep over," Eion remarked candidly. "How could anyone possibly link up with the *Maine* if we don't even know where she is?"

A long pause. Scott eyed the young ensign warily, then responded, "Well, let's take a look-see anyway, just to be sure."

"All right Captain, we'll give it a go, but I'm not optimistic we'll find anything."

Minutes later, the trio marked an unidentified surface ship—the *Kansong*—as their first suspect traffic crossing the max speed circle. Soon afterward, her course changed, as if she were steering an intercept course on the *Maine*. Five minutes after that, they marked her as their prime suspect once she clipped the teardrop. Finally, after stepping through the next twenty minutes of recording, one frame at the time, their worst fears were confirmed. The unidentified ship intercepted the *Maine*'s most probable course— were she adrift.

"So Colonel Mason was right," Gary Ellie sighed. "Never thought it possible."

"I woulda never believed it." Eion shook his head slowly.

"This isn't conclusive proof," Scott cautioned. "Neither is that eighty-seven-cent accounting error, but they're too suspicious to ignore."

Dumbfounded, Eion and Gary Ellie agreed, but were at a loss as to how to proceed.

Thinking ahead, Scott continued. "No one'll believe it—not at first." Looking in Gary Ellie's eyes, she continued quietly, "Colonel Mason needs to see this . . . here— now. We're gonna need help and lots of it."

The trio called immediately for reinforcements. Mason and Napper arrived before the dust settled.

Gary Ellie summarized their eighty-seven-cent accounting discrepancy. Mason felt it could be significant, but at this early stage of investigation, it was hard to know for sure.

Eion highlighted significant clips from ClearWater's ocean surveillance. After they'd played the recording and teardrop overlay, Slim rubbed his brow. "I don't want to jump to conclusions here. This chance intercept could be a coincidence—but I doubt it. I don't know the odds of their courses crossing, but it's an enormous ocean. The size of these ships is insignificant by comparison." He paused, then spoke to Sam. "Let's call in our satellite photo reconnaissance group . . . get a positive I.D. on that ship. Give them the exact time and location of our possible intercept. Correlate our data with theirs. Let's see what they've got."

Sam agreed, then raced out of Eion's office.

Sorting through his options, Mason struggled to think ahead of their problem. Facing the camera, Slim addressed Scott. "Think it's time you and Tristan packed your equipment," he sighed. "Collect your receiver plus any test gear you'll need. Unless you've got a better idea, I'm afraid you're both headed to an old, dilapidated P-3 base on Kiska."

Scott cut her eyes toward Mason's. "Sub hunt?"

Looking away from the camera, Mason nodded, clearly uncomfortable with their prospects. "Plan on installing your receiver and tactical display in a P-3." He looked up again, studying Scott's expression. "Think you can handle it?"

"You've gotta be kidding me." Scott's face brightened. "Dry land, long runways. Not to worry, Colonel. You get us there, we'll cover it. Besides, it's a good idea; our Clear-Water receiver'd come in handy during a sub hunt, no doubt about it."

Mason's apprehension eased following Scott's support of his idea.

"There's one other thing though, Colonel. An idea I've been mulling over."

"What's on your mind?"

"I've gone round and round with this, sir, but always come down on the same side of the fence. I'll admit we don't have conclusive proof of malice, but we've got strong reasons to be suspicious. As I see it, there's only one way any rendezvous could have taken place." Scott paused to let her point sink in.

During her silence, Mason filled in the blank. He'd concluded the same thing earlier that afternoon. "Some way, that ship's skipper knew the *Maine*'s location."

Scott agreed. "We're facing the very real possibility that our submarine position database could have been compromised."

Mason's throat felt dry. "It's possible," he gulped. The idea sounded worse when someone else said it out loud. "Any suggestions? How do we plug the leak? What should we do?"

"Unless we're lucky, Colonel, don't plan on finding any security leaks quickly. Think about it. If someone's on the inside working against us, it could take weeks, maybe months, to ferret 'em out."

Mason sighed agreement.

"I propose we corrupt the information they're after. Screw up the sub posit database with random errors; consequently, if it's stolen, it can't be used against us."

Mason's expression turned melancholy. In his gut, Slim felt she was right, but ClearWater's database had been in service several months and U.S. military forces around the globe were already depending on it.

"I can guess what you're probably thinking, Colonel, but

in the short term, it's the only way to guarantee our database won't be used against us. It's the only way to be sure."

"You're absolutely right." Mason stiffened his resolve. "It won't be easy, but I'll get on it immediately. We've got a great many hurdles to clear before making this happen, but like you say, it's the only way to be sure."

After jotting down a few notes, he shifted topics, addressing Eion in a more confident manner. "Don't breathe a word about this to anyone. This is hot. As of this minute, you report directly to me. The admiral needs to see this immediately and Craven's gotta know. Send them both a copy of your log and animation file ASAP."

"Will do, sir," the ensign remarked above the noise of his clattering keyboard.

Shifting his gaze to Gary Ellie, he continued. "Let me know if that eighty-seven cents turns up."

"Could be an accounting software bug, or could be something significant." The young man shrugged, not knowing what else to say.

"And one other thing, Gary."

"Sir?" His feeling—tentative.

"Check our computer network security."

"I'll do my best, sir, but . . ." Gary Ellie sighed, feeling overwhelmed.

"But what, son?"

"Honest, Colonel, Scotty's right. Unless we're lucky, we won't find anything, not fast anyway. It's like looking for a needle in a thousand haystacks."

Missing On Patrol, 12/27/2008, Sat., 12:22 P.M.
COMSUBPAC

Eastwood's hot line rang inside COMSUBPAC.

"Admiral, this is Colonel Mason."

"Hold one second, Colonel, while I put you on speaker-phone. My staff's here and I want them to hear what you've got to say."

A click followed by "You're on."

Mason cut to the crux. "Any word on the *Maine*?"

"Nothing. Nothing at all." Over the speakerphone, the admiral's voice sounded hollow, like someone talking into the end of a pipe. "The *Maine* hasn't responded. It's as if the ocean's just swallowed her up."

"Admiral, something's gone terribly wrong." Mason cleared his throat. The admiral leaned forward, but did not speak. "I believe we know why the *Maine* never responded. Somehow, some way, she's been hijacked." Mason went on to explain while the admiral watched the intercept played back on his computer screen.

Time and time again, Admiral Eastwood zoomed in on the apparent intercept point and played through the recording. Reluctantly, the admiral concurred with Mason's observation. "It's not conclusive proof, but you're right about one thing. It's too suspicious to ignore." Admiral Eastwood zeroed in on the ocean's depth in the suspect area. "Our DSRVs may not do us much good here. On paper, they can't operate below five thousand feet, but I'll run it by our experts and see what they think."

He looked across his desk at one of his staff. "Bring our DSRV driver onboard, the one stationed at Ballast Point. Call him . . . tell him our situation. See if there's anything he can do. If he thinks there's a chance, we can have the *Avalon* on station in less than twenty-four hours." The *Avalon* was one of the Navy's quick-reaction submarine rescue vehicles stationed on NAS North Island, San Diego.

"Aye, aye, sir," the youngest staff member responded on his way out the door.

Once the DSRV issue was being worked, the admiral rubbed his forehead, thinking through what to do next. That depth could be a problem for their DSRV. He looked to the staff remaining in his office. "See what else we can do. Contact Woods Hole immediately and get their deep-submergence vehicle on it. *Alvin* can cover the depth with no problem . . . scour the area. If they left any traces, we'll find them." The admiral paused, then shook his head dejectedly. "No, on second thought, we could have a problem getting her on station quickly. *Alvin*'s a research vessel, not built for rapid deployment. Her operations are tied to a mother ship and she's a slow mover."

"I'll give it a go, sir . . . let you know what I find out." A second junior officer left the room, leaving only the senior officers behind with the admiral.

The admiral's mind raced ahead. "What else do we have in the region? We could get a pair of Orions over the area in a hurry . . . right?"

One senior staffer hurriedly logged into the workstation located along the office wall. Without wasted motion, he entered the location of the trouble spot, then queried their database for U.S. naval and Air Force resources available within a fifteen-hundred-mile radius. Almost immediately, an image of a loose-leaf asset notebook appeared on screen. Within seconds, he thumbed through the notebook with a series of mouse clicks, tabbing over to the section marked P-3 Orion. "Yes sir. Looks like P-3s could be there inside of eight hours." One click later, the young man was reviewing a list of Los Angeles–class attack submarines closest to the area. "The *Cheyenne*'s closest to the mark— could be on station in ten hours, maybe less."

Studying the large, global view of the Pacific displayed on his monitor, the admiral prodded further after a few moments' reflection. "The Seventh Fleet just completed a joint PacRim exercise with Japan." He paused, tapping his fingernail against the desk three times. "Where are the carriers?"

A few clicks later, the staffer continued. "The bulk of the Seventh Fleet's located in and around the Sea of Japan—well out of operating range. Our two carrier groups there won't do us much good, not in the short term." As the officer continued absorbing fleet location data, his expression brightened following a few more clicks. "The *Stennis* is here, sir. We may be in luck." A blinking carrier icon appeared on the admiral's monitor west-northwest of the Hawaiian Islands. Seconds later, the entire *Stennis* battle group appeared on screen. "She's on loan from the Mediterranean, pulling a three-month PacRim deployment. They're heading back to Pearl now, but we could extend her Pacific tour, send the entire battle group north . . . use her ASW capabilities . . . and her attack sub." There was a pause while the officer ran through some range and fuel figures. "Assuming adequate jet fuel reserves onboard, her Vikings could fan out over the area from the southwest. Allowing time to get her planes on the flight deck, coordinated planning, mission briefings, and midair refueling, I'd estimate their time to station—maybe eight hours, ten hours tops. Her attack sub, the *Topeka*, could pull away from the battle group en route. Worst case, she'd make the *Maine*'s last known location in thirty-six hours, although she'd probably arrive in less . . . maybe thirty-four. That's the best we can do on a short fuse."

"Good. We were lucky. Typically, we wouldn't've had a carrier within two full days' steam of trouble." The admiral held his hands together, perfectly still, pondering their situation. "*Topeka?* Who's her skipper?"

One click yielded "Commander Slay Hawkins, sir."

"Excellent. Hawk's the best we've got, none better."

Rubbing his fist in his palm, the admiral's expression brightened. After another few moments' reflection, he continued speaking out loud to let the others know what he was thinking. "What I'd like to do, I cannot do . . . not yet anyway. I need a plan. First off, we need to call our boomers and guided missile subs back to the barn."

"All of them?" a senior staff officer asked, initially taken aback.

"Everyone we've got patrolling the Pacific. If the *Maine*'s a renegade, we'll have to kill her. We sure as hell don't want to kill one of our own by mistake."

"We'll need a plan and presidential approval," another senior staff officer added.

"No doubt about it," the admiral pressed on. "Second, I'd like to throw everything we've got into the search . . . anything in the Pacific that'd be any help . . . any help at all. Divert the *Stennis* north immediately, extend her stay. Get her Vikings in the air ASAP. Move the *Topeka* on station with all possible speed. In this scenario, the *Stennis* is the hunter for a change, not the target."

"We're placing our carrier at risk, Admiral," one senior officer cautioned.

"Obviously," Eastwood snapped back. "Finally, we need to let our allies know what's going on . . . better let the Russians and Chinese know too. This sudden activity's going to draw a lot of unwanted attention. We've got to make our intentions clear well in advance. Could be easily misinterpreted if we're not careful."

His staff nodded agreement.

The admiral held his head in his hands, searching, sorting through what to do. What was a reasonable response in light of their best available information? And then it became clear, as if a dense fog had lifted. He rubbed his hands together and spoke in a quiet, deliberately clear voice. "Call the remainder of my staff back from leave. Treat this situation as an emergency action. Split into two groups—long and short fuse. Focus on the short fuse first. I need op plans and I need them now. First, get the Orions and Vikings in the air—every ASW aircraft we can get our hands on—combing the area as quickly as possible. Put together an op plan to coordinate their coverage. Second, order the *Cheyenne* and *Topeka* to scour the area. We don't need any additional approvals so get cracking. Set it up— make it happen—right now." Two senior staff members rushed out the room on a mission.

"Third, put together a sub recall plan to bring our missile boats—all of them, boomers and guided missile attack—back home."

"I'm on it." Mason heard from a voice fading in the distance.

"Fourth, put together a search plan that uses everything we've got that'd help. I mean it, everything . . . the whole nine yards. Redeploy the Seventh Fleet, empty Pearl Harbor if you need to, but the *Maine* must be found."

"Aye, aye, Admiral." The room emptied as fast as the admiral issued orders. Only a half dozen senior staff remained.

"Finally, put together a plan identifying everyone we should inform about what's going on. If the *Maine* is a renegade, we're going to need all the help we can get—and I think we should ask for it. Maybe the Brits or Japanese would lend a hand. Japan has more than a hundred Orions, over fifty Aegis destroyers. We've trained like hell together. Let's take advantage of it now!" *Hell, the Russians and Chinese may want in on the act,* he thought. *That would complicate things, make a bad situation worse.* He shook his head, clearing the distraction.

And the remaining officers raced out the room, single

file, leaving the admiral alone on the line with Mason. Satisfied his showstoppers were being worked, the admiral returned to Mason's call.

"You got any idea about why anyone would steal a guided missile submarine?"

Lots of ideas . . . none of them good ones, Mason thought but did not say. "We're working the question now in real time, Admiral, but we don't know—not yet anyway."

A long, protracted, silence.

"Maybe it's not as bad as you fear, Colonel. She could be in trouble . . . might be down. We've received no ransom letter or ultimatum."

"I could be wrong, Admiral, and I hope I am, but in cases like this, you go with your gut."

"We don't have one shred of hard, physical evidence." The admiral's tone was hopeful. "We're really just guessing."

"I'm afraid it's only a matter of time, sir. For now, it's a judgment call."

The admiral thought out loud, reflectively. "We always knew this could happen, but I never thought I'd live to see the day."

"None of us did, Admiral."

CHAPTER ELEVEN

"So this is tech-head heaven?" Eion asked with a hint of sarcasm in his voice. His gaze was fixed on the USSPACE-COM comp center—an equipment-filled, auditorium-sized room situated behind a seemingly endless wall of one-way viewing glass.

"It's an amazing place," Gary Ellie responded with a wide grin. "Technology changes so fast, the network's under constant flux, almost takes on a life of its own." Gary Ellie escorted Eion through a series of security doors into the basement of the building. Entering the comp center, he continued. "I feel like a kid in a candy store! It's so cool, like school never stops. You learn something new every day."

"I like the candy store part," Eion quipped, looking a little bewildered. "Any women?"

"Sure, but they're all out on leave this week. Most went home for Christmas."

"Figures. Any prospects about my age?"

"Yep." Gary Ellie picked up real quick where this was going. Like an unyielding force of nature, you can't fight it and win. "Listen, we don't have much time now, but I can give you an overview in two minutes. Pull up a chair."

"My pleasure." After carrying a foam-lined equipment case down two flights of stairs, Eion's arm needed a rest.

They sat down at a Sun workstation. Following a burst of keystroke clatter, Netscape's web browser appeared on screen. One bookmark later, Gary Ellie displayed a pictorial org chart of the comp center staff.

To Eion's delight, it was loaded with ladies. "Excellent!"

"Isn't technology wonderful?"

"I see what you mean." The ensign's eyes sparkled with four, maybe five possibilities.

"I'll e-mail the URL, and you can check out everyone's home page once this thing blows over."

"Cool. Like you said, it's a great place to work."

Gary Ellie logged off, then escorted Eion through the spacious comp center.

Surveying the room, Eion noticed the comp center looked in turmoil—like a large factory floor. On second thought, maybe transition was a better word for it. Sections of the room were either being demolished, under construction, or cordoned off as finished operational areas. "Please Pardon Our Appearance" signs were scattered about the floor, yet the operational spaces in the center of the room appeared reasonably well ordered.

One corner of the large room was roped off as boneyard storage—a resting place of old computer equipment not in use, but too expensive to throw away. Another corner— stacked high with unopened boxes from Sun Microsystems—was set aside for storage of new equipment, but the operational space in the center of the room had the pretty-maids-all-in-a-row look about it Eion'd expected to see. Overhead, cable racks and large air ducts ran suspended from the ceiling. Beneath them, a raised floor covered yet more cable racks and air returns. Eion knew the comp center's connecting nerves and backbone were hidden beneath the floor and overhead out of sight. Sorting through this dense equipment and wiring maze—thousands of wires, fiber-optic cables, network routers, bridges, hubs, and multiplexers—would be a nightmare without some sort of automated guide.

They had to find the network management workstation if they were going to make any headway with their security investigation. Gary led him through a maze of new equipment boxes toward the center of the cavernous room.

Off in one corner, Gary saw what he'd been looking for, the HP network management workstation—their guide through the chaos and clutter of the comp center. Looking around the rows of equipment, it wasn't at all clear which equipment was doing what, which were operational, or who was talking to who. But that HP system would *tell all* in a matter of minutes.

"This is it." Gary Ellie pointed to the large computer monitor labeled "The Boss." "Best place to go for an overview of the network."

"All right. I'll set up the cameras, you load the software."

Eion opened his equipment case, removed two video cameras, and focused them on Gary Ellie.

The lieutenant smiled for the camera, then loaded their video conferencing software on the HP computer. Once it was installed, he rebooted the system, and they were ready to ping the *Yorktown*.

To Gary's surprise, the network ping was successful. "Colonel Mason said they'd set up restricted network access for the *Yorktown*, but I still can't believe our security folks approved it."

"Frankly, I don't expect they had much choice in the

matter. Besides, this satellite link's triple encrypted. No one's going to compromise it anytime soon."

The lieutenant agreed, then set up the video conference call in a few mouse clicks. Scotty's face appeared on screen within seconds.

After a brief exchange, the trio got down to business and the good news was Scotty knew the HP system. "That's a break," she said, feeling a welcome sense of familiarity. "HP makes good stuff, easy to use and reliable."

While Gary Ellie logged on the HP system locally, Scotty attempted to log in from the *Yorktown*. As quickly as she began typing, she was prompted to enter the network management password.

Seeing her dilemma, Gary responded. "The whole network's only got this one password, Scotty. It's "hp_open," all lower case."

"Who else knows it?" Scott asked offhand.

"Everyone with access to this room."

Scott grimaced. "You mean the entire comp center staff?"

"That's about the size of it, nineteen or twenty people. Occasionally, we cover for each other. As a result, everyone knows the password because everyone needs to know it."

"Yeah, I understand, but it won't make our detective work any easier, will it?" Scott entered the password, then clicked on the network road map icon. Immediately, a map of the United States appeared on screen. Everything Scott saw, Gary and Eion saw. Highlighted in red were links running between USSPACECOM and other naval bases—including the Pentagon—scattered about the country. One link ran to Pac Comm, San Diego; another to COMSUB-PAC, Pearl Harbor; another to COMSUBLANT, Norfolk. "Looks like we're hard-wired into the defense grid."

Both the ensign and lieutenant agreed.

This isn't going to be easy, Scott thought. "You were right, Gary. I'm not really sure where to start. This problem's like looking for a needle in a haystack . . . half the size of the earth. You got any suggestions?"

Gazing at that maze of red lines, the lieutenant felt overwhelmed.

Scott heard only his sigh.

"Who's responsible for the Wide Area Network?" she asked. "Who connects all our comp centers together across the country anyway?"

"AT&T. They're the only outfit big enough, with the network expertise to tie it all together."

"I think we should rope them in on this. Security breaches must be a source of constant concern to them as well." Scott paused for a moment and considered what it might take to quickly engage the resources of AT&T. "In my experience, the only thing that makes AT&T move quickly is money, big money, and it'll take an excellent mover-shaker type to make it happen. Colonel Mason thinks a great deal of General Craven. Might be a good idea if he were involved. Something about the enormous size of it all makes me think we're in over our heads."

"Big money drives big companies. . . . no surprise there," Eion offered. "From what I've heard about Craven, if we point him in the right direction, he'll run with the ball. I'll talk to the colonel about it."

Pointing to the screen, Scott pressed on. "What do these red lines mean . . . the ones connecting our military bases?"

Gary Ellie responded on queue. "The red color means the data carried outside any military comp center is triple-encrypted . . . that's as secure as we get. I've been told it'd take our best supercomputers a zillion years to break the cipher, but somehow, I find that pretty hard to believe."

"It's only as secure as the people running the network," Scott observed, then guessed what the green-colored lines meant. "Can I assume these green lines inside the comp center mean clear text?"

"Green means clear text and more," the lieutenant agreed. "Cables are shielded inside the building, but the data's not encrypted. Fact is, they're double shielded . . . pressurized with air to help detect illegal taps. The width of the line reflects how much data travels across each connecting pipe. The fatter the line, the more data's moving through the pipe. As you probably figured out, the military controls the comp center end points while AT&T links them together."

"So we get AT&T to worry about their wide area network security, and we worry about the end points." Scott sighed. There were so many end points. She'd need to narrow them down, limit the number of suspect comp centers.

"Which comp centers use ClearWater data?" she wondered out loud. *Check the connection list inside the edge router,* she reminded herself. Scott changed her display to a window showing all the computer equipment connected in the building. Immediately, the image brought order to the equipment and cabling chaos. The screen showed a collection of box-shaped icons, lined up by row and column, all neatly connected.

Next, she zoomed in on the basement, and there it was. A box-shaped icon labeled "Firewall Router" appeared near the right-hand edge of the screen. On the left side of the icon, six skinny and medium-width green lines appeared connecting other equipment inside the building. On its right side, one fat, bright red line was displayed leaving the building. A notation above the red line read: "To/From AT&T Wide Area Network."

Without a moment's hesitation, Scott double clicked the

router icon and began wading through seemingly endless lines of information and pictures. But Scott knew what she was after and wasn't distracted by information she didn't need. She dived deeper and deeper into the router's innards, until she opened its heart. With one final click, she displayed the essence of the router—its routing table—on screen. The table struck Scott as long—the longer the table, the more locations using ClearWater data—but not nearly as long as it might have been.

"Gary?" she asked. "How about you two printing out a copy of this table and highlighting every outside data circuit? I'll do the same."

Five minutes later they compared notes. Scott opened. "What'd you find?"

"I counted twenty permanent data connections to the outside world."

"Me too. That's not so great, but it could have been worse."

"Could have been as many as four hundred," Eion said, counting the total number of lines in the table.

"But it wasn't," Scott breathed a sigh of relief. "And it looks like we don't support telephone calls at all."

"That's right. As a rule, nothing or no one inside our comp center can make any phone call outside the building. It's all a matter of security and unauthorized computer access."

"I'm glad to hear that," Scott said without pretense. "That eliminates one piece of straw from our haystack." She perused the list, sighed, then spoke quietly. "I'll translate this gibberish into English . . . generate a destination for each of these circuits."

"Good idea," Gary agreed. "We'll need to know the bases that use ClearWater data when we talk to the colonel."

Scott thought ahead. What next? "What's the most valuable information you maintain there?"

"Sub posit data," Gary responded immediately. "That's a no-brainer."

"Presumably, any of the comp center staff could access the data?"

"Yep." Gary Ellie pulled up the duty roster on screen.

Eion's interest perked up.

"Eion, let's poke around while we have the chance. A few of the comp center staff will return from leave tomorrow. The rest'll be back in a week."

"Only too happy to help, Gary." Eion feigned a serious expression. "I'll look into the women first."

"Knew we could count on you."

"The sooner we face it, the better," Scott affirmed. "If you were going to smuggle information out of the comp center, how'd you go about it? Take sub posit data for example. How'd you get it out of the building?"

Gary's face went blank for a few moments, then he responded by pulling a CD out of a desk drawer. "If I wanted to walk out of the building with a snapshot of every submarine location we know, I'd query the sub posit database and store that information on CD. They're easy to use and easily concealed." A pause, then his expression darkened. "But there's a problem with this approach . . . the video surveillance cameras." The lieutenant pointed to a camera suspended from the ceiling behind him. Scott acknowledged it, then he went on to point out a series of cameras continually scanning every square inch of floor space.

"Where do your video feeds go?"

"Everything's recorded on tape . . . including the conversation we're having now. But there's one other problem that I didn't think to mention . . . and its probably important. It's got to do with the nature of this sub position information. Its value is fleeting. It's only useful if it's maintained in real time. Our submarines are constantly moving. There's real strategic value in knowing where they are now, not where they've been."

"You're absolutely right . . . so how'd they do it?"

"How'd they do what?"

"Set up a data comm link that periodically updates sub positions in real time."

Gary Ellie shook his head in disbelief as he scanned the room. "I'm sure it must be possible, but at this stage, I honestly don't have a clue." He walked over to one of their intercom boxes, a push-to-talk speaker/microphone combination located on every desk. "When we need to speak with anyone outside this room, we have two alternatives." The lieutenant pointed to a small, government-gray box. "Either we use the building intercom or a portable phone."

Eion picked up the intercom, studied it carefully. "Only a power cord? No speaker wires?"

"That's right. Voice is carried over the power lines inside the building, but not outside. Voice is filtered off before leaving the building."

"Can I see your portable?"

The lieutenant handed over his small phone.

"What's its range?"

"Not far . . . inside the building, I think. Repeater sites are scattered about, distributed across every floor."

"That's interesting. Any wireless computer data links used inside the building?"

"No, but I see where you're heading. The comp center's not emag tight, but it's monitored round the clock for suspect radiation."

"So how could anyone smuggle data out of this building over a real-time data link?" Scott asked rhetorically. "Can't be an acoustical link, no windows on the outside wall. Can't use the power lines, they're filtered. Can't use the phone lines, don't have any. Can't use radio frequencies, they're monitored round the clock."

"I don't know, Scotty." A pause. "How much data we talking here?"

"For now, strip it down to the bare bones. One sub, and she's a slow mover."

Gary Ellie queried the sub posit data base, examining the last known location data for the *Maine*. "Ballpark estimate . . . we're talking fifty bytes every few minutes . . . that's practically zero."

"Maybe we've overlooked something. Maybe moving such a small amount of information opens up some data link technology that we've missed. Maybe infrared . . . who knows? I think we need an expert. We're taking on water faster than we can bail."

"Sure, put another cry for help on the list for all the good it'll do." The lieutenant's mood was not optimistic.

Scott felt like she was being swallowed up, sinking deeper and deeper into a bottomless pit of quicksand. The closer they looked at their security problem, the more obvious it became they needed an immediate, large influx of highly specialized, technically skilled people. For a brief moment, she began questioning her sense of judgment. Then she examined the image on screen one last time.

Thousands of miles of connecting cables—some buried under land, some under sea—thousands of pieces of computer network equipment, part of it owned by the U.S. government, part by AT&T. Twenty military computer centers stretched half a world apart, linked together by a network so complicated it almost defied description. Few people could fully comprehend a network this complicated, let alone make it work.

No, Scott thought. *There's nothing wrong with this picture and there's nothing wrong with my judgment. If the Maine's been hijacked, somewhere in this maze of indescribable complexity, there's a leak.*

Following a long pause, Scott heard the lieutenant say, "Maybe the videotapes or comp center log files will give us some clue." The sound of his voice brought her back from her seemingly endless journey.

Moments later, she spoke, not to Gary's suggestion, but her own thoughts. "Could we monitor sub posit queries? You know what I mean . . . trace all requests made for our most sensitive data."

"Yes, but unfortunately that's the information everyone's interested in. We respond to thousands of queries every hour."

"I've got this sinking feeling," Scott sighed. "I don't know, information overload I guess." She felt the energy draining from her body with every passing minute . . . almost as if she were slowly shutting down, ceasing to function.

The lieutenant nodded his understanding. "Onboard a submarine, it's called data shock. It's a self-protection mechanism, I think. Overload people or computers with too much information, they'll freeze up on you every time."

The Choctaw, 12/27/2008, Sat., 05:15 P.M.
Sarge's Diner

Normally, Sarge's Diner was a popular place with college students and faculty alike, but over the Christmas holiday, the place was practically deserted. A small, reasonably priced restaurant, Sarge's featured good food—fried shrimp a specialty—friendly service, and a wonderful fifties-like atmosphere. The place was a throwback to a bygone era—shiny, stainless steel kitchen, porcelain fixtures, spin-top counter stools, and a mechanical cash register with a wonderful ring to it, all housed in a building built like a dining car.

Late Saturday afternoon, the stools lining the long counter were empty but for two small children spinning around. A dozen or so patrons gathered inside, scattered among the booths. One group of four older men got together regularly every Saturday afternoon in their corner booth for the blue plàte special and a game of cribbage.

Except for two middle-aged Choctaw Indian men, Sarge knew every face—considered each a regular. *Faces are vaguely familiar,* Sarge thought. *Probably truck drivers, judging from the road atlas they're studying.* He'd seen them before, but not often. Both men had thick dark hair, dark skin, and wore khaki uniforms, but one was considerably larger than the other, carrying the beginnings of a trucker's pot.

Both ordered the shrimp special, then shortly afterward, a stranger walked in.

"Howdy." The stranger spoke to the dominant figure behind the counter. "Mind if I use your phone?"

Cocking one eyebrow, Sarge replied, "Pay phone's in the corner against the back wall."

The stranger acknowledged Sarge's pointer and began thumbing through the phone book yellow pages. In the automobile section, he found what he was looking for— the phone number for NAPA Auto Parts. The stranger jotted down the seven-digit local number on a Post-it note, along with the words "air filter," then warily eyed the greasy telephone handset.

Without hesitation, he cleaned the handset with his handkerchief, then placed a local call—not to the NAPA dealer, but to the Choctaw Indian's trucking dispatch office on Highway 64. As expected, an answering machine responded. He spoke after hearing the beep.

"Is this NAPA Auto Parts?" A pause. "Is this 555-2862?" Silence. "Listen, I'm in a jam. If anyone's there, would somebody pick up?" Grumbling "wrong number" moments later, he hung up the phone.

Depositing two more quarters, he dialed again, this time entering NAPA's phone number. An answering machine reported NAPA closed for the day, but that came as no surprise. After recording the same message a second time, he left his Post-it note stuck alongside NAPA's yellow page listing and went on his way.

Not recognizing the stranger's face, Sarge took quick note of his car tag. Mississippi license plates lined his parking lot with one exception—Alabama. *A good ole boy,* Sarge concluded from the gun rack mounted inside his red-clay-covered pickup.

Half an hour later, the larger of the two Choctaw men called their dispatch office. As expected, his answering machine picked up. On hearing the beep, the Choctaw entered a three-digit access code, playing back his voice mail.

"Is this NAPA Auto Parts?" he heard the stranger's voice say. Once it played through, he pressed *d, deleting the message, then hung up. Opening the phone book, he methodically thumbed through the yellow page automobile listings, one page at a time.

And there it was.

Lifting the Post-it note off the page, he tucked it away in his shirt pocket. He'd need this information to read his AOL e-mail later that evening.

Both Choctaw Indians entered their dispatch office—a low-budget, hole-in-the-wall type of operation. Studying the Post-it note, the smaller man sat down in front of their PC and clicked the AOL icon. When prompted for his login, he entered TRUCKERMAN. At the password prompt, he entered air_filter.

Once logged into America On-Line, he read his e-mail. As expected, the first e-mail on his list was sent FROM: TRUCKERMAN, TO: TRUCKERMAN—apparently e-mail TRUCKERMAN sent to himself.

But it wasn't.

By convention, they shared their TRUCKERMAN login with the good ole Alabama boy, and as expected, he'd sent them e-mail. Interestingly enough, the threesome never kept AOL service long enough to accumulate any bill. Like thousands of others across the country, after using their fifteen free hours, they'd cancel their subscription and sign up with someone else—typically NETCOM or AT&T's WORLDNET.

After hot-linking through AOL's home page, the Choctaw clicked GET MAIL. Within seconds, AOL's mail server downloaded e-mail into their PC, then he logged off. Total session time—less than three minutes start to finish.

The small man displayed their e-mail on screen. As expected, it looked like gibberish. Next, he stuck the Post-it note about eye level on the plastic casing bordering his monitor screen. Clicking the DECRYPT icon, he filled in an on-screen form.

Encrypted File Name	TRUCKERMAN mail
Decryption Key	6015552862
Decrypted File Name	Clear Text Message

(Clear Form)   (Submit)

Once complete, he clicked SUBMIT, decrypting the file. Opening the file named "Clear Text Message," he displayed it on screen.

```
Unification Play Is Go. Deploy Immediately.
Target ELF Station Wisconsin. Target ELF
Station Michigan.
Take positions Wednesday, Dec 31, 1:00 A.M.
Central Standard Time.
Expect Launch Authorization Code between
1:15 and 3:15 CST.
```

Eyeing his partner, the small man released a long, protracted sigh. "Sooner or later, I knew it'd come to this."

CHAPTER TWELVE

Motivation, 12/27/2008, Sat., 06:35 P.M.
USSPACECOM

"Our worst case scenario's playing out before our very eyes," Mason lamented. Over video link, Scott noticed his temples looked red, raw from constant rubbing. "The *Maine*'s disappeared without a trace. She hasn't established communications, we haven't detected her, and no locator buoy's been released." The colonel surveyed the faces around the table, making eye contact with each individual on his team before continuing. "She's down, or she's a renegade."

Lieutenant Gary Ellie gulped. "So our investigation's no longer just an exercise."

"That's about the size of it." Mason took a sip of water, then struggled to convey his request in an even tone. "For now, I'd like us to focus our discussion on a single topic—motivation; what's an SSGN good for anyway? I've got a few ideas but I'd like to hear what you folks think. So tell me, why would any country steal a nuclear-powered guided missile submarine?"

Napper sighed, meeting his friend's gaze eye to eye. "To blow up something."

Mason began taking notes on his laptop. "OK . . . why would they want to do that?"

"Revenge," Scott said tiredly. Her voice was stone cold. "Many countries didn't exactly embrace ClearWater with open arms. Nothing would delight them more than to turn our own technology against us. I remember reading about the protests last summer. China and Russia were most vocal of all. They felt threatened—almost violated—by our leapfrog in surveillance technology."

The lieutenant recalled his first impressions of Clear-Water. "You're right . . . kinda caught me off guard too. When I first heard about it in school, I thought the whole idea of illuminating the world's oceans was so cool, but to me, it was just another piece of the star wars armada . . . you know, business as usual. But for these people, it was an emotional thing . . . like we'd invaded the privacy of their own homes or something."

Round the table, there was a long pause as Mason organized his thoughts. "Forty-one countries maintain submarine fleets. Many felt ClearWater unveiled their submarine forces, placing them at risk during a first strike scenario. As a result, several countries—India for one—now consider their submarine force obsolete. Others view them as viable, comparable to their surface fleet, but their element of stealth is gone. Some countries are still sorting through this issue and don't know what they think—but they know they don't like it. It's a *have* versus *have not* sort of situation.

"For a few months last summer, ClearWater was like an emotional, heartfelt cause . . . a rallying point for the United Nations. The Russians and Chinese had a field day with the press. Every country in the Middle East backed them up. Even India joined in. I agree with Scotty's point.

Nothing would delight them more than to see our own technology used against us."

"Indian protest is understandable," Napper explained, "but not fundamentally menacing. Were we in their shoes, we'd do the same. They're in the throes of naval expansion and use submarines to defend their carrier battle groups." Sam began speaking with his hands. "What about the Russians and Chinese? They view ClearWater as a first strike technology—the next step up the ladder of nuclear escalation."

Mason grimaced. "The Russians invented the technology in the first place and they're working around the clock to leapfrog what we've done. I read their satellites are already better than ours—operate down to 150 meters. The Russians have the capability and they're in the process of deploying it as we speak. Part of their network's already operational."

"Ceaseless, futile effort." Napper sighed, slowly shaking his head. "This race never ends."

There was a long pause, then Scott offered another possibility. "Maybe blackmail."

"Historically, political blackmail has always been a concern . . . been a concern as long as we've had missile boats," Mason confirmed, "but there's been no blackmail letter or communication."

"We couldn't be blackmailed and not know about it, could we?" Gary asked.

"No." Napper responded in a confident tone. "If we were being blackmailed, eventually we'd hear about it."

After a short pause, the lieutenant spoke again tentatively, like he wasn't convinced. "Would anyone benefit by starting World War III?"

The group's knee-jerk reaction was unanimous—a

resounding NO. On second thought, however, Eion added one point in support of Gary Ellie's motive. "They could destroy something, something important like Moscow, and make it look like the United States was responsible."

The lieutenant's eyes bulged out. "That's a happy thought."

Slack-jawed, no one felt like eating anymore. A gloomy, melancholy mood washed over the group.

"Sounds like a real-life *Fail-Safe* scenario—trading Moscow for New York." Referring to the novel *Fail-Safe,* Mason shook his head slowly, clearing his mind of this morose thought. He couldn't afford to think about that now. No one could. It was debilitating, the consequences too horrible to imagine.

"They could operate the guided missile boat as a deterrent, like we do." Gary Ellie was bright, young, and full of ideas.

"Could be, but I don't think it's very likely." Eion hated to dampen the lieutenant's idea, but this deterrent idea was a long shot. "Vigilant, round-the-clock deterrence requires a deep harbor, two or three submarines minimum for one patrol, and more land-based maintenance support than you'd ever believe possible."

"Could she kill other subs, other boomers . . . maybe even attack our carriers?"

"They'd need a ClearWater data link for weapon guidance," Scott observed.

"Carriers would absorb any cruise missile attack like a sponge," Eion added in a matter-of-fact tone. "They'd never even come close."

Undaunted, the lieutenant continued without skipping a beat. "They could sell the weapons, maybe take the boat apart. There's value in reverse engineering, there's value in figuring out how we make these ultra-quiet, high-speed boats."

The group nodded. "A possibility." Gary spouted off ideas faster than the group could think, certainly faster than Slim Mason could type.

Finally, silence.

"I think we're overlooking one important possibility," Scott said quietly, holding back until she sensed a slow-down in the young lieutenant's output stream. A long pause followed while the group caught their breath and refocused. Once she had their attention, she continued. "What's the effect on the Navy when one of our sub-marines turns up missing?"

Blank stares, followed by a rapid-fire series of guesses.

"Denial?"

"Disbelief?"

"Panic?"

Mason spoke next, summarizing the day's activities for the group, then concluded. "Losing the *Maine* unified the Navy and provided a central focus across all the armed services—everyone's pulling together in this crisis."

"That's true," Sam chimed in. "There's been support for search-and-rescue operations from the top down. Poli-tics virtually disappear in life-and-death situations like this."

"But if she's a renegade," Slim added, "there'll be a consolidated effort to wipe her off the face of the earth." On this final point, there was strong agreement, and then there was silence.

"Did we get it right, Scotty?" Eion asked in a delibe-rately light tone of voice. "What? . . . What exactly are you saying?"

"Losing the *Maine* diverts our attention . . . right?"

The team nodded, but remained silent. Scott was leading them where she wanted them to go; they were willing, and she knew it.

"Diverts our assets . . . right?"

"It does that," Mason offered, his mind racing ahead. "In a big way."

"And she draws fire."

Scott's idea struck home with Mason immediately. He spoke quietly at first, but as he heard the sound of his own voice saying these words, his confidence increased. He didn't like what he heard, but what he heard himself saying was undeniable. "It will, in all probability, divert our entire Pacific fleet. The Seventh Fleet may be redeployed, moved away from the Sea of Japan. Pearl Harbor could be emptied, turned out to sea. Our missile boats'll be called back . . . Every action seems destabilizing."

"My point exactly, Colonel. If she's a renegade, she'll divert the Pacific fleet and she'll draw fire."

"She'll draw fire, the likes of which has not been seen on this earth since World War II," Slim said grimly, still not feeling satisfied. "But I'm missing something, somewhere. Where does this leave us?"

"With no one guarding the store, Colonel. When the police pull out, chaos rules . . . happens all the time."

And Mason understood. *Should have seen it coming,* he thought, impressed with Scott's line of reasoning. "OK then, let's identify the store. Who're we policing?"

"I still don't get it," Gary said, feeling a bit frustrated. He wanted to play, but didn't understand the rules. "We've got forces scattered all around the world."

Mason thought for a moment, culling out what he wanted to say. "What I mean is this. Who'd stand to benefit from this diversion?"

Feeling overwhelmed, Gary shrugged his shoulders.

Resonating with Gary's dilemma, Napper struggled to get his hands around the problem. "Say, Slim, can't we narrow the scope a bit?"

"Yeah, good idea," Mason's team chimed in with unanimous approval.

After a few moments' reflection, Mason smiled and nodded agreement. "I think we can do that. What if we divide our who-done-it problem into three smaller parts. First, who could profit when the Seventh Fleet's being drawn away from the Sea of Japan? Second, who might take advantage of Pearl Harbor being emptied, and finally, who's gonna benefit when our missile boats are called back?" Inwardly, Mason was pleased with their shifting focus. It was as if the group were leading itself, feeding on its own best ideas while rejecting the improbable. *Awesome team of people,* Mason thought to himself, *just awesome!*

A few minutes later, Gary Ellie returned with a CD-ROM version of the world atlas. As soon as he flashed a map of the Pacific Rim on screen, China, Russia, and North Korea stood out immediately as suspects.

"China's enormous," Eion sighed. "Their navy's expanding and they've got a submarine fleet."

"They've already got missile boats and so do the Russians for that matter," Napper said. "Why would they take one of ours?"

"Who knows?" Eion shrugged. "Reverse engineering? Acoustic signature acquisition?"

"Could be, but I doubt it," Napper countered. "Russia's swamped with economic problems of her own. She has trouble enough keeping her own navy afloat, let alone ours. As for China, China's one of the best customers we have. They're modernizing their infrastructure at a phenomenal rate; it's growing faster than anywhere else in the world. Our best companies have set up God knows how many factories over there to help 'em—state-of-the-art, high-tech facilities too, not sweatshops. I tell ya, it doesn't make sense they'd cut off the hand that feeds 'em."

"We both have a tremendous lot to lose," Scott added by video. "What about North Korea?"

"Unpredictable." Napper grimaced, shaking his head. "They've had their eyes focused on South Korea my entire life."

"That's right, Sam, and our troops pulled outta South Korea last fall—both Army and Air Force, as I recall." Mason rubbed his temples, his voice contemplative. After a few moments' hesitation, he spoke to Eion. "Could you pull up our current troop disposition in South Korea?"

Eion sat down behind the computer keyboard and began clattering away.

"One Army division, that's it, sir. That's all we have left in South Korea."

"Hmph." Mason paused. "Where are our closest reinforcements?"

Eion flashed a map showing the Ryukyu islands, Japan and Korea. "Okinawa and the Japanese mainland."

Scott's eyes met Mason's on camera. *Bingo.*

"That's right," Scott spelled it out for the young lieutenant. "South Korea could be cut off if the Seventh Fleet were diverted. South Korea would be vulnerable."

"Undeniably," Mason acknowledged and Napper agreed.

"North Korea does have a navy," Scott added, "but I don't know much about it."

"Standby, Scotty." Eion double clicked an icon labeled "Jane's Fighting Ships." Everything Eion did, Scott and the team could see on screen. Within a matter of seconds, the screen read:

```
              Korea, North
        Democratic Peoples's Republic
          Strength of the Fleet . . .
```

After studying Jane's write-up, Eion summarized North Korea's navy in one line. "They're optimized for cutting sea supply lanes."

"You're sure about that?" Scott queried.

"That's my read, Captain," Eion smiled, "and Jane agrees."

"The hell you say," Sam muttered under his breath.

"Without the United States breathing down their back," Mason observed, "they'd be free to pillage the store."

"The shoe fits," Scott confirmed.

"It makes sense," Napper acknowledged, "but how'd they pull it off? How'd they hijack the *Maine*?"

"Yeah," Eion frowned, thinking out loud. "Doesn't look to me like they have the wherewithal to capture one of our missile boats."

"I can't speak to that," Mason stated flatly, "but South Korea will be vulnerable when the Seventh Fleet is diverted. That fact is undeniable."

"Why would they attack?" The young second lieutenant, Gary Ellie, wanted to know.

"They've been trying to unify Korea as long as I can remember," Sam assured Gary, "ever since the Korean War."

Mason's mouth twisted to one side. "I don't like it, but it holds together. I'll ask General Craven to have SAT recon take a look." Slim surveyed his team. "Are we ready to shift gears here?"

"Next!" Gary grinned, and the group agreed.

"What happens when Pearl Harbor's turned out to sea?"

After a short discussion, it wasn't clear that anyone would profit when Pearl emptied. Attacking an empty harbor didn't make sense and an invasion of the islands seemed out of the question. More to the point, there were no surface fleets in position to support a Hawaiian invasion.

Finally, to Mason's surprise, calling back our missile boats was considered a good thing. Fact was, positioning our missile boats closer to home increased flight time to target, giving Russia and China more time to react, a little more breathing space, comparable to head room in a crisis.

Shortly afterward, the team ran out of viable ideas so Mason shifted the subject. Looking into the camera, he asked Scott, "What's the latest on that missing eighty-seven cents?"

"Tristan's still working the issue, but he's learned one thing. There's no problem with the accounting software. Someone reactivated an old login and, as a result, had no valid project case number to charge their computer time against. We don't know who did it, but it could be significant."

"I expect you're right." Mason checked his watch. "What's the latest status on your chopper?"

"We're nearly set here. Should lift off in about three hours. Tristan's got the equipment ready. Chopper arrived a couple hours ago. From what I heard, the pilot had a little trouble finding us, came aboard on fumes, and set down pretty hard. The shop's pulling maintenance on her now. Kiska's pushing the outer limit of the Sea King's range and they want to make sure we make it."

"Good idea," Mason chuckled, shifting his group's focus once again back to motive. Summarizing those most plausible, his team narrowed their list down to the big three: revenge, diversion, and blackmail.

Following a wrap-up conversation about who might benefit from diverting U.S. Navy forces, the team determined they couldn't know for sure, but North Korea topped their hot suspect list.

Brigadier General Robert Craven would carry the ball from here.

Craven, 12/27/2008, Sat., 07:30 P.M.
Cheyenne Mountain, CO

Hell, Slim! You don't want much, do you? Craven thought reading Mason's "Urgent" e-mail. It was a lengthy laundry list outlining the additional support Mason needed—yesterday. On first read, his knee-jerk reaction—disbelief.

Checking his watch, Craven noted twenty minutes until his conference call began with Mason, then he studied his e-mail again, this time more carefully. It came as no surprise to find Mason's reasoning sound. In addition, the support he'd requested, in context of this renegade sub problem, wasn't exaggerated.

Craven looked over the list again, ordering priorities in his mind. *FBI support: 160 background investigations delivered overnight—yeah, right. NSA support: 100 technical head count, government computer security specialists, flown all over the United States. MAC can provide the airlift, but we're dealing with the U.S. government here, not Federal Express. AT&T Network Security—no idea how many head count we're talking here, hundreds anyway, but no matter what, that's going to take big money. CIA photo recon and intell support—routine—can do. Eastwood's covering Navy search and rescue . . . good, one less thing to worry about. That leaves me the rest of the U.S. government plus AT&T. What a bloody mess . . . Merry Christmas.*

Craven saw that Mason's e-mail came with attachments, a video clip, a viewgraph presentation, several pictures, and a URL pointing to the personnel records of the submarine crewmen. The URL was like a home address and house plan combined, telling Craven where to find the crew's personnel records—which computer held them, and exactly where to look. Craven double clicked on the crew URL and a list of the 160 crewman appeared on screen. None of the names looked familiar, but that was no surprise. Submariners live in a closed community.

Next, he double clicked the video clip, playing back the square-wave pattern and apparent intercept sequence. As the video played, a sound track of Eion's voice summarized the relevant points on screen. *This video evidence isn't airtight,* Craven thought, *but it's impossible to accept as coincidence in light of the circumstances.* Then he clicked on a viewgraph presentation narrated by Linda Scott, a series of animated color pictures showing an overview of the United States military computer network. Military comp centers—the network end points—were shown in green, AT&T connecting links were shown in red. With each passing slide, Craven became more convinced Scott was right. Without a large, coordinated influx of highly specialized technical people, the scope of their security problem was overwhelming; it could be intractable, but he wouldn't quit without a fight. Next, he examined Scott's list of suspect comp centers, and finally, he read the team's heads-up regarding North Korea and their synopsis on motive.

Craven wrinkled his brow. *North Korean diversion?* He'd known Mason most of his military career and knew him well enough to know he wasn't kidding. No doubt about it, this was a cry for help. It was an intriguing story, but lacked hard, supporting data. That's where his satellite reconnaissance organization came in. He reread the colonel's heads-up again, scrutinizing his request for goosed-up satellite surveillance more carefully. This time around, however, Craven sensed a subtle hint of desperation in Slim's tone.

Instinctively, the general scrunched his face into a scowl. He'd never known Mason desperate before. *Angry, yes, and when he's angry, his Southern heritage comes shining through.* Slowly, Craven's expression relaxed. Over the years, he'd stood behind Mason's judgment on many occasions and never regretted it, never regretted it even once. That meant a great deal to Craven. From the beginning, theirs was a professional relationship built on mutual trust and admiration. Over the span of Mason's career, their relationship had deepened into a lasting friendship. The man stood for everything Craven admired, a man who lived each day honorably with faith in God and selfless concern for others. Above all else, Craven knew the man would do the right thing or die trying. After a few moments' reflection, he phoned the head of his satellite recon organization. *What the hell,* he groused, *Mason could be right.*

In less than twenty minutes, Craven reviewed firsthand the most important information Mason's team had uncovered during their investigation. He knew their concerns now, fully understood them. Mentally and in spirit, he felt with them . . . part of the team.

But he didn't like what he saw.

Their two conclusions, God forbid, were inescapable. *In all probability, the* Maine*'s a renegade. And above all else, time's the crucial element.*

• • •

Mason and his team sat along one side of their video conference table facing a wall lined with video monitors and TV cameras. Scott and Roberts conferenced in from the *Yorktown*. At 8:30 P.M. sharp, a video picture appeared on screen of Craven sitting alongside a large computer monitor. Scott noticed Craven's jaw muscles tense when the red light flashed over their TV cameras.

In addition, Scott watched a large gathering of Craven's staff grouped around him, busily reviewing the information they'd e-mailed Cheyenne Mountain earlier. At first, it was a curious feeling. Over their video conference link, Scott heard the sound of her own voice inside Cheyenne Mountain, narrating her story about their apparent security leak. She smiled. Somehow, hearing the sound of her own voice played back made her feel better about their situation, but only for a moment. When she heard her *needle in a haystack* summary of their problem, she felt herself grinding to a halt—again. Still, she agreed with her conclusion and would stick by her guns. They needed well-coordinated, specialized technical help, and needed it immediately.

Once Craven recognized they were on the air, he addressed his entourage, commanding their attention. "Listen up!" Within a matter of seconds, all playbacks ceased. A hush enveloped the room. Having their attention, Craven opened the meeting. There was no introduction, no exchange of pleasantries, no *getting to know yous*. Nearly all present knew one another and time was of the essence.

Craven squinted, facing the flood lamps, looking into the bank of cameras. He spoke abruptly in his *cut the crap and get down to business* tone. "I want to keep this meeting short." Without waiting for agreement, he continued.

"Reviewed your work . . . understand it."

"We're only beginning to scratch the surface, General,"

Mason said, "and looks like we really opened up a can of worms."

"If you're right—and I think you are—we're in one hell of a mess. If the *Maine*'s a renegade, time's critical . . . time's everything. I'll jerk the right chains . . . get the help you need, but it'll take time . . . too much time, damnit . . . three or four days minimum. We're talking reality here. Face it. Plan on too little, too late. If the *Maine*'s a renegade, we're driven by some enemy bastard's time table and they're not dragging around. For now, focus on the things we control directly . . . like the SPACECOMM comp center."

"Makes sense," Gary Ellie agreed quietly. "After all, our comp center provides ClearWater's brain."

"Thought about your motives." Craven pressed on. "I opt for revenge . . . It scares the hell out of me."

"Why revenge?" Mason asked.

"Can't be blackmail. We'd know about it. Diversion doesn't scare me. Let chaos rule—to hell with 'em. We've got a world to save." Craven intentionally sidestepped the North Korean angle, testing Mason's resolve.

"What about our pitch on North Korea?"

"Your case struck me as a little weak."

Mason stammered a moment, then his eyes met Scott's. Without conversation, their communication was clear. *Put up or shut up.* "Now hold on just a cotton pickin' minute here, General. North Korea coulda done it, we can't prove they didn't. We . . . we . . . we can't say for sure one way or the other. Think about it, will ya? We already pulled our troops outta the South and once the Seventh Fleet's diverted, the South is vulnerable. I . . . I think they're gonna attack."

Struggling to maintain his tough-as-nails expression, inside Craven grinned ear to ear.

"Anyway, all we're asking for's a look-see," Mason concluded. "We need your support."

Cotton pickin'. Slim's words revealed he was worked up and he was *sincere*. Craven's expression relaxed around his eyes. "I considered the possibility you might be right about this, Colonel. My satellite recon outfit's all over this one. If North Korea's up to anything, we'll nail 'em."

Taken by surprise, Mason stammered again, then settled down to his slow, even cadence. "Well, thank you, General, thanks a lot. At first, I got the impression you might be trying to brush us off."

"Not for a minute, Slim, but don't get me wrong. I said what I think. Revenge scares the hell out of me, but you could be right with this North Korean angle. We'll see. I understand Ozzie's planning to comb the area, recall his missile subs, and throw everything we've got into the search."

"That's right."

"Good. I think he should do exactly that. Priority one—find her. If she's moving, wipe her off the face of the earth—before it's too late."

"We're hoping . . . praying for a miracle," Mason said without apology.

"Truth is, we're depending on miracles." Craven felt exasperated, hemmed in . . . out of options. "As I see it, the only hope we've got is that the *Maine*'s down. God willing, we could find her . . . maybe save the crew. Otherwise, we're screwed."

PART FOUR

Malice

CHAPTER THIRTEEN

No Mistake, 12/28/2008, Sun., 03:31 P.M.
Onboard the USS *Topeka*
A Los Angeles–class Attack Submarine

The commanding officer of the USS *Topeka*, Commander Slay "Hawk" Hawkins, sat in his cabin caressing his favorite familygram. Recalling memories of the birth of his daughter, Hawk quietly read his weekly forty-word allotment—for the hundredth time. He'd been home when his first child, Mary Anne, was born. He remembered the indescribable joy that comes with being there, the inexplicable feeling of loving a tiny, wrinkled person you don't even know. He sighed deeply, wishing he were home to see his new son. *At least everyone's OK,* he thought. As fate would have it, seven pound, two ounce Trevor Hawkins had been born last week, with his dad at sea.

Slay Hawkins graduated from the U.S. Naval Academy in 1990, but didn't meet the right woman until he was thirty-six years old. His wife, Jo Anne, gave birth to Mary Anne two years ago, and now Trevor was nearly one week old.

Someday, he'd be nicknamed "Terror" Hawk, his father thought and grinned. Slay liked that sound; it conjured up a great image with an adventurous ring to it.

The captain's daydreaming was cut short by a call from

the control room. "Flash message traffic, Skipper. You'd better come take a look." Hawk hit the deck moving.

"The *Maine*—a renegade?" Hawk balked, his stomach tightened scanning the message. "That's impossible! Clay McCullough's her skipper. There must be some mistake."

A pause followed.

When Hawk spoke again, he was subdued . . . melancholy. "Holy mother of God . . ." He looked up, making eye contact with his XO. "They're sending the entire Pacific fleet after her."

The XO broke eye contact, his face muscles tensed, but he did not speak, at least not immediately. After absorbing the skipper's mind-numbing disclosure, the XO's mouth felt bone-dry. "What are our orders, Captain?"

"Come to periscope depth, check our SSIXS message traffic, then proceed with all possible speed to the *Maine*'s last confirmed location." His mind raced ahead, playing through this horrific scenario, the one he'd never believed possible. Envisioning the situation back at Pearl, his expression saddened. Smartly squeezing his forehead, the captain summarized the situation. "Unless I'm missing something, Admiral Eastwood won't take any chances with this. If she's in open ocean, he'll nuke her."

The XO took a slow, deep breath, followed by a long, protracted sigh. "You're convinced, Captain? . . . This one's for real? Maybe it's a loyalty test or something?"

Struggling to conceal his despair, the skipper studied the message again, looking for some clue, some hint of hope. Finding none, his forlorn expression revealed his innermost thoughts. Looking again into his XO's eyes, he conveyed a sense of strained anxiety. "I know Clay McCullough, know him well . . . know his family. We've been friends since high school." At this moment, for the first time in his life, the captain felt an inescapable sense of being completely alone in the crowd. "No, there's no mistake. We're going to kill the *Maine*."

Excruciating Pain, 12/28/2008, Sun., 02:13 P.M.
USS *Maine*

"Aaaaggghhh!" Mandrone's right eye felt filled with blistering, red hot sand. His head throbbed as if he'd been clubbed with a wooden mallet. Any movement in his right eye brought about sudden, excruciating pain. Fact was, it hurt so badly he could barely open his other eye. Six hours after having his cornea lopped off, Mandrone found he couldn't rest, his visibility limited to a narrow slit through the swollen lid of his good eye. *Unbelievable.* Had Mike been able to open his injured eye at all, he'd have seen something resembling a red cherry tomato covered in thick, crusty mucus.

Mandrone knew he was in the captain's cabin alone, lying on a fold-down bunk. Squinting, peering through the slit in his good eye, he rolled on his side, checking the ship's status display mounted adjacent to him.

"Aaaaggghhh!" The pain was debilitating, every exposed nerve on fire. Lying absolutely still for what seemed an eternity, the agony eased slightly.

In the low light, Mandrone read their position, speed, and depth. *Looks all right,* he thought, but his confidence was shaken. The pain inhibited his ability to think clearly, almost prohibited him from thinking at all. *Better check my messages . . . something's gotta give here.*

"There are no new messages on the server" flashed on screen. Peering at the display through his tearing good eye, the captain finally read it on his third try. *Good, no news is good news.* Pressing the time clock icon on screen, he heard the words "zero-three-fifteen Zulu" repeated by a luscious female voice. Shutting both eyes, the captain lay absolutely still, concentrating, hoping to relieve the pain. After performing some mental arithmetic, estimating their distance-from-rendezvous, he smiled a sinister, self-satisfied type of smile. *They could send the entire Pacific fleet for all the good it'd do. Two million square miles of ocean . . . no chance in hell.*

Momentarily distracted, Mandrone instinctively pulled himself upright, increasing pressure on both eyes with the strain. To his anguish, sitting up caused more pain than he'd ever experienced in his life. Over the course of six hours, Mike's eye had transitioned from an inconvenience to an immobilizing force. No doubt about it, he was going to need some help. Before standing, he switched on the light, peering through his watery squint, searching out the telephone handset.

He was in agony! Light slashed through his eyelids like a white hot knife. Covering his face with a pillow, Mandrone killed the light, then groped for the phone.

Finding it, he spoke directly to Ash Wilson. "Medic!"

Carrying the ship's first aid kit, the chief sonarman entered the darkened room to find Mandrone restless, lying flat on his back. "What happened, Captain?"

Mandrone explained.

"I need some light, Captain . . . Can't examine you in the dark."

Mandrone raised one hand in acknowledgment, covered both eyes, then flinched as light flooded the room.

The sonarman's expression turned to a tight-lipped frown. He'd seen the symptoms of corneal abrasion before. After inspecting the captain's thickened eyelid and crusty mucus discharge, he knew what to do.

Pulling out a small bottle of Tetracaine, a topical anesthetic, the sonarman placed two drops in the captain's eye. Within thirty seconds, Mandrone could open his good eye without pain. In a minute or so, he could pry open his injured eye—partway. Seeing the bloodshot eyeball, the sonarman winced. He was doubling as a medic because it was necessary, not because he liked it.

"I can't tell you the extent of your injury, Captain, but you've scratched your eye . . . badly, I think . . . probably the cornea. I don't have anything for infection on me, but we've got some Tobrex in the dispensary. I'll clean it first, go get the Tobrex for infection, then treat it with warm compresses for the next few hours."

Mandrone nodded understanding. "Give me something for the pain. Patch me up, but I've got to stay alert."

Filling a coffee cup with water, the chief sonarman placed four Tylenol in his hand. "I'll check on it, but take these for now."

Mandrone eyed the medication suspiciously. "What is it?"

"Tylenol."

"Hell of a lota good that'll do."

Journey to Kiska, 12/28/2008, Sun., 04:30 P.M.
Onboard a Sea King

Whop whop whop . . .

Commander Dixon eased up on the collective and the immense helicopter lifted off, ponderously at first, but gradually accelerating. The old Sikorsky H-3 Sea King was a monster of a helicopter—counting rotor blades, over seventy feet long, sixty feet wide, weighing over nine and one half tons. Considering its size, Dixon always said it flew like any other, only not as agile.

During takeoff, Scott knelt behind Dixon and the copilot, never missing a beat. Her eyes, ears, and nose took in everything. She felt the steady vibration from the main rotor bouncing her up and down. She smelled the stench of hydraulic fluid and burning jet fuel. The flight instruments glowed a dull red. Every few seconds, she scanned them, making sure all systems operated normally. Black night and overcast skies eliminated any reference other than the *Yorktown*.

Suddenly, she realized they were airborne.

Imperceptible liftoff, Scott thought. *This guy is good. No wallowing, no bouncing tail.* She watched out the cockpit as they cleared the *Yorktown*'s superstructure, rotated downwind, tucked, and accelerated forward.

Scott was impressed by Dixon, even though he struck her as a bit cocky. From behind his seat, she observed his seemingly relaxed concentration, his hands loose on the controls, his eyes cutting from instruments to the receding helo pad below. No apprehension, no confusion, no indication that this was anything other than routine.

Satisfied with their cockpit crew, Scott went aft to the large cargo bay looking for Tristan. It was dark and loud. Military aircraft are designed for function, not comfort. Stacked against the rear wall, fastened with heavy fishnet strapping, equipment crates were piled head high. Lining its outer walls were hard fold-down seats and bunks. There she found Tristan tense, white-knuckled, looking pale as a ghost.

Scott assured him he had nothing to worry about. Their mission was, after all, nothing more than a long taxi run to Kiska. In-flight dangers were real, but routine. Still, Tristan was not convinced, wanting to talk metal fatigue and rotor failure. Scott recognized that Tristan's imagination had gotten the best of him, but his mind seemed irreversibly made up. Bone-weary, once she'd done all she could, she climbed in her bunk and collapsed, fast asleep.

Tristan wondered how she could sleep at a time like this. The noise was deafening, the bay floor shook, and the lights kept flickering. Looking from across the cabin, he thought Scotty was a piece of work, a study in relaxation. Her head rolled back and forth following the jerking motion of the helo. Through it all, her eyes remained shut, her expression passive, arms limp. No worry, no hint of fear.

No one would shoot at them, she had said, so why worry?

Tristan worried about metal fatigue because he understood more than he ever wanted to know about stress loads placed on helo rotors. Mechanical things wear out, weaken with age, and Tristan expected this Sea King might be as old as he was. *Another happy thought,* he mused.

Overhead, the helicopter's turboshaft engines, now running at their rated power, were guzzling fuel. The aircraft was approximately six hundred fifty miles southwest of Kiska, pushing the Sea King's cruising range to the limit. Even with its external fuel tanks capped off, this distance gave them little margin for error. Consequently, other than compensating for winds aloft, their course ran a perfectly straight line.

By the time Scott fell asleep, they were traveling one hundred eighty knots, fifteen hundred feet over the inky black water of the Pacific.

Lifesaving Ballet, 12/27/2008, Sat., 09:10 P.M.
San Diego, CA
Ballast Point

When the colossal C-5A Galaxy transport plane arrived at NAS North Island, ground crews were ready, swarming around the behemoth like worker bees attending their queen. Once the gargantuan plane lumbered to a stop alongside the cargo hangar, its nose pivoted upward, exposing a cavernous, empty cargo hole. On queue, an access ramp lowered into loading position, then without fanfare, a powerful low-rider towing vehicle labored slowly up the incline into the cargo hole, pulling behind it a custom-built flatbed trailer.

Centered on the flatbed, strapped securely to her cradle assembly, rested the *Avalon* DSRV and all the equipment necessary to search for the *Maine* and rescue her crew, were rescue operations required. Trailing single file behind the DSRV, her crew followed, bringing up the rear.

Beautifully orchestrated—every player knew their part in this quick-turnaround process—countless hours of planning and practice lay behind this lifesaving ballet. In fact, saving lives formed the glue which bound these players together. Their goal: deliver the DSRV's crew and rescue equipment to any point on earth within twenty-four hours and rescue any downed submariner in less than forty-eight. Over the years, their lifesaving skills had been polished to that of a fine art—no wasted motion, no wasted time—load 'em up and ship 'em out.

Once the load master had triple-checked the cargo straps, he spoke briefly to the maintenance chief, then signaled the flight crew using his walkie-talkie. "Load's secure, gentlemen. Fuel's topped off and maintenance is complete. She's ready to roll."

Five minutes later, with her throttles wide open, hauling down the runway, the C-5A Galaxy rotated skyward, lumbering off the ground into the darkness, gradually banking west—heading for Pearl.

Where Are the Carriers?, 12/27/2008, Sat., 08:00 P.M.
Pearl Harbor, HI
CINCPACFLT Operations Headquarters

The briefing for CINCPACFLT (Commander-In-Chief, U.S. PACific FLeet) began with an overview of their carrier situation. To no one's surprise, there wasn't much to talk about. By the year 2008, the total U.S. carrier fleet had dwindled to eleven active carriers. Of these, only three were available to the Pacific fleet commander-in-chief. For better or worse, one of the three was homeported in Yokosuka—with strings attached—to fulfill the U.S. military commitment to Japan.

Describing the salient elements on his first viewgraph— a high-resolution satellite photo still warm from the printer—the staff officer opened. "The carriers pictured here at Yokosuka are the *Harry S. Truman,* homeported in Yokosuka, and the visiting *Ronald Reagan.*"

CINCPACFLT noted the photo's date and time stamp, then checked his watch. *Current information,* he concluded. *Only ten minutes old.*

Seconds later, the room darkened and the projected satellite picture changed to a grainy, greenish-black video image of a Nimitz-class aircraft carrier plus her battle group, heading northeast under full steam. Text surrounding the flat-top identified the nuclear-powered supercarrier as the USS *Stennis,* located 33N 165E, west of the dateline, west-northwest of the Hawaiian Islands. On a second overhead screen, the staff officer projected a map showing the Pacific Ocean bordered on the north by the Aleutian Island chain, on the west by Japan. "We've diverted the *Stennis* battle group northeast toward the *Maine*'s last confirmed position, here, approximately forty-five degrees north, one seventy-five east." After marking both the battle group's destination and current location east of Tokyo, the officer continued. "Their destination's a thirty-five-hour sail, but she'll have Vikings over the area in six hours, maybe less." Overlaying their constantly expanding, circular search region, the speaker sketched an alarmingly small, pie-shaped air operations area, originating from the carrier.

CINCPACFLT considered speed, location, and ASW capabilities of the supercarrier, then questioned the speaker. "How many air-worthy sub hunters she got?"

Two quick keystrokes into his laptop computer and the carrier's flight complement flashed on the overhead projection screen. Highlighted, the answer read:

```
ASW Viking 18 2
```

"Nearly a full complement, sir. Two down for maintenance."

CINCPACFLT nodded approval. "Current weather?"

One keystroke later:

```
Visibility: 8 miles
Ceiling: Unlimited
Wind: 270 deg @ 4 knots
Temperature: 34°F
```

"Forecast?"

"Slow-moving storm front's approaching the area. Conditions will degenerate over the next four to six hours."

Figures. Visible even in low light, CINCPACFLT's tension showed as muscles flinched about his temples. *One of the few things in life you can count own. Bad weather when you need it least.*

Pressing on, undisturbed by the prospect of any surface storms, the Pacific submarine commander pushed his one-line agenda. "Japan's losing the *Reagan* and *Truman*—at least temporarily—to the central Pacific." Admiral Eastwood presented his proposal to CINCPACFLT as a done deal.

After a brief deliberation on readiness and availability, CINCPACFLT closed the discussion.

"In all probability," CINCPACFLT observed, "our defense readiness condition will increase to DEFCON One once the President commits the Pacific fleet to the search. Prepare for this. As of now, all leave is cancelled. Recall every ship's complement that could help in the search. Above all else, get our ASW flight crews back on board. Move both battle groups east . . . to the outermost limits of their operational range. By the time they're in position, God willing, we'll have Presidential approval to sail east at battle speed, committing the fleet to full-scale deployment."

"There'll be an aircraft carrier gap in the Western Pacific," observed the senior intelligence officer. "Inherently destabilizing. Cheyenne Mountain reports North Korean troops closing on the DMZ, could be division strength. Something's coming down there, we're not sure what."

"If we're lucky," CINCPACFLT spoke in an expressionless tone, "this gap will be short-lived. Is South Korea plugged into this?"

"Yessir, they're hot-wired. General Craven's got 'em tied in over satellite link. They're analyzing everything we see in real time."

"Good. What do they make of it?"

"They're not sure yet, but they're concerned. Their own intelligence sources have been warning them about an attack since we withdrew last fall, so our heads-up didn't come as a complete sur—"

BEEP! BEEP! BEEP! suddenly erupted from the officer's shirt pocket. Instinctively, he removed his calculator-sized PalmPilot and read the e-mail flashing on screen. "Priority message from Cheyenne Mountain, sir. Our latest satellite photos show North Korean soldiers decked out in gas masks and full chemical warfare gear. It could be a drill, but the South's not taking any chances. They're going on full alert. From all accounts, General Craven's got their attention. If the North attacks, they'll be ready."

"Then we've done everything we can do, at least for now," CINCPACFLT concluded. "We've got problems enough finding the *Maine.*"

"To increase our own chances of success," Admiral Eastwood pressed, "we must activate an often overlooked resource." The room hushed. "The Japanese operate over one hundred P-3 Orion 2000 ASW aircraft, four times more than our Seventh Fleet." Eastwood scanned the officers again, looking for support, and found heads nodding affirmative.

"Their surface fleet has three times as many Aegis destroyers," a naval commander added, supporting Eastwood's implicit proposition. Collectively, every officer present, surface fleet and submariner alike, agreed.

Given the encouraging reception and the U.S. Navy's high regard for Japan's naval forces, a second surface fleet commander spoke up once the room hushed. "We share technology, equipment, weapon systems, and know-how with Japan."

And then, the testimonial floodgates opened.

"We've done it for years."

"It's a matter of policy."

"It's more than a policy, it's part—a big part—of our naval culture in the Pacific."

"They land on our carriers routinely during RimPac exercises."

"Together, we've kept peace in the region over sixty years."

Once the group collectively said what they felt they should say, they went silent, waiting for their leader to make his decision. They didn't have to wait long.

"We maintain a high degree of interoperability with their navy by design." CINCPACFLT acknowledged the point, inwardly pleased with the emerging coalition.

Admiral Eastwood recognized consensus when he heard it and pressed for closure. "We need as much blue water ASW help as we can get and we need it now."

"If the Japanese're willing," CINCPACFLT concluded, "we'll get it."

"God willing, we'll get it quickly," Eastwood added. *It may already be too late,* he didn't say.

After scheduling follow-on planning meetings, the large conference room cleared except for Admiral Eastwood and CINCPACFLT. The commander of the Pacific submarine fleet remained alone with CINCPACFLT, cornering him for a heart-to-heart.

"The size of the sub hunting force we need depends on the potency of our ASW technology. I mean, since available technology provides only modest search and detection ranges, our ASW forces must be correspondingly larger to fill the gap."

CINCPACFLT studied Eastwood for a moment, a little puzzled at first, then decided his admiral had something he needed to say. "Take a seat, Ozzie, and spell it out. What're you talking about?"

"We downsized too fast, faster than technology could take up the slack."

CINCPACFLT's expression remained impassive.

Eastwood needed support on this issue, and pressed his point with the old man. "Let me put it another way, Admiral. We're in one helluva mess because we gutted our ASW forces, and technology hasn't back-filled the hole."

CINCPACFLT decided to speak frankly. "This should have been our primary imperative when retooling our ASW forces, but it was not. It all came down to congressional politics on a limited budget and we screwed up. Maintaining an ASW force is like maintaining a road. You don't get votes for maintaining anything, you get votes for building new roads, new bridges, new ships, and new high-tech systems."

"ClearWater promises an operational counterweight for our declining force structure, but we're not there yet. ClearWater technology covers shallow water, littoral ASW . . . Great for diesel subs but we're screwed in blue water. Missile subs run quiet and deep . . . Ya can't find 'em, no way in hell . . . Can't trail them without a nuclear attack sub."

"The challenge presented by technology is like sifting wheat from chaff . . . identifying advances that'll have the greatest impact," CINCPACFLT lamented.

"There's no cheap ASW solution, no high-technology panacea, not yet anyway."

The room went absolutely silent . . . seemed like an eternity to Eastwood. Finally, CINCPACFLT spoke again, addressing the crux of the matter. "How long we got?"

"Before the *Maine* makes her move?"

CINCPACFLT nodded, his mouth twisted slightly to one side.

"I don't know, sir, but my gut tells me we're on a short fuse."

CINCPACFLT swallowed, then spoke in earnest.

"My gut's a bloody knot."

COMSUBPAC and CINCPACFLT were of one mind, but their prospects weren't pretty.

• • •

Later that evening in CINCPACFLT headquarters, Pearl Harbor, a series of emergency joint ASW planning meetings were held, focusing on long-term contingencies. Senior officers from the Japanese Navy, U.S. Air Force, and U.S. Navy participated. Gone were the days when the U.S. Navy had resources to go it alone. During the Cold War, the Navy kept ASW to itself, but with the demise of the Soviet Union and dwindling blue water ASW resources, all that changed. Joint ASW planning represented a dramatic change of mind-set for the Navy, but it reflected the reality of their near impossible, two-million-square-mile search situation.

Everyone present clearly understood one harsh, mathematical fact: *Time favored the renegade because their search area increased as the square of the* Maine's *distance from rendezvous. Worst case, their search area expanded as the square of the time elapsed since rendezvous.*

Given the vast search area, coordinated ASW hunter-killer groups would sweep their assigned areas on schedule, and in turn. Regrettably, losses were part of planning, losses were expected. Before the hunt was through, accidents would happen, equipment would fail, human errors would occur, and as a result, good people would die—statistically unavoidable.

But successful, combined ASW is about orchestration with minimum loss.

Air Force aircraft plus Marine Harriers, launched from land and sea, would flood the search area with a type of radar optimized for periscope detection.

In addition, Air Force tankers would replace Navy S-3 tanker aircraft from the carrier battle group, freeing Navy aircraft for specialized ASW tasks.

Surface ships, including the three carriers, would deploy updated ASW helicopters with improved dipping sonar—SH-60F Oceanhawk, SH-60R LAMPS, plus the SH-60B Seahawk.

Updated IUSS (formerly SOSUS) shore-based listening posts would triple their analyst staff immediately; otherwise they'd be swamped with more data than they could possibly digest.

Coast Guard cutters would be readied for service ASAP with Navy sonarmen—sub hunters—integrated into their crews.

Satellites would be repositioned, targeted over the vast renegade submarine operating region. The Joint Worldwide Intelligence Communication System would be prioritized for submarine data and antisubmarine warfare briefings. Navy units would collect any and all communications intercepts that could aid the ASW effort.

Blue water submarine hunting demands that large, three-dimensional ocean regions be searched. Four attack submarines, one from each carrier battle group plus the *Cheyenne,* would sanitize four quadrants—each quadrant a vast, three-dimensional volume of ocean—working outward from the *Maine*'s last known position.

Everyone agreed, it was a great viewgraph story . . . a super plan on paper, but it'd require time, lots of time—days, weeks, even months. Given Presidential approval and the emperor's consent, they could pull together everything they'd need to comb the region; their long-term prospects looked good, but in reality, they were driven by Mandrone's schedule.

In reality, there was no long term.

With the demise of the Soviet Union, most believed our blue water ASW problem had disappeared.

But submarines were there all the time, operating silently, submerged deep beneath the surface.

CHAPTER FOURTEEN

Slow, But Sure, 12/28/2008, Sun., 11:28 A.M.
Kiska

It looked like a winter scene in the northern Pacific from
World War II: a makeshift runway, deeply rutted roads,
Quonset huts, and frozen mud.

Kiska Air Base consisted of one patched-up runway,
two Boeing KC-135 tankers on loan from the Air National
Guard, four P-3s, and a dozen freshly refurbished Quonset
huts. The place had been set up practically overnight, and
already, everyone stuck there was talking about going
home after this blew over.

"Colonel Mason was right about one thing," Tristan
noted, surveying the airstrip. "This base is dilapidated."

"So tell me something I don't know," quipped the
young pilot, Lieutenant Billy Ray Briggs. "It's been
deserted for years, but every so often the government needs
the strip and repairs it."

Lieutenant Briggs flew the P-3 that would carry Scott,
Tristan, and their equipment. Eventually, every operational
P-3 would get similar military-grade receivers; however at
this early phase of prototyping, these sub hunter radios
were available only in very limited supply. In addition,

they didn't operate over the full mil-spec temperature range, so you had to give them special treatment, run 'em extra cool.

Sitting behind Billy Ray and Tristan inside a P-3 cockpit, Scott listened without comment. Unquestionably, she'd sized up Briggs and was concerned. He struck her as immature, wet behind the ears, and short on training. Six months out of flight school, it seemed all he'd done for the U.S. Navy was chase drug runners. It wasn't clear he or his crew knew anything about hunting submarines, and this had Scott wrestling over what to do.

Billy Ray was straightforward with Scott. They'd flown simulated sub hunts, but never over open ocean, engaging real submarines. During the Cold War, hunting submarines was principally the job of the P-3C Orion, but over the last fifteen years, they'd been relegated to tracking drug runners.

Orions carry sonobuoys which may be dropped from the air. Once deployed, the sonobuoy sinks via tether to a programmed depth, listens, then plummets to the depths of the ocean floor. Sonobuoys are limited in power, and once used, they're spent. Besides sonobuoys, Orions carry the ISAR (Inverse Synthetic Aperture Radar), which displays a detailed black-and-white image of an object, instead of just a blip. Embedded in its distinctive tail boom, each P-3 carries a MAD (Magnetic Anomaly Detector) that senses perturbation in the earth's magnetic field caused by submarines. Even the latest MAD equipment has very limited range and may only detect disturbances within eight hundred yards either side of the plane. To achieve this requires low-altitude flight, which limits ISAR and visual search performance. P-3Cs also carry FLIRs (Forward-Looking InfraRed scanners), to detect thermal scars from a nuclear sub in shallow water. But again, the technology suffers from range limitations.

Without a good place to start, sonobuoy, ISAR, MAD, and FLIR technologies are not up to pinpointing a submarine's location in deep-water searches of open ocean. The oceans are simply too deep and too wide. ClearWater's surveillance technology was designed to augment, not replace, our existing ASW arsenal by providing enhanced visibility into the ocean depths on a global scale.

Tristan and Scott walked aft to the sensor cabin. Scott seemed distracted, but Tristan didn't push.

"How long's it gonna take to install?" she asked, referring to the radios.

Tristan looked overhead, then pulled down a plastic cover lining the top of the P-3 fuselage. What he saw came as no surprise, but nevertheless it was disappointing to see it in person. The fuselage was plastered with hydraulic lines and electrical cables. Somehow, Tristan had to find an opening through the maze, a place to mount his antenna on the topmost region of the fuselage. Clearly the job wouldn't be easy.

"Rerouting these lines, then punching the hole's going to take most of the time. Probably couple'a days anyway. Installing the radio and wiring power's going to be a cinch by comparison."

Scott studied the overhead section of the fuselage with a flashlight, then sighed, forcing a smile. "Well, let's get to it!"

Stalled, 12/29/2008, Mon., 10:05 A.M.
CINCPACFLT Headquarters, HI

Pearl Harbor's video conference room was packed wall-to-wall with the admiral's staff, and it was stuffy. The air felt heavy with humidity, almost oppressive. Conversation was muted, movement was minimal, as everyone sat staring across the table at the wall of video monitors. In Washington, a dozen video cameras provided pictures to CINC-PACFLT headquarters from inside the cabinet meeting room. As had become the custom, naval brass stationed in Hawaii attended the President's emergency meetings by video link. Both submarine and Pacific Fleet commanders waited apprehensively in Hawaii for the meeting to begin.

USSPACECOM conferenced in by video bridge. Mason and Craven were reviewing the Pacific fleet's location when a solemn group of big shots and naval brass began crowding into the cabinet room.

The secretaries of Defense and State arrived first, followed by the CIA and FBI directors, the chairman of the Joint Chiefs, then the White House chief of staff. The national security advisor, NORAD, and NATO representatives filed in, hurriedly followed by a white wave of naval dress uniforms. Fact was, the better part of the remaining space was occupied by naval brass filing in from the Pentagon.

One thing struck Mason as odd. With all these people present, discussion would be limited; there was no other way. Conclusion: The President's decision must have already been made.

After a few moments, the door opened. Everyone stood as the President walked in. He hurriedly scanned the faces on his TV monitors first, surveyed the room, found his seat at the head of the table, then sat down.

The meeting began with a nod of his head.

The secretary of defense summarized the situation from a military standpoint. First, he reviewed the threat. The *Maine* was an Ohio-class boat retooled for guided missile attack; a sub hunter equipped to attack submarines and surface ships. Armed primarily with guided missile torpedoes, stripped of her intercontinental ballistic missiles, she posed no major threat to land targets. In conclusion, the SecDef projected a map of the Pacific, identifying all locations of air and sea forces in the region.

Once the SecDef sat down, the secretary of state evaluated the risks of starting a war by suddenly mobilizing the Pacific fleet, pulling out of the Sea of Japan. Next, he speculated on the message total Pacific fleet commitment would send to our enemies, then spoke about the destabilizing effect it would have on countries in the Pacific Rim, Russia, and China. Political risks were considered and weighted heavily because the United States had only recently pulled out of South Korea.

Publicly, South Korean leaders were confident regarding their own security. Privately, however, they were increasingly jumpy due to the North's annual winter maneuvers near the DMZ and the prospect of America redeploying the Seventh Fleet. Even now, they were poised on full alert, watching these exercises around the clock. As a result, the SecState's recommendation was to stall on total fleet commitment, don't do anything fast. If we don't have a confirmed problem, don't risk another Korean crisis by overreacting in haste.

Finally, SecState argued we should inform our enemies—and allies—of our situation through every available channel, but readily acknowledged it'd take time.

"We don't know if the *Maine*'s lost or a renegade," Admiral Eastwood insisted, breaking in over video phone. "And mobilizing the Seventh Fleet, stocking provisions, positioning them where they could do some good, . . . all this takes time."

"How long until we know if the *Maine*'s been lost?" The secretary of state spoke in a polite, but detached tone, offering the appearance of concern, rather like returning a courtesy.

"Twenty-four to forty-eight hours," snarled COMSUB-PAC, neither moved nor impressed. "We should assume the worst, plan for it. Positioning the fleet will take time enough if we deploy them now." *If the* Maine*'s a renegade,* Eastwood thought, *it may already be too late.*

"If she's a renegade," the secretary of state offered calmly in a soft-spoken voice, "if we get confirmation, we'll reconsider our decision in light of the political situation at the time."

Mason's conclusion had been correct. The secretary of state's demeanor telegraphed confidence. The deciding votes had already been taken; the President's decision had been made. Political considerations carried the day. Overruling dissenting votes from COMSUBPAC, CINCPACFLT, the secretary of defense, and the chairman of the Joint Chiefs of Staff, in the final analysis, the President's political considerations prevailed. All other priorities were rescinded.

"My decision represents a compromise," the President began in a less than persuasive tone. "We should stall before totally committing the Pacific fleet, but we don't ignore the problem. Commit the *Stennis* and *Reagan* to the search, but keep *Truman* on station in the sea of Japan . . . Don't wanna solve one problem only to create another. And keep us posted. If the situation changes, we'll take another look.

"In addition, recalling our submarine forces is inherently dangerous . . . Redeploy them well outside the *Maine*'s search area, but don't recall them. They could be useful if the *Maine*'s a renegade, but in all honesty, gentlemen, I doubt very seriously if it'd ever come to that. It's not possible; we've never had a submarine hijacked, and even if it were possible, it simply doesn't make any sense. What plausible motivation could be behind such an act of piracy and why should it happen now, in peacetime?" Hearing his own words, the President shook his head slowly, convincing himself once again that his reasoning must be sound. Assured by the sound of his own voice, he continued. "The lion's share of our efforts should focus on finding our downed submarine and rescuing the crew, if any rescue is possible. If the situation changes, if by some unimaginable circumstance we confirm she's a renegade, we'll reevaluate our alternatives in light of the political situation."

The President paused, surveying his audience, then spoke to his ambassador to Japan. "Mr. Ambassador, I'm afraid you've got a great deal of work to do. Run interference for us. Socialize our situation across the Pacific Rim, warn them what we may be up against. Solicit their support if possible, but they absolutely must understand what we're up against."

Once the ambassador to Japan nodded, the President stood and reassured his constituency. "Sometimes, when dealing from a position of power, it's best to let the dust settle . . . Don't do anything quickly. Sometimes, it's better to do nothing at all."

If the President had been dealing from a position of power, of benevolent control over the situation, he might have been right.

But Mandrone was calling the shots.

Transmit ELF Bell Ringer, 12/30/2008, Tue., 05:35 P.M.
ELF Station, North Korea

Inside a darkened radio room outside Pyongyang, North Korea, a junior naval officer reviewed their first outbound communication for the *Maine*. Checking his watch, he concluded the time had come.

Picking up his telephone, he dialed the Weather Channel equivalent for North Korea's military forces. After confirming that sea conditions in the *Maine*'s vicinity hadn't changed substantially during the past hour, the young officer hung up the phone, satisfied he'd done the best he could. Picking up his grease pencil and checklist, he lined through the most significant item— glassy seas.

Moving hurriedly across the floor to the encryption gear operations panel, he carefully recorded their newly activated crypto keys. Earlier that evening, the *Maine*'s crypto codes had been entered manually, verified, and enabled by their radio technician. The officer's responsibility was to double-check his work. Following a tedious, bit-by-bit comparison of each long key, the officer lined through another item on his checklist. Although prone to input error, each crypto key had been entered correctly.

Across the room, standing alongside an enormous transmitter loading coil, a second electronics technician signaled the go ahead. His ELF antenna tuning procedure had been completed. Dwarfed by an array of massive, thirty-foot-tall helix coils, the officer approached the technician immediately. Within minutes, he'd verified the technician's tuning efforts—maximum power would indeed be delivered to their antenna.

Returning to the control console, he handed his message over to their radio operator, satisfied everything was ready. "Send it."

Modeled after a Russian ELF station, built of Chinese radio and antenna components stolen from former Soviet designs, North Korea's ELF radio station lacked the range and good geographical location enjoyed by the superpowers, but in the final analysis, all that really mattered was that it had range enough for the communication task at hand. Without any stretch whatsoever, North Korea's ELF station could extend its slow-speed submarine transmissions deep underwater, well off Russia's Kamchatka Peninsula.

In a land quilted with patches of farmland, North Korea's ELF station looked like any other patch from the air. On closer inspection, a plus-shaped transmit antenna could be identified if you knew what to look for, but the ELF antenna complex had been disguised to look like part of North Korea's AC power grid. From a distance, the poles and long wire looked convincingly like power lines. Beneath the antenna wires supported aboveground, unseen by surveillance cameras overhead, the wires were connected to a poor grade of iron-bedrock, which served as part of the transmit antenna. The combined wire and earth circuit produced a strong ground wave signal which penetrated deep underwater, propagating reliably beyond the international date line.

Communication Established, 12/30/2008, Tue., 09:01 P.M. USS Maine

Mandrone stood motionless by the periscope pedestal in the control room, his injured eye tearing, bandaged with an ocular patch. In his shirt pocket he carried a small bottle of the topical anesthetic Tetracaine for pain. Tetracaine retarded healing, but offered his only viable alternative for continuing his mission while keeping mentally alert.

Megadoses of Tylenol hadn't worked and any other painkillers either made him drowsy or knocked him out cold. More than anything else, he felt disgusted with himself for letting it happen, but even in retrospect, he didn't see any way to have anticipated the accident. Who'd have imagined tending the dead would've resulted in such a debilitating injury?

"Conn, radio" squawked over the intercom. Back in the radio room, the newly installed rack of Chinese radio gear flashed green, coming alive with message traffic. "Our new crypto gear's locked in, sir. Receiving ELF flash traffic. It's one of ours . . . the one we've been waiting for."

Mandrone lifted the 1MC handset. "Radio, conn. Read it."

Moments later, "Glassy motion" echoed from his handset.

Mandrone translated the coded message, then spoke over the intercom. "Our first signal has arrived, gentlemen. So far, so good. Topside . . . surface should be glassy. Stateside, our missiles're moving. Will keep you advised."

Following a short pause, Mandrone punched up his radio room over the 1MC. "Radio, conn. Anything new topside?" The *Maine* sat motionless, flying a tethered antenna buoy, continually eavesdropping on U.S. surface fleet and aircraft communications.

"No change, Skipper. Closest contact remains two P-3s maybe four hundred fifty miles east."

"Very well. Prepare our SLOT buoy with minimum wake-up delay."

"Aye, aye, Skipper." Forward in Electronics Maintenance, an electrical engineer began removing the black nose cover off the SLOT buoy's front end, exposing its gyroscopically stabilized antenna and watertight transmitter compartment. Satisfied, he connected a power umbilical to the buoy—a three-inch-diameter cylinder shaped much like a miniature torpedo. As the SLOT's brain cycled through a series of diagnostics, the electrical engineer placed a RF detector alongside the buoy's transmit antenna, then programmed the buoy for a thirty-second, smooth surface wake-up delay. His objective—verify the buoy's satellite uplink frequency.

Less than one minute later, a bright green trace swept across his HP spectrum analyzer screen, showing the buoy's transmit power signature—shaped like a series of sharp peaks. Methodically, carefully, the engineer navigated his vertical line cursor across the screen, coming to rest over the tallest peak. After measuring the signal's center frequency and spectral width, the engineer concluded the RF section was ready.

Once the RF transmitter testing was complete, guidance system umbilicals were attached and a mechanical engineer went to work verifying both the buoy's pointing mechanism and gyroscopic platform stabilizer—a military-grade version of steady-cam technology. Within limits, the mast-shaped buoy must partially protrude above the ocean's surface, oriented north to south, maintaining a stable, near vertical orientation, independent of the ocean swells . . . or so the theory goes. All these conditions must be met before the buoy can mechanically point its small dish antenna skyward, southwest above the equator, toward the Chinese relay satellite parked over Sumatra. Not surprisingly, SLOT buoys work most reliably in glassy seas with clear skies overhead. Still, SATCOM provides one of the most secure means for sending a message from a submarine, offering on-line encryption plus low probability of intercept. The signal can only be intercepted by a receiver situated near the buoy's line of sight with the satellite.

Minutes passed waiting for the buoy gyros to spin up to speed. Once stabilized, the buoy and NAVCOMM equipment chatted over its data link umbilical, updating its guidance system with the *Maine*'s current position. After completing a series of integrity tests, the mechanical engineer configured the buoy's gyroscopic platform, antenna pointing mechanism, and finally programmed their message. When all buoy systems flashed green, both engineers reassembled the black nose cover, then loaded the buoy into its three-inch launch tube.

"SLOT buoy's warm and ready to launch, Skipper."

"Very well," Mandrone said. "Sonar, conn. Verify surface conditions."

"Conn, sonar, aye."

Forward in the sonar room, their acoustics engineer positioned himself in front of a specialized piece of equipment which operated something like a fathometer. It transmitted short sound pulses over a narrow beam to the ocean's surface, then listened for echoes from the air-water interface using underwater microphones mounted on the *Maine*'s topside. A counter circuit and computer converted time delay into distance, ultimately drawing an accurate picture of the ocean surface overhead. After studying the surface profile— an almost perfectly straight line—for a couple of minutes, the sonarman knew that Mandrone would be pleased.

"Glassy sea topside, sir, surface is calm."

Excellent. "Radio, conn. Launch the buoy."

"Aye, aye, sir."

Several minutes later, its mask shape slowly breached the surface, vertically oriented, suspended in a controlled hover, exposing eighteen inches of its six-foot length to the open air. Pointing its antenna to a programmed elevation above the southwest horizon, as the mast waned side to side, the gyroscopically stabilized positioning system compensated, holding the antenna true. Thirty seconds after the buoy sensed glassy surface conditions, it transmitted an encrypted message skyward to the Chinese relay satellite parked over Sumatra. Following a brief pause, it transmitted again, then again. Once the message had been repeated sixteen times, the buoy's brain executed its final terminal sequence—a programmed self-destruct. Ballast ports opened below the waterline, low-pressure air vented with a hiss, water flooded in, and the buoy sank to the eighteen-thousand-foot depths of the Pacific floor . . . without a trace.

Overhead, a relay satellite received the encrypted radio signal, shifted its frequency, then downlinked it to North Korean and Chinese earth stations.

But only North Koreans could decrypt the short message.

Loop Closure, 12/31/2008, Wed., 12:09 A.M.
Satellite Earth Station, North Korea

Outside, the earth station looked like an antenna farm . . . rows of eighteen-meter satellite dishes planted across an open field, pointing predominately south, above the horizon. Inside, the earth station equipment building looked more like a cable TV headend, a room packed floor to ceiling with satellite receivers, decryption equipment, and display monitors. As was typical, all this equipment ran around the clock, requiring only a minimum of technician support on site. This night, the earth station decryption technician, radio operator, and officer in charge had been put on alert to make sure nothing went wrong. Early on, all was quiet, but suddenly . . . the *bong, bong, bong* from an inbound signal bell echoed about the room.

About 12:10 A.M. local time, the North Korean radio operator nearly jumped out of his chair. Seconds later, the *Maine*'s acknowledgment message flashed on screen. Without hesitation, he informed the officer in charge, who immediately placed two calls. One to the ELF transmit station outside Pyongyang, the second to Naval Operational Headquarters.

Translated, his two-part message took only moments to convey: *We've contacted the* Maine. *She's ready, in position, awaiting downlink.*

Off Load, 12/31/2008, Wed., 12:53 A.M.
Sixty Miles South of the DMZ

Somewhere off the coast of Kangnung, South Korea, a telephone pole–sized antenna mast protruded above the surface, standing fast against the waves, stoically facing the darkness. Beneath the black cylindrical column beat the heart of a submarine, a North Korean diesel-electric, the newest and quietest in the fleet.

"Comrade Captain, things are going just as expected." The second in command appeared genuinely pleased. "Radio reports we have received orders to release our commandos."

"Good." The captain checked his watch. "Seven minutes early. That is very good."

Forward in the control room, an orchestrated frenzy of activity began to unfold. Over the course of the next hour, thirty highly trained special warfare experts swam out the submarine's airlock toward the coast. Aside from carrying American-made firearms, ammunition, communication and reconnaissance equipment, two things were telling. First, each soldier carried a South Korean army uniform, and second, each carried lightweight protective gear to counter against gas attack.

Enable Sub Posit Data Link, 12/30/2008, Tue., 08:32 A.M.
USSPACECOM Computer Center

In life, there are always people who perceive themselves as somehow better than the rest . . . for any number of ill-founded reasons. More often than not, these people feel put upon because they're never recognized. Most grow bitter over time, many become very negative about their plight in life, many feel trapped, but statistically, a small percentage will reinforce their puffed-up self-image by secretly, silently, betraying the sacred trust of others. Air Force Captain Traci Dutton was such a woman, and in her position of trust inside USSPACECOM's computer center, her high-tech acts of treason were in many ways more damaging than the Walker spy ring.

Sitting behind her old, gun metal gray Steel Case desk in an office doubling as an equipment storage room, Captain Traci *with an i* Dutton surveyed her cluttered empire. Not much to show for a lifetime of school, dedication to country, and hard work, but she didn't care really, not anymore. Inwardly pleased with herself, she looked around her squalidly wretched hole, feeling strangely satisfied, almost amused, by her status quo. *The equipment stored in my office alone costs more than I'd make in a lifetime working here,* she thought and smirked. The anger she'd felt, the resentment that'd festered throughout her life, had found an outlet, one that would soon change her economic position in life. She deserved better and someday she'd get out of this dump and start her own business, probably consulting with the U.S. government. *That's where the big money is . . . in consulting.*

Checking voice mail, her answering machine reported five new messages. Punching the number 2 button on her phone, she began listening, jotting down notes as necessary. The first message, she regretted, would require work, no way out of it. Some network user was having a problem accessing some server, nothing unusual about that. *Tweak the router's filter,* she thought, *give him access permission and we're in business.* Punching the # key, Dutton advanced to the next message. The phone earpiece howled, chirped, and chattered as if talking to a FAX machine.

Pressing another key sequence on her phone, she rewound the FAX message, then played it back again. During the playback, she measured the duration of the message using her watch. Forty-five seconds long; once the message stopped, she didn't breathe. Distracted, she forgot to breathe until her body gasped for air. Clearing her throat, she skipped forward to the next message. Again a FAX machine's chatter, this time thirty seconds in duration. Anticipating her next message—*FAX chatter, fifteen-second duration*—she sighed, thinking ahead to what she must do. Playing it back, a FAX chirped, fifteen seconds ticked off, then the speakerphone went silent. Dutton's mouth twisted slightly as she hung up the phone, leaving her fifth and final message unopened.

This three-message signal was no mistake. She'd been expecting it, but never knew when. Only two things mattered at this juncture. She was prepared—her equipment was on line, tested and ready. And she knew exactly what to do.

In her position of trust as senior network and system administrator for the USSPACECOM computer center, Traci held the keys to the kingdom.

CHAPTER FIFTEEN

Born to Hunt, 12/31/2008, Wed., 10:35 A.M.
48N 174W
Southwest of Dutch Harbor, Aleutian Islands

One hour after takeoff, three-fourths of the P-3's crew struggled to relax, hoping to get some sleep en route to station. Normally, they fell asleep like they'd been drugged, but this mission was different. In less than one and one-half hours, Scott, Tristan, and the eleven-man crew of Patrol Squadron Ten would attempt to prosecute—find, pinpoint, and kill—one of their own, and this was no exercise. They carried a single Mark 101 nuclear-depth bomb earmarked solely for this purpose. Knowing the fate of millions could lie in the balance didn't make it any easier.

In their souls, they felt torn, each hoping the admiralty had made some horrific mistake. Each member of the crew hoped the *Maine* was down in shallow water; each hoped the *Maine* could be found, her crew rescued. Professionally, however, everyone knew the admiralty was probably right; the *Maine* was indeed a renegade—nothing else made any sense. Nevertheless, privately and unspoken, the Orion's crew hoped their sensors would remain silent, hoped they wouldn't detect the *Maine*. It's one thing to kill a historical foe, quite another to intentionally destroy one of your own.

There was disconcerting news regarding their training for the mission at hand as well. Although each crew member had logged hundreds of hours in the P-3, not one had ever located or tracked a nuclear-powered guided missile submarine. Back in the heady days of the Cold War, P-3 crews flew a lot, two-thirds of the time on contact. Once you found your foe, you flew continuously around the clock, typically stalking five days nonstop, all the while rotating both aircraft and crews. More often than not, the submariners never knew they had company topside. During the Cold War, Orion crews were the only in the military to train against the very forces they might one day fight. Back then, if Russian Admiralty wanted to know where their submarines were, they'd find out where the P-3s were operating—or so the story goes.

But today was different.

Tracking drug runners with their eyes and radars, Orion crews seldom used wet sonobuoys or BTs (BathyThermographs) at all. Requiring radically different skills, antisubmarine warfare is far more technically demanding than eyeball work. Like landing on a carrier, ASW skills require regular, repeated honing, and if unused, the skills perish. In reality, antisubmarine warfare requires highly trained team players maneuvering about a three-dimensional chess game, seldom played these days. Those who've been there know it takes all this and luck—lots of luck.

Forward in the cockpit, Lieutenant Briggs, Captain Scott, and the copilot sat three abreast with Scotty riding shotgun, centered between the men, slightly to their rear. While Billy Ray and his copilot flew the plane, Scott monitored her ClearWater tactical display for contacts and scanned the horizon. Considering her flight crew's limited experience, she felt better working inside the cockpit.

Situated immediately behind them in the sensor cabin, their cherub-faced navigator, Lieutenant jg Dale Tew, continually informed them of their position and maintained radio contact with the outside world. The remainder of the crew, including Tristan, wrestled fitfully with sleep.

Tactical Coordinator Russell "Rusty" Riley, an athletic man about thirty, rested uneasily behind his flight station. Rusty had been a promising baseball star in high school, with aspirations of playing in the pros, but like so many others, his career was cut short by injury. His job as tactical coordinator, or Tacco, was to decide where to drop buoys, and to direct the search until the *Maine* was found.

Beyond the Tacco sat Jerry "JT" Taylor, a mouthy, immature kid with a seldom practiced, but keenly important job. His responsibility as electronic countermeasures operator was to protect the plane from enemy radar and missiles. Gazing open-eyed at his blank screen, JT wished he was back home in Texas. Seemed like everybody got to go home but him. His two older brothers were there with his mom and dad now. He'd already missed Christmas, looked like he was going to miss New Year's too. No way he'd sign up for another hitch. He was getting short. Six months from now, he'd be a free man. *Look out, Austin, here I come!*

Next to JT, gazing across the aisle into space, sat the MAD (Magnetic Anomaly Detection) equipment operator. Behind him, a bespectacled young man nicknamed Radar leaned back in his seat, expressionless, staring at his radar screen. Further aft, on the floor next to a buoy rack, Tristan, the ordnance man, and the in-flight technician lay awake, staring blank-faced at the ceiling. Behind them lay pilot number two and the flight engineer, both

awake on their bunks, both thinking about the 160 men
onboard the *Maine*.

The only comfort they found in their mission, and there
was precious little, was the fact that the *Maine* could be
anywhere within two million square miles of ocean. Even
operating at top proficiency, given adequate blue water
ASW resources, it'd take a miracle to find her. In an odd,
backhanded sort of way, the Orion's crew found that their
low probability of success made this mission somehow
more bearable.

Without an immediate, vast influx of highly trained
ASW resources, they believed their hunt was futile. Truth
was, the U.S. Navy no longer maintained effective blue
water ASW forces, and the admiralty knew it. With the end
of the Cold War, the underpinnings of ASW crumbled.
Over the past twenty years, ASW forces thinned, matching
the perception of a similarly shrinking menace.

But the perception was wrong.

This renegade crisis situation would command wide
attention and priority throughout the Navy, the Pentagon,
and Congress. Trouble was, there was no time to plan, no
time to counter, only time to react.

Unless the *Maine* made a noisy blunder or consciously
chose to show herself, they'd never find her.

There was no conversation over the P-3's intercom, no
sense of levity, no thrill of the hunt, only the monotonous,
eternal droning of the turboprop engines working against
the wind.

Denied, 12/30/2008, Tue., 04:31 P.M.
USSPACECOM Computer Center

Admiral Eastwood heard from Washington first, then forwarded their reply without comment to Colonel Mason

and his staff. Scott's recommendation for introducing random errors into the sub position database was denied. She had suggested this because corrupting the database was the only way to make sure, if the data was stolen, it couldn't be used against them. At this juncture, they had two reasons to suspect malice, but no conclusive proof.

Unfortunately, direction from Washington regarding this matter was crystal clear:

```
Introduce No Deliberate Errors, random or
otherwise. If the Air Force has a security
problem, solve it.
```

As Mason knew, the highly classified sub posit database was strategically sensitive and already in operational use by the government. Corrupting the sub posit database at the government's request would open a contractual can of worms, giving ClearWater's prime contractor a legitimate, legal excuse to further delay new features; result: needless additional costs to taxpayers.

In addition, professional politicians had their own agendas—it was an election year, ClearWater costs were veering off course, and Washington was searching for a scapegoat. Approving corruption of this strategically sensitive database would promise an end to even the brightest political or military star.

Intentionally scrap the whole database now?

Not likely, not in our lifetime.

Keys to the Kingdom, 12/30/2008, Tue., 04:38 P.M.
USSPACECOM Computer Center

Traci Dutton had worked over changes to her program script countless times, so it came as no surprise that it

worked flawlessly. Indeed, Traci believed her coding skills
consistently surpassed those of her peers. Sleazy corporate
climbers had made their promotions claiming credit for her
work, but now, at long last, she'd found a financially
rewarding line of work for herself, and an employer who
recognized her potential up front.

From her comp center office, Traci remotely logged into
the renegade workstation and transferred her program file
to a location where it could run, creating her desired effect.
It's not that she had to think about it, really. The keystrokes
for moving programs and running them at a predetermined
time were wired into her fingers. As a computer network
administrator, that type of activity defined the heart of her
day job.

Her program was, in effect, a form of wiretap, querying
the posit database for submarine locations operating in the
Pacific region. Eavesdropping, she stole sub positions, then
transmitted them to her overseas employer.

ELF Site Attack, 12/31/2008, Wed., 01:28 A.M.
Upper Michigan

The eighteen-wheeler was surrounded by darkness,
wooded wilderness and rolling hills. From a distance, the
tractor-trailer rig looked as if it had pulled over for the
night. Though the tractor cab was dark, the driver didn't
sleep. Behind a wooded hill, off a rural road in Upper
Michigan, the Choctaw driver sat up late, anxiously awaiting a call.

At 1:31 A.M. local time, telephone company records
would later show, Motorola's Iridium satellite rang his
mobile phone. The Indian answered before the second
ring, thus completing his international call. He didn't

speak, but depressed the pound key on his phone, signalling all was ready. The North Korean caller replied by depressing two number keys, first four then six, on his phone pad, signaling the Choctaw to GO. After repeating the pattern three times, the caller hung up.

Without pausing to reflect, the Choctaw turned off his phone, crawled out of the cab, and opened the rear loading doors of his semitrailer. Next, he crawled into his sleeper cab and powered up his auxiliary hydraulic pump.

Technically, his trailer was a cruise missile TEL (Transporter Erector Launcher), an armored boxcar disguised as an ordinary semitrailer. Once he'd achieved hydraulic pressure, he activated a large hydraulic cylinder which pivoted the trailer upward, front end high. When the tilt indicator read sixty degrees, he shut off the lift and a hinged forward door swung down. Last of all, he gave the flight profile software one final diagnostic run. Five minutes later, he had his answer. As expected, his ground-launched advanced cruise missile checked out air worthy.

The key ingredient, the flight profile software, was already loaded. Every digital terrain contour map had been assimilated in the missile's computer memory hours ago. The missile's radar altimeter was active, ready to measure terrain altitude data. The inertial guidance system had spun up, ready to roll.

Watching a countdown timer close to zero, the Choctaw leaned forward, simultaneously rotating two switches.

At the extreme rear of the missile, a Type 106 solid-propellant rocket motor ignited. The boost-phase power-plant generated six thousand pounds of thrust, propelling the missile well clear of the trailer in a blinding flash. Lost in the darkness, unseen from the ground, four tail fins and its wing deployed. Seconds later, the underbelly air intake

spun out, the booster rocket jettisoned, and the cruise
engine fired.

Target: ELF Station Michigan

Vertical Ascent , 12/31/2008, Wed., 09:35 P.M.
USS *Maine*

Topside, it was pitch-black . . . middle of the night. Five
hundred feet below, red lights preserved Mandrone's night
vision so he could see the surface. From the helmsman's
chair, Ash Wilson and the *Maine*'s autopilot worked as a
team, maintaining her depth and course with machine-like
precision. Mandrone looked on in absolute silence, periodically plotting their position by hand. The only sounds
echoing about the room were pops and clicks from sonar.

Forward, just off the control room, the sonar man listened intently, correlating, triangulating, plotting . . . infer-
ring bearing from even the faintest, most distant sounds.
Using their towed hydrophone array, the sonarman heard
the snap-crackle-pop of shrimp, plotted the astounding
maneuverability of whales, and struggled to isolate the
bearing and distance of a single probable target . . . *potentially a submarine,* he suspected, *off to the southeast.*
Range could be as little as fifty, maybe as great as one hundred fifty, miles. At this point, he couldn't call range with
any confidence. When tracking distant targets using passive sonar, submarines must maneuver an extended period,
collecting data all the while, before triangulating bearing—and determining range was tougher still.

Mandrone walked aft, sensing the pulse of his small
crew, taking a look-see around the engine room. The contrast was striking. Instead of the eerie red glow of the control room, Mandrone squinted his good eye under the harsh
white-green glare of fluorescent lights. Replacing live pops

and clicks from the sonar room were the low, mechanically resonant rumblings of a fully loaded power plant playing in concert with the high-pitched, whining steam turbines.

Here in the *Maine*'s throbbing heart, power flowed into the propeller, sending her further into harms' way. Mandrone found his nuclear engineer operating their reactor power plant, tending their machinery in an analytical, nearly clinical fashion. The middle-aged North Korean looked away from his gauges momentarily, locked his calibration wheel in position, then stood to meet Mandrone. After reviewing the engine room status, discussing their situation gauge by gauge, Mandrone asked how he was holding up.

"The waiting's the hardest part, Skipper."

"It won't be much longer now," Mandrone said. "If all goes well, expect to hover inside of two hours."

The reactor operator nodded understanding.

Mandrone could not fight off the feeling that every turn of the propeller, every spin of the turbine took them closer to their grave. When they were detected, how long before their steel tube was vaporized or crumpled into a mass of twisted metal wreckage?

Mandrone shook his head to clear the doubt. In spite of his bravest attempts, he had to admit something to himself. He was afraid, but admitting it didn't make him feel any better. Fear of the unknown was worse than apprehension; more a feeling of strangulation he couldn't shake, yet the feeling was somehow strangely familiar.

Thinking back, Mandrone searched his memory, suddenly realizing it was the Gulf War. It'd been years since he'd thought of it, but it was the same feeling. Not since his first cruise missile patrol in the Persian Gulf had he felt the same fear. Then, as now, he faced the unknown feeling absolutely inadequate.

Fear of the unknown—that gnawing uneasiness resulting from lack of information and understanding. His first submarine deployment, bound for the Persian Gulf south of Iraq. Remembering back, he felt it in the pit of his stomach. Choke points aplenty, not much maneuvering room . . .

During the Gulf War, Mandrone's job was cruise missile launch director. It was his job to plan and execute a cruise missile attack on the Iraqi mainland that would cripple the Iraqi communications capability with one strike. Practice against land-based dummy targets under mock hostile conditions in a New London simulator was one thing, quite another in the crowded, no-place-to-hide waters off the Iraqi coast. *What if they were detected? What if they were attacked? What if he choked in a clutch, when the chips were down?* He'd seen it in his dreams a hundred times. *Inexperienced, full of self-doubt, and young, much too young,* he thought with a grimace.

Then came that darkest night . . . Mandrone faced his fear then and put the issue behind him—until now. He remembered it like it was only yesterday . . . shortly after midnight, January 16, 1991. His blood pressure rose, his face flushed, his hands trembled, then steadied. Mandrone felt faint, weak kneed, then he quit imagining what might happen and started fighting like he'd been trained to fight. Once moving, his paralyzing inertia disappeared; his fear vanished.

Mandrone's recollection of war was shattered by an intercom announcement echoing about the boat.

"Captain, radio. ELF message indicates our satellite link should be operational now."

"Radio, Captain. Prepare for downlink. Reel in antenna buoy."

"Radio aye," Mandrone heard, punching the 1MC. "Sonar, conn. Talk to me."

"All clear, Skipper. One target bearing southeast, range: fifty miles minimum, probably more."

"Very well, sonar."

"Torpedo room, meet me in control. Man the planes and pumps."

"Engine room, all stop. Free wheel the prop."

"Aye, aye, Skipper."

Torpedo One and Two joined Mandrone in Control.

As Mandrone entered, his eyes focused on the men at the *Maine*'s diving controls, strapped in their leather bucket seats. The skipper stood behind Ash and Torpedo Two, assuming the duties of diving officer. Mandrone was now responsible for holding the *Maine* motionless, five hundred feet below the surface—a delicate task, but nothing compared to what they'd do next.

Forty-five minutes later, the *Maine* had slowed to a standstill, dead in the water, drifting with the current. For purposes of steerage, her control surfaces were useless.

Mandrone and his crew knew what they must do to avoid detection from ClearWater satellites racing overhead—a slow, perfectly vertical ascent toward the surface without forward motion.

"Bring her up slowly to periscope depth," Mandrone said with a tone of apprehension in his voice he could not hide. "Full vertical planes."

Following Mandrone's tune-and-tweak commands, Torpedo One starting lightening the ship. Standing by a long bank of flow control valves, he gently manipulated a series of levers. The distinctive whir of pumps filled the room as seawater ballast was pumped out fore and aft. The eighteen-thousand-ton submarine began to drift upward, slowly at first, like an enormous balloon.

Mandrone sensed the deck shifting beneath his feet, inclining nose high, listing slightly to starboard. Depth had been the mask that veiled the *Maine* under its cloak of darkness; now they were deliberately taking the ship up where danger lay. Still, so long as they moved with the current, ClearWater couldn't detect them, and Mandrone understood this full well.

"Four fifty," Mandrone said, calling out the depths as she came up. "Four hundred . . . three fifty . . . Speed's increasing, gentlemen, three hundred." Mandrone need say no more. Before the words left his lips, he heard the noise of water flooding back into the tanks as Torpedo One slowed their ascent. If the *Maine* breached the surface and skies were clear, chances were she'd be detected by satellites passing overhead or downlooking aircraft radar.

"Secure flooding," Mandrone instructed.

Flipping several switches, Torpedo One closed the vents. The *Maine* slowed her ascent, stopping about ten feet shallow of periscope depth. Following a few trim adjustments to level the ship, the *Maine* settled down to periscope depth, ready.

A submerged Trident submarine, stationary in the water, is like a mammoth, unwieldy balloon. Normally, it rises using forward motion to control its depth, planing up or down. Without forward movement, the submarine drifts up or down depending on its trim and buoyancy.

And buoyancy's a tricky business—even the temperature and salinity of the ocean strongly affect it. Here, under the Pacific, Mandrone was staking the ship's stealth on their ability to make the *Maine* do something she was never designed to do—rise straight up at a predetermined speed, then stop on a dime.

Once stabilized at periscope depth, Mandrone raised their low-profile ESM (Electronic Support Measures) mast. Within a matter of seconds, the electromagnetic sniffer told Mandrone what he wanted to hear. Topside, their passive eavesdropping antenna remained quiet. Radio frequency signatures from GPS and ClearWater satellites were present as expected, but overall, signals between 2.0 to 40.0 GHz were quiet; no airborne ASW radars flooding the surface, and consequently, no worry their larger search periscope would be detected.

Once Mandrone verified the surface safe for their larger periscope, he performed two tasks simultaneously. With one seamless motion, he lowered the sniffer while raising their main tactical mast—the search periscope. Without wasted motion, he began his three-sixty sweep, scanning the surface with his good eye. As Mandrone became accustomed to the dim light, he surveyed the surface looking for motion, surface ship lights, or planes. With his horizontal three-sixty scan complete and recorded on Super 8 videotape, Mandrone surveyed the airspace directly overhead through a fisheye lens, looking and listening for any signs of ASW helicopters. There were none.

After verifying the surface clear, Mandrone began using the periscope as a navigational sextant, taking fixes on celestial bodies overhead. A sextantlike device was installed on the *Maine*'s periscope and Mandrone calmly, methodically, snapped off sightings as the stars faded in and out of the clouds. At the press of a button, the nav computer's disk chattered, recording the time and measured angle of each sighting. Using their celestial nav computer, Mandrone calculated their position based on accurate angle measurements and the exact time of each observation.

His final navigational task was updating their NAVSTAR Global Positioning System. Unless the GPS system had been intentionally compromised by the Americans to mislead them, it should provide latitude, longitude, and height above sea level within twenty meters. Seemingly the ultimate navaid, its complexity makes manual verification impossible, and, therefore, its results suspect. Used in conjunction with other navaids, it provides an independent assessment of position, but not their only estimate. Once the GPS receiver displayed its new posit, Mandrone compared it against their celestial nav computer. To his relief, they agreed within expected tolerances. With his sanity check complete, he updated his gyrocompass and inertial navigation systems. When launching any missile attack, it's important to know where you are and where you want your missiles to go. They knew where they were—now—with a high degree of confidence. Once engaged, the satellite link would download target posits—coordinates specifying where their missiles would go.

Meanwhile, the radioman activated the stub aerial atop the tactical mast, and began intercepting HF and UHF communications. Processing equipment continuously swept frequency ranges in use, passively listening, tracking them randomly hopping about. Several minutes later, the radioman reported results of his sweep.

"Conn, radio. Judging from the limited traffic topside, either they're observing radio silence, or we're alone."

Mandrone couldn't conceive any large-scale sub hunt or search-and-rescue operation taking place without continuous, widespread radio chatter. "Radio, conn. Excellent, activate the downlink."

"Radio, aye." Aft in the radio room, the radioman entered a series of numbers—frequency, azimuth, and elevation—into his SATCOM computer. Moments later, the satellite antenna on the main tactical mast was engaged. Protruding above the water, their conical spiral antenna rotated southwest, pivoting into position above the horizon, pointing toward the relay satellite fixed over Sumatra. Less than sixty seconds after Mandrone's request, the

Maine's SATCOM link status indicator turned green. "Downlink's acquired, Captain, fully operational, running error free."

Depressing the intercom, Mandrone addressed the crew. "Topside, weather is calm; we're clear horizon to horizon. Sonar reports one contact . . . submarine bearing southeast, range in excess of fifty miles. Radio is clear, scope is clear, downlink is active. Gentlemen, we are ready for business."

Dogleg, 12/31/2008, Wed., 02:41 A.M.
ELF Station, MI

The advanced C-variant missile rocketed along a darkened valley at over five hundred miles an hour, skimming two hundred feet over the trees, its one-thousand-pound warhead bound for ELF Station Michigan.

Flight over land is a compromise between flying too high, risking detection by radar, and flying too low, risking a crash. North Korean mission planners had long ago resolved this compromise, and their instructions had been loaded into the missile's computer prior to launch.

As the missile approached a sheer cliff face through the black night, the program increased its altitude, pitching the nose up just in time to clear the rise. Had this maneuver been visible, the casual observer could be forgiven for counting the missile lost.

Recognizing the southernmost spoke of the ELF antenna, the missile armed its warhead, then followed the long wire toward the transmitter building.

Screaming overhead, the missile's position estimate became increasingly precise as it streaked toward the ELF transmitter building, unaffected by snow on the ground. In less than one-hundredth of a second, the missile's computer brain shifted gears to the terminal phase of its mission.

With the lights of the transmitter building in view, the missile executed a pop-up/terminal-dive maneuver, entering a climb just before reaching target. Once overhead, the missile rolled 180 degrees and dove through its final suicide maneuver, impacting the top of the building in a vertical attitude.

For a moment, the missile appeared consumed by the mammoth structure, but the eerie stillness was short-lived. The deception was simply a matter of programmed timing. Once the warhead penetrated the roof and upper two floors of the building, it entered the cavernous loading coil room containing the transmitters. For it was here, mission planners reasoned, an explosion would do the most harm, and it was here the detonation device triggered.

The explosion and subsequent fireball erupted hundreds of feet into the air, shattering everything in its wake.

When the building lights went dark, the lives of seven local Michigan families were changed forever. Three grandfathers were taken, two fathers, one son, an expectant mother, and her unborn child died horribly that night, blown apart by the shock wave, ripped open by shrapnel, or crushed under debris.

But from a mission planning perspective, the strike was considered a complete success. ELF Station Michigan was silenced with minimal collateral damage.

Approximately forty-five seconds later, six more American families suffered a similar fate and ELF Station Wisconsin dropped off the air.

CHAPTER SIXTEEN

ELF Dropout, 12/31/2008, Wed., 09:45 P.M.
USS *Maine*

Aft in the radio room, ELF receivers operated round the clock, in constant one-way communication with American Command Authority. As a result, computer monitors constantly scrolled ELF messages across their screens, periodically dumping information, one message at a time, to the printers. One printer handled boat business—missile operations and FYI communications about contacts in the area. The other, marked with a red heart-shaped valentine, handled familygrams—lifeline messages for the crew.

Every hour or so, the radioman collected hard copy from these printers, then read it, fluorescent yellow marker in hand. Sitting down at his desk, he hurriedly scanned through these messages, highlighting anything that might impact their mission. Most messages were operational or FYI in nature, but regrettably, many were familygrams for the *Maine*'s crew which would never be delivered. A hurried read of these familygrams revealed the birth of a son, Nathan Paul Bradley, to the chief sonarman and a new baby daughter, Laura Carol Lewis, to the engineering officer. *Life's good, but it's not fair,* the radioman observed, feeling he now better knew the crew. *Submariners perish, but life goes on, continually renewing itself.*

As the radioman read through the last of their message traffic, a vibrating buzzer suddenly blared an ear-piercing racket, sounding like a home fire alarm. Startled and caught off guard, the radioman spun a one-eighty, swiveling around his chair, scanning the room in near panic for fire or flashing red lights. He didn't need to look far. Within arm's reach, immediately behind him, every American ELF receiver flashed critical alarm.

Reacting instinctively, the radioman pounded the ALARM CUT OFF switch, silencing the buzzer. Standing by the frame stacked top to bottom with sixteen receivers, the radioman pressed status display buttons on each unit. Immediately, a pattern emerged with each liquid crystal display reading: "Link Down: Loss Of Signal." Although the radioman had anticipated this alarm, he paused several minutes before reporting to the captain, making sure this signal loss condition was permanent, not just another transient hit. It was out like a light with no hint of recovery.

"Conn, radio. American ELF link has been severed."

"Very well, radio. Secure the ELF antenna . . . reel her in."

"Radio aye."

"Things should begin picking up for us shortly, gentleman," Mandrone announced over the intercom. After a few moments' thought, he began sounding off orders. In reality, the crew knew the sequence, having practiced the routine many times before.

"Sonar, stow the towed array."

"Prepare countermeasure for deployment."

"Engine room, we'll need some steam. Prepare to engage the impeller during launch."

"Weapons Officer, set missile status to 1SQ. Anticipate manual preset download."

Looking across the control room, Mandrone spoke to his torpedo crew. "Man the forward torpedo room. Load tubes one and two for a SAM strike. I'm expecting company topside."

Subs Come Shallow, 12/31/2008, Wed., 09:12 P.M.
One Thousand Miles Southwest of the *Maine*
Onboard the *Wyoming* (SSGN-742)

The guided missile submarine *Wyoming* was patrolling deep, somewhere over the Kuril Trench, when her vital ELF communication channels suddenly fell silent. Aft in her spacious three-man radio room, red alarm lights flashed trouble, every ELF radio blinking *Loss of Signal.* After fifteen seconds without communication, the severity of the alarm situation automatically escalated. The situation was bad, and getting worse. Apparently, their ELF signal carrier had dropped out, leaving no possibility for recovery. Forty-five seconds later, the alarm severity went critical, demanding the attention of the skipper.

The *Wyoming,* like all missile submarines, must maintain continuous one-way communication with her National Command Authority to sustain credibility as a deterrent force. Consequently, their communications plan provided backup procedures for reestablishing communication if their ELF link failed. As a result, the *Wyoming* came shallow, relying on their backup VLF radio system for communication with the American mainland.

Across the Pacific, ELF communication links dropped out, and in response, America's deepwater missile submarines came shallow, reestablishing VLF communication with their National Command Authority.

Within seconds, ClearWater detected their position and subsequently logged them into its sub posit database. Meanwhile, Traci's renegade software continually searched for every naval target within reach of the *Maine*'s missiles.

Ultimately, an electronic copy of this information was stolen as quickly as it was sorted.

Download, 12/31/2008, Wed., 10:16 P.M.
USS *Maine*

"Conn, radio. Downlink under way." Transported at the speed of light, then downloaded into the renegade sub via satellite link, Mandrone's missiles were soon made ready to fire.

"Very well, radio, show us what you've got." In an instant, small Russian and American flag icons began flashing on screen. A Mercator map bordered by Russia, China, Alaska, and Hawaii appeared across the large twenty-one-inch flat-screen display suspended above the plotting table.

Mandrone printed hard copy of the map display, laid it out hurriedly across the plotting table, then studied each target location without comment. Marking the *Maine*'s approximate position with a pencil, he felt pleased their position wasn't in the posit database, not yet anyway. Next, he examined the target data, noting the exact distance and range of the submarine contact to the southeast. Circling it, Mandrone recognized this was their closest and most immediate threat. They'd take her out first.

Over the course of their training, they'd visited and revisited their best target strategy. Their objective: maximize probability of kill. Their solution: overkill—three nuclear-tipped, guided missile-torpedoes per target, geographically dispersed, assuming each was closing on the *Maine*. Mandrone understood that from the onset, when the *Maine* launched her first weapon, she'd become the target, her location detected by satellite in a matter of seconds. Operationally, they'd assumed any submarines, surface ships, and aircraft within range would close on the *Maine* immediately, with all possible speed. Odds were, every guided missile sub within range would target the *Maine* within minutes, launching autonomous retaliatory attacks as fast as their missiles could be programmed. Moreover, every attack sub and aircraft in range would do the same.

And these attacks wouldn't be conventional, but nuclear warheads.

Every commander attacks with the most effective weapons at his disposal, and in the case of a renegade submarine, Mandrone and his crew anticipated an all-out attempt to wipe them off the face of the earth.

All things considered, their hit list wasn't everything Mandrone had hoped for, but it was a typical day's showing. In summary, their target data identified three American missile boats, two Russian, plus two fast attacks, one closing from fifty-five miles southeast.

After Mandrone mentally planned their attack, he sat down behind his computer keyboard and began assigning targets. The whole missile assignment process was a drag-and-drop affair, requiring only a few seconds per target. Mandrone clicked missile one, dragged it from the *Maine,* then dropped it on the *Cheyenne*. Next, he entered the *Cheyenne*'s estimated course and speed, assuming she'd close on the *Maine* once they began launching their missiles. Repeating this drag-and-drop procedure time and time again, less than five minutes later, twenty-one missile-torpedoes had been assigned seven live targets.

Once the target display stabilized, Mandrone lowered the search periscope, then addressed the crew. "Gentlemen, we have five missile subs plus two fast attacks in range; one's an immediate threat—a fast attack—to our southeast."

"Diving Officer, submerge to launch depth and prepare to hover. Make it a slow, vertical descent."

"One-five-zero feet, aye," Ash replied, opening the vents. Sinking sixty feet is a far simpler maneuver than a controlled, vertical ascent.

Hearing water rushing into the main ballast tanks, Mandrone continued over the intercom. "Maneuvering, make ready to engage the screw."

"Torpedo room, give me status on tubes one and two."

"Surface-to-air weapons loaded, warm, and ready for download, sir."

"Very well," Mandrone acknowledged, then spoke to Missile Control. "Weapons, make ready to launch. Anticipate targets will close using all available speed. Download coordinates and torpedo presets—three missiles per. Designate firing order: one through ten, fourteen through twenty-four. That is all."

Sonobuoys, 12/31/2008, Wed., 10:18 P.M.
Onboard A P-3 Orion

Moving over 220 mph, skimming across the black depths of the North Pacific, two P-3s searched for the *Maine* operating as a hunter-killer team. At seven hundred feet, Lieutenant Briggs banked sharply to the right, fast approaching his drop point due north of the *Maine*'s last known location. Scott felt every maneuver, scanned every instrument, but focused primarily on her tactical display.

"I'm planting a line east-west," Billy Ray announced. "Select what you need, I'll punch 'em in."

"Space 'em one thousand yards apart," Rusty responded. "Stand by for buoy drop."

"Okay, buoys away now, now, now!" yelled Briggs, pressing the pickle. The pilot banked sharply again, circling back over the buoys, listening.

Nothing, then suddenly Scott saw an American missile sub coming shallow on her tactical display. First, one appeared over the Kuril Trench, then another, and another. Tristan ran a series of diagnostic tests, then assured her nothing was wrong with their equipment. Unbelievably, American missile subs were, in fact, coming shallow across the Pacific, as if on queue.

Without hesitation, she contacted Mason via video link and began puzzling through the mystery.

The Page, 12/31/2008, Wed., 02:19 A.M.
USSPACECOM

Back at USSPACECOM, Mason and his staff found themselves playing catch-up, reacting to a series of seemingly unrelated, rapid-fire events.

Slim Mason's beeper went off with annoying, alarmclock precision. Retrieving the phone number, he didn't recognize the area code . . . Wasn't Washington, Hawaii, or Alabama. Following a brief discussion, Scott suggested the area code sounded familiar from her days at the University of Illinois . . . Could be a Michigan area code. Mason borrowed a phone on the screening room floor and returned the call. It was busy.

After redialing five or six times, Slim finally heard ringing at the far end, then almost immediately, it stopped . "Lieutenant Marcy Yates, ELF Monitoring Station."

Mason identified himself.

"Colonel, you're on our list of people to notify when something goes wrong here. I just spoke with Admiral Eastwood and he said we should speak immediately. The essence of what I need to tell you is this. My facility monitors the quality of our submarine transmissions around the clock. Within the last fifteen minutes, both our Michigan and Wisconsin ELF sites dropped off line. Let me be perfectly clear on this point, sir. All our ELF transmissions have stopped, we don't know why. We've tried contacting our people on site without success."

There was a long pause as Mason absorbed the situation. Recognizing Mason's hesitation, the lieutenant guessed what Mason might be thinking, and addressed his suspicion directly.

"There's nothing wrong with our monitoring equipment, sir. In addition, both ELF sites have independent, stand-alone AC power plants plus redundant transmitters. We don't believe this signal loss is due to any electrical power or equipment failure."

Following another pause, Mason asked in an even tone, "What do you make of it?"

Her response was as immediate as it was direct. "I don't have one shred of physical evidence to support my suspicion, sir, but I think we've been attacked. Don't ask me how or why, I don't know, but there's nothing else which explains the loss of both sites . . . plus, like I said, they don't answer the phone. We've tried contacting both sites by phone and radio. Get nothing. I think we've been attacked and it's going to take some time to sort through the details."

"I agree with your assessment, but I hope you're wrong." Mason struggled with what to do. "Do we have any bases near our ELF sites?"

"Not that I know of, sir. These sites're in the boondocks."

"Thanks," Mason concluded. "I've got friends at Cheyenne Mountain. I'll give 'em a call, take a look-see."

"Please keep us in the loop, sir."

"Will do, Lieutenant."

Satellite Pix, 12/31/2008, Wed., 02:29 A.M.
USSPACECOM

"We don't know if anyone survived." Craven's voice sounded subdued over speakerphone. "Choppers're en route as we speak."

The mood inside the Pacific screening room was somber as Mason eyed two satellite photographs on screen. Scott studied the same pictures inside the P-3. The caption beneath one photo read "ELF Station Wisconsin After Attack;" the other, "ELF Station Michigan After Attack." In many respects, both photographs looked alike—each a high-altitude pass, each a night shot, each the thermal image of a bright green, smoldering hot crater set in dark contrast against cooler surrounding woodlands.

"How about superimposing before and after shots of the Michigan site?" Scott requested.

"Will do," sounded an unfamiliar voice over the speakerphone. Miles away, inside Cheyenne Mountain, a Photoshop technician manipulated satellite image files, closing one named "Wisconsin After," opening another named "Michigan Before."

Inside the Pacific screening room, Mason observed the technician's work progress on a device known as a mirror monitor—a large thirty-six-inch screen displaying exactly what the technician saw inside Cheyenne Mountain. Scott watched from the P-3. The mirror monitor idea was simple—identical screens, remote locations.

With a click and drag of his mouse, the Photoshop technician positioned one translucent image, "Michigan Before," over "Michigan After." After selecting reference crop marks on each image, he pulled down his graphics tool palette, clicked ALIGN, then the power of digital image manipulation came into focus on screen. Almost as if by magic, the images shifted, coming into perfect alignment. In closing, the technician clicked SHARPEN—his final touch-up operation—and the composite image was quickly redrawn with striking clarity.

The image looked like two slides, aligned, laid over each other. One shot taken immediately before the explosion, the other soon after. An enlarged, translucent image of the ELF transmitter building overlaid the greenish crater.

Once the enhanced picture appeared, Scott grimaced. She'd seen similar destructive patterns from conventional cruise missile attacks before. "Judging from the crater's symmetry, whatever caused this explosion entered the transmitter building through the roof, dead center . . . perfectly vertical terminal phase, zero lateral motion."

"Cruise missile attack?" Mason asked.

"Most likely, sir," Scott replied, "But there's more. Did you notice the time stamp on both photographs? Looks to me like these sites were taken out simultaneously."

"That's right," Craven added over the speakerphone. "Perfectly timed. We think each site was hit by a single conventional warhead, and both attacks occurred less than one minute apart."

"That sounds like the way we'd do it," Mason lamented, exhaling a long, slow sigh.

"Think about it, sir," Scott offered in a supporting tone.

"Whoever hit our ELF stations was well supported, well connected, and well coordinated."

A look of stark terror flushed across Mason's face. *So was the outfit that hijacked the* Maine.

Ripple Launch, 12/31/2008, Wed., 10:30 P.M., 09:30 ZULU
50N 172W
USS *Maine*

Without warning, Mandrone made his open field run.

"Missiles're programmed, Captain," sounded an overhead speaker. "Download's complete. Two minutes to 1SQ."

Mandrone felt he should say something at this juncture, something motivational or profound, but the words wouldn't come. He'd thought through his speech a thousand times before, but now, facing real targets, he couldn't remember what he'd wanted to say.

He felt like an addle-headed schoolboy.

Is this all there is?

Squinting through his good eye, he gazed at his launch manual, finding some comfort in its familiar procedures.

"Ship's at launch depth, Captain," Ash announced from the diving console. "We're ready to hover."

"Very well," Mandrone replied, snapping out of his malaise. In the blink of an eye, his instincts took over, picking up the ship's pulse without skipping a beat. "Maneuvering, engage the impeller."

"Aye, aye, Captain."

"Diving Officer, begin hovering."

Setting diving planes and rudder controls on autopilot, Ash stood, leaving behind his aircraft-style steering yoke. Walking a few feet to his left, he surveyed the *Maine*'s massive ballast control panel. Hurriedly, he scanned the maze of switches governing the boat's ballast and trim tanks. The name of the game was to stay neutrally buoyant during launch.

Surrounded by a kaleidoscope of colored indicator lights, Ash meticulously ballasted the sub, maintaining ordered launch depth within tight tolerances. Once stabilized, he delegated launch depth control to the electronic hovering system. The hovering system compensates for changes in the boat's weight—changes which occur once a missile leaves the boat. When the sub gets light, the system admits water into a huge tank. If too heavy, it expels ballast water, balancing the boat fore and aft.

Minutes later, vent and pump indicator lights settled down to a predictable duty cycle—a trickle-in, pause, pump-out sort of pattern. Satisfied the hovering system had reached steady state, Ash buckled back into his driver's seat. Releasing the autopilot, he manned the helm, ready to counter each whip to stern created during launch. (Heaving thirty-four-foot missile-torpedoes skyward requires momentous thrust, and as a consequence, rocks the boat.) Set in position, he signaled Mandrone.

On cue, Mandrone spoke into the intercom . . . this time, to the missile control room. "Weapons, report missile status."

"Status is 1SQ, Captain."

"Very well, equalize missile tube pressure to launch depth, then open outer doors."

"Aye, aye, Captain." In the missile control center, the weapons officer punched the pressurize switch for missile one, then monitored an array of flashing lights, shifting from red, amber, to green.

Pssssssssssss.

Compressed air hissed from tube one, equalizing pressure with the sea. Inside the missile control center, tube one's equalization light flashed green. Without pausing to think, the weapons officer instinctively opened the outer muzzle door. For a few brief moments, the sound of hydraulic pumps whined, pushing the missile door up and over, slamming it soundly against the stops with a dull, hollow, metallic *thunk*.

The sound was unmistakable.

With the success of missile one behind him, he proceeded with machine-like precision, working down a column of pressurization switches marked two through ten—skipping eleven, twelve, thirteen—picking up with fourteen through twenty-four.

Pssssssss. PsssssssssssssssSSSSSSSSSSSSSSSSsssssssss.

Simultaneously pressurizing, twenty tubes transitioned the missile control panel into a virtual Christmas tree of lights. The weapons officer waited, finger poised on the outer door switch for missile two. Once the flashing stopped, once every green indicator glowed continuously, he marched downward along the switch column, feeling the satisfying detent of each mechanical switch engaging through his fingertip. He counted twenty clicks.

And with every click, the pitch of hydraulics dropped, pivoting each door skyward.

Thunk, thunk, thunk, . . . thunk, thunk.

In the background, above the hydraulic whine, the rapid-fire succession of missile doors slamming open, one at a time, echoed throughout the boat.

. . . *eighteen, nineteen, twenty.* Mandrone grimaced, counting open doors. *The sound of Armageddon.* With hydraulic pumps now quiet, he checked his watch. *Right on schedule.*

Without comment or fanfare, Mandrone walked to the launch panel immediately aft of Ash's diving control station. Columns of indicator lights showed each missile's operational status and at the bottom of the panel—an ignition switch.

Mandrone knelt down on one knee, squinting, focusing his good eye on the stainless steel switch. Holding the launch key between his first finger and thumb, he dragged it across the launch panel, slightly marring the enamel surface. Inching across the top of the raised switch, Mandrone felt the keyhole, a dark blurry crevasse. Once he felt the launch key settle in over the slit, he rotated it out to ninety degrees, turned it slightly, then, once aligned, slid it into the keyhole. Standing braced against the launch panel, Mandrone rotated his key, locking it fast with vise-grips, completing one-third of the circuit required for missile launch.

Listening to sounds over the intercom, Mandrone sensed the launch sequence taking on a momentum of its own. In other parts of the boat, his officers worked through checklist after checklist, making sure the *Maine* and her twenty-one targeted missiles were ready.

"Radio, conn. Any comm traffic topside?"

"Two P-3s bearing east southeast, Captain. Range two hundred ten miles."

Good, Mandrone thought. *Should give us maybe half an hour.* "Sonar, conn. Any last-minute trace of trouble?"

"Negative, Captain. Sonar is clear inside fifty kilometers."

Excellent. Nothing can stop us now. "Torpedo room, make ready all torpedo fire-control and surface-to-air systems. We won't be alone out here for long."

Inside the control room, Mandrone's breathing tensed, though he consciously tried to regulate it. Rubbing the stubble on his face, he clenched his teeth at the thought of his next task. *Another damn keyhole.* Following several failed attempts, he finally bagged it, inserting his last launch key into the panel by the periscope. Two out of the three switches required for launch were now closed.

Moments later, "Weapons, this is the captain," rang out over the intercom. "Request weapons status." Suddenly, the boat fell perfectly quiet, almost as if its heart skipped a beat.

A long pause followed while the weapons officer individually checked each targeted missile. Once final tests were complete, the seemingly endless silence was broken. "Conn, Weapons. Status is 1SQ. Missile flight profiles're programmed; onboard torpedo presets provisioned for maximum search range."

"Very well." Releasing their missiles wasn't something Mandrone relished, but in the final analysis, he believed they might destroy a significant fraction of the world's nuclear arsenal with one blow—if they were lucky. Drawing a deep breath, then releasing it slowly, two distinct syllables rang out over the intercom. "Fire one."

The words seemed to linger in the air, endlessly reverberating about the boat.

Everyone braced for a jolt.

The weapons officer squeezed a pistol-grip trigger, completing the launch circuit, firing a steam generator system located at the base of number one. Roaring to life, a fixed position rocket ignited, directing its white-hot exhaust plume on a body of water in the bottom of the launch tube. Moments later, steam pressure catapulted one skyward. Meanwhile, the dome-shaped top of the missile tube closure was shattered by explosive charges. As the dome top ripped apart, a thirty-two-ton missile-torpedo, encased in a watertight capsule, erupted violently toward the surface.

After catapulting upward thirty feet, a solid rocket booster ignited, ramming the torpedo-shaped capsule to the surface. Once clear of the water, explosive bolts jettisoned its buoyant canister as spring-loaded tail fins snapped into position, guiding the massive cylindrical form through a 180-degree roll about its long axis. Cutting the darkness like a strobe, two blinding pyrotechnic flashes followed; both flank doors opened and two large wings swung out. Completing its metamorphosis to air-breathing flight, an air scoop pivoted downward, its booster jettisoned, and an internal gas cartridge fired, starting the turbofan engine. Control surfaces responded immediately, laying the missile-torpedo over gently, assuming a slightly nose-high attitude. Moments later, it descended to a cruising altitude of fifty feet, pulled a U-turn banking southeast, then sped away into the night.

Down below, the giant sub shuddered, then bounced. A muffled *whoooooooosh* engulfed the boat. Her stern whipped about from the enormous forces thrusting missile one skyward from its tube. Even before the missile breached the surface, the dampened roar of solid stage booster ignition reverberated about the boat, momentarily overwhelming their sonar.

Compensating for weight loss, the vacant tube flooded immediately.

"One's away and clear, Captain," Weapons reported, but didn't need to say.

Once the shifting deck stabilized, Mandrone spoke to his diving officer.

"Ready at the helm?"

Ash eyed the ballast control panel. *Steady state, ballast cycling normally.* Looking over his shoulder, he shot Mandrone a thumbs-up.

"Very well," Mandrone continued. "Gentlemen, there's no turning back now." A pause. Launching all twenty remaining missiles would take approximately twenty minutes, start to finish. "Weapons, commence ripple launch."

Everyone braced as the boat bounced.

Whoooooooooooosh .

Seconds later . . . the roar of thunder.

As Mandrone knew well, America had no assets within short-range striking distance, and consequently, nothing could be done to terminate their launch sequence mid-stream. Having trained for this job all his adult life, Mandrone held every advantage. Instinctively he knew he'd win.

Do You Hear What I Hear? 12/31/2008, Wed., 10:46 P.M., 09:46 ZULU
Fifty-five Miles Southeast of the *Maine*
USS *Cheyenne*

What the . . .

The *Cheyenne*'s chief sonarman played back the sound—*unbelievable*—then played it back again.

But the recording left no doubt.

"Conn, sonar. Missile launch detected bearing northwest. I repeat—launch detected bearing northwest. Range: unknown . . . probably in excess of forty miles."

"We closing, Skipper?" the XO asked immediately.

"Negative. Area's gonna get hot as hell. Bring her to periscope depth for SATCOM. We've gotta know who's out there."

"Aye, aye, Skipper." The XO repeated the captain's order. "Diving Officer, come to periscope depth."

"Radio, conn," continued the skipper. "Send this message: Emergency—stop. Missile launch detected northwest—stop. Request range to target and orders ASAP . . ."

"Conn, incoming emergency flash traffic," interrupted the radioman. "It's a bell ringer, sir. We're ordered to periscope depth for SATCOM."

"Good. We're running the same wavelength."

CHAPTER SEVENTEEN

God Help Us, 12/31/2008, Wed., 02:46 A.M., 09:46 ZULU
USSPACECOM

America's crisis—for that matter, the crisis for all the world—came with the launch of the first missile-torpedo. Suddenly, from the middle of nowhere, the *Maine*'s first missile launch was detected.

Standing watch overlooking the Pacific screening room floor, Ensign Eion Macke punched his telephone autodial. Recognizing Colonel Mason's voice at the other end, he spoke abruptly. "Missile launch detected, sir. Could be our bogie."

Stunned, but not completely surprised, Mason responded instinctively. "Where'd they come from?"

"ClearWater can't I.D. the sub, sir, but launch location's near the dateline, well off Russia's Kamchatka Peninsula. The boat left no wake trail; it just suddenly appeared, but it's gotta be our boomer. Nothing else makes any sense. Sudden heat from the launch was detected by satellite."

Following a brief pause, the colonel asked, "What do we know?"

"We detected a single cruise missile launch during its boost stage—and it's a big one. Judging from the heat signature, it's one of ours. Tracked it a few seconds then lost it in sea clutter."

"Bearing? We know its course?"

"Negative, Colonel. We're not certain which way it's headed, but if it's one of ours, we've gotta assume it's hugging the deck. No surprise there, but God only knows where it's headed."

Closing his eyes, Mason lowered his head, placing the bridge of his nose against his fingertips. His voice was quietly subdued, now a faint whisper. "What about assets? Anything nearby?"

Suddenly, a second red missile icon flashed on the big board.

Spellbound by the blinking icon, Eion and the entire Pacific screening room staff abruptly fell silent, as if everyone's heart stopped.

Mason heard Eion gasp, followed by muffled commotion. "Hold one, sir."

Moments later, a console operator tapped his headset, snapped to attention, then signaled Ensign Macke from across the floor. He held up two fingers.

Eion nodded understanding. "Another one, sir. Second launch confirmed."

Holy mother of God.

Across the country, top brass from Washington to Pearl Harbor watched these events unfold—transfixed by disbelief, powerless to stop them.

Arm the Weapon, 12/31/2008, Wed., 10:46 P.M., 09:46 ZULU
Killer Orion

Scott cringed watching the renegade missile launch on screen. After a few moments' thought, she typed a brief e-mail message to their radio operator, then turned around where she could see him. Lieutenant junior grade Dale Tew looked like an angelic child with ink black hair, smiling eyes, rosy cheeks, and a chubby face. She keyed her throat mike and spoke. "Dale, we've got trouble."

He'd made eye contact with Scott before she'd finished her heads-up and didn't waste any time getting on it. Before she'd offered any additional explanation, Dale Tew scanned her e-mail, then shifted into high gear. Switching radios, he engaged his voice scrambler and began speaking hurriedly. "Flight Control, Flight Control, this is Sea Hunt. Do you read me? Over."

A pause.

"We read you, Sea Hunt. Standby one."

Within minutes, the Orion crew obtained permission to close, arm their weapon, and eliminate the *Maine* from the U.S. naval register.

Counterattack, 12/31/2008, Wed., 09:47 P.M., 09:47 ZULU
USS *Wyoming*

Miles off the Kamchatka Peninsula, in the vicinity of the Kuril Trench, a near vertical column of blue-green laser light suddenly appeared flitting about the ocean's surface. For a few brief seconds, the beam illuminated the back of the *Wyoming*.

"SLCSAT download complete, Captain. Missile status is 1SQ."

"Very well, then." The skipper's expression turned grim. "Fire one through eight in rapid order."

Everyone braced as Weapons pulled the trigger.

Whooooooooooooosh.

The giant sub's stern whipped, then bounced.

With her location compromised, once all eight missiles were airborne, the *Wyoming* ran an active sonar search, combing the area for contacts. Their search revealed nothing within a radius of twenty miles but the captain knew that could quickly change. Once her sweep was complete, the skipper countered by diving deep, running a high-speed egress from the area.

The skipper fully intended the *Wyoming* and his crew should live to fight another day.

Destination Unknown, 12/31/2008, Wed., 10:49 P.M.,
09:49 ZULU
USS *Cheyenne*

"Captain, radio. Flash SSIXS traffic from COMSUBPAC."

"Read it."

"Missile launch acknowledge. Destination unknown. Course unknown. Missiles cannot be tracked against sea clutter. P-3 Orion closing to prosecute. *Wyoming* backup attack in progress."

Back in the radio room, another light flashed green.

"Heads up, Captain. Target database download complete. Check your display."

A map flashed on screen showing the *Maine*'s position to the northwest. Text surrounding the submarine-shaped icon blinked red: "4 Missile(s) Away."

Friendly Tracks, 12/31/2008, Wed., 02:50 A.M., 09:50 ZULU
Cheyenne Mountain

General Craven studied the big board feeling frustration. Projected on the wall, he saw a large percentage of the overall picture unfolding in the Pacific, but the things he wanted to see most—tracks of missiles launched from the

Maine—he could not. Cheyenne Mountain could detect stealth cruise missiles launched during their boost phase due to the twelve-second burn of the Type 106 solid-propellant rocket motor, but once it fell away and the missile transitioned to its turbofan cruise engine, their best sensors were useless. Practically speaking, they could detect cruise missiles for about ten seconds as they breached the ocean's surface, then they went blind.

On the other hand, stealth missiles programmed as *friendly* were tracked in flight using a two-way satellite link. Once the *Wyoming* launched its eight missiles, they periodically reported their positions to Cheyenne Mountain and were displayed on screen racing toward the *Maine*.

Warning, 12/31/2008, Wed., 10:50 P.M., 09:50 ZULU
Killer Orion

Searching in tandem with a second P-3, using the Orion's look-down radar in a bi-static configuration, Scott detected cruise missiles heading toward two American fast attacks, the *Topeka* and the *Cheyenne*. In the blink of an eye, her ClearWater tactical display flashed red, showing both subs vulnerable, both engaged in satellite communication, languishing near the surface at periscope depth. Both were sitting ducks, but the *Cheyenne* was clearly in greatest peril only fifty miles southeast of the *Maine*.

Scott reasoned the missile-torpedo must be programmed to fly to a fixed position on the ocean's surface. Once on the mark, the torpedo must enter the water, search, and close on its target. It's the only way they could operate without real-time guidance along the way. Alarmed by this revelation, she warned both skippers via radio then convinced Mason to scramble everything within attack range of the *Maine*'s missiles.

Jam the Planes, 12/31/2008, Wed., 11:01 P.M., 10:01 ZULU
USS *Cheyenne*

"Sea Hunt, say again."

Dear Lord, please help us. "Captain, radio! The *Maine*'s launched its missiles at us."

Checking his watch, the skipper's face scrunched into a scowl. *Six-to-eight-minute flight time max.*

"They're the big ones, sir. Presumably, nuclear-tipped. Danger is imminent." The radio operator kept talking, but the skipper didn't hear. Bringing down the periscope, he mentally ran ahead of his ship, sorting through what to do.

"Torpedo room, load AT's in tubes one and two and step on it."

Forward in *Cheyenne*'s very bowels, a whirlwind of activity took place though remarkably little was said. To minimize loading time, activities occurred in parallel. Two torpedomen moved the 3,400-pound AT (Anti-Torpedo) torpedo onto its loading tray while another swung open the breech door and conducted a quick inspection of the number one torpedo tube. Once that was complete, the loading ram slid the AT torpedo into firing position and two torpedomen converged on tube one like bees to honey. One torpedoman connected the guidance wire and sealed the breech door. The second checked tube integrity, making sure all connections and seals were set. Remarkably, this well-orchestrated affair required less than ninety seconds, start to finish.

But topside, after ninety seconds, the inbound missile-torpedo had traveled another fifteen miles, thirty percent of its total programmed journey.

"Diving Officer," the skipper ordered, "get her down fast, below the layer; make your depth four hundred feet. Jam the planes; give me maximum down angle. Keep your wheel amidships."

He turned, speaking into the intercom. "Maneuvering, make turns for full battle speed, pronto."

As the skipper studied their tactical situation, his jaw muscles tensed. The *Maine* was well out of range of his torpedoes, and their complement of cruise missiles were designed to take out surface ships. There had been no time to reload their vertical launch tubes for sub-to-sub attack.

"Out of range and on the run," he groused. "What a way to enter a shooting war."

Classic Bunt Maneuver, 12/31/2008, Wed., 11:03 P.M., 10:03 ZULU
Onboard the Cruise Missile Targeting the *Cheyenne*

Once airborne, its journey took only seven minutes. Had there been daylight, the *Cheyenne*'s communications mast would have been clearly visible from the cruise missile's vantage point.

Closing on the *Cheyenne,* the missile-torpedo entered its terminal phase, executing a classic bunt maneuver. Its bombay doors jettisoned, then the missile's nose pitched up, lobbing the torpedo forward in an arc toward the mast. A drag shut slowed the torpedo's descent, but on entering the water, it was ready to hunt.

Torpedo in the Water, 12/31/2008, Wed., 11:04 P.M., 10:04 ZULU
USS *Cheyenne*

Forward in the sonar room, the unmistakable, high-pitched whine of the pump-jet impeller was detected as the torpedo swam its serpentine search pattern.

"Captain, torpedo in the water! Bearing three-three-zero!"

"Range?"

"No range yet, but it's *really* close."

"How close?"

"Sounds like it's on top of us, sir."

The skipper went pale. "All stop."

"All stop, aye."

"Weapons, enable snapshot fire control."

"Snapshot, aye."

"Countermeasures, launch decoys."

A pause. "Decoys away, Captain."

"Flood tube one and open outer door."

"Flooded, Captain," Weapons replied.

"Sonar, range?"

"Not yet, Captain."

"Weapons, run an AT out shallow for one hundred yards, bearing three-three-zero, and step on it."

"Aye, sir."

Weapons ham-fisted a red button. When the torpedoman heard the whoosh of the launch, lights on the weapons officer's fire-control panel turned green. From the bowels of the boat, an antitorpedo variation of a Mark 48 thrust out of tube one. Engaging its pump-jet impeller, the AT torpedo swam away, spooling guidance wire out its tail.

Using his joystick, a young fire control technician swam the AT out one hundred yards, listening all the while through the torpedo's seeker head. Regrettably, running fast swamped the sensor with flow noise and the young technician never heard a thing.

As the AT ran out shallow, their nemesis ran in underneath.

Ping . . . ping . . . ping . . . ping-ping-ping . . .

"Conn, sonar. It's acquired us, Captain!"

Ping-ping-pingpingpingpiinng!!! rang out over the intercom.

"Captain, it's taken the bait, locked on the decoy, passing below us."

"All ahead flank!" *No, no, dear God in heaven, not below us.* The captain knew that with shallow-water detonation, explosive forces inevitably escape out the weakest point in their surroundings—toward the surface.

Pi-pi-pi-pi-pi-p i i i i i n n n n g g g g !
BARROOOOM!!!

Mercifully, like the young fire control technician, not one of the 133 souls onboard heard a thing.

The tactical nuclear explosion detonated below and behind the *Cheyenne,* heaving her stern completely out of the water. From a distance, the hull appeared to break apart at its assembly points, imploding bottom up with the passing shock wave. Hurled upward by a massive bubble of superheated steam, erupting skyward like a killer volcano, the collapsed hull sections were scattered willy-nilly across the ocean surface like milkweed carried on the wind.

Knuckle, 12/31/2008, Wed., 11:04 P.M., 10:04 ZULU
USS *Topeka*

The surface was an eerie calm as the *Topeka*'s electromagnetic sniffer extended out of the water under a starlit sky. It disappeared moments later, replaced by a telescoping communications mast. Once its antenna elements were fully extended, Skipper Slay Hawkins pressed the TRANSMIT button identifying themselves to the submarine satellite information exchange system, interrogating the satellite, signaling they were ready to receive their SSIXS message traffic.

On queue, a barrage of prioritized messages were downlinked as fast as the submarine's satellite receiver could absorb them. The entire exchange took only a matter of seconds.

As messages from COMSUBPAC and CinCPAC flooded in, one radio operator printed them out, another read them, sorted by priority.

Meanwhile, aft in the comm shack, a third radio operator recorded communications channels occupying UHF and HF frequencies. Scanning across the aircraft bands, the third operator suddenly recognized the name *Topeka* crackling above the background noise.

A pause, then again.

"*Topeka,* this is Sea Hunt. Do you read me? Over."

The signal was faint, but distinct enough to be sure.

"Sea Hunt, this is the *Topeka*. We read you. Over."

During the next two minutes, the radio operator experienced a kaleidoscope of emotion ranging from distress to disbelief, but the greatest of these was fear.

"Conn, radio," boomed an excited voice over the intercom.

Concerned, Hawk decided to put on his headset and switch off the loudspeaker. He opened a channel to the radio room and prompted, "OK, whaddaya got?"

"Captain, we received an unscrambled voice communication direct from a Navy P-3, operating out of Kiska, I think. They've located the *Maine* two hundred and forty miles northwest of our position. They're confident they found her, and what's more, she's launched an unknown number of missile-torpedoes in our direction. They believe they've got our name on 'em, sir, and suggested—hell, skipper, they insisted—we clear the area with all possible speed."

Hawk was stunned. "Are you sure about this?"

"Positive, sir."

"What's come in on the SSIXS?"

"Message traffic confirms the *Maine*'s posit, sir. And the *Cheyenne*'s about a hundred ninety miles to our northwest, roughly between us and the *Maine*." About that time, the ClearWater downlink flashed on the boat's tactical display, affirming the *Cheyenne*'s position.

"What the . . ." The chief sonarman's jaw fell slack. He rewound the audiotape and played it back slowly, piping it onto his waterfall display. There was no mistake. The acoustic signature of any thermonuclear explosion possesses a nightmarish, Armageddon-like quality to it. For the first time in his life, the sonarman felt as if he were nose-to-nose with death, staring the Grim Reaper squarely in the face. "Conn, sonar" blared over the 1MC. "Thermonuclear explosion to our northwest, Captain. They got her, they killed the *Cheyenne*."

Hawk felt an icy knot in his stomach, but didn't let that detract from the problem at hand; they could be next. Years of training and endless drills provided him the resolve to drive this situation home.

"Gentlemen, they're shootin' at us." The skipper's expression, the look in his eyes, conveyed the gravity of their plight.

Instantly, everyone understood this was no drill. The mood in the control room shifted only slightly, almost imperceptibly. Submariners fight like they train.

"Diving Officer, put a knuckle in the water. Right full rudder! All ahead flank!"

As the periscope seated with a thunk, Hawk spoke to the TSO (Tactical Systems Officer) standing by his fire control console. "Countermeasures, make ready your three-inch tubes. Load decoys for a full spread."

Hawk grabbed an overhead handhold as the *Topeka* rolled hard right. Punching the intercom, he continued snapping orders. "Torpedo room, I need four ATs and I need them now."

While the *Topeka* churned a knuckle, the skipper delayed his next order, allowing the torpedomen time to load their weapons. From a distance, the *Topeka* flew tight circles through a gradual spiralling dive, trashing the ocean into an aerated emulsion. Although the knuckle consisted only of air bubbles, it reflected sonar sound like a stationary submarine, as if the *Topeka* were leaving a ghost image of itself behind.

Less than five minutes later, a winded voice boomed over the intercom. "Forward tubes loaded, Captain."

"Very well." Focusing his gaze across the control room, he spoke directly to the diving officer. "Take her down fast, below the layer! Make your depth five hundred feet, maximum dive angle."

"Five hundred feet, aye."

Hawk grabbed an overhead handhold as the deck fell away, then spoke to the weapons officer. His voice was quietly restrained, but everyone in the control room heard his order clearly. "Once we're level at five hundred, put an AT in the knuckle."

The sonarman grabbed his headphones—surface transient, sounded like an impeller spinning up.

As he confirmed this call with one glance at his waterfall display, the chief sonarman's pulse ratcheted up a notch. His next report to the skipper was the one every sonarman dreaded most. "Torpedo in the water, Captain. Bearing zero-four-five."

"All stop. Quick quiet," Hawk ordered instinctively.

Moments later, the sonarman heard the Mk-48 searching for targets, pinging shallow water in the layer above them. The torpedo's sonar head electronically steered its beam, guiding the weapon through its search to target. Tirelessly, the torpedo scanned its forward half hemisphere, listening for reflected sound. Its speed was slow at first, to conserve fuel, but once its full scan was complete, the pump jet propulsor diverted its thrust, causing the torpedo to align itself headlong on the knuckle. Three hundred fifty feet above the *Topeka,* well aft off her starboard side, the Mk-48 sonar reduced its search area, limiting its field of view to that of a narrow tunnel, converging its sonar energy on the knuckle. Now lined up and focused, its acceleration to target was amazing. In a matter of seconds, its closing speed clocked over sixty knots.

Below in the *Topeka,* the range-gaiting ping of the torpedo rang in the sonarman's ears.

"Conn, sonar. It took the bait, Captain! It's moving away from us, making a run for the knuckle."

Hawk knew it wasn't over till it was over. "Sonar, estimated run time to target?"

"Two minutes, Captain, three minutes tops. Best we can do, sir. Torpedo's closing on the knuckle from the northwest. Bearing three-one-five."

"Weps." The skipper made eye contact with his weapons officer. "Whaddaya hear?"

"Can't hear anything outside the knuckle wall, Skipper." His tone conveyed frustration, nervous anxiety.

Hawk expected the AT's sensors would be deaf inside the knuckle, but occasionally you get lucky. Sometimes, acoustic holes open up through a knuckle as the mass of air bubbles rearrange themselves. "Weapons, swim the AT clear of the knuckle so you can hear. Run it out to the northwest a couple hundred yards. Arm the EMAG fuse and . . ."

Hawk's voice dropped off.

"And what, Skipper?" Weapons asked.

Hawk cocked his head, answering with a deliberately calm, but forceful tone. "We've got time, so take it slow and don't let this one get away."

Slowly, the technician swam his tethered weapon northwest, outside the wall of bubbles, listening all the while through the AT's sensor head. Almost immediately, the technician's ears perked up. "I've got something, sir. It's coming in!"

"Can you lock on the incoming signal?"

"Signal is acquired, Captain. Signal is locked. AT's ready for auto-run to target."

"Don't polish the cannon ball with this shot, Weps. Just get it in the ballpark."

"Aye, Captain." The weapons officer's voice sounded a bit more relaxed as he flipped a switch enabling automatic proximity detonation.

"Range one thousand yards and closing, Captain."

"Forewarned is forearmed."

"Auto-enable is set for proximity detonation, Captain. We'll kill it in the ballpark."

BARROOOOM!

As the Mk-48 streaked over the AT torpedo, its EMAG fuse detected the Mk-48 and went off where it would do the most good, directly beneath it. Luckily for the *Topeka*, the Mk-48 ADCAP and AT torpedoes were close relatives, siblings from the same family, both variants manufactured by Hughes. Consequently, the AT inherently knew a great deal about killing Mk-48s, and did so with remarkable precision.

The conventional explosion ripped the nuclear-tipped

torpedo into twisted metal. Fuel exploded in the torpedo's tail section, disemboweling the pump jet propulsor from its shroud, shattering the guidance computer into hundreds of components, from circular-shaped circuit boards to computer chips. Forward in the torpedo's business end, while guidance control and acoustic sensors were totally obliterated, the nuclear warhead sank intact, spiralling down eighteen thousand feet to the bottom of the Northern Pacific.

Hawk and his crew breathed a sigh of relief. Everyone hoped the danger had passed, but only the young and inexperienced believed the worst was over.

"Weapons," the captain ordered, "put one AT in the knuckle, and another where the last AT exploded."

Hawk and his control room crew hurriedly critiqued their torpedo kill scenario, then set up again, waiting for another.

They didn't have to wait long.

CHAPTER EIGHTEEN

Fight the Boat, 12/31/2008, Wed., 11:05 P.M., 10:05 ZULU
USS *Maine*

"Outer missile doors are closed, Captain."

"Very well. Make ready to fight the boat." Looking across the control room, Mandrone spoke to Ash Wilson. His tone had a no-nonsense ring of urgency to it. "Diving Officer, come to periscope depth."

"Periscope depth, aye, Captain."

"Engine room, make turns for twelve knots."

"Depth is nine zero feet, Captain."

Mandrone acknowledged Ash's comment, then raised the main periscope, ESM mast, and both periscope sleeves.

Mandrone surveyed the surface through his mast camera, then pulled a quick survey to zenith. No lights—nothing. At first glance, they were alone, horizon to horizon. "Radio, whatdaya got?"

"All's quiet topside. Sniffer screen's blank."

"Maybe so, but they know we're here. I feel it. We're not alone. Activate the search radar. Let's see who's out there."

"Aye, aye, Captain. Three-sixty sweep's in progress." Three-fourths of the way through the first sweep, a blip appeared on the green phosphorus screen. Without hesitation, the radioman circled the aircraft blip with his light pen, electronically sweeping the sector time and time again. Almost instantly, their radar acquired the aircraft's return signal and locked on. No mistaking that blip.

"Radar contact, Captain. Aircraft heading straight over us. Spectral return pattern matches a four-engine turbo-prop. Bearing one-three-five degrees. Range: two-zero miles. Altitude: five thousand feet and climbing. Speed's pushing two hundred knots."

"Radio, say again. One aircraft? One aircraft only?"

"Aye, Captain. Designate radar contact Romeo One."

"Very well. Activate laser range finder. Illuminate Romeo One."

"Aye, aye, Captain." The radio operator clicked an icon labeled "Range Finder," and a picture containing gun-sight crosshairs instantly appeared on screen. Next, after selecting Romeo One, he dragged it across the screen, dropping it squarely centered on the crosshairs.

Topside, a pipe-shaped laser housing mounted on a hydraulic cylinder erupted upward from the periscope mast. When completely extended, the laser housing pivoted about its mast, pointing to—and continuously tracking—Romeo One. With the low-power laser in position, a short flash of light was emitted, reflected back from Romeo One, and its round-trip time measured. Ultimately, the round-trip time was converted to target range, accurate within inches. The entire process took less than forty-five seconds. "Target is acquired. Laser is locked."

"Torpedo room, make SAMs ready in all respects. Download tubes one and two. Designated target is Romeo One."

After tubes one and two had been flooded, both outer doors were opened and the tubes were ready. "Conn, torpedo. Proximity fuses set. Breech doors are sealed. Tubes one and two now ready to launch."

"Weapons, fire one."

Pressing the firing button on his launch control panel, the weapons officer directed high-pressure air on a piston, creating a water ram, thrusting the surface-to-air missile capsule forward into the sea. Once it was clear of the bow, heading toward the surface, the outer door closed.

Seconds later, the SAM breached the surface, erupting explosively from its watertight cocoon. Hearing ignition overhead, Mandrone punched his stopwatch. Flight time to target—approximately twenty-five seconds.

Prosecute, 12/31/2008, Wed., 11:05 P.M., 10:05 ZULU
Killer Orion

Painted flat gray, the P-3 looked ghostlike, but was almost impossible to see against the night sky. Inside, focusing only on the *Maine,* Scott gazed at their ClearWater display and summarized the situation for pilot Billy Ray Briggs. "Twenty-one missiles away and counting."

For Billy Ray, this bomb run was all that existed now. His life felt compressed into this single moment. Everything depended on how well he flew. Closing fast from the southeast, they were climbing to twenty-five thousand feet for their high-altitude drop. No matter what, he had to fly his plane to the release point.

With eyes caged on instruments, he watched the release marker advance steadily toward the *Maine* at 220 mph. Once the marker disappeared off screen, the Mk-101 nuclear-depth bomb would drop clear of the bomb bay, plummeting downward, allowing the Orion time to escape the blast.

Wheeling around to his final course, Billy Ray felt an odd, anesthetic-like dullness creeping over his senses.

"X-band illumination!" JT yelled from his countermeasures console back in the sensor cabin. "Signal's hot, sir. She'll see us."

Forward in the cockpit, Billy Ray hesitated, considering their situation.

"She musta surfaced," Scott prodded. "Nothing else's in the area."

"The *Maine* carries twenty-four missiles," Billy Ray insisted, "so what the hell happened?"

"It's not important." Her tone—matter of fact. "Get on the countermeasures."

"Could be a fire onboard, or maybe they ran outta targets," Rusty guessed. "If they heard our radio chatter, maybe they know we're coming. Who knows?"

"I know one thing," JT whined. "We got our ass hanging out up here, man. We're freaking exposed as all get out!"

"X-band warning's important," Scott insisted dryly. "Get on your countermeasures."

"Take it, Rusty," Billy Ray snapped. *Give me a freakin break!*

Rusty began barking orders. "JT, standby countermeasures. Activate broadband jammer on my signal. Standby chaff. Standby flares."

"Radar, pinpoint the source. She must have something showing above the surface."

Radar punched a few buttons, activating their ISAR (Inverse Synthetic Aperture Radar) image display. ISAR showed a detailed black-and-white image of an object, instead of just a blip, but some part of the sub—even if it's just the periscope—must be above the waterline. Seconds later, an image appeared on screen revealing two masts protruding above the water, trailing twin wakes.

Following a long pause, Billy Ray punched intercom. "Hey Radar, what gives?"

"Found her, Lieutenant . . . Two masts dead ahead."

"Listen up," Rusty interrupted, reading target data off his console. "JT, activate jammer. Radar, set detonation depth to three hundred feet. Target bearing dead ahead. Range: two-zero miles. Lieutenant, continue climb to twenty-five thousand for high-altitude drop. Copilot, keep your eyes glued to the surface."

Moving at two hundred twenty miles per hour, the P-3 shook, jerked, and rattled, climbing through the turbulent air at five thousand feet.

"Contact!" yelled the copilot. "Possible missile launch. Bright white flash off the surface . . . dead ahead!"

"SAM?" Billy Ray snapped.

"Could be . . . Lost visual . . . Can't find it."

An insane warble howled over the pilot's headset. "I think it's got us."

"SAM inbound, coming up our butt."

"Where? Where?" Scanning the sky for white rocket exhaust, Billy Ray fought back the urge to urinate.

"No trace."

"Bloody wonderful." From five thousand feet, the Orion was a slow, sitting duck with little altitude to trade and precious few options. "JT, punch chaff. Now, now, NOW!"

Countermeasures ham-fisted the chaff release. Small explosive charges ignited and four canisters filled with thin metallic strips flooded down into the slipstream.

Chaff, 12/31/2008, Wed., 11:06 P.M., 10:06 ZULU
USS *Maine*

"What'ya see on radar?"

"Countermeasures, Captain. Jammer's hot and probable chaff; sector's washed out—filled with it."

Mandrone watched the exhaust plume trail off on screen. Seconds later, a bright flash appeared on their periscope monitor. "Radar?"

"Lost in the chaff, sir. Can't say for sure."

Yank and Bank, 12/31/2008, Wed., 11:07 P.M., 10:07 ZULU
Killer Orion

"Hold on to your butts." Billy Ray jammed the throttles forward to the stops, pitching the Orion's nose up, rolling wing over behind the chaff cloud. *Hang on baby—give, give.* Both pilot and copilot knew they were stressing the airframe beyond its elastic limit, pulling Gs their aircraft was never designed to sustain.

A one-inch circle popped up as Radar frantically punched buttons under his radar screen. If the submarine remained within the circle, the weapon would vaporize the target.

"Mark target position now . . . now . . . NOW!" Radar barked over intercom.

"Negative! Negative!" yelled the copilot, eyes racing frantically across his flight controls, hands touching every switch. Moments later, he found it. "Closing bomb bay doors NOW!"

Suddenly, the black night sky lit up with a blinding flash, followed immediately by the sound of an explosion. The Orion shuddered forward with a lunge as an explosive shock wave passed over them, leaving in its wake fire and ruin. One bomb bay door was blown away. The other dangled precariously, flopping unconstrained about its hinges.

"Fire!" The lieutenant heard a panicky voice over the intercom—sounded like JT.

Smoke from electrical fires filled the rear cabin, flooding in from shorted bomb bay cabling and damaged jamming equipment. Grabbing an extinguisher, JT smothered the flames with dense foam.

"Three's burning," the copilot snapped, pointing out the window. A cadre of failure and alarm lights blazed wall-to-wall. "Losing hydraulic pressure."

"Killing three. Cut over backup hydraulics." Punching his throat mike, the pilot continued. "Rusty, damage control."

Silence.

"Rusty?"

A pause.

JT put down his extinguisher, holding on with each step, maneuvering forward through the cabin to Rusty's station. First thing he noticed, Rusty lay face down on his desk, arms limp, dangling at his side. JT touched his shoulder gently at first, then firmly. No response. Pulling Rusty back by the shoulder, JT noticed his head remained limp, flopping about his neck. His desk, clearly visible now, was covered by a thick pool of blood. Spilling over, it saturated Rusty's flight suit, then dripped to the floor.

Gently, JT lifted Rusty's head with his hand, feeling a warm rush of his blood, gushing forward under pressure. Rusty was dead, his face blown away, but his heart fought on, refusing to give up.

At the touch of his face—a soft, bloody pulp—JT convulsed. Where Rusty's face had been, only a gooey cavity remained. JT examined his hand—coated in a dark, wet, sticky, viscous substance—dropped to his knees, and threw up on the floor.

The pilot heard gagging over the intercom. "JT?"

"Rusty's dead, Lieutenant." JT's voice broke.

"How 'bout you? Everyone else all right?"

A sob. "Something hit his head, Lieutenant; took his face clean off. There's a hole back here size'a my fist."

Suddenly, within the span of a two-second sweep, a distinctive peak shape appeared across Rusty's ECM threat screen. JT didn't need to look twice. He'd seen this signature before.

"X-band illumination, Lieutenant! They're looking for us again."

Burn Through, 12/31/2008, Wed., 11:08 P.M., 10:08 ZULU
USS *Maine*

"Radio, talk to me."

A long pause.

"Jammer's clear, Captain. Chaff cloud's breaking up. She's on the far side—pulling away."

"Lock laser on target. Illuminate Romeo One."

"Aye, aye, Captain. Romeo One is locked."

"Torpedo room, download tube two and make ready to fire."

Seconds later, "Tube two has been reconfigured, Captain, and is ready in all respects."

"Fire two." Seconds later, Mandrone watched a second missile exhaust plume streak off into the darkness.

Final Flight, 12/31/2008, Wed., 11:08 P.M., 10:08 ZULU
Killer Orion

Billy Ray saw it first, out of the corner of his eye—another white flash off the surface.

The cockpit crew frantically scanned the ink black sky below, knowing their best chance to avoid the surface-to-air missile was to pick it out of the darkness, then outmaneuver it. They saw nothing, as if the missile had disappeared off the face of the earth.

"JT, dump chaff, flairs, whatever ya got . . . now, now, NOW!"

A muffled sob.

"Punch it, JT! Punch it!"

"I got it." Scott heard Dale Tew's voice over the intercom, but it was already too late.

Suddenly, an insane warble racked their ears, and this time Billy Ray's bowels let go. When the red MISSILE light flashed, the Orion felt very fragile, vulnerable, and terribly exposed . . . a prisoner entombed in its own airspace, with no place to hide.

The copilot spoke without hope. "Ditch her."

"Chaff away! Jammer's busted!" Dale Tew screamed above the engine noise, struggling back to his station.

"Radio," Billy Ray snapped. "Send signal—we're going in." Dale Tew was already ahead of him.

The last thing Lieutenant Billy Ray Briggs would remember was a blinding, radiant white flash. He saw the light, but never heard the the explosion.

White Flash, 12/31/2008, Wed., 11:09 P.M., 10:09 ZULU
USS Maine

Seconds later came the bright white flash of an explosion followed by a secondary, lingering yellow fireball. "Radio, I think we got her."

"Kill confirmed, Captain. Romeo One is dead."

"Give me a three-sixty."

"All clear topside, Captain. Radar's clear horizon to horizon."

"Very well, our job's finished here." Mandrone lowered

both masts and protective sleeves, then began issuing orders to vacate the area with all possible speed, masking their escape from satellite eyes. "Diving Officer, hard down on the dive planes. Engine room, all ahead full."

As her screw spun up, a rooster tail spray fluoresced on the surface.

Survival, 12/31/2008, Wed., 11:09 P.M., 10:09 ZULU
Killer Orion

Airborne shrapnel gouged holes in the Plexiglas window on his side of the plane. One tiny fragment penetrated Billy Ray's neck, piercing his carotid artery, exiting below the ear. A second, larger fragment shattered his left arm, ricocheted off his rib, then ultimately lodged in his lung.

Grabbing his neck with his right hand, Billy Ray slumped forward against the yoke, shoving the Orion into a dive.

Stunned by the blast, Scott looked at the pilot, failing at first to grasp what had happened. Over the intercom she heard gurgling punctuated by JT's screams. Time seemed to stand still until she heard Billy Ray's voice.

"I'm hit," he gurgled into his throat mike, coughing, spitting up blood. When she saw blood spurting between his fingers, she knew what to do.

She looked to the copilot for help, but he was out cold. His eyes were open, bulging out, staring into space. No way to judge the extent of his injuries now.

With two engines feathered, and the Orion plummeting downward in a suicide dive, Scott worked her way behind Billy Ray, pulling him upright against the hard back of his seat. He clutched her arm firmly, heaving himself up and out of the way, then collapsed in a pool of blood on the floor, both eyes rolled back in their sockets.

Checking her instruments, she saw that the needle on the airspeed indicator quivered at four hundred knots, and she nearly panicked. Reflections off the ocean's surface were coming up fast.

"Strap in tight!" she yelled over the intercom. Her shoulder harness engaged and held her firmly against the seat back. *Now reduce your airspeed, and fly the plane!* She had to pull out without shearing off the wings. She couldn't know how much stress her wounded P-3 would take, but knew to go with her gut.

Instinctively, she grabbed both active throttles, pulling them back through the taxi range, across the detent to maximum reverse, hard against the stops. Within seconds, the pitch of both propellers turned backwards, delivering the maximum reverse thrust—2,770 shaft horsepower— each Allison could muster. With almost unimaginable force, Scott felt herself thrown forward, slung off the seat, cut by the straps. The effect of sudden reverse thrust during their terminal speed dive was profound. Though the roar from the big Allison turboprop engines was deafening, they held together, slowing the plane with gut-wrenching deceleration.

Unyielding, Scott grasped the yoke, pulling it slowly to her chest, leveling the plane at two hundred feet as their airspeed dropped below one hundred fifty. Satisfied, she eased forward on the throttles and took account of the plane. Its right wing had a tendency to drop, but she countered with trim, and the plane seemed to right itself.

Under the red lights flashing in the cockpit, Scott noticed black bloodstains covering her flight suit where Billy Ray had grabbed her. Keeping one hand on the yoke, she reached for the pilot, searching for his wounds. Blood spurted from his neck and below his ear, but he was still alive. She couldn't reach the copilot on the far side of the cockpit, but noticed both his arms limp, dangling. She engaged the autopilot, hoping to free herself and help him. For a moment the system flashed green, giving a glimmer of hope, but something was busted somewhere. Green turned red when the autopilot failed to hold the plane straight and level. After one best effort attempt, the autopilot disengaged and Scott smelled smoke tainted by the distinctive odor of Bakelite burning—telltale signs of an electrical fire. She couldn't see the fire spreading behind the cockpit instrument panel but its symptoms were becoming all too evident. Green lights turned red, red lights went dark. Instruments and alarm lights were dropping off line like flies, failing one by one, losing power.

Recognizing she needed help, Scott glanced again at her instruments. The plane wouldn't fly itself and she couldn't be distracted now. Cold, certain death raced by below and she knew they'd get no second chances.

She keyed her throat mike. "Tristan, we've got two injured in the cockpit. Can you come forward?"

"Be right there" echoed over the intercom. "The damage is extensive back here but the fire's out." He'd been completely silent through their ordeal, and Scott was relieved to hear his voice.

"And Rusty?"

"We can't do anything for him now."

Another quick glance at the fuel gauges told Scott they were still in big trouble. She keyed her mike and began rattling off orders.

"Dale, we're leaking fuel like a sieve. Radio our position and stay strapped in, we're gonna get wet. JT, position both rafts and our first aid kit by the emergency exit over the wing, and step on it. We can't stay aloft much longer."

"What's the point? We're shark chum, man. We'll all wind up like Rusty."

Something finally snapped inside Scott. "Put a lid on it! You do your job, we'll get rescued before anyone knows we're missing."

JT looked across the isle. Dale nodded an affirmative from behind the radio set. "*Topeka*'s eight hours away."

"Rescue, well-uh . . . good idea." JT nodded his head, liking the way it sounded out loud. "I'm on it, Captain."

"Tristan, how about moving our wounded aft. Once they're set, strap 'em down and get your life preserver on. We're gonna need 'em."

"I'll agree with you there," Tristan paused. "I never learned to swim."

Over the next few minutes, Scott brought the plane down slowly to a sea skimmer altitude, twenty feet above the ocean swells.

Checking her airspeed, she decided to dirty up the control surfaces, using her flaps like air brakes, increasing the plane's drag to slow it down. To safely ditch the plane, she had to further reduce airspeed, but her cockpit was still glowing red with alarms. From all accounts, the flaps were undamaged, but Scott couldn't be sure.

Holding her breath, she said a prayer as she dirtied the plane, extending the main flaps first, a few degrees at the time. Lockheed would have been proud, and rightfully so. As both sets of flaps ran out in unison, the aircraft slowed, bucking hard against the turbulence, nevertheless staying stable all the while. With flaps fully extended, she pulled back harder on the yoke, slowly bringing the nose up. The Orion buffeted and jerked, but kept flying in preparation for final touchdown.

Scott couldn't imagine any better way to ditch her, so she skimmed the surface, slowing the plane, nose high, until it stalled. About the time she felt her controls go slack, she pitched the nose up sharply and the Orion fell out of the sky, slipping down tail boom first, skidding to an eventual belly flop. Her subsequent slide wasn't pretty, but aside from a few stiff backs from the impact, no one else was hurt.

A crash landing on twenty-foot seas in the pitch-black of night is a nightmarishly frightening experience for anyone lucky enough to live through it. Fear comes with catastrophic loss of electrical power, total darkness, and the onrush of cold seawater. That feeling of being alone, trapped inside a tube, unable to find your way out; a horrible way to die.

A second equally frightening characteristic about water landings is how fast an aircraft sinks. Three minutes after the Orion skidded to a stop, the crew were clearing the aircraft. Four minutes after touchdown, the Orion slipped beneath the surface without a trace.

It wasn't long before Scott heard the drone of their partner P-3 approaching. After marking her position with flares, the second P-3 began methodically lining the area with sonobuoys.

Three members of the Orion's crew were dead, another near death, but seven survived the ordeal.

Forward in their life raft, Scott applied pressure to the tiny punctures in Billy Ray's neck while Tristan immobilized his shattered arm. Trembling with cold from the wind and ocean spray, JT held the flashlight while Dale tended the emergency radio beacon. He, more than anyone, was optimistic. Their beacon was working perfectly and help was on the way. For a bad situation, their prospects seemed pretty bright, at least for now.

Occasionally, between twenty-foot swells, Scott glimpsed marker lights from the second raft astern. It was a devastating sight. Rusty, the copilot, and the flight engineer lay dead along with three survivors she didn't know very well—Radar, the MAD operator, and the flight technician. She grieved for the dead and deliberately focused on helping the living. Still, in spite of her best efforts, she felt the very pulse of Billy Ray's life ebbing away, her ungloved hand sticky with blood.

Who is this woman? Tristan gazed at Scott in wonder. *Young face, old eyes,* he thought. *Probably seen more death than most.*

Constant tension had drained her, exhaustion overwhelmed her, everyone underestimated her, but somehow she survived. "What're you thinking?" he prodded gently.

Scott's expression never wavered. When she replied, her voice was distant and detached. "You don't want to know."

"No, I'm serious. I don't have any idea what's on your mind."

"You're not going to like it, but you'd figure it out for yourself soon enough anyway."

"Try me."

Scott let out a tired sigh, then struggled to convey her concern clearly. "We're pitted against one of the most formidable adversaries in the world."

Tristan reflected on the events of the past few days, reluctantly appreciating the skill, cunning, and utter ruthlessness of their nemesis. "I agree with your appraisal, Scotty. He's certainly kept us scrambling so far."

"As long as he controls the *Maine,*" she continued, "he's one of the most powerful people on earth."

"Undeniably."

"Well then," she pointed toward the dark horizon, "you see that P-3?"

Tristan saw its lights; JT's ears perked up.

"If they locate the *Maine*," she paused, making eye contact with Tristan, "we're expendable."

"Right, right. And I was gettin' short too," JT whined, waving his flashlight.

After a long pause, Tristan wiped his brow and sighed. "Yes, it follows."

"I underestimated him once," Scott added quietly, "but never again."

"What are their chances?" Tristan asked. "Think they'll find him?"

"They've got a good starting point to work from," Scott observed objectively. "JT, whaddaya think?"

"I sure as hell hope not," he responded with a knee jerk. A few moments later, he continued, thinking out loud. "Yeah . . . yeah, right. It's real deep here . . . and they had time. If that skipper's smart, he could dive below the layer, make a run for it, and they'd never find him, not with a single P-3 anyway."

"He's smart, and he's clearly not suicidal," Scott concluded. "I'd give him the benefit of the doubt."

Minutes later, Scott surveyed her situation, feeling lucky to be alive. "We never know when death will come," she lamented. "Life's so fragile, but we take it for granted every day, like we'll live forever."

It was almost as if Billy Ray heard her voice, woke up, and opened his eyes. She held his head gently in her lap as he struggled to speak, but couldn't form the words. Scott heard air rushing in, but only a gurgling sound emerged. Over the next few seconds, his eyes revealed a desperate desire to live, an eagerness to survive, and for a fleeting moment, she felt encouraged. He grabbed her arm, but his strength faltered quickly. His grip fell slack, his breathing stilled, then in the blink of an eye, he was gone.

She saw his eyes change when it happened. That spark of life extinguished; in its place a cold, gray, unfocused gaze, an empty look that's left after the soul is gone.

Watching life ebb from Billy Ray, seeing how quickly life disappeared, Scott was changed by those few seconds, changed by how desperately he tried to hold on.

She'd remember that look in his eyes for the rest of her life and, from that moment forward, vowed to live every day like it was her last.

CHAPTER NINETEEN

Tough Words, 12/31/2008, Wed., 05:15 A.M., 10:15 ZULU
White House

It came as no surprise that the President and his staff had been asleep when the call came. The last report they'd been given assured them all that everything that could be done was being done to locate and rescue the crew of the USS *Maine*. The water was deep though, and there was little hope the crew would be found alive. Yes, there was the possibility she'd been hijacked, but for practical purposes, the probability was so small, it was considered impossible. After all, in the history of the American Navy, no one had ever hijacked a nuclear submarine. There were numerous, well-thought-out safeguards in place to prevent it. Besides, no one except the U.S. Navy even knew where they were at any given moment, and sometimes even they weren't sure.

But the reality was a U.S. Navy nuclear-guided missile submarine had been hijacked, and American nuclear-tipped missiles were in the air now, bound for targets unknown. The President must be told.

The single most telling experience on the President's résumé was what was missing. The commander in chief of the United States Armed Services had never served a single day in the military in his entire life, and more troubling than this, he seemed almost proud of it. He'd never experienced the gut-wrenching fear that comes when people you don't know start shooting at you, yet he had few reservations about risking the lives of others.

In all fairness, he was a good economic leader during peacetime, but in times of crisis, the man lacked moral integrity; he didn't know what he believed beyond his polls and profit-loss statements. You might risk a fraction of your life savings on a man of his caliber, but you'd never risk the lives of your children. When political decisions become matters of life and death, moral principles of decency must take precedence over the ledger.

This President, like many modern-day American presidents, had spent his life accumulating wealth, power, and possessions. He was a businessman by profession, an accountant by training, and instinctively felt ill at ease if the numbers didn't add up.

Well, tonight, they didn't add up, but like all consummate politicians, he was also a fine actor.

Given a good script, he could inspire confidence from even the most skeptical military leadership. Regrettably, tonight there was no script, and as he'd come to find out, there was no viable plan. There was only the chaos of the moment, lots of questions, great oceans of conjecture, but no definitive answers.

The White House conference call had been set up hurriedly. The President was cold, bleary eyed, sitting in his robe by the speakerphone in the Oval Office. At this moment, he felt more like a prisoner in solitary confinement than the President of the United States. Surrounding him, poised at every entrance to the room, stood secret service men to protect him, but for the immediate problem at hand, they were no help at all.

Looking around the room, waiting for the phone to ring,

the President felt like the loneliest man on the face of the
earth. One secret service man offered him coffee, but it had
tasted like muddy water mixed with warm milk. The President didn't know what to expect from this conference call,
but he knew no one would wake him at five o'clock in the
morning to tell him good news.

Finally, the phone rang. Participants on the call hurriedly identified themselves one by one, in rank order.
Those closest to the President identified themselves first,
and to his relief, his two most trusted advisors, Clive
Towles and Dr. Russ Singleton, were on the line. In addition to his national security advisor and secretary of
defense, the secretaries of the Air Force and state joined
the call with the CIA director, CINCPACFLT, Admiral
Eastwood, and two voices the President didn't recognize
from USSPACECOM, General Robert Craven and Colonel
Slim Mason.

The President was taking names and organizations
down on paper as meeting introductions progressed from
around the country. He'd learned years ago that sometimes
it wasn't important what was said, one need only know
who attended a meeting to determine its significance. Considering the time of the conference call, and those present,
the President concluded this meeting was a show-stopper.
National security must be at stake.

Once introductions drew to a close, the President
opened without even a hint of grace. "I don't have an
agenda for this meeting, gentlemen, but let me assure you,
I'm not here to hear myself talk. What's the problem?"

There was dead silence over the line for a moment, then
Dr. Singleton, the secretary of defense, made his opening
remarks setting the tone for the meeting. "It's the *Maine,*
Mr. President. We've experienced one horrific turn of
events in the Pacific."

A pause. The President did not speak.

"We have a nuclear missile crisis on our hands, Mr. President, and time is of the essence. Our problem is to determine the right thing to do in a matter of minutes. Our agenda's restricted to three items, and unless you steer the conversation outside these areas, our discussion will be limited to these points. First, Colonel Mason will quickly summarize what's happened. Next, we must infer what the Russians're thinking and how they'll respond. Finally, we must decide what we're going to do, then execute. Colonel Mason knows more about this situation than anyone and I've asked him and General Craven to bring us up to speed. Colonel, if you would, please tell the President what we know and answer any questions as honestly as you can. Tell him what you think, but keep it short. This is not the time for missed or unspoken communication."

From his office inside USSPACECOM headquarters, Colonel Mason reluctantly stepped up to the task. In his hand he held a few handwritten notes, everything he'd organized in advance for his first meeting with the President. Maybe in his heart he knew it was coming, but the reality was, he'd been given less than five minutes to prepare. As ClearWater project director, Mason had become accustomed to Washington looking over his shoulder, but this kind of high-pressure visibility he could do without. "Mr. President, I regret to inform you the *Maine* has been hijacked and fifteen of our latest nuclear-tipped missiles are in the air, presumably armed, bound for destinations unknown."

Mason paused, waiting for some audible feedback, some sense his words were finding traction.

The President's initial reaction could best be described as stunned, but after a few moments, the terrifying consequences of Mason's statement began to sink in. The President felt a kaleidoscope of emotions, covering the full spectrum from fear to rage, but as a matter of opening strategy, he elected to simply say nothing. He sensed his blood pressure rising, probably shooting through the roof, but for now, he'd listen to what the colonel had to say.

"At this point, the *Maine* has launched a total of twenty-three missiles, twenty-one nuclear-tipped plus two conventional sea-to-air. Six nuclear-tipped missiles have reached their targets, resulting in the loss of the *Cheyenne,* one of our Los Angeles–class, fast-attack submarines. So far, it seems the *Maine*'s skipper's not taking any chances, allocating three missiles per target. As it turned out, another fast attack, the *Topeka,* was also the target of a three-missile salvo, but warned in advance, she was able to avert destruction."

Mason heard the President utter a muffled "Thank God" over the speakerphone, then he continued.

"Two sea-to-air missiles also found their mark, bringing down one of our P-3 Orion aircraft."

"How many dead so far?" the President queried. Over the speakerphone, his voice sounded perplexingly detached, something like Dragnet's Seargent Joe Friday, *Just the facts, ma'am.*

"These numbers haven't been confirmed, but we expect all aboard the *Cheyenne,* one hundred thirty-three men, were lost. We believe there were some survivors from the P-3; however, at this point, we can't say who or how many. Please understand, Mr. President, those remaining airborne missiles are our immediate problem. We don't know where they're going, but in all probability, they're heading for naval targets. Considering the missile-torpedo nature of the weapons, we believe any naval vessel, any surface ship, possibly any submarine, within the *Maine*'s two-thousand-mile reach could be in peril."

At this moment, the President was like a powder keg.

"We have some fix on these missiles, right? We can shoot 'em down, can't we?"

"We can't detect these missiles without special bi-static radar, sir. We don't know where they are. They could strike anywhere in a twelve-and-a-half-million-square-mile area. They're low cross-section sea skimmers and nothing we've got in our inventory today can track these missiles over such a vast span of ocean as this."

Mason's answer provided the spark that set him off.

"Could they be headed for land?" the President demanded bitterly.

Mason cleared his throat. "Yes, sir. They could detonate over any land target within a two-thousand-mile radius of their launch position."

Inside the Oval Office, a map centered near the international date line off Russia's Kamchatka Peninsula flashed on the President's television screen. Overlaying the map, a four-thousand-mile-diameter circle revealed possible targets. Mainland China lay on the outermost fringes, but clearly the Kamchatka Peninsula, Alaska, and Japan were in immediate danger. Superimposed over each country were separate countdown timers, ticking off the seconds.

"Unless we take action now, we're powerless to stop them, Mr. President," General Craven added. "We have no viable missile defense system. Neither does China, Japan, or Russia for that matter. We're at the mercy of the renegades who targeted our missiles against us."

"What's the Russian reaction?"

"They haven't been told officially, Mr. President, but they know something's up. So do the Chinese. Their shoreline's lit up like a Christmas tree. Normally, they blink their radars on then disappear off the air, but not this time.

Radars're going active and staying active across the whole of China, Russia, and the Kamchatka Peninsula."

"You're telling me millions of innocent people could be wiped off the face of the earth by our own weapons and we're defenseless, powerless to do anything about it!"

"Pardon me, Mr. President, but we're getting off track here," Mason offered almost apologetically. "I believe naval targets are most likely at greatest risk. I say this in light of what's happened. So far, they've only gone after naval targets. Our long-range, deep-water submarine communications have been sabotaged, and the fact is, they held back three missiles. If these renegades were bent on world destruction, they would've launched everything they had. I think they ran out of targets, Mr. President; in fact, I'm afraid our own missile submarines could be at greatest risk, but it's only a hunch. We haven't uncovered any hard evidence to support my suspicion, but if ClearWater's been compromised, it's possible."

"Originally, I'd assumed our ELF transmitters were attacked either as a diversion, or to disrupt submarine communications," Admiral Eastwood added, supporting Mason's suspicion.

"When they lost their comm link," Mason continued, "we detected our missile submarine's coming shallow to establish VLF communication."

"That behavior is consistent with what we'd expect. They're obliged to reestablish communications with their command authority." Following Admiral Eastwood's lead, the commander of the Pacific fleet acknowledged Mason's observation as well founded. Although never spoken, CINCPACFLT, Eastwood, and Craven were aligning themselves behind Mason because they knew the President would be looking for consensus.

The call went silent for a few moments, then Clive Towles, the President's closest council and national security advisor, conceded Mason's point. "Insufficient data to form any solid conclusion, but what you suggest makes sense. It does answer a lot of questions."

Once his national security advisor put the issue of Mason's credibility to bed, the President asked the obvious question.

"How long before the crisis comes? How long until these missiles could penetrate Russian airspace?"

Mason checked his watch, then whipped off some fast mental arithmetic to double-check the countdown timers on screen. "The timers on your screen are correct, Mr. President. Fifty-one minutes, thirty-six seconds minimum to the Kamchatka Peninsula."

Mason heard a primitive grunt, as if the President had been punched in the solar plexus.

I could kick myself for not seeing this coming, Mason thought. *Classic data shock, too much information too fast. I thought the timers were obvious, but did I miss the mark or what? At least he's beginning to comprehend the immediacy of the crisis and that's a good sign.*

The President requested a sanity check after studying the numbers flashing on screen. "Two hours one minute to the Alaskan coastline?"

"Yes, sir, but understand Alaska's not the problem. Neither is Japan. I'm told we've got 'em both covered. A small percentage of China's navy's at risk, possibly some elements of her submarine fleet, but Russia's the problem."

"I don't follow you, Colonel. Tokyo must be a target."

"Let me backfill here quickly, Mr. President." General Craven said. "I'm pretty close to what's happened with air defense. In three hours, twenty minutes, these missiles could be over Tokyo, but we're taking action now to head off disaster. Japan's with us on this, they're already on alert. Everything they've got that could help's in the air. Everything we've got's been scrambled. We've got time and resources, we can defend Japan. Alaska is ditto. Mainland China's out of range, so's most of her fleet. Believe me, Russia's the problem here."

"Gentleman." The President's eyes narrowed. "We have a crisis, we have a decision to make, and no time to socialize it with anyone. You'd better have one helluva plan." His tone was one of subdued rage.

"We have four alternatives, Mr. President," Clive Towles offered. "General Craven and Colonel Mason have one proposal, but the War Plans Division of the Defense Department has studied this accident scenario at length and recommends a different course of action."

"Considering we've had a nuclear mishap, what do our defense planners recommend?"

"Scramble our forces around the globe immediately, Mr. President. Come to DEFCON One." The secretary of the Air Force was emphatic on this point. *The Navy screwed up and, as usual, Air Force to the rescue—standard operating procedure.*

"As I understand it, the Russians can detect our missile launches," Mason said grimly. "Don't they know our missiles are already airborne? Won't they consider our move to DEFCON One a prelude to war?"

"The colonel's point should be considered," General Craven and Admiral Eastwood agreed. "We know they detected the nuclear detonation which killed the *Cheyenne*. Unless they're sleeping, they detected the conventional explosions set off by the *Topeka*, but we can't be sure." Instantly, voices over the speakerphone welled up in support.

"We have clear consensus with your concern, Colonel

Mason," Clive prompted. "Please answer the question, Mr. Secretary."

The secretary of the Air Force conceded without acknowledging the significance of Mason's observation.

"Unless they're behind this hijacking," Dr. Singleton added, "they have no better idea where those missiles are headed than we do."

"You've hit on the crux of our dilemma," Clive observed. There was an intriguing sense of revelation in his voice. "Are the Russians behind this hijacking? Can they be trusted?"

"Gentlemen, let me remind you that they insisted hijacking was a strong possibility from the beginning." Dr. Singleton's Southern accent broke through. "Their satellite pics plainly showed the *Kansong* with her port side doors open, but we didn't trust 'em. We preferred to believe the photographs had been doctored. The possibility that one of our submarines, one of our finest submarines, had been hijacked was absolutely unthinkable."

"Nevertheless, they have the technology," the Air Force secretary countered.

"We believe they have technology which renders the ocean transparent to a depth of one hundred fifty meters, but it's not fully deployed," the CIA director added, following the secretary's lead. "It is possible they could have known where the *Maine* was located off their coastline. It stands to reason, if we could detect her, they could detect her as well."

Building on this groundwork, the secretary of the Air Force laid DoD's cornerstone. "The War Department understood this, Mr. President, and as a result they believed Russia was behind this hijacking from day one. Think about it. If the Russians hijacked the *Maine*, they'd use it against us, don't kid yourself. They'd stage this whole thing to make it look like our accident, and the first thing they'd do is take out our missile boats, sink them before we can launch our retaliatory strike. It all adds up, Mr. President. Colonel Mason said it himself, our own missile boats are at greatest risk. They'd stage it such that we fired first; that'd give 'em all the excuse they'd need. If we approach 'em with our tail tucked between our legs, we'll be playing into their hands. I tell you, Mr. President, it's a trap. They know we'd never intentionally strike first. They staged this hijacking to throw us off balance, to make us vulnerable to a first strike."

There was a rise in background noise over the conference line, still one voice broke through. "The Cold War's over."

Dumbfounded, not knowing what to say or do, the President sat silent a few moments. Everything added up, but nothing added up. He didn't know what to believe.

Clive Towles took advantage of the silence to ask the obvious. "Do we have any evidence the Russians are behind this?"

"As of this moment, we have no evidence whatsoever who's behind this hijacking and to state otherwise is an outright lie." Admiral Eastwood was adamant regarding this point. "We don't believe any terrorist organization is behind it, but we have no legitimate reason to convict the Russians."

"They have the technology, they have the resources, and they have the organization," the Air Force secretary pointed out evenly.

"And the Chinese do not," the CIA director added, "not yet . . ."

"Bullshit!" Admiral Eastwood interrupted. "So do we, but we don't use them to hijack Russian missile boats and start a nuclear war!"

"The Russians don't want to start a nuclear war with us," the secretary of state reasoned analytically. "Neither do the Chinese. We've got billions invested in both countries covering everything from burgers to high-tech factories. We're one of the biggest markets they've got and one of their biggest investors. There's no value proposition in it for them."

Hearing these words, the President felt as if a heavy cloud had lifted. "It's the economics. You don't kill a good customer."

"And one other thing," the secretary of state added. "Russia knows we lost the *Maine,* that's a fact. The entire international community knows this."

"Did they really believe we lost her?" the President asked.

"I think so, sir. We're turning cartwheels to find her. Japan and Britain are involved in the search. Russia showed us their satellite recon and offered to help, so'd China."

"Good." Mason breathed a quiet sigh of relief. "That might be useful if the time comes."

"For now, I think we should give Russia and China the benefit of the doubt," Clive Towles concluded, knowing the President would be waiting for his judgment.

"I concur," Dr. Singleton said simply, then he pressed forward with his own analysis. "If we move to DEFCON One, they'd be puzzled, Mr. President, but the Russians wouldn't let our action go unchecked, and understand, if they go on alert, the Chinese will follow. In all probability, they would consider our move to DEFCON One a prelude to war, and believe me, they'll goose up their own defensive posture, moving us three notches closer to nuclear war. In this respect, they're no different than we are. When they increase their readiness, we follow in lockstep."

"But say we go to DEFCON One, what then?" The President liked the idea of DEFCON One; it sounded conservative, like the safest thing to do.

"If our missiles enter Russian airspace," the secretary of the Air Force explained, "we have three options—first-strike, fail-safe, or do-nothing. The War Department recommends first-strike and I agree, it minimizes our losses. Launch an all-out strike immediately before they can retaliate. Otherwise, we're defenseless."

Stupefied, the President's jaw fell slack. He couldn't believe what he was hearing. Suddenly, DEFCON One didn't sound so safe anymore.

"This is insanity," the secretary of state erupted in a knee jerk. "We won the Cold War."

Admiral Eastwood's eyes widened, but he recovered. "You're proposing Armageddon."

Expecting this recommendation would surface eventually, Clive was surprised it emerged so quickly. Nevertheless, he'd thought through his reply in advance and quietly, concisely articulated what he believed. "Americans are not mass murderers. We don't annihilate millions of people because we can't defend ourselves against our own weapons."

"The Russians know this," the secretary of the Air Force cautioned. "Their plans may depend on it."

"It's an axiom," Clive replied, his voice was tougher. "It's not negotiable."

Hearing these words, the President knew he could sell that reasoning to anyone and prodded the conversation forward. "Next option."

Instinctively, the secretary of the Air Force was a fighter, but at this juncture, he decided not to press. First-strike held academic appeal, it represented DoD's party line, but mass destruction is something no one in his right mind fights for with passion. "The fail-safe alternative offers an eye for an eye, Mr. President. We had an accident; accident's happen right? So we sacrifice comparable cities, like in the novel. They lose Moscow, we sacrifice New York."

The silence that followed lasted almost forty seconds, then Dr. Singleton spoke quietly. "Work around it, people."

"Wheeler warned this could happen fifty years ago," General Craven acknowledged.

"Yeah, but that was then and this is now," the secretary of state stated in disbelief. "Economics, Chernobyl, and Reagan won the Cold War. I thought fail-safe and this mutually assured destruction insanity were supposed to be behind us."

"They have the capability to wipe us off the face of the earth," the SECDEF warned. "Their submarine-launched ICBMs may be targeted against us in a matter of minutes."

"You can't make this stuff up," Mason reasoned softly. "Real life always plays out stranger than fiction."

"I believe we're all familiar with the fail-safe alternative," Clive concluded somberly. Having read the Burdick Wheeler novel, the majority of those on the conference call were painfully aware of this realistically plausible scenario. "The similarities between our situation and *Fail-Safe* are almost unbelievable. We may need to invoke this alternative, or possibly offer U.S. territory in trade, but I recommend we consider these only as a last resort."

"I agree," Dr. Singleton said. Consensus was reached on this point in a matter of seconds.

"Next option," the President prompted. "The clock's running."

"We could do nothing at all, Mr. President. Wait and see what happens."

"These alternatives offer the President no viable options," the national security advisor growled.

Unseen by anyone, the lines in Mason's face, especially those around his mouth, deepened. "We're gambling with the lives of millions of people. The future of everyone and everything we care about hinge on the decisions we make here, now. I believe we have an additional alternative, Mr. President. We've got bi-static look-down radar systems that can track these missiles at close range. We could help the Russians find 'em, possibly shoot 'em down."

"Sort of a look-down, shoot-down alternative," the Air Force secretary quipped sarcastically, checking his computer screen. "You've got forty-eight minutes."

"I thought of it as lending a hand, Mr. Secretary, but you're right about the time. It may be insurmountable."

"Well intentioned, but naïve, Colonel. You don't know the Russian mind. They're proud people. They'd never allow armed American planes in their airspace. Mark my words, it won't happen, not in my lifetime."

"Mr. Secretary, somehow, someone's got to defend their coastline plus their navy. I'm talking about their missile boat bastions and any surface fleet in missile range. If their air cover can't defend their fleet against a missile-torpedo attack, they'd better get out of the way. Our best estimates have these missiles targeting fixed positions, and these advanced torpedoes can search a twenty-mile radius. Best case, the Russians move twenty miles any direction and they're out of danger."

"My staff agrees with the colonel's assessment, Mr. President." The commander in chief of the Pacific fleet summarized their position. "Desperate situations demand desperate measures. Everything we've got in the *Maine*'s reach is already on alert, either braced for a missile-torpedo attack or racing at flank speed to get out of the way."

"Right now, the Russians're wondering what we're up to," CINCPACFLT concluded, "and without additional information, their generals will react exactly the way I would. They'll attack first and ask questions later. At the very least, we should call them and spell out the situation. We'd expect no less from them."

A pause.

"Call 'em, see if they go for it," Dr. Singleton said softly, casting his lot with the admiral's camp.

"I'm supposed to call the Russian President and tell him in forty-eight minutes he could have American nuclear-tipped cruise missiles breaching Russian airspace." The President rubbed his hair and scrunched his face into a scowl. "What does the Department of Defense recommend?"

The secretary of the Air Force hesitated, then spoke with noticeably less confidence, as if he were repeating the party line. "DEFCON One; first-strike."

"America will never strike first as long as you're President." Clive's voice cut in with authority regarding this fundamental matter of principle.

The President acknowledged his national security advisor's point, then to his surprise, Colonel Mason summarized his pitch.

As Mason spoke, his confidence increased with every word. "I urge you to call the President Czernienko and explain our situation, Mr. President. Spell out the fail-safe option up front, convince him we're in earnest, then offer to lend a hand. And no DEFCON One. Remember, these missiles may not be heading into Russian airspace at all." In truth, it wasn't much of a plan, only a series of hunches, but with missiles possibly only minutes away from Russian airspace, Mason's proposal represented the least of all possible evils.

"The colonel could be right, Mr. President," Clive agreed. "This problem could solve itself."

Unconvinced, the President grimaced, but said nothing.

Plowing ahead, Clive Towles addressed the group in a tone that said *keep it short*. "Gentlemen, is there anything else that should be said?"

The line fell silent, seemingly without end. Though unspoken, everyone knew the time had come and understood that in all probability their decision would be irrevocable.

"Mr. President, I believe we're now in agreement." Clive pushed for closure. "I move we adopt the colonel's proposal and our acceptance should be unanimous."

There was no further discussion.

"I think we're ready to talk to the President Czernienko," Clive prodded.

There was a sigh over the line, then the President acknowledged his council's advice. "Clive, you and Russ pick up your private line. The rest of you gentlemen, please stand by. We'll need you."

CHAPTER TWENTY

The Call, 12/31/2008, Wed., 05:26 A.M., 10:26 ZULU
White House

The President looked over the array of buttons on his phone, then pressed the one labeled "Operator." "I need to speak to President Czernienko immediately on a matter of utmost urgency."

"Yes, sir." Over the President's speakerphone, a series of telephone touch-tone sounds could be heard, followed immediately by a fast busy signal. The pattern repeated a second time with similar results. "His satellite phone is busy, Mr. President. So's his cell phone. For some reason, all Moscow's trunks are busy."

"What time is it in Moscow?"

"About one-thirty in the afternoon."

"Send him a priority message on his pager. Please request he communicate with me over our secure line. It's not as convenient, but it won't be busy."

In Washington, three to four minutes passed in silence, waiting for the Russian president to respond.

Suddenly, noise erupted over the speakerphone, the sound of telephones and alarm bells ringing nonstop in the background. Judging from the racket, Moscow sounded more like the floor of the New York stock exchange during a peak trading period. "Hello," barked a gruff voice. "This is President Czernienko."

"Hello," the operator said. A pause. "Hello, President Czernienko, can you hear me?" Background noise from Czernienko's Moscow office dominated the speakerphone connection at his end and the operator's voice couldn't break through. Clive, Russ, and the President could hear the operator and all the commotion in Moscow, but President Czernienko could not hear them. Having dealt with speakerphones and noisy rooms many times before, the operator instinctively pressed the pound key on his phone keypad three or four times. In Moscow, the Russian President heard the distinctive sound of a touch-tone phone.

"Someone is playing with buttons on your end," Czernienko said, then he hit the speakerphone mute key. Back in Washington, the line went quiet.

"The President of the United States is calling, President Czernienko," the operator said. "The President's national security advisor, Clive Towles, and secretary of defense Russ Singleton are also on the line. We are having trouble breaking through your speakerphone. Would you please pick up your handset?"

President Czernienko leaned forward and picked up the phone. "Say again. Who is on the line?" he requested abruptly. Clearly, this former naval admiral was accustomed to giving orders.

"Clive Towles and Dr. Russ Singleton," the President spoke for the first time. "My national security advisor and secretary of defense." Clive and Dr. Singleton introduced themselves briefly so Czernienko could recognize their voices.

"Why do you call?" Czernienko interrupted bluntly. Judging from the harshness in his voice, the man was already out of patience and overstressed. His voice implied no exchange of pleasantries, no getting to know you; no relationship, strictly an us-versus-them proposition.

"We need to discuss a very serious turn of events in the Pacific."

"You're calling about your missile attack and nuclear detonation off Kamchatka?" Czernienko's English was remarkably concise. "My experts informed me of this thirty-five minutes ago."

"Yes, and to inform you that this apparent attack is not of our making. It would be a mistake, a terrible mistake, to conclude the United States is behind this."

"You deny responsibility for this attack?"

"No, we take full responsibility for the situation, but we did not launch these missiles. This is an isolated incident involving the *Maine*; it is not part of any attack or war plan sponsored by the United States. It may be a problem which peacefully resolves itself, but we are deeply concerned. I urge you to not take any action which cannot be reversed. One of our submarines has been hijacked and we're calling to tell you everything we know about it. Time is short and it could have the most tragic consequences if this situation were misinterpreted or misunderstood."

For a moment, former Admiral Czernienko remembered his own security and technology concerns as a senior naval officer in the Russian navy. Even today, when he was the Russian president, technology changed faster than his people could keep up, and security concerns were considered passé. After a brief reflection, he spoke in an even voice. "We too have been concerned about submarine hijacking for many years. As we showed you, our satellite reconnaissance photographs suggested this possibility, but I wanted to hear what you had to say."

"My people are at a loss to explain how it happened, or why it happened, but we know fifteen nuclear-tipped cruise missiles remain in the air, each launched from a position approximately 725 miles east of Kamchatka."

"Hold for one minute. I understand time is short, but we here must move to another conference room. The speaker-phone is necessary; my generals must hear what you have to say."

"Very well, but please hurry."

Staring at the pendulum of the grandfather clock, the President waited, and waited an interminable amount of time.

"Clive," he said in a tired voice. "Cut to the chase; tell them what we know, the implications, and what they should do next. Either they'll believe us or they won't. There's no time for discussion, analysis, or fixing blame."

"I will do exactly that, Mr. President, and dear God, please let 'em trust us."

"I pray our missiles don't penetrate Russian airspace," Singleton stated flatly, without apology.

The President did not speak. All his life he'd done without God, never felt he needed Him until now.

"We'll do our best," Clive said, "that's all we can do, but in the final analysis, our fate's largely out of our hands. What we do's important, don't get me wrong, but whatever we do better be right. It all boils down to where those missiles go and how the Russians react. Think about it; how much of this situation's in our control?"

The President's mood shifted toward the morose with the each passing minute. Five minutes and twenty-eight seconds later, President Czernienko's voice cut in with authority.

"There is no time for introductions. Some of my staff were—how do you say it? They are good military men but had difficulty dealing with this volatile situation. We are ready now."

"The *Maine* is a renegade, she has launched her missiles," Clive spoke somberly, "and there is no time for analysis. In as little as thirty-eight minutes, American nuclear-tipped cruise missiles could begin penetrating Russian airspace."

An increase in background noise was punctuated by Czernienko's question. "What exactly do you mean?"

"We do not know the targets. We believe they're targeting naval vessels, but we can't be sure. They could detonate over land, that can't be ruled out completely, but we don't believe it likely. All I can tell you with absolute certainty is that this is a tragic mishap. It is not a trap or part of a larger strike. As you may already suspect, we have lost one aircraft, one attack submarine, and we almost lost a second."

"We suspected this but did not know for sure," Czernienko acknowledged.

"The target area is shown inside the circle on the map we sent you. We take responsibility for this accident; those are our missiles; we're trying to detect them and blow them out of the sky, but as you can see, the area is vast and our coverage is limited."

"Their missile's range is greater than we anticipated," a soft baritone voice observed quietly from Moscow.

"It's the latest, most fuel-efficient version we've got."

"How long can these missiles remain airborne?" the baritone asked.

"It varies with speed and altitude, but plan on four hours." Clive Towles checked his watch. "In three and a half hours, the missiles will have expended their fuel, but the torpedoes search a twenty-mile radius before they expend their fuel. I can't say how long they might search; I'm sure hours in their slow-hunt, fuel-conserve mode, but I'll find out." There was the muffled sound of a background conversation while Clive checked with Admiral Eastwood on the other line. "The length of time these torpedoes hunt depends on how they're programmed at time of launch. If they hunt nonstop, it's a matter of hours, but they may hunt for a period, then sleep for days, only to wake up when a known target, a recognized noise source, approaches."

"Is there any way to disable or destroy the weapon without setting off the nuclear warhead?" the baritone continued his query.

"Yes, there is. Our experts will convey this information to your people immediately."

"That is good," the voice concluded.

"But what if we fail to shoot them down?" Czernienko asked bluntly. "What if your missiles rain death down on Russian cities? What then, Mr. President?"

"We are prepared to do whatever we must do to avoid a nuclear exchange," the President said. "We offer immediate aid and reparations, U.S. territory, or if necessary, we are prepared to sacrifice comparable cities."

Over the conference line, there was a brief discussion in Russian from Moscow, then President Czernienko summarized their position. Clive only made out part of the conversation, but it sounded like President Czernienko's support was on the decline. "I understand. We would like to leave our options open until this situation has played out, however, if the time comes, Mr. President, Moscow will designate the comparable American city and its elimination must be immediate, within an hour."

A pause.

"Let's hope it doesn't come to that." Clive spoke for the President.

"What do you propose we do in the time we have remaining?" Czernienko asked, his tone final.

"I would like to cut to the chase, President Czernienko," Clive said. "Defend your coastline and your Navy, the missile boat bastions and any surface fleet in missile range. Get your air cover aloft and move your missile boats north, under the ice, until the danger has passed. If your air cover can't defend the fleet against a missile-torpedo attack, move them out of the way. We believe these missiles are targeting fixed positions so move 'em twenty miles or more and they'll be out of danger."

"Our Pacific fleet's doing the same thing." Dr. Singleton summarized. "Everything we've got in the *Maine*'s reach is already on alert, either braced for a missile-torpedo attack or racing at flank speed to get out of the way."

"We detected significant increases in air cover over both Japan and Alaska," the low baritone voice observed. "Is this the explanation?"

"It is."

Again, there was the noise of background conversation over the conference line, followed by the sound of movement as the Russian high command rushed out of the room to deploy their defensive forces.

"What are the chances you will detect and shoot down these missiles before they enter Russian airspace?"

"Very low. We've deployed a squadron of fleet defense forces east of Kamchatka; however your coast is vast and our defensive net has many holes. We ask permission to enter your airspace if necessary."

"Denied." There'd be no discussion, no negotiation. "If the missiles get past your fleet defense, our radars can detect them."

"That is true, but they're flying low. Our experts tell us you'll only detect them for the blink of an eye, then lose track of them."

"What is the possibility these missiles will get through?" Czernienko asked bluntly.

"I'm not sure I know what you mean," the President responded.

"What do your experts say? What are the chances these missiles may get past your defenses and ours?"

"I'll answer this one." Dr. Singleton spoke for the first time. "We've run through the simulations a thousand times, President Czernienko. If our missiles do enter Russian airspace, three out of four of the missiles will get through unless you can get over them. The missile's maximum radar cross-section exists looking down on its back. Your best chance is to vector your look-down radar aircraft to the areas where missiles are detected and use them in a bi-static configuration. We typically operate in synchronized teams where one plane carries the transmitter, two or more carry separate receivers."

"Is there anything else you wish to say?" Czernienko asked.

"One request. We ask a radiation-hardened phone line be set up between your coastal defense headquarters and our Pacific fleet communications center in Hawaii. If our forces detect these missiles, we need a mechanism for getting messages to your people in the field."

"We can do this, but there is little time for you to help. Very little time to brace against an attack, maybe enough time, but I doubt it. I will leave the line open."

Mason had trouble believing it himself, it all happened so quickly, but within a matter of minutes, everything within the *Maine*'s reach—including most elements of the Russian, U.S., and Japanese military—went on alert, either bracing for a missile-torpedo attack or racing at flank speed to get out of the way.

Hunter Orion, 12/31/2008, Wed., 11:46 P.M., 10:46 ZULU
Life Raft

The surface winds were picking up as the Pacific storm front roared through the darkness. The seas were rough and getting rougher by the minute, but even above the howling wind, Scott could hear the roar of the Orion's turboprop engines sweeping out an expanding, circular search pattern overhead. From the pitch of the engines, she'd guessed the hunter Orion was dropping sonobuoys around the *Maine*'s last confirmed position.

"I can't stand it any longer." She heard Dale Tew's voice from the far side of the raft. "I've gotta know. With the surface churning up like this, they may have found her."

"It's kinda strange, almost like a death wish," Scott said softly, clutching her necklace, a gift her husband, Jay Fayhee, had given her back in high school. "I'd like to know too, but if they find her, we're toast."

"Yeah, but I still gotta know. I'm sure we got a few minutes left on the battery." Dale put on a featherweight headset, radioed the hunter Orion searching overhead, then spoke again to Scott.

"Nothing so far, but with a hot starting point like this one, they're sure they'll find her if their fuel holds out. No way she'll elude 'em for long."

Knowing only made the waiting worse. For every shivering, cold, wet soul in the raft, hope seemed to vanish. Praying silently, Scott thought of home and the three things that meant more to her than anything else in the world: her husband, her father, and the children she'd wanted since high school, but never had.

Unthinkable, 12/31/2008, Wed., 06:08 A.M., 11:08 ZULU
White House

For Mason and everyone else holding on the President's conference call, the waiting was the hardest part. Watching the clock on the wall, watching the countdown timers on screen wind down, hoping nothing would happen, hoping he'd wake up and it'd go away. Had they done all they could do? Had anything been overlooked?

Suddenly, a beep sounded over the call, indicating the President, Clive Towles, and Russ Singleton were rejoining the conference bridge.

The President opened without delay, apparently picking up a conversation already in progress. "Do the American people understand we have absolutely no defense against these renegade missiles?"

"No, not really," the SECDEF, Dr. Singleton, observed dryly.

"No one likes to think about it, sir," Clive added grimly. "It's almost unthinkable, and besides, you said it yourself, missile defense is a budget breaker; it's damned expensive."

"But if the Chinese or Russians retaliate, there won't be any budget."

Even over the phone, Mason could tell the President was shaken. In a matter of seconds, the President's stress turned again to frustrated rage.

"Colonel Mason," the President snapped. "You're telling me any crackpot who launches a missile can wipe out our largest cities and we're powerless to stop it?"

Slim took a deep breath, then replied as evenly as his racing heart would allow. "Not just any crackpot, sir, but in practice, what you say is true. It takes skill, brains, courage, and organization, but with the proper terrain information an enemy could put a missile down the chimney of the White House."

"Jeez, Slim." Mason heard Craven grimace over the speakerphone. Sounded like he was in the next room.

"Maybe my White House chimney comment was too close to home," Mason conceded, "but your point stands, Mr. President."

"After all the money we spend on defense, I simply cannot believe it."

"With all due respect," the national security advisor said frankly, "this is a reality of the world we live in today. It took this renegade submarine to rattle our cage, but it's been this way all along."

Detection, 12/31/2008, Wed., 11:34 P.M., 11:34 ZULU
Russian Radar Station Outside Olyutorsky

Bleary-eyed, nursing his cup of coffee, the radar operator struggled to concentrate on the green screen. He'd been told to keep a close eye for low-flying cruise missiles and knew they'd be difficult to detect. His interest peaked when he noticed a single blip on screen at close range, but within a matter of seconds it vanished. He couldn't calculate the speed with any certainty and guessed it was either a flock of birds or ground clutter; nevertheless, he recorded the time of detection in his log, started his recorder running, and set his timer, just in case. He was a relative newcomer in the radar business, but couldn't recall ever detecting birds during the middle of the night in the winter. He remembered detecting birds at night during the spring mating season, but with the exception of owls, all the birds he could think of in the region slept at night during the cold winter months.

Curiously, fifty-eight seconds later, another blip suddenly appeared at close range and nearly the same place. With grease pencil in hand, the technician marked the blip's position on his green screen. It too persisted a few moments, then vanished. Although only visible for a few seconds, the technician judged its speed might be in excess of five hundred knots heading north. He wasn't sure what it was, but it was no bird.

Fifty-six seconds later, he saw the blip for a third time, same location, same duration, and decided to report it to coastal air defense headquarters. While on hold with his recorder running, he detected three more blips, each spaced approximately one minute apart.

After he transmitted the radar recording to his coastal defense controller, a well-rehearsed sequence of events happened in rapid succession.

First, Moscow was informed of the invasion, then reflexively, the Russian bear bristled from the threat. As if preprogrammed, its military machine was automatically elevated to full alert status, yielding all available forces ready for combat: Missile submarines raced to shelter beneath polar ice; every remaining land-based ICBM carrying a MIR warhead was programmed for launch, targeting scores of American cities; pilots and planes were scrambled across the continent at a frenetic pace.

In addition, four Ilyushin Il-76 Mainstay look-down radar aircraft—the Russian equivalent of the American E-3 Sentry AWACS—were vectored well north of the city of Olyutorsky. Two patrolled as a bi-static team over land, north of the Koryak range; the second pair over sea, circling just south of the missile boat bastions between Polyarnyy and Kolyma.

Across the country, armies of men rushed to station, hundreds of aircraft streamed toward the coast in swarms, radar stations ran hot, communications channels filled to capacity, orbiting antisatellite weapons maneuvered into strike position, and countless missiles hurled headlong to the edge of the precipice.

But the miracle wasn't the might of the machine, it was

the soul of the soldier. Although poised on a hair trigger, moving forward with seemingly unstoppable momentum, no one, not one person, went over the edge.

Within a matter of minutes, China responded in lockstep with their neighbor's increase in air activity. They didn't know the cause for Russia's alarm, not yet anyway, but they would not be caught in a shooting war with either their aircraft parked on the ground or their ICBMs sleeping dormant, still cold in the tubes.

In an eerie, almost surreal sense, the vast majority of the world's population continued through the motions of their daily lives, never skipping a beat, oblivious to these potentially apocalyptic events.

Minutes after the coastal defense controller reported the invasion to Moscow, Czernienko informed the American President. At 11:34 P.M. local time, the first American cruise missile penetrated Russian airspace. Technically, a state of war now existed between the two nations.

Data Link Down, 12/31/2008, Wed., 04:44 A.M., 11:44 ZULU
Cheyenne Mountain

"It's a long shot, but it's sure as hell worth a try," Craven agreed. "Are our antenna arrays configured?"

"They're ready, General," the satellite controller responded. "Footprint's steered over Kamchatka, all available missile comm frequencies enabled."

"Tell me, is the missile's tactical data link normally enabled? Do we know?"

"McDonnell Aerospace set us straight on it, sir. Bottom line—the two-way link's a security risk, so it's normally off unless explicitly enabled by the flight profile download. Early versions were susceptible to jamming and any missile radio transmissions potentially compromise its position."

"Figures, but it makes sense, sounds like the way we'd do it. Send the query anyway, let's see if any of 'em respond and tell us their position. Maybe those bastards made a mistake configuring the missiles, maybe we'll get lucky and they'll talk to us."

The satellite controller clicked on an icon labeled "Advanced Cruise Missile Communications Module." Moments later, an outbound message folder appeared on the controller's screen, positioned alongside the *Maine*'s twenty-four missile icons. With a final sweep of her mouse, the controller grouped the missiles together, dragged them across her screen, and dropped them into the outbound message folder labeled "Missile Query." In a few millionths of a second, twenty-four encrypted, individually addressed "Where are you?" messages were created and placed in the outbound transmit queue.

Less than one-half second later—the time it takes light to travel from Cheyenne Mountain halfway around the world via satellite link—six data comm computers woke up, each housed inside its own cruise missile. Once fully alert, each checked the administrative status of its data link, found it was down, threw away its incoming message, then went back to sleep.

Flying eight hundred feet above cloud-covered Koryak mountain peaks, bound for the Russian missile boat bastion in the Eastern Siberian Sea, each of the six advanced stealth cruise missiles heard Cheyenne Mountain's query message, but not one responded.

Mandrone's missiles had been hurriedly programmed and he didn't have the flight path imagery of Russia required for TERCOM (Terrain Contour Matching) guidance. As a result, each stealth cruise missile used its NAVSTAR Global Positioning System receiver in combination with an onboard radar altimeter to navigate over Russian terrain. The guidance system pulled in signals from GPS satellites and its altimeter, then compared them to its programmed flight path. When they disagreed, the guidance system steered the missile back on course, effectively driving its horizontal and vertical position errors toward zero.

Incoming, 12/31/2008, Wed., 10:47 P.M., 11:47 ZULU
South of Petropavlovsk Submarine Base, Kamchatka
E-2C Hawkeye Radar Reconnaissance Aircraft
Operating from the Aircraft Carrier USS *Reagan*

"I think we've found 'em, sir" crackled over the Hawkeye's intercom. "Three of 'em anyway." The air-intercept controller put his headset down and hurried the length of the E-2C, the carrier-based aircraft with a rotating, twenty-four-foot Frisbee-shaped radar dome on top.

At first, the images on screen seemed like some kind of war game, but it was no game. This was the real thing, a nuclear-tipped nightmare playing out in real time.

"Three missiles bearing two-two-zero degrees, sir."

"Data link status to the *Reagan*?"

"Data link is go, sir. They've got the same picture we see."

"Good. Extrapolate missiles' course and plot. Any targets jump out at you, obvious or otherwise?"

A line suddenly appeared on screen. "Running over a whole lot of nothing, sir; a lota water."

"Display everything you've got in the area—aircraft, surface ships, submarines, everything. Any hits?"

"Nothing, sir, at least nothing obvious. Missiles do intersect the *Wyoming*'s track though." The radar technician studied the plot for a few seconds and overlaid additional course detail. "That's odd."

"Whaddaya mean?"

The technician took his grease pencil and circled the spot where the missiles' projected course would soon intersect the *Wyoming*'s. "This is where the *Wyoming* launched her missile strike against the *Maine*." Next, the young technician drew X's over a Russian antisubmarine frigate and Akula fast-attack sub, both closing at flank speed toward the *Wyoming*'s missile launch location. "This could be a disaster in the making."

A sick feeling of nausea rose from the pit of the officer's stomach.

"How far's the *Wyoming* from her launch position now?"

The technician measured the distance on screen using two cursors, then translated the length to distance. "About fifty miles away, sir, and moving at one helluva clip."

"How 'bout the frigate?" The Akula was moving faster, but closing from much farther away.

Another quick measurement. "Thirty miles and closing fast. I'd estimate she's making at least twenty-two knots, maybe more."

The officer held his breath as the three cruise missiles closed on the position where the *Wyoming* had launched her missile strike against the *Maine*. One by one, each missile slowed to approximately three hundred miles an hour, apparently beginning its terminal maneuver, but the missiles never disappeared from the screen.

Undetected by the E-2C Hawkeye's radar, each cruise missile climbed to an altitude of three hundred fifty feet, jettisoned its bombay doors and parachute-retarded torpedo, then continued true to course in level flight. This diversionary *keep 'em flying* behavior was no accident, the tactic designed to mask the torpedo launch from the peering eyes of look-down radar.

After a few moments studying the missile blips on screen, the air-intercept officer shook his head. He couldn't put his finger on it exactly, he didn't have any clear confirmation of his suspicion, but he didn't like what he saw. "Radio *Reagan* a heads-up, make sure they see this, three missiles detected."

Two hundred miles southeast of the Hawkeye, in the darkened combat direction center of the USS *Reagan,* a large group of people swarmed around the missile plot. The tactical action officer had already sized up the situation and was relaying his urgent recommendation to Washington via satellite link. Within a matter of seconds, his top-priority e-mail message was electronically forwarded to Moscow and relayed without bureaucratic delay to Russia's coastal defense forces.

Almost unbelievably, with both Russian and American military pulling together, the communications links worked, and worked effectively. Both the Russian frigate and the Akula came about immediately, egressing the area with all possible speed.

And finally, although already out of danger, the *Wyoming* was warned. "Torpedoes in the water fifty miles aft. Don't stop, don't loop back."

CHAPTER TWENTY-ONE

Mechanized Death, 1/01/2009, Thu., 12:59 A.M., 11:59 ZULU
Life Raft

Scott, Tristan, JT, and Dale listened as the Orion's droning engines slowly faded in the distance.

"That's curious," Tristan said.

"Maybe they found something." Dale turned on the radio and spoke briefly to the departing hunter.

After laying sonobuoys for an hour, the crew's plans quickly changed after recognizing they must clear the area, making way for eight incoming, nuclear-tipped missile-torpedoes en route from the *Wyoming*.

The crew had the option of taking the missiles out and continuing their search; however, after reviewing their fuel status, they elected to rendezvous with their tanker and let the torpedoes pick up the hunt where they left off.

Dale pondered this news for a moment, debating if he should share it, then scanned the darkness. The night sky was overcast, visibility from their raft practically zip. Nothing good could come of discussing it; no one could see the inbound missiles anyway, so why spell it out? "Tanker rendezvous" was all he said.

No one pressed for details. No one really wanted to know, not anymore.

• • •

Minutes later, unseen by the survivors, a single cruise missile flew by overhead, ultimately releasing its torpedo seventy miles east of their raft. Scott heard its small turbofan engine approaching, cut on her flashlight, and made eye contact with Dale. Even through the darkness, his expression telegraphed *don't ask.*

She didn't. More than anything else, she wished she could see Jay one last time, just to say good-bye.

Ring of Fire, 1/01/2009, Thu., 01:01 A.M., 12:01 ZULU
MK-48 Nuclear-tipped Torpedo

At an altitude of three hundred feet, explosive bolts flashed, penetrating the darkness, bomb bay doors on *Wyoming*'s southwesternmost missile blew off and fell away. Out of the weapon's bomb bay, a massive three-thousand pound telephone-pole-sized cylinder rotated downward, business end first, with a drogue chute deploying out its tail. Dangling in a near vertical attitude, the parachute released as the nuclear-tipped torpedo neared the surface, plunging the ominous, loglike object into the black ocean depths below.

The ADCAP came to life entering seawater—transitioning to a relentless, suicidal killing machine. As anyone who's survived an ADCAP attack will testify, the Mk-48's an awesome weapon to have on your side, but a death wish if turned against you. It's agile, fast, and smart—a frighteningly effective combination with a twenty-eight-mile range, electronically steerable sonar, plus an uncanny ability to home on specific targets. Downloaded at time of launch with the *Maine*'s acoustic signature, this ADCAP was programmed to seek out and destroy her.

Sustaining barely enough speed to maintain steerage,

stabilized at a depth of three hundred feet, facing northeast toward the *Maine*'s launch location, the ADCAP's sonar listened attentively, passively scanning the enormous volume of water in front of the weapon. There was much to hear, the faint pinging from distant surface ships and active sonobuoys, whales singing, sharks—countless hundreds of them—rushing, panicked bait fish, whoops, snaps, crackles, pops, gurgles, clicks, honks, and hisses, but the torpedo's sonar processing (called Fast Fourier Transforms) could not discern any submarine-generated sounds nearby.

Finding no submarine close at hand, the torpedo shifted to its long-range search mode, accumulating signals for a much longer period of time from each direction. Not surprisingly, the lower the ratio of submarine sound to ambient noise, the more difficult the detection problem. Predictably, ultraquiet submarines at extreme range take longer to detect and often produce false alarms.

After scanning forward repeatedly, the ADCAP detected nothing comparable to the *Maine*'s signature. Unconvinced, the weapon's sonar went active, relentlessly steering its narrow beam forward in a tedious, row-by-row, TV-like scan pattern. Ping after ping, line after line, the torpedo labored tirelessly listening for echoes reflected off the *Maine*.

If the *Maine* closed within sonar range, it would determine her position and destroy her. Understandably, ADCAP torpedo programmers knew a great deal about killing American, Ohio-class, guided missile submarines.

• • •

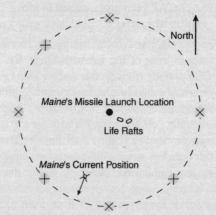

Of the eight missiles launched by the *Wyoming,* one had an in-flight turbofan failure, but seven completed their trip, boxing the compass, surrounding the *Maine* with a torpedo ring one hundred forty miles across. The faulty weapon jettisoned its torpedo such that it could be recovered near the surface in a matter of hours, while the remaining seven torpedoes entered the water hot, setting up an active sonar fence, surrounding the *Maine* with a ring of fire. Within a span of fifteen minutes, every torpedo entered the water on the prowl.

Interestingly, the westernmost torpedo entered the water first and its sonar immediately detected sounds from not one, but two contacts nearby. After their acoustic signals were separated into frequency bands, their telltale low-frequency components revealed that these contacts were not of American origin. Further, based on the received direction of the incoming signals, it could be determined that these contacts were submerged, probably submarines of similar types, origin unknown.

Had the ADCAP been programmed to identify the class of each submerged contact, it could have with a reasonable degree of confidence; it had collected sufficient acoustic information. Had this same information been available to PACSUBCOM headquarters, they could have deduced the submarines' nationality and class almost immediately. What was most telling here was location—the torpedo entered the water approximately six hundred fifty miles east of Russia's Petropavlovsk Submarine Base.

Running the Gauntlet, 1/01/2009, Thu., 01:10 A.M., 12:10 ZULU
USS Maine

Ping . . . . *ping* . . . . *ping* . . . .

"Conn, sonar. Active transmissions; possible torpedo detected off our starboard hull array. Range unknown. Bearing two-seven-zero degrees. Signal is faint, very faint, barely discernible."

Mandrone lay perfectly still for a few moments in his pitch-black cabin, his injured eye bloodred, crusted over, oozing. He couldn't open either eye now; any noise or movement caused excruciating pain. Gently separating his lower eyelid from the mucus, he fumbled in darkness with his medication. Following several missed attempts, he felt a cool drop entering his eye. Fifteen seconds later, relief.

Lifting his handset, he spoke to his sonarman. "We need a range. Can it hear us?"

Ping . . . . *ping* . . . . *ping* . . . .

"Another one, Captain, off our port side, bearing one-three-five degrees. Definite torpedo. Possible Mk-48 judging from active transmissions."

"Range? Can they hear us?"

"Possibly, but I doubt it. No indication they're homing

on us. Transmission signal level is barely above our noise floor. Negligible doppler. I think it's searching, Captain."

"We need a range. Let me know the instant it appears to converge on us."

"The amplitude of both signals is almost identical. Assuming they're similar sources, I'd estimate we're splitting the difference between them, sir. Could be slightly closer to the torpedo off port."

"So we're running the gauntlet. Let me know if anything changes and we need a range. Are they ten miles away or thirty?"

Mandrone entered the control room and noticed its autopilot at the helm. Dimly lit by red lights, Ash Wilson lay stretched out on a mattress, sleeping on the floor.

Ping . . . . . . *ping* . . . . . **ping** . . . . . . *ping* . . . . . .
ping . . . . . . *ping* . . . . . **ping** . . . . . . *ping* . . . . . .

"Conn, sonar. Signal amplitude is increasing off our port side. I think we're moving closer, but still splitting the difference between them. Bearing angle is changing slowly."

"Range?"

"It's a low-confidence call, Captain, but I'd estimate they're both fifteen to thirty miles away."

Mandrone did some quick mental arithmetic. Could they break out running between them? At a range of fifteen miles, no way. Still, at thirty miles, he could split the difference and have an excellent chance. "So either we have a problem or we don't," Mandrone quipped. "Any recommendations?"

"Maintain current heading and speed. If they begin to close, drop a knuckle and dive below the layer."

"Very well, sonar, I concur." Mandrone checked his sound velocity chart to determine the thermocline depth, then walked across the control room to his helmsman's makeshift bed. "Heads up, Ash. We've got trouble."

• • •

Ping . . . . . . ping . . . . . . ping . . . . . . ping . . . . . .

"Port torpedo's search pattern seems to be converging in our direction, Captain. Range unknown, but its not moving, negligible doppler."

Lifting his intercom handset, Mandrone punched up the sonar room. "Good, sounds like it's still making up its mind."

"Probably running its long-range search algorithms," the sonarman speculated.

"That makes sense, long integration times, it can't decide if we're here or not. Probably considers any detection at our range suspect. Any recommendations?"

"Leave it something to focus on, Captain."

"My thinking exactly." Running his finger over the intercom buttons, Mandrone squinted, finally bringing the ship's intercom into focus. "Gentlemen, sonar recommends we leave a knuckle behind as a diversionary tactic and I concur. There is no immediate danger. Once we've settled out, I'll engage Wyley one." The WLY-1 is an intercept system designed for automatic defense against torpedo attack.

Mandrone took his place alongside Ash at the ship control console. Maneuvering the 560-foot-long, 42-foot-diameter submarine demanded a gentle touch on the control surfaces to prevent unwanted noise, but popping a knuckle intentionally broke the rules.

Sitting behind the planesman console, Mandrone took a deep breath, then spoke to Ash. "Signal full power."

Ash turned a knob, relaying the message back to the engine room.

Once they sensed acceleration, Mandrone continued. "Come hard about. We'll take her down to sixteen hundred feet."

In one continuous motion, Ash pulled a tight turn as

Mandrone banked the boat, pushing her bow into a steep, controlled dive. Rolling thirty degrees on her side with a thirty-degree down angle, the *Maine*'s deck felt as if it were falling away. Outside, the corkscrewing movement looked as if the *Maine* were spiraling down an enormous bathtub drain.

Nevertheless, the abrupt maneuver created an enormous mass of bubbles in the water, a decoy acting as a ghost image of the *Maine*. From a distance, the bubble mass reflected sonar pings like a submerged submarine, eventually drawing the focused attention from both nuclear-tipped ADCAPs.

Within five minutes, the port-side torpedo had homed on the distant knuckle, streaking toward it at a speed over sixty knots. Twenty minutes later, with its warhead still unarmed, the guidance computer slowed the weapon to a crawl and began quietly listening. Operationally, the ADCAP must establish a signature match before executing its terminal run.

Meanwhile, closing from the opposite direction, the starboard torpedo followed suit.

Too late, both torpedoes determined they'd been outsmarted by Mandrone's countermeasure, for unlike a submarine, the knuckle didn't move and its acoustic signature contained no low-frequency components. By the time they'd closed on the decoy, their fuel was nearly spent.

Running the quietest submarine ever put to sea, Mandrone dove beneath the layer, eluding sonobuoys, a salvo of incoming torpedoes, and ClearWater detection. Like an open-field runner, he broke out of the box, heading for open ocean. Bold, decisive, an inspirational leader, Mandrone could have been one of the finest missile sub skippers the U.S. Navy ever put to sea.

*Contact Bearing Southeast, 1/01/2009, Thu., 01:29 A.M.,
12:29 ZULU*
Russian Akula-class Attack Submarine
The *Puma*

Renegade or not, when nuclear-tipped cruise missiles penetrate Kamchatka airspace, Russians don't take it lying down. They respond like Americans, doing whatever's in their best interest, continually seeking the upper hand.

And they don't ask permission.

Sixty miles northwest of the *Maine* and running deep, a Russian Akula-class attack submarine patiently listened, passively scanning all points of the compass through its hull-mounted hydrophone arrays. Unknown to PACSUBCOM, though not entirely unexpected, the *Puma* was one of the pickets in a submarine fence erected around Petropavlovsk, Russia's only submarine base with direct access to the Pacific.

Forward in the Puma's sonar room, a seasoned Russian officer worked through a maze of signals, most associated with surface noise, marine life, and an occasional active sonobuoy. His signal processors filtered out most of the noise, but suddenly something changed, something faint and barely discernible emerged that wasn't there before.

Instinctively, he sensed they weren't alone.

The sonarman hunched forward, pressing his headphones tight to his head. Although weak, the signal persisted. Cranking up the volume, he piped the signals through another maze of filters, then watched his visual display. As expected, hundreds of randomly scattered snow flecks on screen coalesced into a series of solid lines during the next few minutes.

These sounds were definitely man-made.

And they weren't Russian.

Without further delay, he spoke into the intercom. "Cavitation noises to our southeast, Captain. Request you reduce speed and conduct a maximum-range sonar search."

"What do you hear?"

"Signal is faint, but definitely mechanical. Judging from its low-frequency components, contact is probably of American origin, could be the renegade, range unknown. Recommend we deploy towed array and run—"

Startled, the sonarman fell silent, grabbing his headphones in disbelief. His eyes widened with recognition, then the veteran officer's complexion turned pasty. "Torpedo in the water, Captain. Signal is faint, actively pinging, possibly homing on the American, I can't say for sure. Definite homing ping. Type unknown, but it's not one of ours."

"Where'd it come from?"

"Unknown, Captain. We detected no launch transient. Impeller's spinning up. Definite contact, sir. Torpedo's beginning its run."

"What about—"

"Situation's changing, Captain, becoming more complicated," the sonarman interrupted. "There's another one, sir, another torpedo, two homing pings now confirmed. Range unknown, but the second one's louder, closer to us. A second impeller's spinning up bearing southwest!" Even as the sonarman spoke, the captain could hear background chatter from the sonar room ratchet up a notch.

A long, tense silence followed as the sonarman tracked changes in doppler and bearing angle. "Second torpedo's closing on the American, Captain. It's louder, but moving away from us, possibly running southeast."

"You're sure it's not heading for us? Could be a trick, some sort of dogleg maneuver."

"Negative, Captain. Torpedo is homing on the cavitation source. Doppler indicates the weapon is moving away from us."

"That is good. We'll run east and triangulate on the American. At this volatile juncture, we must establish their range without compromising our position." The captain briefly reflected on his experience with American tactics, then looked across the control room to his countermeasures officer. "Make ready the noisemakers, just in case."

CHAPTER TWENTY-TWO

Night Hunt, 12/31/2008, Wed., 11:57 P.M., 12:57 ZULU
MiG-31 Foxhound

No one in their right mind flies through weather like this,
thought Russian pilot Dimitri Gorshkov. He knew the cold,
desolate blackness above the Eastern Siberian Sea would
be a lonely place to die, but tonight at least, he had a team
of Mainstay aircraft, his radar eyes in the sky, watching
over him. He also found some comfort knowing his target,
although tough to find, wouldn't shoot back.

Flying through the soup, Dimitri glanced out the cockpit, away from his instruments, but only for a moment.
After watching his aircraft lights illuminate the clouds
engulfing his wings, he estimated visibility limited to ten
feet, if that. Nine hundred feet above the deck, chop buffeted his Foxhound, whipping him side to side about the
cockpit. If he'd had time to dwell on it, he would have felt
nervous about shooting down a nuclear-tipped stealth
cruise missile, but it took every ounce of concentration he
could muster to fly his plane, navigate, and communicate.

"Fox One, you're closing too fast" rang out over Dimitri's headset. "Our signal's intermittent; could be another
false alarm, but the speed's right on this one. Estimated

altitude unchanged, about fifty feet, range to target: twelve miles."

"Mainstay North, request closing vector."

"Reduce speed to six hundred knots, descend to three hundred feet, come to bearing three-four-zero. Acknowledge when you break out of the clouds."

Dimitri backed off the throttles, allowing his Foxhound to descend in a nose-high attitude. "Mainstay North, ceiling eight hundred feet, estimate visibility one-half mile."

"Fox One, do you have the bogey on radar?"

"Negative, can't see him."

The nose of Dimitri's MiG-31 housed a recently upgraded version of the formidable, look-down shoot-down Zaslon radar system—an electronically steered phased-array unit. Dimitri set his radar's output power to maximum, reduced the volume of its search sector, then focused its beam down and forward. Still, nothing shown on screen except black, frigid seawater three hundred feet below.

Modeled after the same concepts that drove the Night Hawk stealth fighter's design, looking somewhat boxy and buglike, coated with a matte black radar-absorbing material, the Advanced Cruise Missile had an elliptical underside which contributed to lift, with a narrow, slotlike engine exhaust out its end. Its exhaust outlet was spread out horizontally, located under a wide, overhanging tail to mask hot gases from infrared sensors overhead. A flush-mounted engine air inlet was set in its composite carbon-fiber body, further reducing its radar signature. Viewed from most directions, the net result was a radar cross-section comparable to that of a small bird, and for practical purposes, its heat signature could not be detected by conventional infrared seekers from any useful range.

• • •

"Fox One, you're converging on target. Reduce speed to five hundred fifty knots. Your position is two miles behind target. Can you pick up anything on your thermal sight?"

Dimitri reduced throttle, then instinctively set his altitude alarm. Flying three hundred feet above the black deck, he didn't want to concentrate on one thing, get distracted, and smash into the sea. Once he had his altitude in check, he routed the thermal camera signal to his cockpit display. "Negative, no infrared lock."

Suddenly, a flick appeared on his radar screen, persisted only for a moment, then was gone. But Dimitri knew all that really mattered was that it appeared at all. "Mainstay North, intermittent radar contact."

Outside, beyond the dim cockpit lighting, Dimitri saw only darkness.

The green blip appeared again, this time persisting longer. He squinted hard, straining to find the missile's exhaust in the darkness. "Range to target, one-half mile. Negative on thermal, negative visual."

Dimitri adjusted the sweep of his radar, focusing all its energy on target. That did it; the blip held fast. Still his thermal scanner was useless and he couldn't get a visual. *Too close, much too close,* he thought. *Locked on target carrying six long-range missiles I can't use.*

Dimitri closed within fifty yards, rolled thirty degrees, and looked down. Seeing only darkness, he raised his clear visor, rubbed his eyes, then tried again. He knew exactly where to look, knew exactly what to look for, but it didn't help.

It must be my eyes.

At forty-four years old, Dimitri's night vision had been fading over the past year, but he hadn't wanted to admit it. This was the first time he'd missed it, but he really needed it now. *What I wouldn't give for a good set of young eyes.*

He could see exquisite detail in rich sunlight, but contrast—differences in brightness—bothered him now and his grays were fading. Shifting his gaze from the comparative glare of his dimly lit cockpit to the black expanse outside was more than his eyes could quickly accommodate. With the moon and stars hidden behind solid cloud cover, he simply couldn't see the black missile's outline against an ink black sea. Maybe no one could.

Dimitri knew his MiG-31 had been optimized for taking out long-range targets using the sophisticated Amos missile; nevertheless, it carried one piece of good ol' stick-and-rudder technology—a conformal-mounted, radar-guided 23mm cannon. The time had come to use it.

Dimitri twirled his altimeter thumbwheel with a grimace, resetting the audible altitude alarm to forty-five feet. Next he toggled a switch enabling his cannon, locking it to the radar and cross-hairs on his heads-up display.

After balling his gloved hand into a tight fist, he allowed his fingers to relax then placed them over the stick-mounted firing trigger. Before descending any lower, Dimitri squeezed off a few rounds, watching tracers streak out into the darkness.

Burr-rump-pomp-pomp!

The staccato sound was sweet.

Satisfied, he began his gradual, carefully controlled descent, keeping the radar locked on target as he maneuvered into position behind it. Scanning the crosshairs on his heads-up display, Dimitri gingerly worked the death dot toward the missile's radar blip, all the while watching the altimeter count down.

Looking forward through his heads-up display, descending through the rough air at sixty feet, Dimitri saw a dim, horizontal sliver of light—engine exhaust—penetrate the darkness exactly where it should be. As he'd learned from experience, the missile was only barely visible to the naked eye looking up its skirt.

As his altitude passed below fifty feet, the rough air caused the distant sliver of light to jerk slightly, but Dimitri's eyes were glued to the death dot. *Closer, closer, closer . . .*

Suddenly, Dimitri heard a female voice—the sound of his flight computer—over intercom. "Pull up, pull up. Altitude warning. Pull up, pull up."

Closer, closer . . . now!

Burr-rump-pomp-pomp-pomp-pomp-pomp!

It was a hypnotic spectacle—tracers racing out, intersecting the distant sliver of light.

Unseen by the Russian, a single 23mm round penetrated the turbofan engine, and within seconds, it had slung itself apart, whipping shrapnel throughout the missile's bomb bay, destroying the torpedo's pump jet propulsor. A second round punctured its primary fuel tank, another sheered off one of the weapon's retractable wings.

A bright flash signaled catastrophic failure—the missile corkscrewed downward with a twisting whipsaw action, then augered into the sea.

Whoop . . . whoop . . . whoop . . . whoop!!! Inside the Foxhound, the landing gear alarm bellowed over the intercom.

Before Dimitri could react, he felt the stick easing back between his legs as both throttles moved forward on their own.

After recovering from the initial shock, he realized his flight computer had taken over and done exactly what she was supposed to do. She simply would not be flown into the sea with her landing gear up. He smiled behind his oxygen mask and spoke fondly to the lady. "Women are always right."

Six Missing, 12/31/2008, Wed., 09:15 A.M., 14:15 ZULU
White House

"Our fighter pilots shot down all six American missiles over the Eastern Siberian Sea," President Czernienko reported. His tone was a combination of satisfaction and relief. "We also confirmed your report of three torpedoes entering the water several hundred miles south of our Pacific submarine base at Petropavlovsk. From our information, six of your renegade missiles remain unaccounted for."

The President of the United States acknowledged Czernienko's count as accurate.

Secretary of Defense Russ Singleton checked his watch. "Wherever those missiles were headed, they're out of fuel by now."

"So we won't find them in the air?" the President asked.

"It's a sea hunt now, Mr. President," Dr. Singleton confirmed. "Wherever those torpedoes are now, I pray we find them before they find us."

"Then, can we assume land targets are out of danger?" Clearly, the President was leading the witness.

"In my judgment, the probability of these remaining missiles taking out any land target is extremely low. For practical purposes, I think our civilian crisis has passed."

"That is good," President Czernienko said stoically, masking his profound relief. Quietly, without comment, he killed off the last of his vodka, then leaned forward across his desk and closed the lid on a small wooden box.

But this was no ordinary box. It was *the box* used to launch Russian missiles against American cities.

Still, the numbers didn't add up for the American president. "We're not out of the woods yet, Russ. Like a bad penny, I'm afraid they'll show up where we least expect them."

"Unless they find us, Mr. President, I doubt we'll ever find them."

Opportunity Lost, 1/01/2009, Thu., 04:45 A.M., 15:45 ZULU
Mk-48 Torpedo

Quietly and without fanfare, the last of the *Wyoming's* eight nuclear-tipped, Mark-48 torpedoes came shallow, then steamed to a stop seventy miles southeast of Scott's life raft. Within seconds of each other, after exhausting their programmed window of opportunity, the torpedoes harmlessly shut down on queue and waited recovery.

Straight Metal Jackets, 1/01/2009, Thu., 06:17 A.M., 17:17 ZULU
Scott's Life Raft

"What was that?" Rubbing his hip, Tristan woke with a start. Something bumped him through the bottom of the rubber raft, hit him hard, shook the whole craft like a battering ram.

"Stay still." Scott grabbed his shoulder, pointing to four black dorsal fins circling their raft.

Tristan's eyes looked bleak. "That's all we need."

"My grandfather flew C-54s during the Korean War," JT sighed softly, "but what he remembered was the sharks."

"That's a happy thought," Dale quipped with a tight-lipped grimace.

"He landed in Kwajalein late one night flying a plane filled with nurses. The follow-on crew took off with an internal fuel tank topped off for the long hop to Guam. They're not sure what happened, but the plane exploded shortly after takeoff. They went to the crash site, but had to call off the search for survivors on accounta sharks. Fourteen nurses and the whole crew lost. Best they could figure, the radioman probably powered up the HF transmitter before getting a fume check, but my grandad never forgot the sharks. When he talked about it, it was like it happened yesterday. It was the fear. Maybe you had to be there, but it scares me to think about it. What chance'd they have?"

"Quiet!" Scott's voice was low, but harsh in a way demanding compliance. Alert, manning her turn at the watch, she studied the ocean's surface, eyes tracking side to side. Soon, she saw another dorsal fin run the surface, then another, following a boiling frenzy of surface churn— schools of smaller fish darting en masse, breaking the surface at high speed, attempting to escape the circling horde.

Instinctively, she reached for her father's single-action Colt .45, the pistol he'd carried throughout his Air Force career. Shivering, she retrieved the cold, hard lump from her soaking pant leg pocket, never taking her eyes from the ocean surface. It was heavy, kicked, and she didn't like it much, but he'd wanted her to learn to shoot a weapon that'd do some good. Her dad always insisted those lightweight 22s weren't good for anything but target practice, and considering the size of these sharks, Scott decided he was right.

Never looking away from the water, operating by feel, she slid a clip loaded with 230-grain hardballs into her handgun. Once it snapped home, she pulled back the slide on her pistol, chambering the round, then double-checked the safety, making sure it was on. As she kneeled upright, both knees spread wide apart in a pool of frigid seawater, her shivers seemed to disappear. In a way, her father was with her, looking over her shoulder, helping her if she needed it. She felt more alive than she could remember, every sense focused on the immediate danger. She could do this; she knew it.

"Dale, radio the raft. Warn 'em, we're surrounded by

sharks, I don't have any idea how many. Best I can tell, they're after the bait fish. Tell 'em to sit tight, dump their shark repellant, don't shoot unless their raft's attacked. I don't think they're after us, but they might get curious."

Hearing Scott's suggestion, JT pulled a small canister from his life vest pocket, tied a cord to it, then tossed the tethered container into the sea. Comparable to octopus ink, a dark blackish pool spread across the surface, surrounding JT's side of the raft. Moments later, in traditional monkey-see-monkey-do fashion, Tristan followed JT's lead and soon they were surrounded by a black pool of india ink. It was supposed to act as a shark repellant, but as to how effective the stuff was, no one really knew.

Suddenly, erupting through the blackness, an enormous head breached the surface, ramming Scott's end of the raft. She fell forward, face down, nearly dropping her pistol over the edge. "They're playing with us," she said, easing off the safety.

"One swipe of those teeth would sink us," Tristan observed succinctly.

"Yep." Scott braced against the edge of the raft. Looking over her shoulder in the dim morning light, she spoke to Dale. "You got a gun?"

"You bet, like American Express, I never travel anywhere on business without it."

"Know how to use it?"

"You kidding? I've been shooting since Boy Scouts."

"Good, you cover your end. How about you, Tristan?"

He looked a little surprised, then shook his head. "No, but I've got good eyes. I'll spot 'em coming in, you pick 'em off." He rose upright, bracing himself against the side of the raft, scanning the surface for motion.

"Billy Ray always carried a Beretta in his leg pocket," Dale offered.

"Good. I'm afraid we're gonna need it."

Scott looked at Tristan, communicating without words. He felt the hard lump on Billy Ray's leg, then removed the pistol and clip. Working the clip into the handle, he fumbled but was determined. After a few false starts, he got it. "I learn pretty quick."

Scott smiled a funny sort of smile. "You load and spot. I'll shoot."

Tristan grinned. "Sounds like a plan to me, chief!"

"JT, how about you?"

"I'm covered," he said, flashing his grandfather's revolver, an S&W K-38 Combat Masterpiece. "Like my grandad said, Pacific Ocean's shark country. Never fly—"

"Incoming!" Tristan yelled, pointing to a large torpedo-shaped silhouette racing toward the raft. "There! There! Shoot! Shoot!"

Scott rotated evenly about her hips as if gyroscopically stabilized, her head and shoulders pivoting as one. As her eyes darted about, scanning the surface, she raised the Colt in front of her, gripping the heavy weapon with both hands.

And there it was, its massive gray head racing toward them, its back glistening in the even morning light. No panic, not yet, she'd wait, couldn't afford to miss.

Steady, wait until . . . it's closing, closing fast, much too fast!

"It's gonna ram!" Tristan yelled.

Relax, exhale, keep it down . . . Now!

THUOOM!!!

A six-inch flame erupted from the barrel. The weapon's mass retarded its kick somewhat; still it climbed slightly, pulling to Scott's weak side.

What the . . . ? The hard ball had no effect at all. She

reacted instinctively, leading the shark's motion—*head shot*—then squeezed the trigger.

THUOOM!!!

It kept coming, barreling forward like a freight train.

Upright, but leaning forward over the raft's edge, Scott lowered her Colt near the water.

THUOOM!!!

Pull down, now!

THUOOM!!!

Her last shots were fired point-blank, nose and head. She was sure she hit it; she saw its empty black eye no more than three feet away.

Everyone looked on spellbound.

Thud.

The raft lurched, but Scott had seen it coming. Teetering over the edge, she tossed her smoking .45 inside and grabbed for the raft.

THUMP!

Suddenly, Dale's end of the raft heaved up out of the water—another shark hit—and Scott fell face first into the sea. Distracted, no one had seen it coming.

Without thinking, everyone converged on Scott's side, nearly swamping the raft, but she was gone without a trace. Ironically, the strapped-down counterweight of Billy Ray's body kept them from capsizing.

Scanning the surface, they saw they were surrounded by sharks, Tristan felt panic unlike anything he'd ever experienced. *She was wearing her life vest, she should surface, but where could she be?*

He felt her head first, underneath his leg, working her way to the outside of the raft, then heard her cry for help. She was directly underneath him and that's all he needed to know.

Yanking off his life vest, braced against the outside wall of the raft, Tristan stood to his knees and began barking orders for the first time in his life. "Dale, hold on to my legs and make sure we don't flip over."

Dale lay face down, his head between Tristan's legs, arms locked around his thighs, chest covering his calves.

Tristan handed JT the Beretta with instructions "Cover me and don't blow my head off."

JT looped the Beretta's tie cord around his wrist, then knelt mid-ship and straddled Dale's waist. Hurriedly, he spun the cylinder of his K-38, snapped it into place, and opened fire on a shark to Tristan's immediate right. It was closest.

BAM!!!

"Go!"

BAM!!! BAM!!!

In the blink of an eye Tristan lunged face forward into the ice-cold seawater, wrapping himself around the raft, using every inch of reach he had to get to Scott. Try as he might, he couldn't reach her.

BLUMP!!!

Even underwater, he could hear shooting.

BLUMP!!! BLUMP!!!

He squirmed, strained and flailed his arms. Topside, Dale cut him a little slack, loosening his grip just enough to add about three inches to Tristan's reach. And it was enough.

BLUMP!!!

He felt her flight suit first, then her life vest.

She was floating face up, working her way toward him. Exactly what happened remained a blur, but as Tristan later recounted, he grabbed her with one hand by the scruff of the neck, then, in one continuous motion, dragged her from underneath the raft, heaved her up out of the water, and flung her face down on the deck.

Stunned, but looking gratefully at Tristan, Scott called it one magnificent Herculean effort. Seconds later, the full impact of her ordeal sank in; she hung her head over the side and began retching uncontrollably.

After the adrenaline and gut-wrenching fear had faded, Tristan couldn't imagine how he'd done it, but in the final analysis, courage made all the difference. In retrospect, he summarized his experience with one line: "Sometimes you don't think, ya just do."

The Shadow, 1/01/2009, Thu., 02:28 A.M., 17:28 ZULU
Off the Eastern Port of Seokcho, South Korea

Climbing toward the surface at a snail's pace, the North Korean spy sub maintained its speed near four knots and eventually leveled off at sixty feet.

"Periscope depth, Comrade Captain," the diving officer reported.

The captain nodded, then looked to his second in command, hoping against hope for good news. Without further prompting, the seasoned veteran hung up the intercom handset. "Sonar reports range to surface contact remains unchanged, forty yards and holding fast."

"That's impossible," the North Korean skipper groused. "This vessel trails us like a dog."

"They mock us, Comrade Captain. How do they do this?"

The North Korean skipper's eyes narrowed in the control room's dim red light. "We stop, they stop. We change course, they follow in lockstep, yet they use no active sonar. They must have aircraft or helicopters overhead."

The captain stood by the plotting table, studying their position. They were heading due north, located three miles inside enemy waters, three miles south of the inter-Korean sea border, only three miles from home.

The North Korean spy sub's bold voyage into enemy waters was perilous at best, but for reasons unknown, they had attracted the attention of a single unidentified surface ship, a contact the captain couldn't shake. Although their espionage mission was a prelude to war, their paramount directive was to remain undetected while delivering commandos safely to South Korean soil. They were painfully aware of ClearWater's detection limits and had operated below its minimums for the entire duration of their tedious voyage. Further, their submarine, a Russian-built Kilo-class diesel-electric, was the newest in Dear Leader's fleet, and was virtually undetectable while running on battery.

And they were on battery, crawling along at a snail's pace. This didn't make any sense.

"What are you thinking?" asked number two.

"We must assume this contact has reported our position and they'll send someone after us. They always do, usually sooner than anyone expects, probably a destroyer from Tonghae." Fatigue was beginning to take its toll on both the captain and his crew. Checking his mission clock, the captain noted it had been over twenty-six hours since they'd made their commando drop and that was long enough. He'd done all he could do for them.

Only three miles from home waters, he must shake this contact. "We'll stay in silent drive for now, ultra quiet, just long enough for me to get a good look at our adversaries. We must know what we're up against. Raise the attack scope."

The whine of hydraulics was silenced by a distinctive metallic thunk as the periscope hit its stops. Catching the small, heat-sensitive search scope on its way up, the captain first surveyed overhead, then spun a full one-eighty, looking directly behind the sub.

Stunned, he pulled away from the scope, rubbed both eyes, then looked again. Regrettably, the picture hadn't changed. He was looking at the back end of a fishing boat, thick hot smoke boiling skyward from her inboard engine. She was in trouble, that much was clear, but from what he could make out, she was going down by the stern, taking water over her transom, and under tow. One, maybe two men were bailing, two more were frantically pumping up and down, working a handcar-like bilge pump, water streaming over the side. Grimacing, the captain realized he had known this could happen, but had believed it would never happen to him. He was better than this.

"All stop," the captain ordered. Seconds later, his worst fears were confirmed. The backwash eased against the boat's transom, its wake stilled. "It's a fishing boat; we're tangled in its net."

"Why doesn't the fool cut us loose?" number two protested.

"I expect they've been ordered to stall us, hold on as long as possible, until help arrives. Raise the main antenna mast." Moments later, their small search scope slipped beneath the waves. Taking its place, a stub aerial breached the surface first, followed by a larger, telephone-pole-sized periscope assembly. Down below, the captain saw the surface was hot; his electronic warfare officer's console screen lit up like a fireworks display.

"Radar activity indicates three, no four surface contacts! South Korean warships, three closing from the south, one from the west. Closest range: six miles, bearing two-seven-two degrees."

"They're trying to cut us off," number two concluded.

"Sonar," the captain snapped. Suddenly, he found himself running out of options.

"Shallow water limits our sonar's effectiveness, Comrade Captain. We must get a diver out, cut and run."

"No time."

"Then we make a break for it; the rigging may give way or his net could fail."

"You forget, Comrade, this is peacetime." The captain clenched his teeth. "They are sinking, this would drown them."

"What do I care?" number two vented. "Then we must blow them out of the water!"

"At this range, the blast could kill us. If it didn't, the destroyers most certainly would. Our orders are to remain undetected. We must not provoke war. Dear Leader's plan depends on this."

"We have been detected, Comrade Captain," the veteran seethed. "What do you intend to do?"

"I would like to make a run for it, but that is not possible. We have only two alternatives—either scuttle the boat or play dead."

The captain stepped back from his periscope pedestal and gazed at the young, wide-eyed faces of his crew. They reminded him of little lost boys, breathless and frozen in time. His career was finished, that much was inevitable, but these young men, they had their entire lives ahead of them; some were new fathers, the youngest of his crew, their helmsman, had not even experienced a woman. He looked across the room at his helmsman's face; he was barely shaving. One glance and he knew what to do.

Lifting his handset, he spoke first to the radio operator. "Signal emergency search and rescue. We have experienced catastrophic engine failure."

Looking across the control room, he motioned to his

diving officer. "Blow all ballast tanks and surface." The diving officer bowed slightly at the waist, acknowledging he understood.

"Engine room. Cut main motors." A long pause. "And short them."

"Comrade Captain?"

"Short them all."

Later that morning, the *Korea Herald* reported:

Stricken Spy Sub Captured Off Seokcho

[Dateline: Thursday—January 1, 2009] Early this morning at 0245 hours, a North Korean spy submarine was found entangled in a fishing net, dead in the water, twelve and one half miles off the northeastern town of Seokcho. The state-run Korean Broadcasting System (KBS) said the defense ministry sent four warships and a helicopter to the area. A Ministry of Defense spokesman confirmed this fact, adding, "Helicopters and warships were ordered in to seize the vessel and protect fishermen known to be in the area."

The vessel, a Russian-built Kilo-class attack sub, was towed to the Tonghae naval base. The crew surrendered to South Korean naval authorities without resistance, requesting return passage to their country once engine repairs were complete.

Afterwards, the North Korean Armed Forces Ministry protested their innocence, insisting these troops had indeed sailed out of Wonsan port on a submarine, but while engaging in routine exercises in their own waters, their submarine suffered catastrophic engine failure, began to drift, and finally found itself trapped in a net. Their own search and rescue efforts were well under way when the South Korean Navy wantonly absconded with their stricken vessel. It was their submarine and they wanted it back.

South Korean officials acknowledge the crew displayed no hostile intent. They sought only surrender and an emergency rescue; however, officials are not convinced by North Korean claims of innocence. They believe this surrender may be an intentional cover-up for another infiltration mission gone bad.

North Korea's explanation may have held up had a South Korean civilian, a taxi driver, not reported a suspicious, three-man reconnaissance team operating near the coast of Kangnung, about 60 miles south of the DMZ. As police tragically discovered—nine were killed during the skirmish—these troops were heavily armed North Korean commandos dressed in South Korean Army uniforms.

By all accounts, this incident was a covert scouting mission and prelude to war. Police found these troops possessed maps showing every airstrip on Kang-Nung Air Force Base, and more telling than this, the dead men carried exposed film of the base revealing excruciating detail. This incident has touched off a large-scale manhunt which is under way as of this writing. Sixty thousand soldiers are currently combing the eastern seaboard for North Korean commandos, and this search has expanded to the DMZ.

Both police and South Korean Army officials insist these North Korean infiltrators should be considered armed commandos, not traditional espionage agents. Early investigations suggest these infiltrators belong to the reconnaissance bureau of the People's Armed Forces, their mission: military reconnaissance, espionage, and assassination. Considering their high level of military training and deadly resistance, these men were armed commandos in every respect and the South Korean government considers this provocation an act of war.

This infiltration incident is the thirty-fourth of its kind since 1990, and as far as South Korea is concerned, "there is no possibility of peace on the Korean peninsula as long as Kim's Pyongyang regime remains intact."

CHAPTER TWENTY-THREE

Rescue, 1/01/2009, Thu., 07:07 A.M., 18:07 ZULU
Life Raft

Tristan saw it first, the *Topeka*'s periscope knifing through the water, towering above the twenty-foot swells.

Dale signaled SOS using JT's flashlight, pointing its beam toward the telescoping mast.

Below in the *Topeka*'s control room, Hawk read their distress message, then signaled Orion survivors: Cavalry is here.

Dale's spirit soared, and his smile was contagious. While he radioed the second raft, Tristan woke Scott.

"Scotty." She felt Tristan's hand on her shoulder. "The *Topeka*'s here." She squinted reluctantly, looking through slits between her eyelids. The only relief she'd found from nausea had been sleep, and right now, the backs of her eyelids looked pretty good.

Sleep also helped pass the time, suppressing her miserable reality.

Peering up from the bottom of the raft, Scott slowly emerged from her Dramamine malaise, shifting positions, struggling to sit. Though not yet fully conscious, she began shivering uncontrollably. Frigid seawater covered her legs, sloshing from one end of the raft to the other.

Instinctively, Scott grabbed the bailer and went to it.
Even after scooping out most of the water, try as she
might, she could not steady her shakes. After eight hours,
her flight suit was soaking wet and her hands looked like
prunes.

Suddenly, the *Topeka* breached the surface.

It took a few moments to register, but when it did, Scott
thanked God for the wonderful sight. From her vantage
point, nothing could have looked sweeter than the silhouette
of the *Topeka*'s sail standing fast against the relentless sea.

Even before she'd stabilized on the surface, Scott
watched a frenzy of activity on top of the fairwater.
Squeezed into the tiny bridge area forward the periscopes,
two human silhouettes emerged in black rubber wet suits.
Immediately, they began rigging the fairwater rails for rescue, installing handrails around the bridge and lookout stations. Once they'd finished, both lookouts secured
themselves to the rigging using a parachute-like harness,
then cast lines to four frogmen poised on the deck below.

High seas made rescue perilous. Atop the three-story
tall sail, one lookout raised the colors. Icy winds howled,
whipping the American flag violently about its mast.
Under calmer conditions, the forward escape trunk
would've been used to bring the Orion's crew onboard, but
today twenty-foot swells washed over the cylindrical hull.
The Orion's crew would board the *Topeka* by climbing her
sail and entering through a small hatch in the floor of the
bridge.

Two frogmen swam to opposite sides of the raft, alongside Scott and Tristan, then began their often practiced procedure for air crew rescue in high seas. One diver stayed in
the water, clinging to the raft, acting as a counterweight for
the second as he hoisted himself and his medical supply kit
onboard.

Without discussion, the first frogman attached a line to the raft and, immediately, Scott sensed they were moving, being drawn slowly toward the *Topeka*.

Scott watched the second diver hurriedly attach individual lines to everyone.

He got to her last, looked her over quickly, then pulled a double take. Frozen in place, he stared at her for a few moments, then his gaze broke into the most peculiar smile. Something was different here. "You're a woman."

The lady forced a smile. "Lucky me. Name's Scott, Captain Linda Scott."

"I'm Steve, Lieutenant Steve York, ma'am . . . sir. I'm a medic." *Skipper's gonna love this!*

"We could have used your help earlier," she said, pointing to Billy Ray's body.

The diver looped the last of his lines around her waist, then checked Billy Ray's pulse. "There's nothing we can do for him now, ma'am."

Minutes later, they came alongside the fairwater. JT climbed the sail first, too juiced up to sit still. His adrenaline was flowing and his eyes were open wide. He clung to the sail ladder like a rock climber dangling over a chasm, his movements exaggerated, deliberate. Climbing up the fairwater ladder, he kept up a steady stream of chatter, encouraging the others. "Let's go, guys, the worst is over. Move it."

Suddenly, without warning, a huge swell sent the raft crashing against the sail, tossing the crew to one side. Before Scott could react, the empty end pitched up and the wind caught it, flipping the raft over.

Plunging into ice-cold seawater, Scott grabbed a handhold on the *Topeka*'s sail. As another powerful wave washed over her, she was swept off the deck, downwind. Her life preserver kept her afloat, but for a few moments she couldn't breathe at all. The sea battered her, rushing up her nose, causing her to gag and choke.

Seconds later, she felt the line draw snugly about her waist. Through saltwater spray and burning eyes, she saw Tristan, Dale, and the diver all tethered to the *Topeka,* bobbing like corks on a fishing line alongside her deck.

Lookouts on the sail pulled Dale in first. Following in JT's footsteps, he grinned despite the torturous conditions, glad to be among the living. Tristan followed next, and finally Scott.

The handholds felt slippery, like wet ice, making Scott's climb up the sail treacherous. Once on the tiny bridge, the foursome followed a ladder down three stories through the control room, where they were rushed off to sick bay.

Word spread like lightning. Less than five minutes later, every man on the *Topeka,* including those who'd been asleep in their bunks, knew they'd taken a woman onboard.

Fresh Water Trail, 1/01/2009, Thu., 07:54 A.M., 18:54 ZULU
USS *Topeka*

"Ocean current data has been assimilated, Captain. Download is complete."

"Very well, bring up all currents surrounding the *Maine*'s missile launch location." Hawk hovered over the plotting table with his bull-built XO, Lieutenant Commander Buck Clayton.

During the Gulf War, this former marine from Sioux City, Iowa, had broken his pelvis after falling eighty feet from a helicopter and couldn't stand still for an extended period without experiencing pain.

Interestingly, Hawk noted, he was standing still now.

Working the numbers, Buck never looked up and hadn't shifted his weight for several minutes.

Using these ocean currents and the renegade sub's last position as a starting point, Buck began working backwards, hoping to sniff out the freshwater discharge trail the *Maine* left behind.

"I think we've got the solution," Buck opened. "Take a look at this video clip."

Hawk studied his protégé's analysis, concentrating on the plotting table display.

"Here's the *Maine* during launch, eight hours ago under one hundred fifty feeta water." A submarine icon flashed on the plotting table's blue water map. Surrounding the sub, an animated pool of fresh white water appeared to grow, spread, and drift with the current. As time passed, the edge of the pool faded to blue as it mixed with seawater.

"Here she comes to periscope depth and takes out the Orion," Buck continued. "Finally, she dives deep, we lose her, and here's her last known location." He marked the spot, then pressed on.

"Now for the magic. We combine the initial position of her freshwater trail with current in the area, run it through our computer allowing for drift the last eight hours, and voilà, it plays out like this." As Buck fast-forwarded his videotape, the freshwater trail began mixing with seawater, drifting slowly across the map.

"Notice, Captain, the freshwater trail drifts to here." Buck circled the most likely location where they'd find the *Maine*'s trail, then made eye contact with the skipper. "The faster we get started, the easier she'll be to follow. The toughest part's detecting her trail when she's shallow because the surface water's all stirred up."

Hawk clicked on the plotting table's depth gauge, displaying water currents deeper below the surface. After a few clicks, the skipper reaffirmed a familiar pattern. "The shallow water's mixed due to surface churn but the deep water's comparatively calm. Ergo, the deeper she runs, the easier she'll be to follow."

Buck agreed, shifting his weight. "Once we detect her, Skipper, we're golden, for a while at least."

"Very well, dump our freshwater tanks en route and take on additional ballast; don't want to contaminate the trail with our own discharge."

"Aye, aye, Captain."

Hawk checked their position on the plotting table for the third time. No doubt about it. They'd already passed through the outer edge marking where the freshwater lake should be.

"Clear water lake detected, sir. Salinity is low, clarity is good. Trail's still warm, definite thermal scar."

Bingo! Hawk checked his watch. In less than two hours, the *Topeka* had sniffed out the freshwater lake the *Maine* left behind. "Trail bearing?"

"Negative, Captain. No egress trail detected yet. Bearing is TBD."

Hawk lifted his handset. "Maneuvering, all ahead slow."

"Diving Officer, commence searching for her freshwater egress trail."

"Aye, Captain." The diving officer translated Hawk's order into two separate orders, the first for the helmsman, the second for the planesman. As the *Topeka* crept forward, the helmsman steered a series of long S-turns, moving in and out of the freshwater, while the planesman slowly varied their depth using a porpoising maneuver.

"Conn, sick bay" echoed over the intercom speaker.

Hawk picked up the 1MC. "Sick bay, whaddaya got?"

"They're stable, Captain. Temperature's back to normal, nausea's passed, they're holding down solid food. Overall, they're in remarkably good shape, considering."

"Thanks, Doc." Hawk addressed the XO on his way out the door. "Buck, take the conn. I'm going to sick bay and check on our guests."

Sick bay was small and crowded because once under way, submariners seldom get sick on a cruise. The doctor gave his go ahead and Hawk immediately sought out Scott. She'd been moved to the privacy of an officer's stateroom.

After a brief introduction, the captain proceeded to pick Scott's brain.

"I understand you and Dr. Roberts were responsible for saving our lives."

"We gave you a heads-up," Scott sighed, "but you saved the *Topeka*. We didn't do the *Cheyenne* much good though, did we?"

"We needed time to lay a smoke screen, and your warning made it possible. Don't underestimate your contribution, Captain. You did all you could do and I'm forever in your debt."

"I did what anyone else would have done under the circumstances."

"From what I've been told, you saved the lives of your air crew as well."

"They're fine people, sir, none better in a pinch, but they're not my crew," Scott lamented. "They're Billy Ray's crew, and he's dead."

"They consider themselves your crew now, Captain Scott."

"Really?"

"And they're grateful to be alive."

Scott's eyes got a little cloudy.

"With your permission, Captain, I'd like to make you and your air crew honorary members of the *Topeka*." Hawk pulled a black nylon baseball cap out of a box with their logo patch—"USS *Topeka* SSN 754"—stitched across the front.

Scott didn't know what to say at first, then found the right words. "Speaking on behalf of my crew, we'd be pleased and proud to be part of your organization, Commander."

Hawk presented her the cap, saying, "Captain Scott, my crew call me Hawk."

Scott put on her hat, smiled, and met Hawk's gaze eye to eye. "Hawk, sir, my crew call me Scotty."

Following an extended conversation with Scotty regarding the *Maine*'s disappearance, Hawk came to respect his formidable nemesis.

"As I see it, our adversary's not suicidal and, clearly, he's not stupid." Hawk paused, imagining their roles reversed. "In all likelihood, he's only made one mistake: The renegade skipper probably believes the *Topeka*'s been destroyed. It's my job to make him pay for that error."

Scott nodded in agreement.

"And there's one other thing, Scotty, and it'll be easier for us both if I speak frankly. We need to have a heart-to-heart talk and I'm not very good at beating around the bush."

Scott didn't know what to say initially, then studied his eyes. For some unfathomable reason, something about his expression reminded her of her father. "Sure, Commander. Say what you need to say."

"Thank you, Scotty." Immediately, the tension in his eyes and mouth relaxed. In the blink of an eye, Hawk looked ten years younger. "I put out the word and you'll be safe here."

"I'm not sure I follow you, Commander. I can take care of myself."

"So I've noticed, but when you move about, I'd feel better if you stay outta ops and had an escort. I ran this idea by the chief of the boat . . ." He stopped midstream.

Scott felt like she was left hanging. "Yeah, and?"

"He volunteered for the duty," Hawk grinned. "My crew's as good as they get, but we've already been at sea for three months and now we've got another job to do. We're gonna have our hands full trailing the *Maine* and can't get you ashore for days. Truth is, you're a distraction and I'm concerned. My crew's gotta keep icy; we can't get sidetracked or we'll get killed."

"Am I under arrest?"

"No, but I'd consider it a great personal favor if you'd allow the Chief to escort you about, and please, confine your movements to our dining and off-duty areas. Once things loosen up a little, we'll give you a tour of the boat, but for now, if you'd stay clear of the operational areas, it'd help us both."

"Are you married, Commander?"

"Yes." Hawk reached in his pocket and pulled out the most fascinating wallet. It contained no money, credit cards, or driver's license, only pictures of his family from front to back.

Scott studied the pictures of Hawk's wife and daughter carefully. "Your daughter?"

Hawk smiled slightly, nodding. "Yeah, that's Mary Anne; she's a very precocious two. My wife just had our second child, a boy named Trevor, a little over one week ago."

"Trevor, that's a nice name. I'll bet you wish you could've been there."

"I'll say, and you never get that chance again, never. There's just something magic about it." Scott detected a sadness in Hawk's voice that hadn't been there before, then only moments later, his eyes began to smile. "You know, I was there when Mary Anne was born, and I remember it like yesterday. It was the most amazing thing, the most wondrous thing I've ever experienced in my life. When

Mary Anne was born, she was all red and purple and wrinkled, but when I saw her, when I got to hold her, for the first time in my life, I felt love for someone I didn't even know. That's the amazing part; I didn't even know her, but I loved her more than my own life. Maybe it doesn't make any sense, I mean it doesn't when you think about it, and I still can't explain it, but I've never been the same since."

Hawk paused while Linda took his words to heart. She wanted children more than anything else in this world.

"My wife's already given Trevor a nickname I kinda like," the commander concluded. "She calls him Terror Hawk. I think it's got a nice ring to it."

"Yes, it conjures up a distinctive image, doesn't it?" Scotty joked. "And this is your wife?"

"Yeah, that's Jo Anne." Hawk grinned like a love-struck kid.

"You write her often?"

"Every day. By the time we get back to port, she'll have a book."

By now, Scott had decided what she thought about Hawk. "Well, Commander, I suppose it's my turn to speak frankly now."

"I wish you would."

"I think you're overreacting with this escort business, but I could be wrong. This is your ship. You know your crew, and clearly you've got your priorities straight. Looks to me like you've got a wonderful family and it wouldn't be right for me to jeopardize their daddy. I've got some letter writing to do myself, so if you'd get me some pens and paper, I think I'll stay put for a while."

"I understand this goes against your grain, Captain Scott, but I assure you, you won't regret it. And I thank you on behalf of my family and my crew."

"Yeah, yeah." Scott winked at Hawk. "Just don't forget

my paper. I've got a book of letters to write. We thought we were going to die out there, and more than anything else, I wanted the chance to make things right with my husband. Now, if you'll excuse me, I've got some catching up to do."

Before Hawk could respond, Scott heard the muffled background noise of the intercom, then the doctor suddenly appeared. "Captain, you're wanted in the control room."

"Found her trail, Captain. Intersected it headlong." The XO drew a straight line across the plotting table as Hawk looked on, then continued. "We've got two possible bearings, either thirty degrees northeast or two hundred ten degrees southwest."

"So which way they'd go?" Hawk chuckled.

"Follow the yellow brick road."

"I'll tell you something, Buck." The captain shifted to his no-nonsense voice. "That skipper's one helluva bad witch. I've gotta feeling we're going to need all the brains and courage we can muster over the next few days just to stay alive."

"What'd you do in his shoes?" Buck shifted uneasily. "Stand and fight?"

"No way! I'd get the hell outta Houston. Let's take a look at the bottom charts."

One mouse click later, an extensively detailed bottom chart overlaid the plotting table map display.

Studying the charts, Hawk didn't know exactly what he was looking for, but instinctively he knew he'd recognize it when he saw it.

And there it was. The southwesterly course intersected the Mariana Trench.

"The renegade skipper's running southwest," Hawk concluded, "making his run for deep water trenches off Guam. That's where I'd go if I wanted to disappear. One spot's nearly thirty-six thousand feet deep. You could ditch a sub there and it'd never be found." Much like Mandrone, Hawk had trained all his adult life for this job. He was good at it and recognized that for the moment the *Maine* held the advantage.

The XO pondered what to do. "Should we request help? Someone to cover the northeast trail just in case?"

"Absolutely, and see if we can pull any fast attacks outta Guam."

"You thinking ambush?"

"Yep, I'd like to bushwhack 'em. Release a SLOT buoy; signal COMSUBPAC details of the situation, and request assistance."

"Aye, Captain."

Hawk looked across the control room. "Diving Officer, come to course two-one-zero and continue your freshwater search."

Weaving a continuous series of S-shaped turns, moving in and out of the *Maine*'s freshwater discharge stream, the *Topeka* crept slowly toward the *Maine*.

Hawk knew the *Maine* held a ten-hour lead. He couldn't know she was in full retreat, running quiet and deep, moving faster than the *Topeka* could possibly follow.

Meanwhile topside, protected by expansive air cover extending six hundred miles across, the *Stennis* and *Reagan* carrier battle groups closed on the *Maine*'s last confirmed position with all possible speed.

Briefing, 12/31/2008, Wed., 02:55 P.M., 21:55 ZULU
USSPACECOM

Mired in an atmosphere of rampant rumor, hundreds of military professionals affiliated with both battle groups watched COMSUBPAC's situation briefing via data link to find out what all the hullabaloo was about. Privately, Admiral Ozzie Eastwood was pleased his presentation found traction with such a large and distinguished audience of ASW experts. Washington watched along with U.S. naval forces, and for the first time, both Moscow and Russia's Pacific Fleet headquarters were provided translated, closed-captioned programming of a United States naval broadcast. Back inside USSPACECOM, Mason's team listened intently as Eastwood summarized his presentation, drawing the large-scale briefing to a close.

"Gentleman, we've got a score to settle. The *Maine* can't stay submerged forever, and there're only so many places she can hide. Pearl Harbor already looks like a ghost town, and in less than twenty-four hours, the Seventh Fleet'll be under way. We're throwing everything we've got that'll help into this, and I hope it's enough. My primary concern now is time; time's on their side, but we must find her and find her on our own terms. Running out of places to hide must inevitably lead to a final showdown, but stay on your guard."

"At this juncture," Ozzie acknowledged somberly, "the renegade skipper has several options. First, and obviously everyone's gravest concern, he's carrying a boat load of the smartest torpedoes and mines in the world, plus three nuclear-tipped missile-torpedoes. When he's cornered, he could kill one helluva lotta people on his way out, maybe emerge suddenly out of nowhere for one last stand, risking it all for say—a carrier kill."

A map of the North Pacific off the Kamchatka coast flashed on screen. The *Maine*'s most probable track was displayed as a line running southwest, highlighted in red dashes, the *Topeka*'s actual track shown as a solid blue overlay. In addition, originating from the *Maine*'s launch hot spot, an area shaped like a disk sector appeared. The

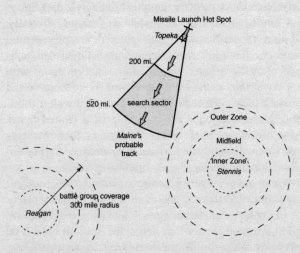

outer arc represented the *Maine*'s most distant position traveling at maximum speed, the inner arc represented her closest probable position cruising a slower, quieter speed.

"The *Maine*'s got a ten-hour lead on us, but she left behind an excellent starting point and probably doesn't know we're on her trail, not yet anyway. The *Topeka*'s been trailing her now over three hours and reported her course bearing two hundred ten degrees southwest, operating in the surface duct at five hundred feet, speed unknown, probably somewhere in the range of fifteen to forty knots. So far, seems she's running scared, not even checking her baffles. In all probability, she's located somewhere in the search sector shown on your screen. Gentlemen, this is classic blue water ASW and it's the same job it's always been—predominately an acoustical business. We've got no high-tech silver bullets to pull us out of the fire. We've gotta detect and positively identify the renegade, accurately resolve her position, then kill her. ClearWater may be of limited use, but don't count on it. Once we get a critical mass on station, we're gonna divide the area into grid squares, then squeeze the box with everything we've got.

"We've got a single P-3 working the search area now, but as you can see, our situation's improving. We've got one additional attack sub en route, tanker aircraft already operating over the sector, S-3 Vikings from the *Stennis*'re minutes away, and *Reagan* air ops tells me their S-3s'll join the fray in two hours, maybe less. Don't get me wrong—thirty-five planes to sanitize sixty-four thousand square miles of ocean plus defend two battle groups—the numbers're stacked against us and all of us know it. To make matters worse, the size of the search sector grows at a rate of two hundred square miles per minute and this rate's increasing. We've gotta cap the growth rate first, bound the box, then shrink it.

"Gentlemen, we've got a job to do and the best eyes and ears in the business to pull it off. I wish you God's speed and good hunting."

Back Door, 1/01/2009, Thu., 11:01 A.M., 22:01 ZULU
USS *Maine*

But Mandrone and his crew weren't suicidal. They were mercenaries with no intention of risking it all or hiding beneath the surface. With only a narrow window open for their escape, Mandrone was running nonstop, racing against the clock, keeping to their tight schedule for rendezvous. He knew it would take hours to mobilize the Seventh Fleet, days before they arrived on station, and used this time to his advantage. At this point, he didn't know exactly when the Seventh Fleet would come, or from what direction, but he knew they'd come.

Through it all, he'd planned a viable back door for escape, depending in part on the North Korean Navy, in part on friends and their own resourcefulness.

Hovering over the plotting table with his infected eye oozing, Mandrone lay out his illusive, deep water escape route to the southwest, ultimately settling by a tiny atoll 145 miles off Guam's Aga Point.

En route to the Mariana Trench, Mandrone occasionally doglegged his course at random intervals, leaving behind a little surprise above every knee. Deploying advanced Mk-60 Captor mines along their way, Mike's crew configured each weapon such that it hovered, suspended in their freshwater trail, listening for approaching submarines. This weapon, actually an encapsulated torpedo, was poised ready for ambush, programmed to hover at launch depth, listening for various submarine types. Like a mine, it lay silently in wait until a sub—or other sound source—approached. But unlike a mine, the encased torpedo woke up with a start, engaged its pump jet impeller, then erupted from its capsule on a sixty-knot run to target.

Not really a cost-effective deployment, Mandrone mused sardonically, *but imagine the skipper's surprise.*

In the near term, Mandrone understood that only another submarine, lucky sonobuoy, or SOSUS sensor array could detect them running ultra-quiet this deep. Mandrone believed you make your own luck and knew the location of every SOSUS array on the Pacific floor. As he saw it, their only seriously legitimate threat—an attack sub in the immediate area—had been destroyed. Unless they suffered a casualty or did something stupid, Mandrone believed they'd make it.

Lost in the Noise, 1/01/2009, Thu., 11:03 A.M., 22:03 ZULU
Hunter P-3 Orion

"Release now, now, now!" rang out over the P-3's intercom.

"Buoy away and clear."

"We're outta business back here," TACCO reported. "That's the last one we've got."

Cruising the deck about two hundred twenty miles an hour, the Orion's pilot pulled back on the yoke, yanking her nose up in a climb, banking through a U-turn. He planned to circle their final sonobuoy three hours, maybe less, until its seawater-activated battery played out.

Circling seventy miles northeast of the *Maine,* the Hunter Orion laid the last sonobuoy it had designed for omnidirectional deep-water operation—designated the AN/SSQ-41. Unfortunately, the crew found themselves with sonobuoys left in their racks, only the wrong type. A regrettable situation, though not unusual. The crown jewels, their most sensitive deep-water buoys with capability for long-range detection, had been expended hours ago around the *Maine*'s missile launch site. Every buoy left onboard was used to localize and track contacts, but so far everything they'd detected had been either a false alarm or a genuine detection later classified as non-submarine.

Even with the latest high-tech aids, classification of an ultra-quiet submarine is no easy task. Classification remained the art of the ASW business (identifying faint echoes as metallic, barely distinguishable from the surrounding reverberation and background noise) requiring a sensitive, well-trained set of ears.

Such acute aural skills were needed onboard the Hunter Orion this day, but like most other P-3 crews, these men specialized in eyeball work, tracking drug runners, not hunting submarines. As a result, the crew listened with their eyes, never using headphones, depending exclusively on signal analysis and visual displays.

But their best efforts at detection and classification had been for naught. The *Maine*'s faint signature wasn't detected because it was swamped, washed out by background ocean noises surrounding the sonobuoy. They were quite literally lost, so far down in the noise that all the signal-processing power in the world couldn't pull 'em out with any degree of confidence.

CHAPTER TWENTY-FOUR

Two Words, 1/01/2009, Thu., 11:10 A.M., 22:10 ZULU
USS *Topeka*

"Can't you give him something for those dry heaves, Doc?" That came from Scott.

"Working on his next meal now." After measuring some clear, viscous solution, the medical officer poured it into Tristan's IV. "Looks like he swallowed more salt water than everyone else put together. Must've panicked."

"We were all scared, but he can't swim. Will he be all right?"

"Sure, he'll be fine. He's just dehydrated, that's all. Be good as new in no time . . . Just needs some rest and a little more of my magic mixture."

Forward in the control room, Hawk and his crew bird-dogged the *Maine*'s freshwater trail. Aft in medical, while Tristan slept for the next eight hours, Scott sat at his side and wrote Jay.

> *Dear Jay,*
>
> *How do I begin to say I'm sorry?*
> *Earlier today, I almost died and all I could do was*

think about you. More than anything else, I wanted the chance to make things right with you, my friends and family. When I thought I was going to die, all I wanted to do was live long enough to tell you I love you more than you can possibly know. I wanted to ask you to forgive me for not being there all these years, wanted to ask for one more chance to start over.

This morning I promised God I'd live the rest of my life like every day was going to be my last, and I meant it with all my heart. I think this was something I knew all along, something we learned as kids growing up in church, but somewhere along the way, my priorities got out of line. I don't know when, but I lost my focus on people, on relationships, on God and the things that are really important in life.

Looking back, I can see it all more clearly now. It's funny the things you think about when you've only got a few minutes left to live. I thought about our happy times growing up together, wished we could relive every one.

Sometimes it seems we never talk anymore, not like we used to. I used to hang on your every word, wonder what was on your mind. Every minute we were together seemed like the happiest time of my life, but somehow, once we were married, the magic faded. It makes me sad to think about it really, but I guess it was our fault for letting it happen. I know I contributed more than my share—I mean, I always knew I had to fly, but somewhere along the way I began trading away little bits of our relationship for my career—and I was wrong. I guess this leads me to what I really wanted to say from the beginning.

I'm sorry and I love you.

More than anything else in the world, I want us to build a wonderful life together. You know we'd talked a

*lot about starting our family. Well, earlier today the
Topeka's skipper, Slay Hawkins, showed me his wallet
filled with pictures of his family. He told me about
being there when his daughter was born, about loving
someone he didn't even know. I mean, he lit up like a
Christmas tree and it set me thinking. When you're
ready, I'm ready to have our children. How do you like
the name Trevor?*

*Everything I've said comes from my heart and it
scares me in a way. I've built my whole life around flying—and you. I'm not the same girl you used to know.
Death has a way of changing a person, but I want to be
true to the kid I was in high school, true to the girl you
knew next door. When I see you again, I pray you'll open
up and talk to me, talk the way we used to talk. I miss
those times, the fun, the magic of your touch, but most of
all, I miss you.*

> *All my love,*
> *Linda*

Tristan blinked his eyes, but did not speak. He felt as if
he'd spent who knows how long dreaming, suspended in
that time between sleep and consciousness, that magic
time before you're fully awake, when all your dreams feel
wonderfully real.

He looked to his left and saw Linda. "Pencil," was all he
said.

A good sign, she thought, glad to hear his voice. After
raising the head of his bed, she placed a pen and pad of
paper in his hand.

Dr. Roberts smiled weakly, then closed his eyes again;
his expression placid.

Scott wasn't sure what this was about, but after a few

moments, Tristan wrote two words—*arbitration hearings*—then his hand relaxed and he drifted off to sleep. Neither word meant anything to Linda.

"You wrote this while you were off somewhere in La La Land," Scott smiled.

It registered immediately. "You know the oddest thing occurred to me while I was dreaming. Since the *Maine* was first hijacked, I've had this strange sense I've been through all this before, just couldn't put my finger on why. I thought maybe I'd dreamed it or something and couldn't really explain it until now. I wish I'd remembered sooner, but sometimes I see things more clearly about the time I wake up. Kinda weird, don't you think?"

"I know exactly what you mean, Tristan, I'm the same way; a lot of people are like that, but tell me, what's this note all about?"

"Six or eight years ago, the Navy contracted one of its officers, an XO, lieutenant commander I think, named Mike Mandrone, to write a book." Tristan paused, struggling with what to say.

"I don't get it. They do that all the time. What's the big deal?"

Tristan took a deep breath then spat it out. "Mandrone laid out how the world would change once ClearWater became operational, and let me tell you, he was rigorous. He examined every detail, every strategic implication and predicted everything that's happened so far; I mean everything, right down to the hijacking and missile launch. He predicted ClearWater would be vulnerable to espionage, then proved this would place our submarine forces at risk. Ultimately, he predicted the United States and her allies would find their own submarine fleets exposed, vulnerable to attack if they came shallow for any reason."

Scott pondered his comments for a few minutes, then asked a pointed question."You're serious? He laid this all out? Sounds like a blueprint for disaster."

Tristan nodded. "Years ago, it seemed too fantastic to lose sleep over, but let me assure you, his work was technically rigorous. Nothing he included was considered a technical stretch by either the engineering or military community."

"Whaddaya think now?"

"In light of what's happened, I'm not so sure. Looks like someone's doing exactly what Mandrone predicted would be done."

"Anything else come to mind?"

"Mandrone was adamant about one point. He always insisted space-based submarine detection technology was a two-edged sword, and politically, this got him into a world of trouble. I've never seen anything like it."

"What'd he mean?"

"For every step forward, we take one step back. Mandrone wanted to make sure we didn't dig ourselves a hole, step backwards, and break a leg. If you think about it, the guy was right. In some ways, we're more secure today, but less secure in others. I mean, we never had a nuclear submarine hijacked before ClearWater became operational, did we?"

Scott understood. "How'd you find out about Mandrone anyway?"

Tristan went on to explain his involvement in the Livermore arbitration hearings, how East Coast politicians and the U.S. Navy railroaded Mandrone out of the service.

"Did Mandrone predict any likely targets for this renegade missile launch?" Tristan had been asleep and couldn't know that the *Maine*'s missile launch had targeted U.S. nuclear submarine forces.

"Targets weren't his primary area of interest, but he did suggest two obvious targets—nuclear submarine forces and carrier battle groups."

"Did he mention ELF . . . ?"

Before she finished her question, Tristan filled in the answer. "Now that you bring it up, I think he highlighted ELF site vulnerability as a weak link." Tristan caught Scott's eye. "This is a little scary."

"We'd better talk to the skipper."

Less than twenty minutes later, Hawk released a SLOT buoy relaying Tristan's observations to COMSUBPAC. Admiral Eastwood called Washington immediately, demanding an immediate answer to one question. "Where is former Lieutenant Commander Mike Mandrone?"

PART FIVE

The Hunt

CHAPTER TWENTY-FIVE

Max Quiet Speed, 1/01/2009, Thu., 01:50 P.M., 01:50 ZULU
USS Maine

"Situation's changing topside, Captain. Listen to this." The sonarman jacked up the volume, then piped his receiver's output over the intercom.

Sounds like chaos on the horizon and it's closing in, Mandrone thought, moving forward to the sonar room. His eye was patched with a makeshift combination of gauze and a band of silver-gray duct tape wrapped around his head. The pain in his eye had settled down to a dull, aching throb, but with no depth perception whatsoever, he had trouble navigating the hatches without banging his shins on the steel bulkheads.

"What do you make of it?" the skipper asked, his good eye meeting the sonarman's. Even through his blurred vision, Mandrone could see that the middle-aged Korean's features were drawn; circles under his eyes revealed fatigue from the continuous duty pulled since the missile launch. Mike made a note, *begin food and sleep rotation now before it's too late.*

The acoustics engineer shook his head, a little bewildered, maybe a little overwhelmed. "I can only guess at this stage, Captain, but the entire noise floor's on the rise.

In my experience, the most likely thing that'd cause an increase in background noise like this would be a carrier battle group, or maybe the Seventh Fleet, moving somewhere in a big hurry."

Mandrone paused for a moment, squinted, then penciled in their approximate position on the map.

"Give me your best bearing."

"It's spread out over two hundred miles, Captain, off our port side."

"Give me your best bearing to the center of the commotion."

"Roughly one hundred thirty degrees."

Struggling to keep his good eye in focus, Mandrone marked the map. "No, it's not the Seventh Fleet. No way they'd approach us off port, not coming in from Japan."

"I'm having trouble keeping track, but I've counted over thirty screws." The sonarman circled a clump of lines on his waterfall display. "I'd wager this cluster's gotta be the carrier. Judging from its bearing, I'd say it's about center of the ruckus."

Mandrone squinted, struggling to examine his sonarman's find. He moved his face nearer the display, then farther away, trying to find a distance where the green flecks would come into focus. After a few moments, he determined he couldn't see clearly enough to extract the details. "How many screws you count?"

"Four, each has five blades."

Mandrone rubbed the stubble on his chin. "You're right, that's probably the carrier."

"And I make out two contacts, possible subs, pinging off port; they're faint, but coming at us."

The captain put his hand on the sonarman's shoulder. "It may sound like pandemonium closing in, but if we play it smart and don't panic, they'll make enough noise to blanket our escape."

The engineer took a short, shallow breath, sensing danger crowding in around them, then suddenly a horrific creaking groan resonated throughout the sub.

The *Maine*'s pressure hull contracted slightly, yielding about the forward torpedo embarkation hatch.

Running this deep, it's the holes in the hull that'll kill you, Mandrone thought, knowing the *Maine* was weakest where large openings pierced her pressure hull. Once her metallic moans fell silent, he listened for the sound of inrushing seawater. As every submariner knows, at a depth of sixteen hundred feet, it doesn't take a very big leak to cause a very big problem.

And somehow, seawater seems to find a way, entering under tons of pressure with sufficient force to sever a man's head or cut through steel.

Mandrone tensed, then spoke over the intercom. "Ash, stand by the ballast control panel. Everyone else, drop what you're doing and check for leaks. Get back to me ASAP."

You couldn't forget the depth—the *Maine* wouldn't let you—but the tension it created kept everyone on edge. It must have been the fear, because there's something fundamentally disconcerting about checking for leaks in a submarine and expecting to find one.

But Mandrone didn't have time to dwell on it. Checking the control room's eight hull-penetrating masts plus the forward escape and weapon-loading hatches took nearly fifteen minutes. And to make matters worse, Mike busted his shin in the process. Overall, the *Maine*'s pressure hull was riddled with tens of holes—missile and torpedo tubes, masts, hatches—and periodically checking them all took time and precious energy.

After his final crewman reported feet dry, Mandrone breathed a sigh of relief, returned to his cabin, then wrapped both shins with gauze padding plus his obligatory—now trademark—duct tape. Decked out in his orange jump suit, with loose bands of tape wrapped around his head and pant legs, Mike would've looked like a comical character had the situation not been so deadly serious. After putting another drop of Tetracaine in his eye, he limped back to the sonar room.

This time, when Mike entered the sonar room, the engineer looked him over from head to toe and just grinned. After a moments' thought, the sonarman reached into his toolbox and handed the captain a well-used roll of three-inch duct tape.

"You need this worse than I do, Captain."

"Hmpt." Mandrone squinted, checking it over with his good eye. "Thank you. You're right, as always." After pocketing the roll, he continued. "Let me hear what you've got out there now."

The sonarman handed him a set of headphones.

"Two probable sub contacts pinging off our port side, Captain; they're still coming at us." His voice revealed apprehension.

Mandrone put his hand on the sonarman's shoulder again. "Trust me on this one; we're running close to crush depth down here. Sea pressure's the biggest problem we've got, not that carrier group, not those subs. I know how they operate and we have the advantage. I've played this game before."

"I hope you're right, Captain."

"The Ohio-class submarine's the quietest ever put to sea. Long as we stay deep and run quiet, they'll never find us. I'll plot an egress course and skirt us around the trouble."

• • •

"Conn, sonar. Something's going on topside. As best I can tell, we're being squeezed. Fifteen contacts, maybe more closing off our starboard side. They're faint, but persistent. Could they be the seventh fleet?"

"I suppose," Mike twisted his mouth, "but I didn't expect 'em so soon,"

For what seemed like the fifty thousandth time, he moved forward to the sonar room.

"I've never seen anything like it, Captain, there's so many screws."

"So what's their spread? They clustered like a battle group?"

"No range at this point, too early to estimate their spread."

"Where's the center of the ruckus?"

"Overall, the noise is centered here, off our starboard side."

Mandrone drew a bearing on his map toward the center of the commotion. "Could be another carrier group, could be a squeeze play. We have no way to know for sure, not yet anyway."

Taking advantage of the situation, Mike dismissed his sonarman with orders to get some food and sleep, then he sat silent for an extended period listening starboard. After a time he shifted directions, listening to the approaching ruckus off port. There was no external indication as to how anxious he really felt. Outwardly, he looked calm and analytical, but inside, his mind raced through countless what-ifs with the nervous energy of a hawk ready to strike. Shifting back and forth, he toggled from port to starboard estimating screw positions, evaluating the changing situation topside against their short list of options.

• • •

Sixteen hundred feet beneath the surface, time seemed to stand still. Hours, seemingly endless hours, passed with Mandrone's ears glued to the headset, his only breaks taken for sandwiches, diet Dr. Pepper, and countless pit stops. His eye was throbbing again, anesthetic wearing off.

Finally, he'd heard enough. At this juncture he had more questions than answers, but judging from the speed and number of contacts, they most likely had separate carrier battle groups closing in from both sides.

Chaos to port heading straight for 'em; commotion to starboard, closing fast, maybe twenty-five to thirty knots. When push came to shove, their options dwindled down to a precious few. No way they could go around 'em both, they'd miss their rendezvous.

Fearless and calculating, Mike Mandrone understood one thing above all else—noise emitted from both fast-approaching surface fleets held the key to their escape. He returned to the control room and plotted their course, splitting the distance between them.

Once he had his plan committed to paper, he read it over again one last time, making sure he agreed with it. He did. It was the submariner's classic quiet play, taking advantage of noise generated when two carrier battle groups approach each other. It played off their silent strengths, but nevertheless demanded courage. This day would be filled with an unrelenting fear of detection. No doubt the crew would be jumpy, but if they kept their wits about them, they'd simply disappear in the background. He'd done this before. If the *Maine* cooperated and they played their cards right, he knew it would work.

Mandrone lifted his handset. "Engine room, slow to fifteen knots. Maintain turns for maximum quiet speed."

"Very well, Captain. Slowing to maximum quiet speed."

"Ash." He looked across the control room. "Maintain

current depth and come to course one-nine-zero degrees. Make it a gradual, ultra-quiet course correction. We've got more company coming in topside than we know what to do with. We're being squeezed between two carrier groups, and in a matter of hours, this place is gonna be about as noisy as an elephant stampede."

The Frenzy Grows, 1/01/2009, Thu., 03:55 P.M., 02:55 ZULU
Aircraft Carrier USS *Stennis*

This would'a made a great movie if it didn't strike so damn close to home, Eastwood thought and grimaced.

Looking down from the primary flight tower, he and the air boss had an unobstructed, end-to-end view of the carrier's flight deck. Inside the Pri-Fly, the motion of the violently pitching deck was amplified by the height of the tower, but they had one consolation—at least they were dry. Outside, the weather was abysmal.

Beneath them, the *Stennis* plunged through massive ocean swells, sending torrents of frigid seawater flooding over the flight deck, cold salt spray raining down on the aircraft. Blue-shirted aircraft handlers had trouble standing upright as they directed the last S-3 to its catapult.

Once the Viking was in position, the jet-blast deflector—a tall steel door which deflects engine exhaust—pivoted into position and the shooter signaled his pilot to rev up. On cue, the pilot brought his throttles to full military power, while overhead, Eastwood watched the Viking's wings shudder, vibrating under tremendous thrust.

Following an exchange of hand signals, the shooter double-checked his catapult settings and made sure the pilot's head was back against the seat. Ready to launch, he arched forward touching the deck, then pointed two fingers toward the bow.

Suddenly, the S-3 was engulfed in a cloud of steam, then it disappeared, lost in the mist.

This spectacle was routine for the air boss, but all the orchestration, teamwork, screaming engines, and power behind a cat shot never failed to inspire Eastwood. *Is America a great country or what!*

Viking squadrons from the *Stennis* and *Reagan* rose from the deck in waves, thirty-five in all, followed by tanker, fighter, and surveillance aircraft.

With well-practiced precision, the seeming chaos of carrier flight operations transitioned into a well-ordered hunt by the numbers game three hundred miles forward. Searching above and below the surface, each Viking scrubbed its assigned grid square using radar and sonobuoys, all the while linking its sonar data back to the *Stennis*. Closer in, dragging their long towed arrays mid-field, surface ships and submarines listened while helicopters sprinted by overhead, dangling their dipping sonars, pinging contacts on demand. Closer still, surrounding the carrier with a circular sonar fence forty miles across, surface ships and helicopters pinged furiously, feeding countless channels of information back to the Combat Direction Center, for the *Stennis* was the information hub of the battle group.

Bird in the Hand, 1/01/2009, Thu., 04:34 P.M., 03:34 ZULU
USS *Stennis*

Inside the CDC, there was standing room only. The place was normally occupied by five tactical organizations, but now the antisubmarine warfare outfit had practically taken over. Even as antisurface and air warfare groups jockeyed for space, all efforts focused on creating a picture of the contact situation over and under the *Maine*'s search sector.

In peacetime, the number of contacts inside their six-hundred-mile-wide area was often alarming; in times of crisis, the numbers could quickly become overwhelming. Consequently, *Stennis* mission priorities reflected a protect-yourself-first, prosecute-the-*Maine*-second type of reality.

Eastwood watched the contact picture coalesce without speaking. His eyes took several minutes to acclimate to the dark room, but once they had, he focused in on the wiry-built tactical action officer situated at the center of the commotion. Behind his horn-rimmed glasses and Gallic nose, the man looked lean, fit, and tough.

"What's our submarine contact situation in the hot zone?"

"Still sorting through 'em, sir, but looks like we have several unwelcome visitors, not sure yet how many."

"That's not surprising," Eastwood said and nodded.

The TAO pulled up several sound tracks from Viking sonobuoys, flashed them on screen, then offered the admiral a headset. "Care to listen?"

"No, I'm tone deaf from my diesel boat days, just tell me what you've got."

"From the looks of these signatures, we've got visitors and they're not made in America."

"Russian?"

"Probably, sir, or Chinese. It's too soon to know."

"How many? This kind of confusion's the last thing we need." Eastwood knew Russian intervention could only aid the renegade. Their communication equipment was outdated, incompatible with America's, so coordination became an immediate problem. In addition, Ruski boat noise would hinder the Americans' own detection capability, and finally, if their submarines approached the battle group, the U.S. fast attacks would have to shadow them.

Operationally, there was no alternative. A lose-lose situation for the Americans, but nothing could be done about it. Eastwood would have protested, but these were international waters.

"Fifteen detections so far. We're localizing them now, Admiral, but experience shows more than half'll be false alarms."

"Yeah, it's the false alarms and foreign subs that tie up resources we can't spare." Eastwood studied the TAO's reaction, sensed agreement, then continued. "I've got a decision to make and I need your input."

"That's what we're here for, sir."

"As I see it, our situation is this. The *Maine*'s trail's growing cold and the *Topeka* needs help. We've gotta assume the *Maine*'s spreading the gap, running faster than the *Topeka* can follow. Right now, that freshwater trail's the best lead we've got, but it's fading fast. You're working four fast attacks from here, and frankly, I need to send one of 'em north. Help me understand the impact—tell me, any of these contacts classified?"

"Five have been classified as probable submarines, sir, but it's too soon to know if they'll pan out. We're localizing 'em now. Once we get a track, we'll close and establish a positive I.D."

Eastwood studied the tactical situation displayed on the large blue screen. Aircraft, ships, and submarines were scattered uniformly across the region. Near the top of the screen, the *Topeka* appeared about a two-hour sail from the attack sub USS *Tucson*. "My bottom line is this. I need to send the *Tucson* north to join *Topeka*. Can you make do?"

The TAO studied the contact picture displayed on the wall a few moments, then responded. "Can I speak off the record, sir?"

Eastwood agreed.

"There's no way we can get by if, and I repeat if, some of these contacts turn out to be Russian subs. This close to our carriers, we'll have to shadow 'em; no way around it and we could run out of fast attacks in one hell of a hurry. But as I see it, my concern's based on speculation while you've got a bird in the hand. I say go for it, get the *Tucson* on her trail before it's too late. I may be shooting myself in the foot with this call, but I think we can make up the loss with air cover. Statistically, half my contacts'll turn out to be false alarms; it'll simply take us longer to ferret 'em out." The TAO smiled thoughtfully, then concluded on a lighter note. "We're tripping over ourselves down there anyway, Admiral."

Signal, 1/01/2009, Thu., 04:58 P.M., 03:58 ZULU
Destroyer USS *Yorktown*

Topside, the *Yorktown* cruised about five hundred feet behind the *Topeka,* providing the ship-to-sub laser data link necessary for one-way, deep-water submarine communications.

That's more like it, the captain thought, catching the latest message traffic bound for the *Topeka.*

Across the bridge, the caustic, slightly built submarine element coordinator squinted. "About time Eastwood got his ass in gear."

The captain nodded, then lifted his handset. "Go ahead, send it."

"Aye, Captain." The *Yorktown*'s radio operator depressed a switch marked "ALIGN." Beneath the keel, several yards behind the *Yorktown*'s sonar dome, a gyroscopically stabilized turret rotated about its vertical axis. From a few feet away, the dome-like blister appeared to launch flashes of blue-green laser light off into the depths of the Pacific. Once the sub tracker homed in, the blue-green light glowed several seconds, illuminating the back of the *Topeka* sixteen hundred feet below. Moments later, this message appeared on Hawk's flat screen display.

```
FR: COMSUBPAC
TO: USS Topeka
Tucson fast attack en route.
ETA two hours.
Will rendezvous on your position bearing
one-five-zero.
Continue to prosecute.
God's speed.
Admiral Eastwood sends.
```

CHAPTER TWENTY-SIX

"Captain, sonar. *Tucson* is on line and in position one thousand feet to port."

Hawk picked up his handset in the control room. "Very well. Commence tactical database assimilation. Tell 'em what they need to know; download our latest trail profiles, then patch 'em through to the conn." Hawk understood that once their databases were in sync, the *Tucson* would know everything about the *Maine*'s freshwater trail the *Topeka* had learned.

"Sonar, aye."

Immediately, Hawk's handset came alive with the distinctive, high-pitched chirping of modem chatter. Sounded like a FAX machine to Hawk, but he knew *Topeka*'s computer was talking to the *Tucson*'s.

Forward in his sonar room, a shelf filled with high-speed modems began blinking as the *Tucson* downloaded data from *Topeka* using their sonar communication system, the equivalent of an underwater telephone. Minutes later, the modem chatter fell silent.

After an exchange of tactical information, including

freshwater temperature, clarity, and salinity data, Hawk spoke with the *Tucson*'s skipper, Ray "Woodie" Wilkinson, an engineer by training and relative newcomer as commanders go, this being his first command afloat.

"You call the shots, Hawk; you've logged all the hours on her trail."

"Very well, Woodie. Load ADCAPs in tubes one and two, twin ATs in three and four. Keep 'em warm and ready to run."

"Load's already in progress; we're matching your load tube for tube."

"Good. The trail's growing cold and we've gotta pick up the pace. You know the ole vent, sprint, and sniff routine?"

"Yeah, but I could use a little refresher."

"Trail contamination's our number one concern here, gotta manage it. We'll dump our freshwater holding tank astern; you do the same and mix it up with your screw. Once you're set, pull ahead of us a thousand yards or so, lock on the trail, then calibrate your sniffer. When your gear's ready, signal. We'll sprint ahead, try to pick up her trail again, then signal once we've got it."

"What about us?"

"You stay on her trail, slow and sure, but when you hear our signal, our roles reverse. On cue, we both vent our freshwater tanks, then you run like the rabbit."

"Tortoise versus the hare." Woodie chuckled over the phone. "Been there, done that, ole buddy. The turtle always wins."

Vent, Sprint, and Sniff, 1/01/2009, Thu., 09:12 P.M., 08:12 ZULU
USS *Tucson* (SSN-770)

"Conn, sonar. Signal from the *Topeka,* Captain. They've picked up her trail."

"Conn, aye." Woodie cut his eyes across the control room. "Diving Officer, vent our freshwater astern. Compensate with the forward trim tank." Typically, nuclear submarines discharge warm freshwater continuously, but the skipper knew this would contaminate the *Maine*'s trail. He understood that the capacity of their freshwater holding tank was minuscule compared to his submarine's unstoppable, artesian well–like capability for creating water; nevertheless, once empty it took several minutes to fill. For a hunter stalking the *Maine*'s trail, this time was of paramount importance because when filling his holding tank, he wasn't discharging freshwater into the sea.

On the downside, while filling their holding tank, the crew's day-to-day existence would revolve around the cyclic availability of water. All in all, everyone's routine meshed into synchronization with the hunt. Crewmen shaved, showered, flushed the toilets, and brushed their teeth on cue, once their freshwater supply accumulated, but before it was vented to the sea.

Woodie heard the rush of compressed air evacuating the ship's precious freshwater supply to the sea. Once the holding tank indicator on the ballast control panel glowed "LEVEL ZERO," the diving officer closed the discharge valve, and for a while at least, the *Tucson* could run without dumping heat into the ocean.

This was important because their own warm freshwater contaminated the *Maine*'s trail by producing a thermal scar. Fact was, they tracked the *Maine* by measuring the salinity, clarity, and temperature of her freshwater trail relative to surrounding seawater. Typically, her trail was less salty, clearer, and slightly warmer than nearby ocean water.

"Tanks're trim, Captain, fore and aft."

"Very good." Woodie picked up his handset. "Maneuvering, make turns for thirty knots." Looking across the control room, he instructed, "Helm, steer well around the *Topeka*; give her a wide berth."

Sewer Pipe, 1/01/2009, Thu., 08:53 P.M., 08:53 ZULU
USS *Maine*

Bong! bong! bong! bong! bong!

"Captain, Captain, something's gone wrong with the air!" Ash sounded panicky over the intercom.

Forward in Sonar, Mandrone's mind raced through a dozen possibilities. His gut tightened into an icy knot at the thought of fire or, worse yet, that poisonous gas. "What's the problem?"

"Mass spectrometer alarm, Captain. My read's methane, but I need to check it."

"Shit!" Mandrone mumbled, exasperated. "Put the boat on autopilot and go to it." Mike had forgotten about dumping their sewage tank and knew methane to be explosive. In modern nuclear submarines, heads can be used anytime. Sewage is collected in a holding tank and discharged at the skipper's convenience.

Mandrone rushed to the control room as Ash headed aft to the atmosphere monitoring equipment.

A few minutes later, Ash's voice sounded over the intercom. "Significant levels of methane have accumulated in our holding tank, Captain. Traces have permeated the crew's berthing spaces and been detected in the crew's washroom."

"Are the levels dangerous, Mr. Wilson?"

"In the holding tank, yes. Recommend we evacuate it immediately."

"Very well, this is a better time than most." His meaning: No sewage-sniffing submarine was nearby.

Ash returned to the control room and opened an air valve, pressurizing the tank with sufficient force to empty it at a depth of sixteen hundred feet.

Mike felt his ears pop first. "Hold it, Ash. Something's wrong here."

Ash felt it too and closed the valve.

The effect that followed was like being suddenly immersed in the sewage pit from hell.

Invisibly filling the submarine, a wave of stench flooded forward from the head, washing over them like a foul wind. The toxic shock literally choked their breath away.

"My god!" Mike gagged. Picking up his handset, he spit out his order. "Suck rubber! Suck rubber!"

Everyone grabbed his emergency breathing gear, struggling to get into the rubber face mask before nausea overwhelmed him. They made it except for the sonarman. He'd just eaten, and he retched his guts out on the deck.

Once the crew was stabilized, everyone looked for the air leak. From painful experience, they knew to check the heads first. Stainless steel heads in a submarine are similar to those in a commercial jet. The metal flap at the bottom of the bowl opens during a flush, but normally remains closed unless inadvertently blocked. As it turned out, a flapper valve in one of the heads had been jammed open when one of the *Maine*'s enlisted crewmen died there. No one had bagged his body, he'd been out of the way, but in an ironic way he'd found revenge. Because he had jammed the flapper valve open, the gasses inside the sewage tank had flooded into the submarine when Ash tried to pressurize it.

Saturating the boat from stern to bow, the odor was like a greasy film, contaminating everything it touched—clothes, skin, equipment. There'd be no getting rid of it quickly; they couldn't risk detection by venting at the surface. It would get better—air treatment gear would see to that—but it would take time. In truth, the stench would never go away completely and everyone knew it.

Mandrone felt trapped, buried alive inside a steel sewer pipe. *Things could be worse. It coulda been a fire.*

The Whole Nine Yards, 1/01/2009, Thu., 06:00 P.M., 09:00 ZULU
Homeport in Yokosuka, Japan
Aircraft Carrier USS *Harry S. Truman*

Steaming out of the Sea of Japan with an urgent fury, the Seventh Fleet traveled the road back, licking its wounds, looking to settle the score. But it had taken time to ready this fearsome armada. Once under sail, they sprinted northeast at flank speed toward the *Maine*'s last known location off Kamchatka, only to find that her trail had grown cold, inadvertently trampled by the Russians.

Keenly aware of the American menace threatening their only submarine base with direct access to the Pacific, the Russians had taken action to keep their undersea waterways open, deploying additional destroyers, picket subs, and extensive air cover around Petropavlovsk.

Ruski, 1/02/2009, Fri., 07:21 A.M., 18:21 ZULU
USS *Stennis*

Admiral Eastwood entered the CDC searching for the head honcho. He found him in front of the big blue screen, sandwiched between an army of ASW staff talking to one of his Viking pilots over radio.

As quickly as the tactical action officer signed off, Ozzie interrupted. "Give it to me straight."

"Things are pretty tense here, Admiral." The TAO's

expression telegraphed concern. "I'm outta fast attacks and some contacts are dropping off screen before we get positive I.D. We're shadowing two Russian subs, both confirmed inside the hot zone, plus a third's approaching the area at high speed. I dispatched my last fast attack south a couple hours ago to check out another mechanical contact, and so far, that Ruski's been given a free ride. Don't get me wrong. We're pinging him with sonobuoys; he knows we've drawn a bead on him, but we don't have the resources to challenge him. Best we can do is put a destroyer on his back."

The admiral nodded understanding. "Hold out as best you can. We've got more reinforcements coming, four fast attacks driving north out of Guam, but they're still twenty hours away."

CHAPTER TWENTY-SEVEN

Fatigue, 1/02/2009, Fri., 07:32 A.M., 19:32 ZULU
USS *Topeka*

The *Topeka* had been on patrol over three months now. The men were tired, and critical items were in short supply—they were almost out of coffee. After dodging the *Maine*'s incoming missile salvo, then picking up her trail, Hawk recognized the first symptoms of a disturbing trend. He knew dwindling attention to detail was the first indication they were losing their edge; still, how many times can even the finest crewman read the same gauges and record the same numbers without error?

Hawk sensed his crew becoming mesmerized, performing their tasks mechanically, almost robotically, time and time again. Inwardly, the skipper was concerned his crew was being lulled into a false sense of security, a mode of looking at their displays, but not seeing them, not comprehending the life-and-death significance of what their numbers meant. Their technical crispness, that sense of being on the edge, was clearly beginning to dull. He needed fresh ideas to feed their imagination and wracked his brain searching for out-of-the-box approaches to keep his crew icy.

As a result, Hawk constantly pushed for better ways to

view their tactical situation. He wanted real-time 3-D animation, color moving pictures of what was going on around them, and pushed for new ways to display their sensor data. He challenged them to start out with something simple, then create movies he could navigate through with the click of a button, but these tasks were technically demanding, took a great deal of computer expertise, and after a while, they became just another job for his crew. The fun of the adventure was fading, the thrill of the hunt was gone, and Hawk was running out of ideas.

Homesick, his thoughts drifted back to the Christmas he'd missed with his family, and his heart sank. Struggling to rally, he pulled his Christmas familygram from his pants pocket, but somehow, it only made him feel worse. Studying it, he yearned for his wife and children. The last coded line, *XOX:-)*, expanded into *Hugs and Kisses, Jo Anne.*

God only gives us so many Christmases on this earth, Hawk thought, *and precious few of them when our children wonder at the magic.* As his longing grew stronger, he remembered his mom, dad, and brother.

He thought about his parents' health, then he bit his lip realizing he could count on his fingers the number of times he'd see them before they died. *God only gives us so many springs, and so many falls. Don't even know my brothers' family, not really. Seldom see their children, never met his youngest, don't have a clue about their dreams, probably wouldn't recognize his kids if I saw 'em on the street. Something's bad wrong with this picture,* Hawk concluded somberly, then he thought about his crew and knotted up inside.

How can they stand it? Most of 'em are only kids themselves; many got brand-new babies back home. God help us all, Hawk lamented, then gazing at nothing whatsoever, his eyes clouded over.

He'd remembered his friend, Clay McCullough. *He must be dead, no way he'd give up the* Maine *without a fight, but what about his family? Surely Jo Anne's gotten in touch with Clay's wife by now, but what could she tell her? For that matter, what could anyone tell her?*

Being there, being available when your friends and family need you, that's what's really important!

So what am I doing here?

Making eye contact with his young weapons officer, he thought back to his own choke-point experiences in the Gulf War. At that point, he recognized his crew needed him too, then he cut his eyes across the control room at his XO. Alert, calm under pressure, he brought the phrase *quiet competence* repeatedly to mind. This former marine from Sioux City was long overdue his own command, and Hawk was going to make sure he got the *Topeka,* the best there was.

The Navy had been good to him, but everything's got a limit. Hawk's obligation to his country had been paid in full.

My decision's not about money, he thought, *not about country, it's about family. This'll be my last command afloat, and that's that. When I get back, I'm outta here. Let the kids carry the ball; I gave at the office.*

Hawk didn't recognize it, but his own imagination faded with fatigue. In addition, his ability to think ahead, his talent for placing himself mentally in front of his boat, began to suffer. After hours of the same vent, sprint, and sniff routine, even this most technically challenging exercise, had become tedious.

"*Tucson*'s on her trail, Captain."

Hawk cut a tired gaze across the room. "Diving Officer, you know the drill."

The sound of rushing water echoed about the boat. "Trim, Captain."

Hawk acknowledged the diving officer's feedback, then lifted his handset. "Engine room, all ahead two-thirds."

"*Tucson* is passing one thousand yards to starboard, Captain."

"Very well, sonar. Signal our passing; we are the rabbit."

What kind of hunt was this? Hawk thought, feeling like a caged animal ready to bolt. *The* Maine*'s trail was like an endless, straight road leading nowhere across a featureless desert. Constant depth, probably cruising constant speed, no maneuvering of import whatsoever, gotta be an autopilot driving the* Maine. *Her skipper's either resting, asleep at the conn, or doesn't believe he's being followed.*

Homesick, Hawk's thoughts returned to Christmas and he wasn't alone in his reverie.

What was missing from their equation was fear, but that was about to change.

Ahead, as yet undetected, the *Maine*'s trail doglegged forty-five degrees to starboard. One-half mile above the knee, approximately five miles off *Topeka*'s port bow, a neutrally buoyant, gyroscopically stabilized torpedo-shaped canister hovered, diligently maintaining its watch station inside a small freshwater lake Mandrone had deliberately created.

Deep within the heart of the cylinder, sensors fed the acoustic signature from the onrushing *Topeka* to the Captor mine's computer brain. Not surprisingly, both the mine's weapon control-computer and its encapsulated Mark-46 torpedo knew a great deal about the sonar characteristics of the Los Angeles–class attack submarine and, after a time, established a positive class I.D. Programmed to wait, it focused its passive sonar beam on the *Topeka*

and continued listening. Using the approach angle of the
incoming sound and its sensor's northsouth orientation,
the Captor mine calculated bearing to target.

As time passed and the *Topeka* drew nearer, its bearing
angle changed faster and its signal strength increased.
After measuring changes in target bearing for ten minutes, the weapon estimated the *Topeka*'s range as five
miles. Once the calculation was complete, onboard control software determined if subsequent action was
required.

```
if (range is.less.than
ATTACK_RANGE_MAX_LIMIT){
     then {
          swim_to_target (range, bearing)
          and
          arm_weapon (ONCE_CLEAR_OF_CANIS-
          TER);
     }
     else {
          log_target (range, bearing)
          and
          track_target (range, bearing);
     }
}
```

Ultimately, the Captor mine's computer concluded that
its torpedo should wait. In the interim, the mine logged its
range calculations into hover capsule memory, then continued tracking the *Topeka*, revising its estimated range to target every ten seconds.

Subsequent query of the hover capsule's non-volatile
memory would later reveal the Captor mine logged range

snapshots for an additional seventy seconds before its Mark-46 torpedo swam clear, streaking to target.

Transient, 1/02/2009, Fri., 07:43 A.M., 19:43 ZULU
USS Tucson

"What the . . ." Startled, the sonarman tapped his headset. "Chief, I'm sure I heard something, a transient, something mechanical."

The chief sonarman studied the young technician's waterfall display, a green screen covered with random noise. Suddenly, something stood out. He could see it clearly now, a solid, short green line on screen. The top of the display revealed a transient bearing off the starboard bow.

"It's man-made all right, no doubt about it," the sonar chief grimaced, "but where'd it come from?"

Before the technician could answer, a second transient flashed on screen, this one the unmistakable footprint of a torpedo impeller fearlessly spinning up with no regard for stealth.

"Cavitation, Chief! That sucker's huge!" His voice broke, but the sonar chief knew what he meant. The signal amplitude was frighteningly high, a clear indication its source was nearby.

"Torpedo's beginning its terminal run." The sonar chief went pale. "From the looks of it, one of us, probably the *Topeka,* is the target."

"Conn, sonar! Torpedo in the water. Designate sonar contact Sierra Seven, bearing six degrees off our starboard bow. "

"Range?"

"No position yet, but it's close, real close."

"What we got, Chief?"

"No positive I.D., but sounds like one of ours, probably

a Mark-46. From the transient, I'd say he set us up, Skipper. That asshole knew we'd be overdriving our headlights. Probably a Captor mine, musta missed it. We've been sweeping his trail, but coming in off starboard like that, musta blown right past it." The *Tucson*'s mine-detection sonar looked forward using a one-degree-wide pencil beam, providing tunnel vision and very limited range.

"Where's the *Topeka*?"

"She's fifteen hundred yards off our port bow, Captain, making thirty knots and deaf as a post." Her sensors were swamped by flow noise.

"Warn 'em pronto."

"Sonar, aye." The chief sonarman launched a high-powered ping carrying a message into the *Topeka*'s side.

Sprinting into Harm's Way, 1/02/2009, Fri., 07:45 A.M., 19:45 ZULU
USS *Topeka*

"Conn, sonar! Emergency message from the *Tucson*, Captain."

Stunned, Hawk's Christmas reverie shut down all-stop. For a few moments that seemed to linger for an eternity, he struggled with what to do next. Scanning the control room, he counted nine faces staring back at him. About the time his XO stepped forward, he remembered what to do, focusing on his flat-screen display.

```
MK 46 INCOMING OFF STARBOARD BOW
```

The XO mouthed one word and Hawk agreed. Punching the intercom, he queried his chief sonarman. "Range?"

"Range unknown, Captain."

Ping . . . ping . . . ping . . .

"Chief!" Hawk heard one of the sonar technicians yelp over the intercom. Even as the chief sonarman peered over the young man's shoulder, a solid green line emerged from the noise on top of the waterfall display.

"Torpedo's pinging, Captain. Signal's coming in above our noise floor, bearing twelve degrees to starboard. It's searching, hasn't found us, but it's gotta be close."

"Need a range, Chief, need it now."

"Sonar, aye." A powerful, precision focused *PING* boiled off their forward transducer array toward the incoming torpedo.

"Weapons, put us on busy one." Before Hawk had completed his order, the torpedo, *Tucson*, and *Topeka* icons flashed on the fire control display.

"Range, eighty-one hundred yards and closing fast, Captain. Pushing fifty knots."

Ping . . . ping ping pingpingping . . .

"Torpedo has acquired us and is homing."

"Conn, aye."

PING! PING! PING! PING! PING! PING! PING!!! echoed over the intercom several seconds.

"*Tucson*'s pinging like hell, Captain, playing a long shot. He's trying to overdrive the torpedo's seeker head, confuse it, or pull it off our back."

After a few moments' silence,

Pingpingpingping . . .

"It's got a fix on us, Captain, and won't be distracted."

"Yeah, I figured as much. We make the smartest torpedoes in the world."

Lucky us, the XO didn't say. "We can't outrun it," the former marine observed, shifting his weight uneasily from side to side.

"Not this close," Hawk agreed. *So how'll we use the speed we've got?*

Then, in a fraction of a second, Hawk's plan crystallized without further discussion. "Weapons, pull the Mark-46's crush depth. Can we make it?" It wasn't a question, really, more a statement of intent. His direction kicked off a controlled, simultaneous barrage of activity across the control room, as if the *Topeka*'s brain thought, and its body sprang into action.

Hawk didn't hesitate. "Maneuvering, I need flank speed and I need it now."

Facing his diving officer, Hawk spoke only one word: "Depth." It sounded detached, like reading from a checklist.

"Sixteen hundred feet, Captain. Seafloor's not a problem, twelve thousand feet plus." Typical of Hawk's crew, they were in sync now, running two steps ahead of him.

Meanwhile, Weapons worked through some fast calculations, then ran a sanity check by his fire control console. BSY-1 flashed red. "No can do, Captain. We can't outdive it."

"Then we'll use the thermocline." Hawk charged ahead undaunted. Shifting into overdrive, he began issuing orders in a tight cadence, as if reading from a script. "Weapons, get me a solution on that incoming torpedo. Download the starboard AT. We're gonna need it."

"Sonar, we clear overhead?"

"Aye, Captain. Closest surface contact is twenty-five miles."

Grabbing his overhead handhold, Hawk shifted his gaze across the control room. "Diving Officer, maintain flank speed and give me maximum up angle on the bow planes." With her planes jammed skyward, the *Topeka* streaked toward the surface like an enormous bullet.

"Countermeasures, make ready to deploy noisemakers. Set 'em up pronto! I need a full spread."

Limited Options, 1/02/2009, Fri., 07:48 A.M., 19:48 ZULU
USS *Tucson*

"Weapons, launch starboard AT and blow that torpedo out of the water," Woodie ordered. *Running interference is always easier when nobody's shooting at you.*

"Aye, Captain. Torpedo is away and running true. In two minutes, ten seconds, weapon will be one-half mile off *Topeka*'s starboard bow. Time to target, four minutes, twenty seconds."

"Very well, Weapons. Once you're alongside the *Topeka,* shadow her starboard side. Stick to her like glue."

"Aye, aye, Captain."

"Weapons, we missed anything?"

Weapons' response was instantaneous. "Swim out the portside AT. Bracket the target in case it turns, or does something we don't expect."

"Do it. Run it out, set up a shield, but don't swamp your seeker head. Don't want the target to get past us because we got in a hurry."

"Aye, Captain," Weapons acknowledged.

Woodie sensed something changing beneath his feet. He'd become accustomed to the feel of the deck shifting up-and-down, side-to-side, as they followed the *Maine*'s freshwater trail. For some reason, the rhythm of the porpoising maneuver was changing and this wasn't the first time it had happened. Fact was, it happened more and more often as the trail faded, blending into surrounding seawater.

Looking across the control room, Woodie made eye contact with the diving officer.

"We really lost it this time, Captain. It's completely disappeared. They either sped up or cut off their distiller."

Topeka *first,* Woodie thought. "Log our position, we'll get back to it."

"Conn, sonar," erupted from the intercom speaker. "Hull-popping noises from the *Topeka*. She's changing depth."

"Shallow?"

A pause.

"Sonar, we've gotta know. Enable active sonar tracking and stay with him. He's going to lay a smoke screen, and if we don't take that torp out first, we'll be left blind, lost in the dust, powerless to help 'em."

Forward, the chief sonarman released a series of narrowly focused pings. "He's going shallow, Captain."

"Sonar, advise *Topeka* we're deploying two AT's, a defensive shield beneath their starboard side."

"Sonar, aye."

"Weapons, can our AT's stick with her?"

"Anywhere she can go, we can go, sir."

"Good. Then run 'em out beneath her starboard side." Woodie's mind raced ahead focusing on the most important term in their time-to-target equation. "No matter what, that Mark-46 must not get through. Once Hawk starts kicking noisemakers out his tubes, the situation's gonna get mighty cluttered."

"Captain," Weapons prodded. "If we're not careful, we'll cut our guidance wires."

"Hmph, you're right." Woodie made eye contact with the weapons officer, hearing his concern. "Keep me honest."

"Aye, aye, Captain."

Woodie punched the intercom. "Engine room, all stop."

Above the Layer, 1/02/2009, Fri., 07:50 A.M., 19:50 ZULU
USS *Topeka*

Hawk held fast as the *Topeka* shuddered. When you're bolting toward the surface at flank speed, any forty-degree ascent's a rocket ride no matter what.

Watching their digital depth gauge count down, the diving officer announced, "Captain, approaching the layer." Sound doesn't travel a straight-line path passing through the boundary layer, it bends and Hawk knew it. The idea was to deploy decoys, distract the incoming torpedo, then use this bending to their advantage.

"Very well, launch countermeasures." Hawk wiped his face with his hand, then punched the intercom. "Rig for collision."

Of all the alarms that strike terror in the heart of submariners, only the ear-shattering howl of the collision warning ratchets up the pulse of the entire crew.

"Captain, we're in the layer."

Hawk's experience took over. "Diving Officer, flank speed! Left full rudder! Level us out, zero bubble."

Hawk held on tight as the *Topeka* banked hard, pulling a tight turn to port.

Ping-ping-ping-ping-ping erupted over intercom.

"Conn, sonar. Incoming torpedo closing. Range twenty-two hundred yards."

Tense, Hawk punched the intercom hard. "Sonar, where're those AT's?"

"Below us, sir, starboard side. Range twelve hundred yards."

"Come on *Tucson*, give," Hawk urged Woodie on beneath his breath. Inside the *Topeka*, everything felt sluggish, taking on a sort of surreal, slow-motion quality.

Ping-ping-ping-ping-ping-pi-pi-pi-pinnng.

"Conn, sonar. Starboard AT is pulling away, running to target. It's going deep, it's diving, sir, going after it."

"Go, Woodie, go."

Shield, 1/02/2009, Fri., 07:50 A.M., 19:50 ZULU
USS Tucson

"Target torpedo is ranging, Captain."

"Weapons, can you lock on signal?" Woodie asked.

"Yes, have solid signal lock, can swim to target."

"Do it." The *Tucson*'s skipper knew this marked the end of the Mk-46. The AT was a modified ADCAP torpedo, and at a minimum, the shock wave from its exploding 650-pound warhead would disable the torpedo's sonar seeker.

"Conn, sonar. *Topeka*'s approaching the layer, deploying countermeasures."

"Weapons?"

"We're well below him, Captain. On beam to target."

"Very well. Blow that torpedo out of the water."

Swimming his AT out with a joystick, the weapons officer looked like he was playing a video game.

"Range to target, sixteen hundred yards and closing," the sonar chief said.

Ping.

"AT is on beam," Weapons announced over the intercom. "Kill radius is well clear of the *Topeka*."

Ping.

"Arm the warhead."

Ping . . . ping.

"Range one thousand yards," the sonar chief reported watching a computer-generated image of the two weapons closing.

Ping . . . ping . . . ping . . . ping . . . ping-ping-ping.

"Keep on it," Woodie urged the weapons officer.

Ping-ping-ping-ping-ping-pi-pi-pi-ping-ga.

Too late, the incoming Mk-46 detected the business end of the telephone pole–sized AT swimming down its sonar beam. As quickly as its mechanical systems could react, its pump-jet propulsor kicked hard to starboard, attempting to divert around the AT. Its chances for survival would have been greater if it had not.

BAROOOOM!!!

The hammer blow from the spherical shock wave ripped through the incoming torpedo, rupturing its electronic eardrums, shattering its guidance computer, leaving the weapon dead in the water.

Kill Radius, 1/02/2009, Fri., 07:50 A.M., 19:50 ZULU
USS *Topeka*

Even when well beyond an AT's kill radius, underwater explosions aren't as predictable as you might think.

An ear-splitting explosion heaved the *Topeka* skyward, pushing her up by the bow. Hawk hung on as a blast of seawater crashed against the hull beneath her starboard side. With his hands wet, his grip let go, torn free by the impact of collision. Off balance, thrown down hard, he collapsed against the deck like a rag doll.

Lights all over the sub went out, then came back on as Hawk struggled to his feet. Grabbing the overhead handhold, he sensed the *Topeka* suspended bow-high, listing slightly to port.

Lifting the handset, he demanded, "Damage report!"

His XO took over, querying the ship's spaces stern to bow. It took less than two minutes, and once the reports were in, he filed his. "Superstructure suffered damage,

Captain. Forward trim tank has collapsed. One starboard vent and some duct work outside the pressure hull has been flattened."

"Diving Officer, can we level the boat?"

"Yes, Captain, I think so, but I wouldn't recommend anything too radical, no more sixteen-hundred-foot dives until we take her in for a tune-up."

"Very well. Diving Officer, trim the boat, come to periscope depth, but take it easy."

Flooding her tanks caused a sickening noise which sounded like long metal ducts flexing, bending against torrents of the onrushing sea.

Twisting his mouth, all Hawk could do was grimace.

Cover Your Tracks, 1/02/2009, Fri., 06:51 A.M., 19:51 Zulu
USS *Maine*

Forward in the sonar room, the sound of an explosion woke Mandrone with a start. He rewound the tape, played it back, then played it back again. He couldn't determine range, but from its bearing he knew it could have been one of their Captor mines. There was no way to know for sure, but someone could have been on their trail.

In retrospect, Mike hoped those mines hadn't been a mistake. He'd considered mine deployment effective when they first began their journey south, but once under way, he'd called it off. After laying only two mines, he'd reasoned all surprise would be lost and likened them to a bread crumb trail, marking the route where the *Maine* had been. *And there's that warm water discharge.*

Mandrone had been running maximum quiet speed and understood that the slower they traveled, the better quality trail they left behind. They discharged only so many gallons of freshwater per minute, and as a result, the slower they ran, the more freshwater they left per foot.

It's time to break up our trail, Mandrone thought, *probably past time.* He spoke to Ash over intercom. "Dump the freshwater tanks and gap our trail."

"Aye, aye, Captain. I'll cover our tracks."

When It Rains, 1/02/2009, Fri., 03:04 P.M., 03:04 Zulu
USS *Stennis*

Inside CDC, Eastwood sat in front of a display console wearing a pair of lightweight headphones. On screen, he studied satellite pictures showing the exodus of the Seventh Fleet. He found the surface ships interesting, but what he was waiting to see was real-time video from USSPACE-COM. ClearWater images would show the whereabouts of the Seventh Fleet's submarines and their proximity to the Russian pickets.

"Colonel Mason's on the line, Admiral. ClearWater data link available on comm three." Eastwood selected the channel and his screen was redrawn showing American, Russian, and several unidentified submarines off Kamchatka.

Eastwood studied their numbers and relative positions, angry that he must commit more resources shadowing Russians than hunting renegades.

"This is just in, Admiral" crackled over his headsets. It was Mason's voice. "It could be important."

"Go ahead, Colonel."

"South Korea reported a gas attack on the DMZ. It's not our problem, not yet anyway, but I thought you should know something's up."

"When it rains, it pours," Eastwood snarled. "What's the crux?"

Mason transmitted a written summary from Clive

Towles, the President's national security advisor, plus a few still photos highlighting troop movements. "Apparently they knew it was coming, Admiral. South Korean forces are deployed for combat."

"First I've heard of it," Eastwood quipped. "This renegade situation's totally consumed us."

"South Korea won't roll over and play dead," Mason reassured him. "According to Clive, South Korean military leaders believe the North's attack represents their chance at unification. They'd hoped for peaceful unification, but peaceful unification's no longer an option. No one in the South wanted this war, but everyone knew it would come."

"What are you saying?"

"I'm saying they're ready."

After a series of setbacks, the might of the South Korean military plus its free economy turned the tide against the North. Like a steamroller, the South pushed north toward the capital.

CHAPTER TWENTY-EIGHT

The Wall, 1/02/2009, Fri., 02:18 P.M., 03:18 Zulu
USS *Maine*

Hunched forward inside the sonar room, feeling like he was about to explode, Mandrone pressed his headphones tight around both ears. "When we get out of this mess, I'll never set foot on another submarine as long as I live" was all he'd said, but his feeling went much deeper. *I'm so sick of having my head in the sand I could scream. Once, just once, I'd like to bloody well know what the hell's going on out there! I've never run this slow, this deep, this quiet, this long in my life. I hate it! You can't see squat, you don't have a clue what's going on around you; even with all this sonar signature matching, you're only guessing. I hate submarines, they're so damn confining.* After mentally venting his feelings, Mandrone concluded his bullet-spitting episode when he smelled food. *Maybe I've changed or I'm just too old for this nonsense. I guess subs're no different than they've ever been, I'm just feeling boxed in, that's all.*

Driven by his sense of smell, Mandrone looked over his shoulder as his sonarman returned from the galley with a pair of sandwiches. One squint and Mike focused on his made-to-order turkey sub.

Without skipping a beat, Mandrone chewed his soggy

lettuce while sorting through scores of sounds. He'd been keeping a close ear on their situation since their missile launch and had grabbed only an odd hour's sleep since then.

Remarkably, the former XO had learned to listen in his sleep, a skill developed as a young man during endless hours on patrol. He'd sleep with his headset on, while his ears stayed awake, listening. If even the faintest submarine sound was detected, Mandrone's ears had been trained to wake him with a start, like a mother wakes at the sound of her newborn baby. He couldn't explain how it worked, didn't care, but all his career he'd spent the lion's share of his time submerged in the sonar room and never regretted a minute of it.

A few minutes earlier, he'd been listening to a surface ship plowing through the water many miles north, presumably part of some battle group. Fortunately, they were moving away and weren't a concern. Listening, triangulating, guessing, Mandrone plotted—for the umpteen-hundredth time—his best estimate of what he heard. His map was littered with surface ships, but only four submerged contacts caused concern. After drawing a straight line between them, Mike caught his sonarman's attention by rocking back in his chair, propping his foot on the desk.

"We've got one thing going for us," Mandrone mused. "Everything out there that's movin's hostile."

The sonarman looked puzzled, but didn't reply.

The captain laid out his map, then looked to the sonarman for confirmation. "The way I read it, there's a line of four fast attacks closing from the south. From the sound of it, they're pinging hard and driving fast, too fast to listen. They're overdriving their headlights, swamping their sensors."

The sonarman pulled out his clipboard and compared notes. Circled, he'd written *4 wide sub wall, 10 miles separation, speed 35+ knots.*

"Good, then we agree." Mike nodded.

"What are they trying to do?"

"I expect they're trying to scare us, flush us out like a covey of quail, drive us back toward the battle group."

"Panic." The sonarman gazed at the ceiling. "Cause us to do something stupid."

"But we're not stupid and we don't panic because someone screams."

"You're going to stay the course?"

"I am. We'll maneuver slowly between and below 'em."

"Should work if they don't slow down."

"They've been overdriving their headlights since we first picked 'em up. I don't know why, but they're in one hell of a big hurry to get somewhere fast."

Mandrone couldn't know these subs were racing north to replace those siphoned off to shadow the Russians.

Time Is on Their Side, 1/02/2009, Fri., 03:59 P.M.,
03:59 ZULU
USS *Stennis*

Inside the CDC, Eastwood counted Russian subs and surface ships in the hot zone and shook his head, thoroughly disgusted. "We needed this like we need a hole in the head," he said and grimaced, speaking to the wiry TAO.

The TAO clinched his teeth. "Things could be better, Admiral, but we can't pin it on the Russians."

"I know that, son. Their admirals aren't doing anything I wouldn't do. Believe me, if a renegade Russian sub showed itself off the Bangor coast, we'd be all over it."

"Seemed like the deck was stacked against us, sir."

"That's not the way I see it," Ozzie snarled. "We were too damn slow."

The TAO looked puzzled. "We closed at flank speed, Admiral. Let me tell you, it was one helluva ride."

"The bottom line remains, we were too slow. Too slow to face the facts, too slow to commit, too slow to station, too slow, much too slow. The Russians only made a bad situation worse. I'd guess the *Maine* slipped away hidden by the noise of the confusion. These renegades ran rings around us and now their trail's grown cold. I doubt we'll ever find it again. Even if we do, we won't know it. How do we confirm it belongs to the *Maine*? No way! The *Maine*'s simply too quiet a boat to detect and, tell you the truth, I believe her skipper knows it. You don't stay undetected this long by accident. The guy hasn't made mistakes." Eastwood studied the large tactical display and sighed. On screen, a counter continuously rolled over, updating the size of their ever-expanding hot zone. At this juncture, all that mattered was that their search area exceeded a million square miles. Naval assets were spread too thin now to be effective. The longer the search lasted, the less effective they'd be. "My sense is we're up against a losing proposition here. Time is on their side and all we really know is they're running deep, heading south. Hmph."

Stark Terror, 1/02/2009, Fri., 11:01 P.M., 12:01 ZULU
USS *Maine*

PING! PING! PING!

It's like being tied to the tracks, listening to the sound of an onrushing train. You hear the pitch and volume increase as it approaches, you're stuck, and it's terrifying. If, by the grace of God, you're lucky enough to live through it, the train passes over you, its pitch drops and the roar fades away.

Mandrone had run the gauntlet before, but that didn't make it easy. Even in low light, his forehead glistened with sweat as the *Maine* shot the gap between two onrushing fast attacks. The sonar room was chilled to a nippy sixty-two degrees, but from the looks of Mandrone and his sonarman, temperature didn't matter at all.

Harrowing Sound, 1/02/2009, Fri., 11:11 P.M., 12:11 ZULU
USS MAINE

PING! PING! PING!

I can't stand it, I can't stand it! Part of Mandrone felt a haunting anxiety, that feeling he'd overlooked something. Part of him wanted to yank his headphones off and smash 'em to smithereens. His ears were sore, and besides, why bother? If they were detected, there was nothing they could do about it anyway. They couldn't fight, not pushing crush depth with insufficient crew.

Mike debated piping their sonar over the intercom. There was nothing more they could do, but on the other hand, that harrowing sound would strike fear in their hearts, and fear had its place. Their pulses would ratchet, their senses heighten, their energy would return when they needed it most. On the whole, Mandrone reasoned they'd be less likely to do anything careless if focused on the tremendous threat passing overhead. He toggled the intercom.

PING! PING!! PING!!!

The harrowing sound reverberated down the length of the boat. Inside, no one moved, no one said a word. It was as if the entire crew stopped breathing.

In theory, they should be undetectable positioned

between the passing horde, lost in the flow noise. In theory, Mandrone could hear them, but they couldn't hear him. In theory.

PING!!! PING!!! PING!!! PING!!!! PING!!!!!

Ready to burst, just when it seemed it couldn't get any louder, the pitch shifted. Suddenly, the volume dropped then quickly faded.

Simultaneously, one captain and ten crewmen remembered to breathe.

Together, they'd walked through the shadow of death and it had touched them, left 'em cold and trembling. There was no celebration, only fatigue such as Mandrone had never known.

CHAPTER TWENTY-NINE

The Navigator, 1/04/2009, Sun., 08:45 A.M., *22:45* ZULU
Puluwat, Caroline Islands

It was a scene out of ancient Polynesia. Five young men scurried about three large catamarans packing last-minute provisions for their journey. Nothing was neglected. First, islanders put aboard spare poles, spars, coils of rope, and bailers. Next, their mast, sail, and steering paddle were loaded. Finally, food for their crew plus passengers: taro pudding, nuts, a squealing piglet, breadfruit paste, cooked breadfruit, and fermented breadfruit which would keep for the duration of their voyage. To top it off, a mound of drinking coconuts was tossed in.

Traditional in every way, their great voyaging canoes were constructed from planks lashed together with coconut fiber cord. The hull's framework was bound in the same way, caulked with breadfruit sap. Comparatively lightweight, their graceful lines promised great speed and strength. Under sail, they could cover 100 to 150 miles a day in open sea. Except for its Dacron sails, the Polynesian craft had changed remarkably little for hundreds of years.

Preparations were under way for their five-day journey from Puluwat to a tiny, unnamed land mass 145 miles east-southeast of Guam. Their chosen route was the traditional one, one hundred miles to the north, then across five hundred miles of open ocean, sailing just south of Guam.

King David, a master navigator from the Caroline Island of Puluwat, stood apart from the young islanders. Tattoos marked his legs, arms, and chest. Bronze, wrinkled, with snow white hair, he directed the proceedings with a calm steadiness surpassing everyone present. Only fifty, he'd trained as a navigator more than twenty-five years ago, and had sailed the Carolines ever since. Relying on stars, currents, and ocean swells—traditional navigational skills— King David would guide them toward Guam.

The navigator gathered the rope used for steering; his son-in-law, Tonga, took the helm; the remaining crew shoved their craft clear of shore, and they were under way. Within minutes, they'd slipped out from sheltered waters, to where their sails filled with wind.

Suddenly, their catamarans felt alive, skimming across the sea.

Concentrating intently on the ocean surface, King David stood the next eight hours with his feet planted wide apart on the foredeck, his only movement occasional direction to Tonga, the helmsman. Setting out from Puluwat late morning, he studied the land disappearing behind them to assess the current. As long as they were visible, King David kept the two largest islands, Puluwat and Alet, astern. Once they disappeared, he navigated based on ocean swells, the most helpful being the wave from Altar.

This wave he held on his beam.

Legacy, 1/09/2009, Fri., 4:39 P.M., 07:39 ZULU
Pyongyang, North Korea

Overwhelmed, Kim felt the loneliness, the hopelessness of having nowhere to turn. At the end of his rope, he came home to the palace garden a beaten man. Moving among the thousand-year-old trees, seeking solace from his father's spirit, Kim always found the forest a peaceful refuge, a special place he could go and feel the presence of his family.

But not today.

Struggling to muster his strength, he felt abandoned, empty inside, with a nagging sense that something was missing. Bone-weary, at the lowest point in his life, Kim felt fatigue so overwhelming, so debilitating, he could imagine drifting off to sleep and never waking up. He could envision feeling so tired, so burdened by despair, he'd simply go to sleep and die.

Trying to find his way, Kim recalled happier times in the garden, but to no avail. For a brief moment, he smiled, imagining death as his escape. Now, nearing the end of his life, he felt a kaleidoscope of emotions, but the greatest of these was loneliness. His chest felt heavy, burdened by the sense of futility that comes when the dreams of a lifetime are laid to waste. All his life, he'd valued the virtues of self-reliance and independence. Now, having run out of options, he raised his eyes in agony.

From here, he could look across the clearing and remember life as a child. There, across the open field were the raised banks of a pond, the pond he'd fished with his father. He could remember those days only through faded black-and-white pictures now, the pond overgrown with moss, the fish, like the happy times, a faded memory he could visit only in dreams.

Where was his father now? What would he do? What would he say?

Kim was sure of one thing and one thing only: His father would never give up, not as long as he had a breath of life left in his body. Even in his darkest days, he was never afraid. Admitting this, Kim felt inadequate, sensing that his father's blessing had slipped from his grasp, and ashamed for bringing dishonor to his name. His father had appointed him heir to carry their government forward and unite Korea. He had failed his father and betrayed the hopes of those who died for their country.

Still, Kim had done his best, dedicated his entire political life to this end; no one could have done more. Like his father, he had gambled his Pyongyang regime on Korean unification, but Kim had lost. Within days, South Korean troops would occupy the palace.

It'd be a short war, he'd see to that, but too late he'd learned their war plans had been telegraphed to the South. The *Maine*'s hijacking had proven the deception he'd hoped, they'd amassed the mobile forces needed to win a quick, decisive victory, but too late he discovered they'd lost the element of surprise. *We had good intelligence,* Kim thought, *but South Korea had better, probably planted somewhere in my own organization. There's no time to ferret them out now, but what does it matter?*

For this reason, Kim felt betrayed; not so much angry, but profoundly sad, as if he'd been violated. He had done his best to bring about Korean unification—and it would happen—but the South's victory left no place for him. The world was changing around him, but the new world left Kim a man without a country.

Still, he could find sanctuary in China, but then again no. His heart was in this sacred place. Here he was born, here he was raised, here he'd lived his life, and now as an old man, here he would die.

Kim's breathing was irregular now. Every breath required a conscious effort. If he didn't try, if he didn't force the air in, he'd simply stop breathing altogether.

Only one month ago he'd felt light as a feather, almost

euphoric among these splendid old trees. In retrospect, he could see things more clearly. It had all started with *Scientific American*'s article on submarine detection, a pivotal point in his life. It was February 1993; he was head of the nation's military. Within eighteen months, his father died, and in time, he took over. After a lifetime of planning, laying the groundwork for unification, he'd never imagined the war would come to this. Feeling melancholy and dejected, in a way Kim looked forward to joining his ancestors.

Thinking of this, Kim's heart lightened, though only for a moment. He remembered walking train tracks with his father, feeling the earth shake, listening to the freight engines roar. He and his father knew the train schedules by heart, knew where they were bound in China, and where they'd come from. They loved trains—their smell, their sound, their feel—but like his father, the trains were a distant memory now, a dream from a time long ago.

Sensing the end of his life, Kim treasured these recollections of childhood and family. *Maybe that's a sign,* he thought. *Maybe when you're ready to die, you visit your memories, maybe you go there and live them over again.*

Fearing capture, Dear Leader understood once the wheels of war'd been set in motion, his fate transcended his own control. At this moment in time, his fate seemed predestined and inescapable. In his waning days, Kim considered himself an instrument in some larger plan. *Ultimately, unification will bring together families separated for over fifty years,* he reasoned, *and what a reunion there will be.* Kim smiled, remembering his father. *I won't see the day, but maybe it's enough to unite Korea. I've been true to my father, true to his fallen comrades, and in a roundabout way, Korean unification will be my legacy.*

Unfocused, Kim gazed across the clearing. On the horizon, a thin halo of light hovered above the city, dimly illuminating the early evening sky. Countless times during his life, he'd watched the sun set from this very spot.

Suddenly, the city fell dark without a sound. Every light in the capital extinguished itself, as if someone threw a giant switch. Seconds later, deep, long, rumbling sounds—like distant thunder—rolled through the garden. Faraway explosions underscored what Kim already knew: North Korea's hydroelectric power plants were again under attack.

Lights in Kim's garden flickered, but unlike earlier attacks, this time they began to fade.

Unseen overhead, approaching from the south, a single cruise missile jettisoned its bombay doors, exposing its submunition dispenser to the open air. Loaded with 166 bomblets, each about the size of a soft-drink can, the D-variant Tomahawk updated its range to target, armed its payload, and emerged ready for business.

Then, without warning, the night sky lit up the palace grounds with a blinding flash. Underground fuel tanks exploded, catapulting flaming fuel skyward in an enormous fireball, setting off a devastating series of events. With no time to react, fire engulfed the palace, detonating its ammunition magazine and two well-concealed rooftop missile batteries.

Kim felt the searing heat from nearby explosions inside the People's Royal Shrine. The cruise missile's first bomblet release had done its work, laying a blanket of destruction down within an accuracy of three feet, shattering the very old stone pagoda with armor-piercing explosive force. But the cruise missile mission was just beginning. After dispensing its first batch of bombs, the missile banked sharply, altering its course, heading for the thousand-year-old wood.

For Kim, fear heightened his awareness, and events began unfolding in slow-motion. Initially, he heard a rapid-fire, staccato burst of bomblets coming his way:

boom, boom, boom, Boom Boom, Boom, BOOM! BOOM!!!

They rushed toward him, closing on his position at breakneck speed. Stunned, blinded by the light, he ran for cover, but too late. Mercifully, the air blast knocked him to the ground, unconscious. Fragments pelted the trees all around him, then the incendiary heat blast burned him beyond recognition. Within seconds, the woods were a blazing inferno, the ground blackened and scorched.

From a planning perspective, the mission was a complete success. South Korea understood that as long as remnants of Kim's Pyongyang regime remained intact, Korean unification would remain at risk. It wasn't personal, it was politics. The old guard must die. As such, the attack leveled the palace and surrounding grounds, leaving only charred, smoldering debris in its wake.

A heat-sensitive photograph later revealed that Kim's North Korean palace appeared in many ways comparable to Nagasaki, ground zero. The palace grounds, including the forest, looked as if they'd been crushed by the giant hand of God.

CHAPTER THIRTY

Stood Up, 1/10/2009, Sat., 08:45 A.M., 22:45 ZULU
13° 56' N, 146° 14' E
USS *Maine*

"They may have killed their engines, Captain."

"It's possible, but I was led to believe we'd hear them on the hour, twin five-bladed screws at that." Mandrone took off his headphones and focused on his sonarman, squinting through his good eye. "The way I hear it, our closest surface contact lies east about forty miles."

The sonarman agreed, circling a cluster of vertical lines on his waterfall display.

Mandrone returned to the control room feeling pessimistic about their prospects for an immediate rendezvous. Hunching over his plotting table, he triple-checked their position.

"Are we there yet?" Ash quipped behind the helmsman's wheel.

Mike tried to smile. "We're almost home, Mr. Wilson. Make our depth one thousand feet and take it slow."

Ash tweaked their buoyancy from the dive control panel, then positioned himself at the planesman's wheel, gradually pulling the yoke back into his lap.

Mandrone felt the deck tilting slightly upward and grabbed the overhead handhold.

The hull groaned, creaking ominously as it expanded like a balloon. Mike read these sounds as if the *Maine* were saying *thank you.*

After what seemed like an eternity, at a depth of twelve hundred feet Ash pushed forward gently on the yoke, planing the *Maine* from its ascent. Mandrone released his overhead handhold, but it took another two hundred feet to level the boat. Once they'd checked for leaks, Mike got on with the business at hand.

"Mr. Wilson, float the dual-band antenna buoy."

From the diving control console, Ash released their towed surface antenna. Outside, behind the *Maine*'s missile bay, an inflatable buoy streaked toward the surface, spooling out a retractable steel cable. Running true, stabilized at the surface, Ash shot Mandrone a thumbs-up.

"Radio, conn. Open up VLF and HF channels. Antenna buoy now fully deployed. We're expecting contact at the top of the hour."

Six hours later, nothing.

Mandrone watched over his radioman's shoulder as he clattered away on his computer keyboard.

"Whaddaya make out?"

"VLF and HF bands are nearly filled to capacity, sir. There's more chatter off Guam than I've ever heard, but none of it's earmarked for us."

"Any hits?"

"I've piped every channel through our speech recognition circuits for hours, converted everything to ASCII, then run it all through the computer searching for these keywords." Flashing a particular smile, the radioman pointed to his monitor screen.

Enter comma separated list in   any language ⬍

Keywords Maine, renegade, sub, kill, prosecute, hunt, Korea

Search   Clear Form

"Yeah, and?" Mike pressed.

"Except for Korea, no significant matches." The radioman handed Mandrone a printout regarding the Korean War.

"Hmph, good. Talks have already started, that's excellent." Mandrone smiled for the first time in days. "It's coming down pretty much like you said all along. I'm impressed. I'd hoped you were right, but in my opinion, you never know how a war like that's gonna turn out."

The radioman sighed after a few moments' reflection. "Korea will be united again, though not as Dear Leader envisioned." Unmarried, over forty, and with no close ties in the North, the radioman had seen too much of the world to be an ardent fan of Communism. He had learned what he knew about South Korea from the Chinese, through the observant, pragmatic eyes of its submarine community. Having studied the South's formidable might, the breadth of its manufacturing base, and the wealth of its global economy, he wasn't surprised to learn the war wasn't going as Dear Leader had planned.

Still, in his heart, he wanted to believe Korean unification would be a good thing. Though never a staunch patriot, he couldn't help feeling some sense of loss and uncertainty. It was like experiencing the death of someone you know, the death of something familiar, the death of a culture and the only way of life, he'd known as a child. *Well,* he thought, *at least we've got the money, most of it anyway.*

Mandrone placed his hand on his radioman's shoulder in a gesture of genuine affection, his good eye looking a bit glassy. "I'm bloody glad something good may come out of this. The game's not over till it's over, but the prospects look bright. I agree with you about one thing though, South Korea will rebuild the North. They've wanted to for years and, knowing the United States, they'll probably pitch in too."

After a long silence, the radioman asked, "What about our money, Captain?"

"Assuming the North surrenders, I doubt we'll ever see our final payoff, but that comes as no big surprise, right? Still, with a half million bucks in the bank each, we should be pretty well set when we get outta here."

"Fresh air, fresh vegetables, sunlight—I can't wait to feel the sun on my face." The radioman turned his gaze on six stiff body bags, secured to the wall, standing in the back of the room. "These bodies, this submarine's like a cold, steel coffin."

"I know what you mean. Once we get out of here, I'll never set foot on another submarine as long as I live. What else'd you turn up in the search?"

The radioman returned to his screen. "Aside from junk words like 'roger,' and throat-mike double clicks, the word most often used was 'weather.' Second most popular word was 'ceiling.' "

"Sounds like we're not the focus of any air or surface fleet communication off Guam," Mike said, "not yet anyway."

"That's what I concluded."

"I was concerned our reputation may have preceded us," Mandrone said and snickered.

"It's been ten days since the launch, Captain. We could be yesterday's news by now."

"Yep. Traffic topside sounds pretty normal."

"Are you absolutely certain of our position?"

"Yeah, these are our rendezvous coordinates all right," Mandrone muttered, coming back to reality. "There's no doubt about it. I've checked our position three ways. Something's gone wrong topside. For whatever reason, probably the war, they stood us up. We'll give 'em another hour, and if we don't hear anything, we'll move out of here."

Considering the war was going badly for the North Koreans, neither Mandrone nor his crew were surprised to find themselves stranded. Still, they couldn't help but feel disappointed. Instinctively, without allowing his crew time to dwell on their situation, Mike pressed forward with his backup plan.

"Not to worry," Mandrone said in a reassuring tone over the intercom. "We planned for this contingency from the beginning. We'll make it back all right, just a little later than we expected."

"Engine room, make turns for maximum quiet speed." He looked across the control room. "Ash, come to bearing one-eight-four. We're heading for the flatlands." For the first time in as long as he could remember, Mandrone felt like a cowboy making his way across the range.

Bottomed Out, 1/10/2009, Sat., 10:55 P.M., 12:55 ZULU
12° 49' N, 146° 7' E
USS Maine

"Antenna buoy's deployed, Captain," Ash said. "Cable's running true. Ready to receive on all bands." The long floating wire aerial was in position on the surface, trailing behind the boat.

"Speed?"

"We're crawling against the current, sir, well below ClearWater minimums." Ash read their speed. "Three knots, tops."

"Conn, sonar" suddenly rang out over the ship's intercom. "We're over the plateau, Captain. Depth averages one hundred fifty feet, reasonably uniform surface, suitable for touchdown."

Hunched over the plotting table, Mandrone triple-checked their position—145 miles from Guam, due east off the Santa Rosa Reef—then spoke over the intercom. "Very well, sonar. Engine room, all stop."

Using his mouse to navigate about the display, Mandrone studied a 3-D computer-generated image of the plateau beneath them. *This was the place all right, very few places like it in the world.* The remarkable feature about the bottom terrain was its topography. Effectively, they were parking the *Maine* on a relatively flat plateau near the top of a mountain beneath the sea. Unbelievably, only four miles' travel southeast, the ocean depth plummeted from 150 feet to nearly six miles. Five miles to their northwest, a small atoll emerged above the surface and Mike knew that if everything had gone as planned, King David should be there awaiting his call.

Ash spoke moments later. "Level bubble, zero turns on the screw, Captain. We're completely stationary, dead in the water."

"Sonar, conn. Depth below the keel?"

"Ten feet, sir."

"Very well, Ash, set her down easy."

Grabbing his overhead handhold, Mandrone heard the muffled sound of dense rubber scraping against sharp, rock-hard coral. As she bottomed out, the *Maine* settled nose-high, rolling slightly with a discernible list to port.

Once the boat stabilized, Ash asked, "Why park her, Captain? Why not just scuttle the ship?"

"It's simple really." Mike paused, then spoke evenly, without expression. "I plan to get out alive."

"Whaddaya mean?"

"Think about it, Ash. It takes time and coordination to get everybody to the surface. You go much deeper than this, you gotta contend with the bends. Turns out, one man'll need to make the trip at least twice, maybe more, and the bends'd do a number on him. Besides, I'm the last man out and, like I said, I plan to get out of here alive."

"But we've got timed charges."

"No good. Take a look at this chart."

Ash joined Mandrone by the plotting table.

To the northwest, three explosive dumps; west toward Guam, an enormous submarine operating area and firing range riddled with underwater sound detectors; finally, surrounding them on all sides, the deepest ocean on earth, the seemingly bottomless abyss known as the Mariana Trench.

"Yeah, I see what you mean. It's like we're parked out here on a mountaintop in the middle of nowhere."

Mandrone agreed. "If we scuttled the *Maine* with live charges, they'd hear the explosions and swarm all over us. On the other hand, if I flood her once everyone's out, she'd sink like a lead brick and I'd never make it to the surface alive."

"Yeah, that makes sense; besides, it's not likely they'll come looking for us here anyway."

"Even if they do, they won't find us. Once the *Maine*'s flooded, their sonar's useless. She'll look like part of the seafloor." Mike meant that once they'd vented all air from inside the *Maine,* her reflected sonar signal would drop as if the sub had suddenly disappeared.

"Good," Ash concluded, more optimistic about their prospects.

After releasing their long, floating antenna wire to the surface, Mandrone and his crew listened again to find out what was going on topside. As expected, they received countless channels of radio chatter off Guam, but as best they could determine, all was routine. In addition, it was reassuring to verify that their three-knot crawl speed had masked the *Maine* from ClearWater detection, even at their shallow depth. Finally, after several additional hours' listening, Mandrone and his sonarman confirmed that their nearest surface contact was more than thirty miles away.

Mike checked the wall clock. *Good, it's dark topside, twenty-two minutes and counting. We're nearly set.*

Squinting, he felt each minute drag by. *It's awful, like running on a treadmill watching the clock, time can't pass by quickly enough.*

Finally, after they had planted themselves on the bottom, making sure the coast was clear, it was time to call King David.

"Ash, release the HF buoy."

A protective door opened behind the *Maine*'s sail and a rigid antenna canister streaked toward the surface, spooling out steel cable along the way. In a matter of seconds, the container rocketed less than one hundred feet to the surface, then protruded above the water, ready to transmit.

Ash signaled thumbs-up, then Mandrone bolted for the radio room.

At the bottom of the hour, Mike and his radioman signaled King David over their commercial marine radio.

"King David, King David, do you read me? Over."

For the next few anxious moments, Mandrone and his radioman heard only static.

Their spirits sank.

"King David, King David, this is Pati Point Two. Do you read me? Over."

Static.

Mike grew tense. Memories of King David, their days together on the Pacific, came flooding over him. King David had awed Mandrone with his skills on the sea, watching the waves, following the lights in the sea, watching the stars. He could navigate with or without the stars, with or without land. Once, they'd sailed from Puluwat to Guam to Truk Island and back with no high-tech nav aides at all.

King David had gotten his name because he owned his own island. They'd become friends years ago, when Mike was just out of school during his first Pacific tour. As it turned out, Mike had been in the right place at the right time and saved King David from certain death. They'd been friends from that day forward. Since that time, King David's son and three lovely daughters had grown. Returning as often as he could, he'd taken hundreds of pictures, stayed in touch by letter, and considered them his adopted family.

King David wouldn't let me down. Mike let out a sigh. *We're inside our rendezvous window, two days to spare. He must be out there somewhere.*

"King David, King David, this is Pati Point Two. Can you hear me? Over."

Static.

Click, click, click.

Mandrone counted off a long, ten-second pause.

Click, click.

"Yes! Yes!" Mandrone clenched his fist, euphoric. A sense of elation washed over him unlike anything he'd ever experienced. The whole crew came alive with excitement. They weren't home yet, but they had a ticket.

Rendezvous, 1/11/2009, Sun., 01:16 A.M., 15:16 ZULU
12° 49′ N, 146° 7′ E
USS Maine

Click, click, click. Mandrone timed a ten-second pause. *Click, click.*

Mandrone spoke into the intercom. "Gentlemen, our ride's here. You know what to do."

"Radio?"

"No change with the topside traffic, sir. It's routine."

"Very well, shut it all down, cut power to the bilge pumps at the breaker board, and meet underneath the forward escape trunk." Back in the radio room, the two engineers shut down one piece of gear after another in rapid succession. Once their equipment and computers went dark, they turned out the light and hurried forward, opening every watertight door along the way.

Looking across the control room, Mandrone ordered Ash to open all main vents. "Flood her tanks, Ash. Flood 'em all."

Ash's hands raced along a series of push-button switches on the ballast control panel, each opening a vent to the sea. Within a matter of minutes, he reported all ballast, bilge, and trim tanks flooded.

"Torpedo room, has the diving gear been moved to the escape trunk?"

"Yes, Captain. There's tanks for five."

"Good, break the breech door seals on all tubes and leave the intercom on." The torpedoman switched on his intercom mike, then loosened the inner doors on tubes one through four. After a quick survey of the room, he powered down the weapon system control panel and hurried up to the escape trunk, purposefully opening every watertight door along the way.

"Sonar?"

Behind the dome-shaped end cap of the pressure hull, the sonarman took one last listen, then reported to the captain. "All clear topside. Closest contact forty miles north."

"Good, you know what to do." Seconds later, every waterfall display, every computer, and every receiver fell dark. The sonarman took one final look around the room, said good-bye, then turned out the lights.

"Mr. Wilson, double-check the galley and bunk area. Take a head count and make sure we've got everybody. I'll join you shortly." Mandrone struggled to steady the drops over his injured eye. Over the past few days, his eye had improved, but Mike believed his vision would never recover.

A few minutes later, Ash reported from the escape trunk. "Weapons and Maneuvering are manning their stations, Captain. Otherwise, everyone's here, present and accounted for."

"Excellent, Mr. Wilson."

Mandrone punched the intercom. "Weapons and Maneuvering, please standby."

The captain met the others by the ladder directly beneath the forward escape trunk. Looking over the faces of his crew, he spoke calmly, with a hint of optimism in his voice. "Gentlemen, sonar tells us to expect three-to-five-foot swells topside. It's dark, but King David's directly above us, tied off our floating wire antenna. Send the raft up, but don't inflate it. Stow it in one of their canoes in case we need it.

"Now, let's get going. I'll operate the escape trunk. Ash, get the men in their gear, and remember, for those of you wearing Steinke hoods, whatever you do, don't hold your breath on the way up! We've gotten this far together and I don't want to lose you now. Good luck, watch out for your partner, and I'll see you topside." The Steinke hood was a combination of a life jacket that tied around your chest and a breathing bag that fit over your head.

"All right, men," Ash added, "those of you who're divers, strap on the tanks. For the rest, it's the Steinke hood for you." Mr. Wilson worked hard and fast, getting the men ready to go, one after another.

Once they were ready, Ash grouped each diver with a Steinke-hooded rookie, then prodded them up the ladder. "Two at a time, men. Now up in the trunk with you."

The first two crewmen selected bowed slightly forward as a form of salute to Mandrone, then climbed the ladder. Around the escape trunk perimeter, four battle lanterns shined, cutting through the darkness, illuminating the trunk's interior. Both men closed the bottom hatch behind them, then stood under the donut-shaped air pocket lining the top of the cylindrical trunk. Inside the chamber, sound waves raced around the circular walls, and this effect was a little eerie, like a whisper dome. The diver on one side of the chamber could hear the Steinke hooder breathing as if he were next to his face.

Of the two, the sonarman was the less experienced swimmer. He charged his Steinke hood from the air nozzle inside the trunk as the second diver opened the flood valve, filling the trunk with cool seawater. As the escape trunk flooded, both men kept with their heads deliberately inside the air pocket.

Meanwhile, outside the trunk, Mandrone watched the chamber fill indicator on the control panel below. Once it flashed "FULL," he opened the upper hatch with a flip of a switch. Now completely underwater, the experienced diver pushed the life raft out the hatch and it floated toward the surface. Next up, the diver signaled the sonarman toward the hatch.

When he felt ready, the sonarman ducked under the metal flange centered on the top of the chamber and floated up through the trunk. As long as he remembered to breathe, the sonarman knew, the bends weren't a concern from their depth. He'd never done this before from an American submarine, but he knew the drill. Basically, it was little changed across submarine services. The next stage promised an express—four hundred feet per minute—rocket ride to the surface, a great trip as long as you didn't ram anything on your way up.

After his exit, the diver followed him up at a slower clip.

Meanwhile, at the surface, the sonarman was brought onboard King David's thirty-foot canoe.

Minutes later, everyone around the chamber heard what they'd been waiting for.

Clang. Clang. Clang.

The first diver surfaced, spoke with King David, then followed the steel antenna cable back down to the *Maine*'s lighted escape trunk.

Mike reasoned if there'd been any serious problem topside, he would have heard about it before now. On cue, he closed the upper hatch and drained the trunk for the next pair of swimmers. Once he spoke to his returning diver, things moved quickly.

Ten minutes later, only Mandrone was left beneath the escape trunk. The *Maine* was almost completely quiet now. Mike heard only the sound of blower motors and his own breathing. Satisfied, he lifted a handset hanging over the console.

"Weapons, shut down both the air handler and the water

distillation plant. When you're done, open the outer torpedo tube doors and come to the escape trunk immediately."

Less than two minutes later, Weapons entered the room winded.

Mandrone punched the torpedo room intercom, then lifted his handset to the sound of rushing water. *This is as it should be,* he thought. *Like her crew, the* Maine *will die a silent, painless death, trickle flooding one compartment at a time.*

"Maneuvering, SCRAM the reactor; our job is done."

"Very well, Captain."

Aft in the reactor room, one crewmen went about turning down the *Maine* in an orderly fashion. Fifteen seconds later, the electrical lifeblood of the ship dried up and the sub went dark, illuminated only by emergency battery-powered lights.

Mike sent both crewmen up the chute to the surface, then strapped a Steinke hood around his chest. Once the escape chamber had drained, he noticed the lonely, desolate silence. Illuminated only by battery light, the room fell absolutely silent—except for the distant sound of rushing water.

Mandrone surveyed the room one last time. He felt only disdain, hating submarines more than he'd ever dreamed possible. He set the chamber hatch control on automatic, climbed into the trunk, and left the *Maine* to die, alone.

PART SIX

Epilogue

CHAPTER THIRTY-ONE

Had it not been for the seabirds, the *Maine* would never have been found.

The fishermen who spotted them had been watching the terns a long time. What caught their attention was the way the birds were lined up, all in a row, bobbing up and down in unison. In nautical circles, it's well known that sub skippers have nightmares about towing floating aerial wire near land. It's disconcerting to see a line of seagulls moving through the water sideways.

Sonar scans of the bottom revealed nothing conclusive, but when fishermen hacked off a length of aerial and brought it in, naval authorities acted immediately, vectoring an airborne P-3 over the area. Once the Orion detected a large metal hulk sitting on the bottom, everything happened quickly. The *Tucson* was first to arrive on the scene with its small team of divers. Less than twenty-four hours later, swimmers swarmed the *Maine* like bees around a hive. Following a thorough inspection, Washington decided to raise the boat, remove the dead, and recover their weapons.

X-ray examination in dry dock revealed that extraordinary pressure had weakened the hull, deformed it beyond its elastic limit. Described as premature aging, metal fatigue was given as the reason for declaring the *Maine* beyond her useful service life.

Though badly decomposed, every crewmen was identified by his dental records, save one—Ash Wilson.

USN Commander Clay McCullough's wife asked that he be buried at sea along with the *Maine*. With few exceptions, the surviving families of the crew agreed their loved ones should be buried with him.

A memorial service was held on the flight deck of the USS *Stennis,* nine miles south of a small atoll, east of Guam. One hundred and fifty-nine names were called that day; the *Maine* was formally struck from the U.S. naval registry and committed, along with her crew, to the depths of the sea.

Predictably, military and government agencies investigated the incident after the fact. One internal naval investigation focused on *how they did it,* how the *Maine* was hijacked in the first place. Another addressed motivation, *why they did it* and a third centered about *how they got away.* As it happened, this formal board of inquiry would reveal only speculation as to how Ash Wilson and his nameless renegades may have escaped, though what actually happened was less remarkable.

In truth, Mike Mandrone, Ash, and the rest of his crew sailed south with King David and simply vanished into the fishing fleet of the Caroline Islands. The board considered a slight variation of this alternative as one possibility, but dismissed it as unlikely, too low-tech.

In Pearl Harbor, Ash Wilson and his nameless crew were tried in absentia by a court of military justice. Former XO and author Mike Mandrone was summoned to testify, but never found. Through it all, both the *Kansong*'s captain and former North Korean diplomats denied any knowledge of renegade operations or sabotage activity inside the

United States. Following a lengthy trial, Ash and nameless accomplishes were found guilty of piracy and mass murder. There was no appeal.

The largest reward ever posted by the United States government was offered for information leading to their arrest, but was never collected.

On occasion, Ash Wilson found himself depressed, lying awake at night, haunted by memories of death on the *Maine*. To make matters worse, during the day he found himself tormented by the prospect of wasting his life away on some tiny tropical island. It wasn't that he regretted what he'd done. On the contrary, he missed the thrill of the chase but found himself paranoid, constantly looking over his shoulder, a man with a price on his head, hunted across the free world.

Tragedy began stalking him later that year in New Guinea. In August, an unknown assailant stabbed and robbed him late one evening as he left his favorite watering hole. Local authorities never resolved the ambush. Sixteen months later, Ash was shot, blown away by a shotgun blast outside the same bar, in a fray over twenty-five dollars his hunting buddy owed him. The shooting was ruled justifiable homicide at the coroner's inquest.

"It was like he didn't want to live," his buddy claimed.

Eyewitness accounts corroborated this story. Ash had threatened him with a knife.

Several months after returning to King David's Pacific paradise, Mike Mandrone married the king's oldest daughter, a Carolinian beauty, and started over, a rare opportunity few are granted in life. Though she was twenty years his junior, their marriage would be a happy one. Their union would be blessed with three children, and in later years, Mandrone would claim they kept him young.

Mike found no satisfaction exacting revenge or proving

the points predicted in his infamous book. He didn't dwell on the past, but he never set foot in another submarine or wrote again. His vision was affected from the trauma; bright light bothered his eye, corneal scar tissue blurred his focus.

All this aside, Mike's confident, self-sufficient attitude remained through the years. He was a take-charge kind of guy others looked up to, a natural-born skipper. but in his heart he was a loner and liked it that way.

Working in full cooperation with the FBI and Motorola's Iridium Satellite Division, Colonel Mason's inner circle closed on Captain Dutton within three months. As it turned out, Traci's December phone bill was riddled with numerous, short phone calls to somewhere—as telephone company records revealed—in the Pacific. When confronted with questions about her bill, Traci's attitude triggered a larger, more extensive search of her quarters. Overconfident, like John Walker before her, Traci had gotten sloppy at home. Computer logs confirmed Mason's worst fears. Her spread-spectrum receiver, home computer, and log files were confiscated on the spot, and subsequently used as evidence. That same day, the ClearWater comp center was dissected piece by piece, but the silver bullet, the telltale transmitter, was never found. Everything Traci touched was scrutinized with a fine-tooth comb, but she'd covered her tracks.

As fate would have it, Traci Dutton was sentenced to spend the rest of her life working behind an old, gun-metal gray Steel Case desk in an overcrowded, maximum-security federal penitentiary for women. Ironically, Traci finally got the recognition she'd been seeking. On America's list of notorious traitors, the deeds of Traci Dutton were ranked alongside those of the Walker spy ring. And as with John Walker, the only people who came calling were the press, and soon, even they stopped coming.

Soon, no one came to visit, no one came at all.

North Korea collapsed completely after only six weeks of fighting, and Korean unification, the dream of North and South alike, came to pass.

Mid-year, once South Korea began rebuilding the North, the remainder of the *Maine*'s crew returned to their reunited homeland. No crewman emerged wealthy from their renegade mission, but with a half million dollars each, no one found themselves destitute inside Korea's booming capitalistic economy.

Dear Leader and his military entourage disappeared from the face of the earth, though their bodies were never found. Political analysts believe it's only a matter of time before they emerge again. Like bad pennies, they have a way of turning up.

The Air Force has an unofficial, unspoken, and unwritten policy regarding its heroes—it takes care of its own. Scott wanted a space plane slot at Edwards, had dreamed of it since she first hugged the front tricycle gear of her father's SR-71. Being fully qualified, she got it. Mason saw to that, and as America's first female space plane pilot, she enjoyed full support from her military brotherhood to boot.

Still, things didn't turn out as she'd hoped. Once shipboard, first thing she did was mail Jay's letter. Later, when she and Tristan returned to the States, they got down on their knees and kissed the ground they walked on, vowing never to return to sea again. Exhausted from the sea cruise, Tristan said good-bye and flew to Florida, taking one month's leave to visit friends, family, and Disney World.

As quickly as Scotty could get her hands on a phone,

she called Jay at his Huntsville apartment. In retrospect, she wished she had not. It was a turning point in her life. She'd never forget that distinctively Southern female voice.

"Jay isn't home now," the voice had said, "but we'll be in later if you'd like to call back, or I could give him a message." Linda recoiled as if she'd been burned, struggled to breathe, and felt a crushing, debilitating pain deep inside her chest.

She didn't know what to say, so she said almost nothing at all. Inexplicably, she knew it was over. *It was the way she said his name,* Linda later recalled.

Years after their divorce, she would conclude there was probably nothing she could have said. She found the letter from his lawyer waiting in her mail when she returned home. He sued her for divorce on grounds of desertion. Most of all, Scotty knew she would miss him.

Commander Slay "Hawk" Hawkins was offered his choice of assignments and opted for a land-based command near his family. COMSUBPAC Admiral Ozzie Eastwood considered him one of the top U.S. skippers in the force, on track for the admiralty. In the aftermath following the *Maine* incident, he earmarked Hawk for promotion to his staff as submarine group commander. Turned out, Hawk and his family enjoyed Hawaii, and within one year, his parents joined them.

Once her repairs had been completed, his XO, Buck Clayton assumed command of the *Topeka,* the finest command in the fleet.

General Craven had big career plans for Mason. Reluctantly, Mason agreed to follow Craven's lead, but in his heart he dreamed of returning to his grandparents' farm.

In conclusion, our ASW forces were decimated prematurely, our hopes pinned on a technology star who's time had not yet come.

Any first-generation technology claiming to illuminate the depths of the earth's oceans will have serious operational limitations. Fundamentally, this hasn't been done before because seawater absorbs light like a sponge. The physics of the problem guarantee this will remain true for all time. People, not technology, are again underscored as the most important asset we have for protecting our freedom. Technology's an enabler, but people must remain the most significant, first-order term in our defense equation.

First and foremost in everyone's mind, our ASW forces were given top priority and began rebuilding immediately.

Second, and of no less importance, Americans now understood we're helpless against any incoming missile attack, renegade or otherwise. Clearly, some form of missile defense system is needed—another lesson Mike taught us the hard way. Mandrone demonstrated beyond a shadow of a doubt that our own missiles are more stealthy than we can detect, let alone destroy. Underscoring the significance of this issue, six nuclear weapons fired from the *Maine* were never recovered—by Americans—but that's another story. In response, the United States government backed a space-based, long-term commitment to missile defense and former President Reagan's Strategic Defense Initiative—Star Wars—was reborn.

First conceived as an orbiting satellite armada, this multibillion-dollar missile defense project would come to be called "HighGround."

ABOUT THE AUTHOR

Bill Buchanan, an electrical engineer with Lucent Bell Labs, develops control systems and communication protocols for computer networks. As a former captain in the U.S. Air Force Electronic Systems Division, he helped develop and test a side-looking prototype radar designed to penetrate foliage. He received a master's degree in electrical engineering from Mississippi State University after working as a graduate assistant at NASA. He and his family live in southern New Hampshire, where he's currently writing his next novel.